On the Way to the Wedding

In which:

Firstly, Gregory Bridgerton falls in love with the wrong woman, and

Secondly, she falls in love with someone else, but

Thirdly, Lucy Abernathy decides to meddle; however,

Fourthly, she falls in love with Gregory, which is highly inconvenient because

Fifthly, she is practically engaged to Lord Haselby, but

Sixthly, Gregory falls in love with Lucy.

Which leaves everyone in a bit of a pickle.

Watch them all find their happy endings in:

The stunning conclusion
to the Bridgerton series
by the incomparable Julia Quinn

Avon Romances by
Julia Quinn

JULIA QUINN

ON THE WAY TO THE WEDDING

AVON BOOKS
An Imprint of HarperCollins*Publishers*

This is a work of fiction. Names, characters, places, and incidents are products of the author's imagination or are used fictitiously and are not to be construed as real. Any resemblance to actual events, locales, organizations, or persons, living or dead, is entirely coincidental.

AVON BOOKS
An Imprint of Harper Collins*Publishers*
10 East 53rd Street
New York, New York 10022-5299

ISBN-13: 978-0-7394-6785-5
ISBN-10: 0-7394-6785-9

Printed in the U.S.A.

For Lyssa Keusch.
Because you're my editor.
Because you're my friend.

And also for Paul.
Just because.

Violet Ledger *m.* EDMUND
1766- 1764-1803

ANTHONY 1784-
m.
Kate Sheffield 1793-
The Viscount Who Loved Me
BOOK 2

Edmund 1815-
Miles 1817-
Charlotte 1822-

COLIN 1791-
m.
Penelope Featherington 1796-
Romancing Mister Bridgerton
BOOK 4

Agatha 1825-
Thomas 1826-

BENEDICT 1786-
m.
Sophia Beckett 1794-
An Offer From a Gentleman
BOOK 3

Charles 1818-
Alexander 1820-
William 1822-
Violet 1824-

DAPHNE 1792-
m.
Simon Basset 1784-
Duke of Hastings
The Duke and I
BOOK 1

Amelia 1814-
Belinda 1815-
Caroline 1816-
David 1817-

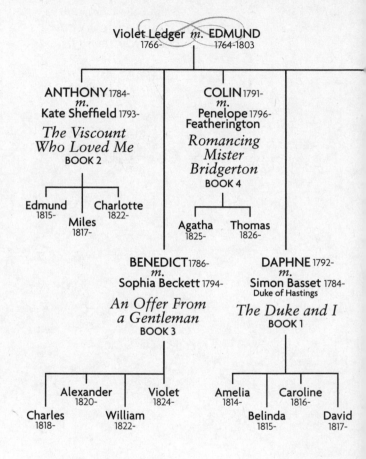

Bridgerton FAMILY TREE

FRANCESCA 1797-
m.1
John Stirling
8th Earl of Kilmartin
1792-1820
m.2
Michael Stirling 1791-
9th Earl of Kilmartin

When He Was Wicked
BOOK 6

HYACINTH 1803-
m.
Gareth St. Clair 1797-

It's In His Kiss
BOOK 7

George
1826-

ELOISE 1796-
m.2
Sir Phillip Crane 1794-
m.1
Marina Thompson
1794-1823

To Sir Phillip, With Love
BOOK 5

Oliver
1816-

Amanda
1816-

Penelope
1825-

Georgiana
1826-

GREGORY
1801-

On the Way to the Wedding
BOOK 8

featuring
Lady Lucinda Abernathy

FOR MORE INFORMATION,
PLEASE VISIT WWW.JULIAQUINN.COM

On the Way to the Wedding

Prologue

London, not far from St. George's, Hanover Square
Summer, 1827

His lungs were on fire.

Gregory Bridgerton was running. Through the streets of London, oblivious to the curious stares of onlookers, he was running.

There was a strange, powerful rhythm to his movements—*one two three four, one two three four*—that pushed him along, propelling him forward even as his mind remained focused on one thing and one thing only.

The church.

He had to get to the church.

He had to stop the wedding.

How long had he been running? One minute? Five? He couldn't know, couldn't concentrate on anything but his destination.

The church. He had to get to the church.

It had started at eleven. This thing. This ceremony. This thing that should never have happened. But she'd done it anyway. And he had to stop it. He had to stop *her.* He didn't know how, and he certainly didn't know why, but she was doing it, and it was wrong.

She had to know that it was wrong.

She was *his*. They belonged together. She knew that. God damn it all, she knew that.

How long did a wedding ceremony take? Five minutes? Ten? Twenty? He'd never paid attention before, certainly never thought to check his watch at the beginning and end.

Never thought he'd need the information. Never thought it would matter this much.

How long had he been running? Two minutes? Ten?

He skidded around a corner and onto Regent Street, grunting something that was meant to take the place of "Excuse me," as he bumped into a respectably dressed gentleman, knocking his case to the ground.

Normally Gregory would have stopped to aid the gentleman, bent to retrieve the case, but not today, not this morning.

Not now.

The church. He had to get to the church. He could not think of anything else. He must not. He must—

Damn! He skidded to a halt as a carriage cut in front of him. Resting his hands on his thighs—not because he wanted to, but rather because his desperate body demanded it—he sucked in huge gulps of air, trying to relieve the screaming pressure in his chest, that horrible burning, tearing feeling as—

The carriage moved past and he was off again. He was close now. He could do it. It couldn't have been more than five minutes since he'd left the house. Maybe six. It felt like thirty, but it couldn't have been more than seven.

He had to stop this. It was wrong. He had to stop it. He *would* stop it.

He could see the church. Off in the distance, its gray steeple rising into the bright blue sky. Someone had hung flowers from the lanterns. He couldn't tell what kind they were—yellow and white, yellow mostly. They spilled forth with reckless abandon, bursting from the baskets. They looked celebratory, cheerful even, and it was all so wrong. This was not a cheerful day. It was not an event to be celebrated.

And he *would* stop it.

He slowed down just enough so that he could run up the steps without falling on his face, and then he wrenched the door open, wide, wider, barely hearing the slam as it crashed into the outer wall. Maybe he should have paused for breath. Maybe he should have entered quietly, giving himself a moment to assess the situation, to gauge how far along they were.

The church went silent. The priest stopped his drone, and every spine in every pew twisted until every face was turned to the back.

To him.

"Don't," Gregory gasped, but he was so short of breath, he could barely hear the word.

"Don't," he said, louder this time, clutching the edge of the pews as he staggered forward. "Don't do it."

She said nothing, but he saw her. He saw her, her mouth open with shock. He saw her bouquet slip from her hands, and he knew—by God he knew that she'd stopped breathing.

She looked so beautiful. Her golden hair seemed to catch the light, and it shone with a radiance that filled him with strength. He straightened, still breathing hard, but he could walk unassisted now, and he let go of the pew.

"Don't do it," he said again, moving toward her with the stealthy grace of a man who knows what he wants.

Who knows what should be.

Still she didn't speak. No one did. It was strange, that. Three hundred of London's biggest busybodies, gathered into one building, and no one could utter a word. No one could take his eyes off him as he walked down the aisle.

"I love you," he said, right there, right in front of everyone. Who cared? He would not keep this a secret. He would not let her marry someone else without making sure all the world knew that she owned his heart.

"I love you," he said again, and out of the corner of his eye he could see his mother and sister, seated primly in a pew, their mouths open with shock.

He kept walking. Down the aisle, each step more confident, more sure.

"Don't do it," he said, stepping out of the aisle and into the apse. "Don't marry him."

"Gregory," she whispered. "Why are you doing this?"

"I love you," he said, because it was the only thing to say. It was the only thing that mattered.

Her eyes glistened, and he could see her breath catch in her throat. She looked up at the man she was trying to marry. His brows rose as he gave her a tiny, one-shouldered shrug, as if to say, *It is your choice.*

Gregory sank to one knee. "Marry me," he said, his very soul in his words. "Marry *me*."

He stopped breathing. The entire church stopped breathing.

She brought her eyes to his. They were huge and clear and everything he'd ever thought was good and kind and true.

"Marry me," he whispered, one last time.

Her lips were trembling, but her voice was clear when she said—

One

In which Our Hero falls in love.

Two months earlier

Unlike most men of his acquaintance, Gregory Bridgerton believed in true love.

He'd have to have been a fool not to.

Consider the following:

His eldest brother, Anthony.

His eldest sister, Daphne.

His other brothers, Benedict and Colin, not to mention his sisters, Eloise, Francesca, and (galling but true) Hyacinth, all of whom—*all* of whom—were quite happily besotted with their spouses.

For most men, such a state of affairs would produce nothing quite so much as bile, but for Gregory, who had been born with an uncommonly cheerful, if occasionally (according to his younger sister) annoying, spirit, it simply meant that he had no choice but to believe the obvious:

Love existed.

It was not a wispy figment of the imagination, designed to keep the poets from complete starvation. It might not be something that one could see or smell or touch, but it was out there, and it was only a matter of time before he, too, found the woman of his dreams and settled down to be fruitful, multiply, and take on such baffling hobbies as papier-mâché and the collection of nutmeg graters.

Although, if one wanted to put a fine point on it, which did seem rather precise for such an abstract sort of concept, his dreams didn't exactly include a woman. Well, not one with any specific and identifiable attributes. He didn't know anything about this woman of his, the one who was supposed to transform his life completely, turning him into a happy pillar of boredom and respectability. He didn't know if she would be short or tall, dark or fair. He'd like to think she would be intelligent and in possession of a fine sense of humor, but beyond that, how was he to know? She could be shy or outspoken. She might like to sing. Or maybe not. Maybe she was a horsewoman, with a ruddy complexion born of too much time out of doors.

He didn't know. When it came to this woman, this impossible, wonderful, and currently nonexistent woman, all he really knew was that when he found her . . .

He'd know.

He didn't know how he'd know; he just knew that he would. Something this momentous, this earth-shattering and life-altering . . . well, really, it wasn't going to whisper its way into existence. It would come full and forceful, like the proverbial ton of bricks. The only question was when.

And in the meantime, he saw no reason not to have a fine time while he anticipated her arrival. One didn't need to behave like a monk while waiting for one's true love, after all.

Gregory was, by all accounts, a fairly typical man about London, with a comfortable—although by no means extravagant—allowance, plenty of friends, and a level enough head to know when to quit a gaming table. He was considered a decent enough catch on the Marriage Mart, if not precisely the top selection (fourth sons never did command a great deal of attention), and he was always in demand when the society matrons needed an eligible man to even up the numbers at dinner parties.

Which did make his aforementioned allowance stretch a bit further—always a benefit.

Perhaps he ought to have had a bit more purpose in his life. Some sort of direction, or even just a meaningful task to complete. But that could wait, couldn't it? Soon, he was sure, everything would come clear. He would know just what it was he wished to do, and whom he wished to do it with, and in the meantime, he'd—

Not have a fine time. Not just at *this* moment, at least.

To explain:

Gregory was presently sitting in a leather chair, a rather accommodating one, not that that really had any bearing on the matter other than the fact that the lack of discomfort was conducive to daydreaming, which in turn was conducive to not listening to his brother, who, it should be noted, was standing approximately four feet away, droning on about something or other, almost certainly involving some variation of the words *duty* and *responsibility.*

Gregory wasn't really paying attention. He rarely did.

Well, no, occasionally he did, but—

"Gregory? Gregory!"

He looked up, blinking. Anthony's arms were crossed, never a good sign. Anthony was the Viscount Bridgerton, and had been for more than twenty years. And while he was, Gregory would be the first to insist, the very best of brothers, he would have made a rather fine feudal lord.

"Begging your pardon for intruding upon your thoughts, such as they are," Anthony said in a dry voice, "but have you, perhaps—just perhaps—heard anything I've said?"

"Diligence," Gregory parroted, nodding with what he deemed sufficient gravity. "Direction."

"Indeed," Anthony replied, and Gregory congratulated himself on what had clearly been an inspired performance. "It was well past time that you finally sought some direction in your life."

"Of course," Gregory murmured, mostly because he'd missed supper, and he was hungry, and he'd heard that his sister-in-law was serving light refreshments in the garden. Besides, it never made sense to argue with Anthony. Never.

"You must make a change. Choose a new course."

"Indeed." Maybe there would be sandwiches. He could eat about forty of those ridiculous little ones with the crusts cut off right then.

"Gregory."

Anthony's voice held that tone. The one that, while impossible to describe, was easy enough to recognize. And Gregory knew it was time to pay attention.

"Right," he said, because truly, it was remarkable how well a single syllable could delay a proper sentence. "I expect I'll join the clergy."

That stopped Anthony cold. Dead, frozen, cold. Gregory paused to savor the moment. Too bad he had to become a bloody vicar to achieve it.

"I beg your pardon," Anthony finally murmured.

"It's not as if I've many choices," Gregory said. And as the words emerged, he realized it was the first time he'd spoken them. It somehow made them more real, more permanent. "It's the military or the clergy," he continued, "and, well, it's got to be said—I'm a beastly bad shot."

Anthony didn't say anything. They all knew it was true.

After a moment of awkward silence, Anthony murmured, "There are swords."

"Yes, but with my luck I'll be posted to the Sudan." Gregory shuddered. "Not to be overly fastidious, but really, the heat. Would *you* want to go?"

Anthony demurred immediately. "No, of course not."

"And," Gregory added, beginning to enjoy himself, "there is Mother."

There was a pause. Then: "She pertains to the Sudan . . . how?"

"She wouldn't very well like my going, and then you, you must know, will be the one who must hold her hand every time she worries, or has some ghastly nightmare about—"

"Say no more," Anthony interrupted.

Gregory allowed himself an inner smile. It really wasn't fair to his mother, who, it was only sporting to point out, had never once claimed to portend the future with anything so wispy as a dream. But she *would* hate his going to the Sudan, and Anthony *would* have to listen to her worry over it.

And as Gregory didn't particularly wish to depart England's misty shores, the point was moot, anyway.

"Right," Anthony said. "Right. I am glad, then, that we have finally been able to have this conversation."

Gregory eyed the clock.

Anthony cleared his throat, and when he spoke, there was an edge of impatience to his voice. "And that you are finally thinking toward your future."

Gregory felt something tighten at the back of his jaw. "I am but six-and-twenty," he reminded him. "Surely too young for such repeated use of the word *finally.*"

Anthony just arched a brow. "Shall I contact the archbishop? See about finding you a parish?"

Gregory's chest twisted into an unexpected coughing spasm. "Er, no," he said, when he was able. "Not yet, at least."

One corner of Anthony's mouth moved. But not by much, and not, by any stretch of the definition, into a smile. "You could marry," he said softly.

"I could," Gregory agreed. "And I shall. In fact, I plan to."

"Really?"

"When I find the right woman." And then, at Anthony's dubious expression, Gregory added, "Surely you, of all people, would recommend a match of love over convenience."

Anthony was rather famously besotted with his wife, who was in turn rather inexplicably besotted with him. Anthony was also rather famously devoted to his seven younger siblings, so Gregory should not have felt such an unexpected wellspring of emotion when he softly said, "I wish you every happiness that I myself enjoy."

Gregory was saved from having to make a reply by the very loud rumbling of his stomach. He gave his brother a sheepish expression. "Sorry. I missed supper."

"I know. We expected you earlier."

Gregory avoided wincing. Just.

"Kate was somewhat put out."

That was the worst. When Anthony was disappointed that was one thing. But when he claimed that his wife had been somehow pained . . .

Well, that was when Gregory *knew* he was in trouble. "Got a late start from London," he mumbled. It was the truth, but still, no excuse for bad behavior. He had been expected at the house party in time for supper, and he had not come through. He almost said, "I shall make it up to her," but at the last moment bit his tongue. Somehow that would make it worse, he knew, almost as if he was making light of his tardiness, assuming that he could smooth over any transgression with a smile and a glib comment. Which he often could, but for some reason this time—

He didn't want to.

So instead he just said, "I'm sorry." And he meant it, too.

"She's in the garden," Anthony said gruffly. "I think she means to have dancing—on the patio, if you can believe it."

Gregory could. It sounded exactly like his sister-in-law. She wasn't the sort to let any serendipitous moment pass her by, and with the weather so uncommonly fine, why not organize an impromptu dance al fresco?

"See that you dance with whomever she wishes," Anthony said. "Kate won't like any of the young ladies to feel left out."

"Of course not," Gregory murmured.

"I will join you in a quarter of an hour," Anthony said, moving back to his desk, where several piles of paper awaited him. "I have a few items here yet to complete."

Gregory stood. "I shall pass that along to Kate." And then, the interview quite clearly at an end, he left the room and headed out to the garden.

It had been some time since he'd been to Aubrey Hall, the ancestral home of the Bridgertons. The family gathered here in Kent for Christmas, of course, but in truth, it wasn't home for Gregory, and never really had been. After his father had died, his mother had done the unconventional and uprooted her family, electing to spend most of the year in London. She had never said so, but Gregory had always suspected that the graceful old house held too many memories.

As a result, Gregory had always felt more at home in town than in the country. Bridgerton House, in London, was the home of his childhood, not Aubrey Hall. Still, he enjoyed his visits, and he was always game for bucolic pursuits, such as riding and swimming (when the lake was warm enough to permit it), and strangely enough, he liked the change of pace. He liked the way the air felt quiet and clean after months in the city.

And he liked the way he could leave it all behind when it grew *too* quiet and clean.

The night's festivities were being held on the south lawn, or so he'd been told by the butler when he'd arrived earlier that evening. It seemed a good spot for an outdoor fête—level ground, a view to the lake, and a large patio with plenty of seating for the less energetic.

As he approached the long salon that opened to the outside, he could hear the low murmur of voices buzzing in through the French doors. He wasn't certain how many people his sister-in-law had invited for her house party—probably something between twenty and thirty. Small enough to be intimate, but still large enough so that one could escape for some peace and quiet without leaving a gaping hole in the gathering.

As Gregory passed through the salon, he took a deep breath, trying in part to determine what sort of food Kate had decided to serve. There wouldn't be much, of course; she would have already overstuffed her guests at supper.

Sweets, Gregory decided, smelling a hint of cinnamon as he reached the light gray stone of the patio. He let out a disappointed breath. He was starving, and a huge slab of meat sounded like heaven right then.

But he was late, and it was nobody's fault but his own, and Anthony would have his head if he did not join the party immediately, so cakes and biscuits it would have to be.

A warm breeze sifted across his skin as he stepped outside. It had been remarkably hot for May; everyone was talking about it. It was the sort of weather that seemed to lift the mood—so surprisingly pleasant that one couldn't help but smile. And indeed, the guests milling about seemed to be in happy spirits; the low buzz of conversation was peppered with frequent rumbles and trills of laughter.

Gregory looked around, both for the refreshments and for someone he knew, most preferably his sister-in-law Kate, whom propriety dictated he greet first. But as his eyes swept across the scene, instead he saw . . .

Her.

Her.

And he knew it. He knew that she was the one. He stood frozen, transfixed. The air didn't rush from his body; rather, it seemed to slowly escape until there was nothing left, and he just stood there, hollow, and aching for more.

He couldn't see her face, not even her profile. There was just her back, just the breathtakingly perfect curve of her neck, one lock of blond hair swirling against her shoulder.

And all he could think was—*I am wrecked.*

For all other women, he was wrecked. This intensity, this fire, this overwhelming sense of rightness—he had never felt anything like it.

Maybe it was silly. Maybe it was mad. It was probably both those things. But he'd been waiting. For this moment, for so long, he'd been waiting. And it suddenly became clear—why he hadn't joined the military or the clergy, or taken his brother up on one of his frequent offers to manage a smaller Bridgerton estate.

He'd been waiting. That's all it was. Hell, he hadn't even realized how much he'd been doing nothing but waiting for this moment.

And here it was.

There *she* was.

And he knew.

He knew.

He moved slowly across the lawn, food and Kate forgotten. He managed to murmur his greetings to the one or two people he passed on his way, still keeping his pace. He had to reach her. He had to see her face, breathe her scent, know the sound of her voice.

And then he was there, standing mere feet away. He was breathless, awed, somehow fulfilled merely to stand in her presence.

She was speaking with another young lady, with enough animation to mark them as good friends. He stood there for a moment, just watching them until they slowly turned and realized he was there.

He smiled. Softly, just a little bit. And he said . . .

"How do you do?"

Lucinda Abernathy, better known to, well, everyone who knew her, as Lucy, stifled a groan as she turned to the gentleman who had crept up on her, presumably to make calf eyes at Hermione, as did, well, everyone who met Hermione.

It was an occupational hazard of being friends with Hermione Watson. She collected broken hearts the way the old vicar down by the Abbey collected butterflies.

The only difference, being, of course, that Hermione didn't jab her collection with nasty little pins. In all fairness, Hermione didn't wish to win the hearts of gentlemen, and she certainly never set out to break any of them. It just . . . happened. Lucy was used to it by now. Hermione was Hermione, with pale blond hair the color of butter, a heart-shaped face, and huge, wide-set eyes of the most startling shade of green.

Lucy, on the other hand, was . . . Well, she wasn't Hermione, that much was clear. She was simply herself, and most of the time, that was enough.

Lucy was, in almost every visible way, just a little bit *less* than Hermione. A little less blond. A little less slender. A little less tall. Her eyes were a little less vivid in color—bluish-gray, actually, quite attractive when compared with anyone other than Hermione, but that did her little good, as she never *went* anywhere without Hermione.

She had come to this stunning conclusion one day while not paying attention to her lessons on English Composition and Literature at Miss Moss's School for Exceptional Young Ladies, where she and Hermione had been students for three years.

Lucy was a little bit less. Or perhaps, if one wanted to put a nicer sheen on it, she was simply *not quite.*

She was, she supposed, reasonably attractive, in that healthy, traditional, English rose sort of manner, but men were rarely (oh, very well, never) struck dumb in her presence.

Hermione, however . . . well, it was a good thing she was such a nice person. She would have been impossible to be friends with, otherwise.

Well, that and the fact that she simply could not dance. Waltz, quadrille, minuet—it really didn't matter. If it involved music and movement, Hermione couldn't do it.

And it was *lovely.*

Lucy didn't think herself a particularly shallow person, and she would have insisted, had anyone asked, that she would freely throw herself in front of a carriage for her dearest friend, but there was a sort of satisfying fairness in the fact that the most beautiful girl in England had two left feet, at least one of them club.

Metaphorically speaking.

And now here was another one. Man, of course, not foot. Handsome, too. Tall, although not overly so, with warm brown hair and a rather pleasing smile. And a twinkle in his eyes as well, the color of which she couldn't quite determine in the dim night air.

Not to mention that she couldn't actually *see* his eyes, as he wasn't looking at her. He was looking at Hermione, as men always did.

Lucy smiled politely, even though she couldn't imagine that he'd notice, and waited for him to bow and introduce himself.

And then he did the most astonishing thing. After disclosing his name—she should have known he was a Bridgerton from the looks of him—he leaned down and kissed *her* hand first.

Lucy's breath caught.

Then, of course, she realized what he was doing.

Oh, he was *good.* He was really good. Nothing, *nothing* would endear a man to Hermione faster than a compliment to Lucy.

Too bad for him that Hermione's heart was otherwise engaged.

Oh well. It would be amusing to watch it all play out, at least.

"I am Miss Hermione Watson," Hermione was saying, and Lucy realized that Mr. Bridgerton's tactics were doubly clever. By kissing Hermione's hand second, he could linger over it, and her, really, and then she would be the one required to make the introductions.

Lucy was almost impressed. If nothing else, it marked him as slightly more intelligent than the average gentleman.

"And this is my dearest friend," Hermione continued, "Lady Lucinda Abernathy."

She said it the way she always said it, with love and devotion, and perhaps just the barest touch of desperation, as if to say—*For heaven's sake, spare Lucy a glance, too.*

But of course they never did. Except when they wanted advice concerning Hermione, her heart, and the winning thereof. When that happened, Lucy was always in high demand.

Mr. Bridgerton—Mr. Gregory Bridgerton, Lucy mentally corrected, for there were, as far as she knew, three Mr. Bridgertons in total, not counting the viscount, of course—turned and surprised her with a winning smile and warm eyes. "How do you do, Lady Lucinda," he murmured.

"Very well, thank you," and then she could have kicked herself for she actually stammered before the V in *very*, but for heaven's sake, they never looked at her after gazing upon Hermione, never.

Could he possibly be interested in *her*?

No, impossible. They never were.

And really, did it matter? Of course it would be rather charming if a man fell madly and passionately in love with her for a change. Really, she wouldn't *mind* the attention. But the truth was, Lucy was practically engaged to Lord Haselby and had been for years and years and years, so there was no use in having a besotted admirer of her own. It wasn't as if it could lead to anything useful.

And that besides, it certainly wasn't Hermione's fault that she'd been born with the face of an angel.

So Hermione was the siren, and Lucy was the trusty friend, and all was right with the world. Or if not right, then at least quite predictable.

"May we count you among our hosts?" Lucy finally asked, since no one had said anything once they'd all finished with the requisite "Pleased to meet yous."

"I'm afraid not," Mr. Bridgerton replied. "Much as I would like to take credit for the festivities, I reside in London."

"You are very fortunate to have Aubrey Hall in your family," Hermione said politely, "even if it is your brother's."

And that was when Lucy knew. Mr. Bridgerton fancied Hermione. Forget that he'd kissed her hand first, or that he'd actually looked at her when she said something, which most men never bothered to do. One had only to see the way he regarded Hermione when she spoke to know that he, too, had joined the throngs.

His eyes had that slightly glazed look. His lips were parted. And there was an intensity there, as if he'd like to gather Hermione up and stride down the hill with her, crowds and propriety be damned.

As opposed to the way he looked at her, which could be quite easily catalogued as polite disinterest. Or perhaps it was—*Why are you blocking my way, thus preventing me from sweeping Hermione up in my arms and striding down the hill with her, crowds and propriety be damned?*

It wasn't disappointing, exactly. Just . . . not . . . un-disappointing.

There ought to be a word for that. Really, there ought.

"Lucy? Lucy?"

Lucy realized with a touch of embarrassment that she had not been paying attention to the conversation. Hermione was regarding her curiously, her head tilted in that manner of hers that men always seemed to find so fetching. Lucy had tried it once. It had made her dizzy.

"Yes?" she murmured, since some sort of verbal expression seemed to be in order.

"Mr. Bridgerton has asked me to dance," Hermione said, "but I have told him that I *cannot*."

Hermione was forever feigning twisted ankles and head colds to keep herself off the dance floor. Which was also all good and fine, except that she fobbed off all her admirers on Lucy. Which was all good and fine *at first*, but it had got so common that Lucy suspected that the gentlemen now thought they were being shoved in her direction out of pity, which couldn't have been further from the truth.

Lucy was, if she did say so herself, a rather fine dancer. And an excellent conversationalist as well.

"It would be my pleasure to lead Lady Lucinda in a dance," Mr. Bridgerton said, because, really, what else could he say?

And so Lucy smiled, not entirely heartfelt, but a smile nonetheless, and allowed him to lead her to the patio.

Two

In which Our Heroine displays a decided lack of respect for all things romantic.

Gregory was nothing if not a gentleman, and he hid his disappointment well as he offered his arm to Lady Lucinda and escorted her to the makeshift dance floor. She was, he was sure, a perfectly charming and lovely young lady, but she wasn't Miss Hermione Watson.

And he had been waiting his entire life to meet Miss Hermione Watson.

Still, this *could* be considered beneficial to his cause. Lady Lucinda was clearly Miss Watson's closest friend—Miss Watson had positively gushed about her during their brief conversation, during which time Lady Lucinda gazed off at something beyond his shoulder, apparently not listening to a word. And with four sisters, Gregory knew a thing or two about women, the most important of which was that it was always a good idea to befriend the friend, provided they really *were* friends, and not just that odd thing women did where they pretended to be friends and were actually just waiting for the perfect moment to knife each other in the ribs.

Mysterious creatures, women. If they could just learn to say what they meant, the world would be a far simpler place.

But Miss Watson and Lady Lucinda gave every appearance of friendship and devotion, Lady Lucinda's woolgathering aside. And if Gregory wished to learn more about Miss Watson, Lady Lucinda Abernathy was the obvious place to start.

"Have you been a guest at Aubrey Hall very long?" Gregory asked politely as they waited for the music to begin.

"Just since yesterday," she replied. "And you? We did not see you at any of the gatherings thus far."

"I only arrived this evening," he said. "After supper." He grimaced. Now that he was no longer gazing upon Miss Watson, he remembered that he was rather hungry.

"You must be famished," Lady Lucinda exclaimed. "Would you prefer to take a turn around the patio instead of dancing? I promise that we may stroll past the refreshment table."

Gregory could have hugged her. "You, Lady Lucinda, are a capital young lady."

She smiled, but it was an odd sort of smile, and he couldn't quite tell what it meant. She'd liked his compliment, of that he was fairly certain, but there was something else there as well, something a little bit rueful, maybe something a little bit resigned.

"You must have a brother," he said.

"I do," she confirmed, smiling at his deduction. "He is four years my elder and always hungry. I will be forever amazed we had any food in the larder when he was home from school."

Gregory fit her hand in the crook of his elbow, and together they moved to the perimeter of the patio.

"This way," Lady Lucinda said, giving his arm a little tug when he tried to steer them in a counterclockwise direction. "Unless you would prefer sweets."

Gregory felt his face light up. "Are there savories?"

"Sandwiches. They are small, but they are quite delicious, especially the egg."

He nodded, somewhat absently. He'd caught sight of Miss Watson out of the corner of his eye, and it was a bit difficult to concentrate on anything else. Especially as she had been surrounded by men. Gregory was sure they had been just waiting for someone to remove Lady Lucinda from her side before moving in for the attack.

"Er, have you known Miss Watson very long?" he asked, trying not to be too obvious.

There was a very slight pause, and then she said, "Three years. We are students together at Miss Moss's. Or rather we were students together. We completed our studies earlier this year."

"May I assume you plan to make your debuts in London later this spring?"

"Yes," she replied, nodding toward a table laden with small snacks.

"We have spent the last few months preparing, as Hermione's mother likes to call it, attending house parties and small gatherings."

"Polishing yourselves?" he asked with a smile.

Her lips curved in answer. "Exactly that. I should make an excellent candlestick by now."

He found himself amused. "A mere candlestick, Lady Lucinda? Pray, do not understate your value. At the very least you are one of those extravagant silver urns everyone seems to need in their sitting rooms lately."

"I am an urn, then," she said, almost appearing to consider the idea. "What would that make Hermione, I wonder?"

A jewel. A diamond. A diamond set in gold. A diamond set in gold surrounded by . . .

He forcibly halted the direction of his thoughts. He could perform his poetic gymnastics later, when he wasn't expected to keep up one end of a conversation. A conversation with a different young lady. "I'm sure I do not know," he said lightly, offering her a plate. "I have only barely made Miss Watson's acquaintance, after all."

She said nothing, but her eyebrows rose ever so slightly. And that, of course, was when Gregory realized he was glancing over her shoulder to get a better look at Miss Watson.

Lady Lucinda let out a small sigh. "You should probably know that she is in love with someone else."

Gregory dragged his gaze back to the woman he was meant to be paying attention to. "I beg your pardon?"

She shrugged delicately as she placed a few small sandwiches on her plate. "Hermione. She is in love with someone else. I thought you would like to know."

Gregory gaped at her, and then, against every last drop of his good judgment, looked back at Miss Watson. It was the most obvious, pathetic gesture, but he couldn't help himself. He just . . . Dear God, he just wanted to look at her and look at her and never stop. If this wasn't love, he could not imagine what was.

"Ham?"

"What?"

"Ham." Lady Lucinda was holding out a little strip of sandwich with a pair of serving tongs. Her face was annoyingly serene. "Would you care for one?" she asked.

He grunted and held out his plate. And then, because he couldn't leave the matter as it was, he said stiffly, "I'm sure it is none of my business."

"About the sandwich?"

"About Miss Watson," he ground out.

Even though, of course, he meant no such thing. As far as he was concerned, Hermione Watson was very much his business, or at least she would be, very soon.

It was somewhat disconcerting that *she* had apparently not been hit by the same thunderbolt that had struck him. It had never occurred to him that when he did fall in love, his intended might not feel the same, and with equal immediacy, too. But at least this explanation—her thinking she was in love with someone else—assuaged his pride. It was much more palatable to think her infatuated with someone else than completely indifferent to him.

All that was left to do was make her realize that whoever the other man was, he was not the one for her.

Gregory was not so filled with conceit that he thought he could win any woman upon whom he set his sights, but he certainly had never had *difficulties* with the fairer sex, and given the nature of his reaction to Miss Watson, it was simply inconceivable that his feelings could go unrequited for very long. He might have to work to win her heart and hand, but that would simply make victory all the sweeter.

Or so he told himself. Truth was, a mutual thunderbolt would have been far less trouble.

"Don't feel badly," Lady Lucinda said, craning her neck slightly as she surveyed the sandwiches, looking, presumably, for something more exotic than British pig.

"I don't," he bit off, then waited for her to actually return her attention to him. When she didn't, he said again, "I don't."

She turned, gazed at him frankly, and blinked. "Well, that's refreshing, I must say. Most men are crushed."

He scowled. "What do you mean, most men are crushed?"

"Exactly what I said," she replied, giving him an impatient glance. "Or if they're not crushed, they become rather unaccountably angry." She let out a ladylike snort. "As if any of it could be considered her fault."

"Fault?" Gregory echoed, because in truth, he was having a devil of a time following her.

"You are not the first gentleman to imagine himself in love with Hermione," she said, her expression quite jaded. "It happens all the time."

"I don't *imagine* myself in love—" He cut himself off, hoping she didn't notice the stress on the word *imagine*. Good God, what was happening to him? He used to have a sense of humor. Even about himself. Especially about himself.

"You don't?" She sounded pleasantly surprised. "Well, that's refreshing."

"Why," he asked with narrowed eyes, "is that refreshing?

She returned with: "Why are you asking so many questions?"

"I'm not," he protested, even though he was.

She sighed, then utterly surprised him by saying, "I am sorry."

"I beg your pardon?"

She glanced at the egg salad sandwich on her plate, then back up at him, the order of which he did not find complimentary. He usually rated above egg salad. "I thought you would wish to speak of Hermione," she said. "I apologize if I was mistaken."

Which put Gregory in a fine quandary. He could admit that he'd fallen headlong in love with Miss Watson, which was rather embarrassing, even to a hopeless romantic such as himself. Or he could deny it all, which she clearly wouldn't believe. Or he could compromise, and admit to a mild infatuation, which he might normally regard as the best solution, except that it could only be insulting to Lady Lucinda.

He'd met the two girls at the same time, after all. And he wasn't headlong in love with *her*.

But then, as if she could read his thoughts (which frankly scared him), she waved a hand and said, "Pray do not worry yourself over my feelings. I'm quite used to this. As I said, it happens *all* the time."

Open heart, insert blunt dagger. Twist.

"Not to mention," she continued blithely, "that I am practically engaged myself." And then she took a bite of the egg salad.

Gregory found himself wondering what sort of man had found himself attached to this odd creature. He didn't pity the fellow, exactly, just . . . wondered.

And then Lady Lucinda let out a little "Oh!"

His eyes followed hers, to the spot where Miss Watson had once stood.

"I wonder where she went," Lady Lucinda said.

Gregory immediately turned toward the door, hoping to catch one last glimpse of her before she disappeared, but she was already gone. It was damned frustrating, that. What was the point of a mad, bad, immediate attraction if one couldn't do anything about it?

And forget *all* about it being one-sided. Good Lord.

He wasn't sure what one called sighing through gritted teeth, but that's exactly what he did.

"Ah, Lady Lucinda, there you are."

Gregory looked up to see his sister-in-law approaching.

And remembered that he'd forgotten all about her. Kate wouldn't take offense; she was a phenomenally good sport. But still, Gregory did usually try to have better manners with women to whom he was not blood related.

Lady Lucinda gave a pretty little curtsy. "Lady Bridgerton."

Kate smiled warmly in return. "Miss Watson has asked me to inform you that she was not feeling well and has retired for the evening."

"She has? Did she say—Oh, never mind." Lady Lucinda gave a little wave with her hand—the sort meant to convey nonchalance, but Gregory saw the barest hint of frustration pinching at the corners of her mouth.

"A head cold, I believe," Kate added.

Lady Lucinda gave a brief nod. "Yes," she said, looking a bit less sympathetic than Gregory would have imagined, given the circumstances, "it would be."

"And you," Kate continued, turning to Gregory, "have not even seen fit to greet me. How are you?"

He took her hands, kissed them as one in apology. "Tardy."

"That I knew." Her face assumed an expression that was not irritated, just a little bit exasperated. "How are you otherwise?"

"Otherwise lovely." He grinned. "As always."

"As always," she repeated, giving him a look that was a clear promise of future interrogation. "Lady Lucinda," Kate continued, her tone considerably less dry, "I trust you have made the acquaintance of my husband's brother, Mr. Gregory Bridgerton?"

"Indeed," Lady Lucinda replied. "We have been admiring the food. The sandwiches are delicious."

"Thank you," Kate said, then added, "and has Gregory promised you a dance? I cannot promise music of a professional quality, but we managed to round together a string quartet amongst our guests."

"He did," Lady Lucinda replied, "but I released him from his obligation so that he might assuage his hunger."

"You must have brothers," Kate said with a smile.

Lady Lucinda looked to Gregory with a slightly startled expression before replying, "Just one."

He turned to Kate. "I made the same observation earlier," he explained.

Kate let out a short laugh. "Great minds, to be sure." She turned to the younger woman and said, "It is well worth understanding the behavior of men, Lady Lucinda. One should never underestimate the power of food."

Lady Lucinda regarded her with wide eyes. "For the benefit of a pleasing mood?"

"Well, *that,*" Kate said, almost offhandedly, "but one really shouldn't discount its uses for the purpose of winning an argument. Or simply getting what you want."

"She's barely out of the schoolroom, Kate," Gregory chided.

Kate ignored him and instead smiled widely at Lady Lucinda. "One is never too young to acquire important skills."

Lady Lucinda looked at Gregory, then at Kate, and then her eyes began to sparkle with humor. "I understand why so many look up to you, Lady Bridgerton."

Kate laughed. "You are too kind, Lady Lucinda."

"Oh, please, Kate," Gregory cut in. He turned to Lady Lucinda and added, "She will stand here all night if you keep offering compliments."

"Pay him no attention," Kate said with a grin. "He is young and foolish and knows not of what he speaks."

Gregory was about to make another comment—he couldn't very well allow Kate to get away with that—but then Lady Lucinda cut in.

"I would happily sing your praises for the rest of the evening, Lady Bridgerton, but I believe that it is time for me to retire. I should like to check on Hermione. She has been under the weather all day, and I wish to assure myself that she is well."

"Of course," Kate replied. "Please do give her my regards, and be certain to ring if you need anything. Our housekeeper fancies herself something of an herbalist, and she is always mixing potions. Some of them even work." She grinned, and the expression was so friendly that Gregory instantly realized that she approved of Lady Lucinda. Which meant something. Kate had never suffered fools, gladly or otherwise.

"I shall walk you to the door," he said quickly. It was the least he could do to offer her this courtesy, and besides, it would not do to insult Miss Watson's closest friend.

They said their farewells, and Gregory fit her arm into the crook of his elbow. They walked in silence to the door to the drawing room, and Gregory said, "I trust you can make your way from here?"

"Of course," she replied. And then she looked up—her eyes were bluish, he noticed almost absently—and asked, "Would you like me to convey a message to Hermione?"

His lips parted with surprise. "Why would you do that?" he asked, before he could think to temper his response.

She just shrugged and said, "You are the lesser of two evils, Mr. Bridgerton."

He wanted desperately to ask her to clarify that comment, but he could not ask, not on such a flimsy acquaintance, so he instead worked to maintain an even mien as he said, "Give her my regards, that is all."

"Really?"

Damn, but that look in her eye was annoying. "Really."

She bobbed the tiniest of curtsies and was off.

Gregory stared at the doorway through which she had disappeared for a moment, then turned back to the party. The guests had begun dancing in greater numbers, and laughter was most certainly filling the air, but somehow the night felt dull and lifeless.

Food, he decided. He'd eat twenty more of those tiny little sandwiches and then he'd retire for the night as well.

All would come clear in the morning.

Lucy *knew* that Hermione didn't have a headache, or any sort of ache for that matter, and she was not at all surprised to find her sitting on her bed, poring over what appeared to be a four-page letter.

Written in an extremely compact hand.

"A footman brought it to me," Hermione said, not even looking up. "He said it arrived in today's post, but they forgot to bring it earlier."

Lucy sighed. "From Mr. Edmonds, I presume?"

Hermione nodded.

Lucy crossed the room she and Hermione were currently sharing and sat down in the chair at the vanity table. This wasn't the first piece of correspondence Hermione had received from Mr. Edmonds, and Lucy knew from experience that Hermione would need to read it twice, then once again for deeper analysis, and then finally one last time, if only to pick apart any hidden meanings in the salutation and closing.

Which meant that Lucy would have nothing to do but examine her fingernails for at least five minutes.

Which she did, not because she was terribly interested in her fingernails, nor because she was a particularly patient person, but rather because she knew a useless situation when she saw one, and she saw little reason in expending the energy to engage Hermione in conversation when Hermione was so patently uninterested in anything she had to say.

Fingernails could only occupy a girl for so long, however, especially when they were already meticulously neat and groomed, so Lucy stood and walked to the wardrobe, peering absently at her belongings.

"Oh, dash," she muttered, "I hate when she does that." Her maid had left a pair of shoes the wrong way, with the left on the right and the right on the left, and while Lucy knew there was nothing earth-shatteringly wrong with that, it did offend some strange (and extremely tidy) little corner of her sensibilities, so she righted the slippers, then stood back to inspect her handiwork, then planted her hands on her hips and turned around. "Are you finished yet?" she demanded.

"Almost," Hermione said, and it sounded as if the word had been resting on the edge of her lips the whole time, as if she'd had it ready so that she could fob off Lucy when she asked.

Lucy sat back down with a huff. It was a scene they had played out countless times before. Or at least four.

Yes, Lucy knew exactly how many letters Hermione had received from the romantic Mr. Edmonds. She would have liked *not* to have known; in fact, she was more than a little irritated that the item was taking up valuable space in her brain that might have been devoted to something useful, like botany or music, or good heavens, even another page in *DeBrett's,* but the unfortunate fact was, Mr. Edmonds's letters were nothing if not an *event,* and when Hermione had an event, well, Lucy was forced to have it, too.

They had shared a room for three years at Miss Moss's, and since Lucy had no close female relative who might help her make her bow into society, Hermione's mother had agreed to sponsor her, and so here they were, still together.

Which was lovely, really, except for the always-present (in spirit, at least) Mr. Edmonds. Lucy had made his acquaintance only once, but it certainly *felt* as if he were always there, hovering over them, causing Hermione to sigh at strange moments and gaze wistfully off into the distance as if she were committing a love sonnet to memory so that she might include it in her next reply.

"You are aware," Lucy said, even though Hermione had not indicated that she was finished reading her missive, "that your parents will never permit you to marry him."

That was enough to get Hermione to set the letter down, albeit briefly. "Yes," she said with an irritated expression, "you've said as much."

"He is a secretary," Lucy said.

"I realize that."

"A secretary," Lucy repeated, even though they'd had this conversation countless times before. "Your *father's* secretary."

Hermione had picked the letter back up in an attempt to ignore Lucy, but finally she gave up and set it back down, confirming Lucy's suspicions that she had long since finished it and was now in the first, or possibly even second, rereading.

"Mr. Edmonds is a good and honorable man," Hermione said, lips pinched.

"I'm sure he is," Lucy said, "but you can't *marry* him. Your father is a viscount. Do you really think he will allow his only daughter to marry a penniless secretary?"

"My father loves me," Hermione muttered, but her voice wasn't exactly replete with conviction.

"I am not trying to dissuade you from making a love match," Lucy began, "but—"

"That is exactly what you are trying to do," Hermione cut in.

"Not at all. I just don't see why you can't try to fall in love with someone of whom your parents might actually approve."

Hermione's lovely mouth twisted into a frustrated line. "You don't understand."

"What is there to understand? Don't you think your life might be just a touch easier if you fell in love with someone suitable?"

"Lucy, we don't get to choose who we fall in love with."

Lucy crossed her arms. "I don't see why not."

Hermione's mouth actually fell open. "Lucy Abernathy," she said, "you understand nothing."

"Yes," Lucy said dryly, "you've mentioned."

"How can you possibly think a person can choose who she falls in love with?" Hermione said passionately, although not so passionately that she was forced to rouse herself from her semireclined position on the bed. "One doesn't *choose.* It just happens. In an instant."

"Now *that* I don't believe," Lucy replied, and then added, because she could not resist, "not for an instant."

"Well, it does," Hermione insisted. "I know, because it happened to me. I wasn't *looking* to fall in love."

"Weren't you?"

"No." Hermione glared at her. "I wasn't. I fully intended to find a husband in London. Really, who would have expected to meet anyone in *Fenchley*?"

Said with the sort of disdain found only in a native Fenchleyan.

Lucy rolled her eyes and tilted her head to the side, waiting for Hermione to get on with it.

Which Hermione did not appreciate. "Don't look at me like that," she snipped.

"Like what?"

"Like *that.*"

"I repeat, like what?"

Hermione's entire face pinched. "You know exactly what I'm talking about."

Lucy clapped a hand to her face. "Oh my," she gasped. "You looked *exactly* like your mother just then."

Hermione drew back with affront. "That was unkind."

"Your mother is lovely!"

"Not when her face is all pinchy."

"Your mother is lovely even with a pinchy face," Lucy said, trying to put an end to the subject. "Now, do you intend to tell me about Mr. Edmonds or not?"

"Do you plan to mock me?"

"Of course not."

Hermione lifted her brows.

"Hermione, I promise I will not mock you."

Hermione still looked dubious, but she said, "Very well. But if you do—"

"Hermione."

"As I told you," she said, giving Lucy a warning glance, "I wasn't expecting to find love. I didn't even know my father had hired a new secretary. I was just walking in the garden, deciding which of the roses I wished to have cut for the table, and then . . . *I saw him.*"

Said with enough drama to warrant a role on the stage.

"Oh, Hermione," Lucy sighed.

"You said you wouldn't mock me," Hermione said, and she actually jabbed a finger in Lucy's direction, which struck Lucy as sufficiently out of character that she quieted down.

"I didn't even see his face at first," Hermione continued. "Just the back of his head, the way his hair curled against the collar of his coat." She sighed then. She actually sighed as she turned to Lucy with the most pathetic expression. "And the color. Truly, Lucy, have you ever seen hair such a spectacular shade of blond?"

Considering the number of times Lucy had been forced to listen to gentlemen make the same statement about Hermione's hair, she thought it spoke rather well of her that she refrained from comment.

But Hermione was not done. Not nearly. "Then he turned," she said, "and I saw his profile, and I swear to you I heard music."

Lucy would have liked to point out that the Watsons' conservatory was located right next to the rose garden, but she held her tongue.

"And then he turned," Hermione said, her voice growing soft and her eyes taking on that *I'm-memorizing-a-love-sonnet* expression, "and all I could think was—*I am ruined.*"

Lucy gasped. "Don't *say* that. Don't even hint at it."

Ruin was not the sort of thing any young lady mentioned lightly.

"Not *ruined* ruined," Hermione said impatiently. "Good heavens, Lucy, I was in the rose garden, or haven't you been listening? But I knew—I *knew* that I was ruined for all other men. There could never be another to compare."

"And you knew all this from the back of his neck?" Lucy asked.

Hermione shot her an exceedingly irritated expression. "And his profile, but that's not the point."

Lucy waited patiently for the point, even though she was quite certain it wouldn't be one with which she would agree. Or probably even understand.

"The point is," Hermione said, her voice growing so soft that Lucy had to lean forward to hear her, "that I cannot possibly be happy without him. Not possibly."

"Well," Lucy said slowly, because she wasn't precisely certain how she was meant to add to *that,* "you seem happy now."

"That is only because I know he is waiting for me. And"—Hermione held up the letter—"he writes that he loves me."

"Oh dear," Lucy said to herself.

Hermione must have heard her, because her mouth tightened, but she didn't say anything. The two of them just sat there, in their respective places, for a full minute, and then Lucy cleared her throat and said, "That nice Mr. Bridgerton seemed taken with you."

Hermione shrugged.

"He's a younger son, but I believe he has a nice portion. And he is certainly from a good family."

"Lucy, I told you I am not interested."

"Well, he's very handsome," Lucy said, perhaps a bit more emphatically than she'd meant to.

"You pursue him, then," Hermione retorted.

Lucy stared at her in shock. "You know I cannot. I'm practically engaged to Lord Haselby."

"Practically," Hermione reminded her.

"It might as well be official," Lucy said. And it was true. Her uncle had discussed the matter with the Earl of Davenport, Viscount Haselby's father, years ago. Haselby was about ten years older than Lucy, and they were all simply waiting for her to grow up.

Which she supposed she'd done. Surely the wedding wouldn't be too far off now.

And it was a good match. Haselby was a perfectly pleasant fellow. He didn't speak to her as if she were an idiot, he seemed to be kind to animals, and his looks were pleasing enough, even if his hair was beginning to thin. Of course, Lucy had only actually met her intended husband three times, but everyone knew that first impressions were extremely important and usually spot-on accurate.

Besides, her uncle had been her guardian since her father had died ten years earlier, and if he hadn't exactly showered her and her brother Richard with love and affection, he had done his duty by them and raised them well, and Lucy knew it was her duty to obey his wishes and honor the betrothal he had arranged.

Or practically arranged.

Really, it didn't make much difference. She was going to marry Haselby. Everyone knew it.

"I think you use him as an excuse," Hermione said.

Lucy's spine stiffened. "I beg your pardon."

"You use Haselby as an excuse," Hermione repeated, and her face took on a lofty expression Lucy did not enjoy one bit. "So that you do not allow your heart to become engaged elsewhere."

"And just where else, precisely, might I have engaged my heart?" Lucy demanded. "The season has not even begun!"

"Perhaps," Hermione said, "but we have been out and about, getting 'polished' as you and my mother like to put it. You have not been living under a rock, Lucy. You have met any number of men."

There was really no way to point out that none of those men ever even *saw* her when Hermione was near. Hermione would try to deny it, but they would both know that she was lying in an attempt to spare

Lucy's feelings. So Lucy instead grumbled something under her breath that was meant to be a reply without actually *being* a reply.

And then Hermione did not say anything; she just looked at her in that arch manner that she never used with anyone else, and finally Lucy had to defend herself.

"It's not an excuse," she said, crossing her arms, then planting her hands on her hips when that didn't feel right. "Truly, what would be the point of it? You know that I'm to marry Haselby. It's been planned for ages."

She crossed her arms again. Then dropped them. Then finally sat down.

"It's not a bad match," Lucy said. "Truthfully, after what happened to Georgiana Whiton, I should be getting down on my hands and knees and kissing my uncle's feet for making such an acceptable alliance."

There was a moment of horrified, almost reverent silence. If they had been Catholic, they would have surely crossed themselves. "There but for the grace of God," Hermione finally said.

Lucy nodded slowly. Georgiana had been married off to a wheezy seventy-year-old with gout. And not even a titled seventy-year-old with gout. Good heavens, she ought to have at least earned a "Lady" before her name for her sacrifice.

"So you see," Lucy finished, "Haselby really isn't such a bad sort. Better than most, actually."

Hermione looked at her. Closely. "Well, if it is what you wish, Lucy, you know that I shall support you unreservedly. But as for me . . ." She sighed, and her green eyes took on that faraway look that made grown men swoon. "I want something else."

"I know you do," Lucy said, trying to smile. But she couldn't even begin to imagine how Hermione would achieve her dreams. In the world they lived in, viscounts' daughters did not marry viscounts' secretaries. And it seemed to Lucy that it would make far more sense to adjust Hermione's dreams than to reshape the social order. Easier, too.

But right now she was tired. And she wanted to go to bed. She would work on Hermione in the morning. Starting with that handsome Mr. Bridgerton. He would be perfect for her friend, and heaven knew he was interested.

Hermione would come around. Lucy would make sure of it.

Three

In which Our Hero tries very, very hard.

The following morning was bright and clear, and as Gregory helped himself to breakfast, his sister-in-law appeared at his side, smiling faintly, clearly up to something.

"Good morning," she said, far too breezy and cheerful.

Gregory nodded his greeting as he heaped eggs on his plate. "Kate."

"I thought, with the weather so fine, that we might organize an excursion to the village."

"To buy ribbons and bows?"

"Exactly," she replied. "I do think it is important to support the local shopkeepers, don't you?"

"Of course," he murmured, "although I have not recently found myself in great need of ribbons and bows."

Kate appeared not to notice his sarcasm. "All of the young ladies have a bit of pin money and nowhere to spend it. If I do not send them to town they are liable to start a gaming establishment in the rose salon."

Now *that* was something he'd like to see.

"And," Kate continued quite determinedly, "if I send them to town, I will need to send them with escorts."

When Gregory did not respond quickly enough, she repeated, *"With escorts."*

Gregory cleared his throat. "Might I assume you are asking me to walk to the village this afternoon?"

"This morning," she clarified, "*and,* since I thought to match everyone up, *and,* since you are a Bridgerton and thus my favorite gentleman of the bunch, I thought I might inquire if there happened to be anyone with whom you might prefer to be paired."

Kate was nothing if not a matchmaker, but in this case Gregory decided he ought to be grateful for her meddling tendencies. "As a matter of fact," he began, "there is—"

"Excellent!" Kate interrupted, clapping her hands together. "Lucy Abernathy it is."

Lucy Aber— "Lucy Abernathy?" he repeated, dumbfounded. "The Lady Lucinda?"

"Yes, the two of you seemed so well-matched last evening, and I must say, Gregory, I like her tremendously. She says she is practically engaged, but it is my opinion that—"

"I'm not interested in Lady Lucinda," he cut in, deciding it would be too dangerous to wait for Kate to draw breath.

"You're not?"

"No. I'm not. I—" He leaned in, even though they were the only two people in the breakfast room. Somehow it seemed odd, and yes, a little bit embarrassing to shout it out. "Hermione Watson," he said quietly. "I would like to be paired with Miss Watson."

"Really?" Kate didn't look disappointed exactly, but she did look slightly resigned. As if she'd heard this before. Repeatedly.

Damn.

"Yes," Gregory responded, and he felt a rather sizable surge of irritation washing over him. First at Kate, because, well, she was right there, and he'd fallen desperately in love and all she could do was say, "Really?" But then he realized he'd been rather irked all morning. He hadn't slept well the night before; he hadn't been able to stop thinking about Hermione and the slope of her neck, the green of her eyes, the soft lilt of her voice. He had never—never—reacted to a woman like this, and while he was in some way relieved to have finally found the woman he planned to make his wife, it was a bit disconcerting that she had not had the same reaction to *him.*

Heaven knew he'd dreamed of this moment before. Whenever he'd thought about finding his true love, she had always been fuzzy in his thoughts—nameless, faceless. But she had always felt the same grand passion. She hadn't sent him off dancing with her best friend, for God's sake.

"Hermione Watson it is, then," Kate said, exhaling in that way females did when they meant to tell you something you couldn't possibly begin to understand even if they had chosen to convey it in English, which, of course they did not.

Hermione Watson it was. Hermione Watson it would be.

Soon.

Maybe even that morning.

"Do you suppose there is anything to purchase in the village aside from bows and ribbons?" Hermione asked Lucy as they pulled on their gloves.

"I certainly hope so," Lucy responded. "They do this at every house party, don't they? Send us off with our pin money to purchase ribbons and bows. I could decorate an entire house by now. Or at the very least, a small thatched cottage."

Hermione smiled gamely. "I shall donate mine to the cause, and together we shall remake a . . ." She paused, thinking, then smiled. "A large thatched cottage!"

Lucy grinned. There was something so *loyal* about Hermione. Nobody ever saw it, of course. No one ever bothered to look past her face. Although, to be fair, Hermione rarely shared enough of herself with any of her admirers for them to realize what lay behind her pretty exterior. It wasn't that she was shy, precisely, although she certainly wasn't as outgoing as Lucy. Rather, Hermione was private. She simply did not care to share her thoughts and opinions with people she did not know.

And it drove the gentlemen mad.

Lucy peered out the window as they entered one of Aubrey Hall's many drawing rooms. Lady Bridgerton had instructed them to arrive promptly at eleven. "At least it doesn't look as if it might rain," she said. The last time they'd been sent out for fripperies it had drizzled the entire way home. The tree canopy had kept them moderately dry, but their boots had been nearly ruined. And Lucy had been sneezing for a week.

"Good morning, Lady Lucinda, Miss Watson."

It was Lady Bridgerton, their hostess, striding into the room in that confident way of hers. Her dark hair was neatly pulled back, and her eyes gleamed with brisk intelligence. "How lovely to see you both," she said. "You are the last of the ladies to arrive."

"We are?" Lucy asked, horrified. She *hated* being late. "I'm so terribly sorry. Didn't you say eleven o'clock?"

"Oh dear, I did not mean to upset you," Lady Bridgerton said. "I did indeed say eleven o'clock. But that is because I thought to send everyone out in shifts."

"In shifts?" Hermione echoed.

"Yes, it's far more entertaining that way, wouldn't you agree? I have eight ladies and eight gentlemen. If I sent the lot of you out at once, it would be impossible to have a proper conversation. Not to mention the width of the road. I would hate for you to be tripping over one another."

There was also something to be said for safety in numbers, but Lucy kept her thoughts to herself. Lady Bridgerton clearly had some sort of agenda, and as Lucy had already decided that she greatly admired the viscountess, she was rather curious as to the outcome.

"Miss Watson, you will be paired with my husband's brother. I believe you made his acquaintance last night?"

Hermione nodded politely.

Lucy smiled to herself. Mr. Bridgerton had been a busy man that morning. Well done.

"And you, Lady Lucinda," Lady Bridgerton continued, "will be escorted by Mr. Berbrooke." She smiled weakly, almost in apology. "He is a relation of sorts," she added, "and, ah, truly a good-natured fellow."

"A relation?" Lucy echoed, since she wasn't exactly certain how she was meant to respond to Lady Bridgerton's uncharacteristically hesitant tone. "Of sorts?"

"Yes. My husband's brother's wife's sister is married to his brother."

"Oh." Lucy kept her expression bland. "Then you are close?"

Lady Bridgerton laughed. "I like you, Lady Lucinda. And as for Neville . . . well, I am certain you will find him entertaining. Ah, here he is now. Neville! Neville!"

Lucy watched as Lady Bridgerton moved to greet Mr. Neville Berbrooke at the door. They had already been introduced, of course; introductions had been made for everyone at the house party. But Lucy had not yet conversed with Mr. Berbrooke, nor truly even seen him except from afar. He seemed an affable enough fellow, rather jolly-looking with a ruddy complexion and a shock of blond hair.

"Hallo, Lady Bridgerton," he said, somehow crashing into a table leg as he entered the room. "Excellent breakfast this morning. Especially the kippers."

"Thank you," Lady Bridgerton replied, glancing nervously at the

Chinese vase now teetering on the tabletop. "I'm sure you remember Lady Lucinda."

The pair murmured their greetings, then Mr. Berbrooke said, "D'you like kippers?"

Lucy looked first to Hermione, then to Lady Bridgerton for guidance, but neither seemed any less baffled than she, so she just said, "Er . . . yes?"

"Excellent!" he said. "I say, is that a tufted tern out the window?"

Lucy blinked. She looked to Lady Bridgerton, only to discover that the viscountess would not make eye contact. "A tufted tern you say," Lucy finally murmured, since she could not think of any other suitable reply. Mr. Berbrooke had ambled over to the window, so she went to join him. She peered out. She could see no birds.

Meanwhile, out of the corner of her eye she could see that Mr. Bridgerton had entered the room and was doing his best to charm Hermione. Good heavens, the man had a nice smile! Even white teeth, and the expression extended to his eyes, unlike most of the bored young aristocrats Lucy had met. Mr. Bridgerton smiled as if he meant it.

Which made sense, of course, as he was smiling at Hermione, with whom he was quite obviously infatuated.

Lucy could not hear what they were saying, but she easily recognized the expression on Hermione's face. Polite, of course, since Hermione would never be impolite. And maybe no one could see it but Lucy, who knew her friend so well, but Hermione was doing no more than tolerating Mr. Bridgerton's attentions, accepting his flattery with a nod and a pretty smile while her mind was far, far elsewhere.

With that cursed Mr. Edmonds.

Lucy clenched her jaw as she pretended to look for terns, tufted or otherwise, with Mr. Berbrooke. She had no reason to think Mr. Edmonds anything but a nice young man, but the simple truth was, Hermione's parents would never countenance the match, and while Hermione might think she would be able to live happily on a secretary's salary, Lucy was quite certain that once the first bloom of marriage faded, Hermione would be miserable.

And she could do *so* much better. It was obvious that Hermione could marry anyone. Anyone. She wouldn't need to settle. She could be a queen of the *ton* if she so desired.

Lucy eyed Mr. Bridgerton, nodding and keeping one ear on Mr. Berbrooke, who was back on the subject of kippers. Mr. Bridgerton was perfect. He didn't possess a title, but Lucy was not so ruthless that she felt Hermione had to marry into the highest available rank. She just could not align herself with a secretary, for heaven's sake.

Plus, Mr. Bridgerton was extremely handsome, with dark, chestnut hair and lovely hazel eyes. And his family seemed perfectly nice and reasonable, which Lucy had to think was a point in his favor. When you married a man, you married his family, really.

Lucy couldn't imagine a better husband for Hermione. Well, she supposed she would not complain if Mr. Bridgerton were next in line for a marquisate, but really, one could not have everything. And most importantly, she was quite certain that he would make Hermione happy, even if Hermione did not yet realize this.

"I will make this happen," she said to herself.

"Eh?" from Mr. Berbrooke. "Did you find the bird?"

"Over there," Lucy said, pointing toward a tree.

He leaned forward. "Really?"

"Oh, Lucy!" came Hermione's voice.

Lucy turned around.

"Shall we be off? Mr. Bridgerton is eager to be on his way."

"I am at your service, Miss Watson," the man in question said. "We depart at your discretion."

Hermione gave Lucy a look that clearly said that *she* was eager to be on her way, so Lucy said, "Let us depart, then," and she took Mr. Berbrooke's proffered arm and allowed him to lead her to the front drive, managing to yelp only once, even though she thrice stubbed her toe on heaven knew what, but somehow, even with a nice, lovely expanse of grass, Mr. Berbrooke managed to find every tree root, rock, and bump, and lead her directly to them.

Gad.

Lucy mentally prepared herself for further injury. It was going to be a painful outing. But a productive one. By the time they returned home, Hermione would be at least a little intrigued by Mr. Bridgerton.

Lucy would make sure of it.

If Gregory had had any doubts about Miss Hermione Watson, they were banished the moment he placed her hand in the crook of his elbow. There was a rightness to it, a strange, mystical sense of two halves coming together. She fit perfectly next to him. *They* fit.

And he wanted her.

It wasn't even desire. It was strange, actually. He wasn't feeling anything so plebian as bodily desire. It was something else. Something within. He simply wanted her to be his. He wanted to look at her, and to know. To *know* that she would carry his name and bear his children and gaze lovingly at him every morning over a cup of chocolate.

He wanted to tell her all this, to share his dreams, to paint a picture of their life together, but he was no fool, and so he simply said, as he guided her down the front path, "You look exceptionally lovely this morning, Miss Watson."

"Thank you," she said.

And then said nothing else.

He cleared his throat. "Did you sleep well?"

"Yes, thank you," she said.

"Are you enjoying your stay?"

"Yes, thank you," she said.

Funny, but he'd always thought conversation with the woman he'd marry would come just a *little* bit easier.

He reminded himself that she still fancied herself in love with another man. Someone unsuitable, if Lady Lucinda's comment of the night before was any indication. What was that she had called him—the lesser of two evils?

He glanced forward. Lady Lucinda was stumbling along ahead of him on the arm of Neville Berbrooke, who had never learned to adjust his gait for a lady. She seemed to be managing well enough, although he did think he might have heard a small cry of pain at one point.

He gave his head a mental shake. It was probably just a bird. Hadn't Neville said he'd seen a flock of them through the window?

"Have you been friends with Lady Lucinda for very long?" he asked Miss Watson. He knew the answer, of course; Lady Lucinda had told him the night before. But he couldn't think of anything else to ask. And he needed a question that could not be answered with *yes, thank you* or *no, thank you.*

"Three years," Miss Watson replied. "She is my dearest friend." And then her face finally took on a bit of animation as she said, "We ought to catch up."

"To Mr. Berbrooke and Lady Lucinda?"

"Yes," she said with a firm nod. "Yes, we ought."

The last thing Gregory wanted to do was squander his precious time alone with Miss Watson, but he dutifully called out to Berbrooke to hold up. He did, stopping so suddenly that Lady Lucinda quite literally crashed into him.

She let out a startled cry, but other than that was clearly unhurt.

Miss Watson took advantage of the moment, however, by disengaging her hand from his elbow and rushing forward. "Lucy!" she cried out. "Oh, my dearest Lucy, are you injured?"

"Not at all," Lady Lucinda replied, looking slightly confused by the extreme level of her friend's concern.

"I must take your arm," Miss Watson declared, hooking her elbow through Lady Lucinda's.

"You must?" Lady Lucinda echoed, twisting away. Or rather, attempting to. "No, truly, that is not necessary."

"I insist."

"It is not necessary," Lady Lucinda repeated, and Gregory wished he could see her face, because it *sounded* as if she were gritting her teeth.

"Heh heh," came Berbrooke's voice. "P'rhaps I'll take your arm, Bridgerton."

Gregory gave him a level look. "*No*."

Berbrooke blinked. "It was a joke, you know."

Gregory fought the urge to sigh and somehow managed to say, "I was aware." He'd known Neville Berbrooke since they'd both been in leading strings, and he usually had more patience with him, but right now he wanted nothing so much as to fit him with a muzzle.

Meanwhile, the two girls were bickering about something, in tones hushed enough that Gregory couldn't hope to make out what they were saying. Not that he'd likely have understood their language even if they'd been shouting it; it was clearly something bafflingly female. Lady Lucinda was still tugging her arm, and Miss Watson quite simply refused to let go.

"She is injured," Hermione said, turning and batting her eyelashes.

Batting her eyelashes? She chose *this* moment to flirt?

"I am not," Lucy returned. She turned to the two gentlemen. "I am not," she repeated. "Not in the slightest. We should continue."

Gregory couldn't quite decide if he was amused or insulted by the entire spectacle. Miss Watson quite clearly did not wish for his escort, and while some men loved to pine for the unattainable, he'd always preferred his women smiling, friendly, and willing.

Miss Watson turned then, however, and he caught sight of the back of her neck (what *was* it about the back of her neck?). He felt himself sinking again, that madly in love feeling that had captured him the night before, and he told himself not to lose heart. He hadn't even known her a full day; she merely needed time to get to know him. Love did not strike everyone with the same speed. His brother Colin, for example, had known his wife for years and years before he'd realized they were meant to be together.

Not that Gregory planned to wait years and years, but still, it did put the current situation in a better perspective.

After a few moments it became apparent that Miss Watson would not acquiesce, and the two women would be walking arm in arm. Gregory fell in step beside Miss Watson, while Berbrooke ambled on, somewhere in the vicinity of Lady Lucinda.

"You must tell us what it is like to be from such a large family," Lady Lucinda said to him, leaning forward and speaking past Miss Watson. "Hermione and I each have but one sibling."

"Have three m'self," said Berbrooke. "All boys, all of us. 'Cept for my sister, of course."

"It is . . ." Gregory was about to give his usual answer, about it being mad and crazy and usually more trouble than it was worth, but then somehow the deeper truth slipped across his lips, and he found himself saying, "Actually, it's comforting."

"Comforting?" Lady Lucinda echoed. "What an intriguing choice of word."

He looked past Miss Watson to see her regarding him with curious blue eyes.

"Yes," he said slowly, allowing his thoughts to coalesce before replying. "There is comfort in having a family, I think. It's a sense of . . . just *knowing,* I suppose."

"What do you mean?" Lucy asked, and she appeared quite sincerely interested.

"I know that they are there," Gregory said, "that should I ever be in trouble, or even simply in need of a good conversation, I can always turn to them."

And it was true. He had never really thought about it in so many words, but it was true. He was not as close to his brothers as they were to one another, but that was only natural, given the age difference. When they had been men about town, he had been a student at Eton. And now they were all three married, with families of their own.

But still, he knew that should he need them, or his sisters for that matter, he had only to ask.

He never had, of course. Not for anything important. Or even most things unimportant. But he knew that he could. It was more than most men had in this world, more than most men would ever have.

"Mr. Bridgerton?"

He blinked. Lady Lucinda was regarding him quizzically.

"My apologies," he murmured. "Woolgathering, I suppose." He offered her a smile and a nod, then glanced over at Miss Watson, who, he was surprised to see, had also turned to look at him. Her eyes seemed huge in her face, clear and dazzlingly green, and for a moment he felt an almost electric connection. She smiled, just a little, and with a touch of embarrassment at having been caught, then looked away.

Gregory's heart leaped.

And then Lady Lucinda spoke again. "That is *exactly* how I feel about Hermione," she said. "She is the sister of my heart."

"Miss Watson is truly an exceptional lady," Gregory murmured, then added, "As, of course, are you."

"She is a superb watercolorist," Lady Lucinda said.

Hermione blushed prettily. "*Lucy.*"

"But you are," her friend insisted.

"Like to paint myself," came Neville Berbrooke's jovial voice. "Ruin my shirts every time, though."

Gregory glanced at him in surprise. Between his oddly revealing conversation with Lady Lucinda and his shared glance with Miss Watson, he'd almost forgotten Berbrooke was there.

"M'valet is up in arms about it," Neville continued, ambling along. "Don't know why they can't make paint that washes out of linen." He paused, apparently in deep thought. "Or wool."

"Do you like to paint?" Lady Lucinda asked Gregory.

"No talent for it," he admitted. "But my brother is an artist of some renown. Two of his paintings hang in the National Gallery."

"Oh, that is marvelous!" she exclaimed. She turned to Miss Watson. "Did you hear that, Hermione? You must ask Mr. Bridgerton to introduce you to his brother."

"I would not wish to inconvenience either Mr. Bridgerton," she said demurely.

"It would be no inconvenience at all," Gregory said, smiling down at her. "I would be delighted to make the introduction, and Benedict always loves to natter on about art. I rarely am able to follow the conversation, but he seems quite animated."

"You see," Lucy put in, patting Hermione's arm. "You and Mr. Bridgerton have a great deal in common."

Even Gregory thought that was a bit of a stretch, but he did not comment.

"Velvet," Neville suddenly declared.

Three heads swung in his direction. "I beg your pardon?" Lady Lucinda murmured.

"S'the worst," he said, nodding with great vigor. "T'get the paint out of, I mean."

Gregory could only see the back of her head, but he could well imagine her blinking as she said, "You wear velvet while you paint?"

"If it's cold."

"How . . . unique."

Neville's face lit up. "Do you think so? I've always wanted to be unique."

"You are," she said, and Gregory did not hear anything other than reassurance in her voice. "You most certainly are, Mr. Berbrooke."

Neville beamed. "Unique. I like that. Unique." He smiled anew, testing the word on his lips. "Unique. *Unique*. You-oo-oooooo-neek."

The foursome continued toward the village in amiable silence, punctuated by Gregory's occasional attempts to draw Miss Watson into a conversation. Sometimes he succeeded, but more often than not, it was Lady Lucinda who ended up chatting with him. When she wasn't trying to prod Miss Watson into conversation, that was.

And the whole time Neville chattered on, mostly carrying on a conversation with himself, mostly about his newfound uniqueness.

At last the familiar buildings of the village came into view. Neville declared himself uniquely famished, whatever that meant, so Gregory steered the group to the White Hart, a local inn that served simple but always delicious fare.

"We should have a picnic," Lady Lucinda suggested. "Wouldn't that be marvelous?"

"Capital idea," Neville exclaimed, gazing at her as if she were a goddess. Gregory was a little startled by the fervor of his expression, but Lady Lucinda seemed not to notice.

"What is your opinion, Miss Watson?" Gregory asked. But the lady in question was lost in thought, her eyes unfocused even as they remained fixed on a painting on the wall.

"Miss Watson?" he repeated, and then when he finally had her attention, he said, "Would you care to take a picnic?"

"Oh. Yes, that would be lovely." And then she went back to staring off into space, her perfect lips curved into a wistful, almost longing expression.

Gregory nodded, tamping down his disappointment, and set out making arrangements. The innkeeper, who knew his family well, gave him two clean bedsheets to lay upon the grass and promised to bring out a hamper of food when it was ready.

"Excellent work, Mr. Bridgerton," Lady Lucinda said. "Don't you agree, Hermione?"

"Yes, of course."

"Hope he brings pie," Neville said as he held the door open for the ladies. "I can always eat pie."

Gregory tucked Miss Watson's hand in the crook of his arm before she could escape. "I asked for a selection of foods," he said quietly to her. "I hope there is something that meets your cravings."

She looked up at him and he felt it again, the air swooshing from his body as he lost himself in her eyes. And he knew she felt it, too. She had to. How could she not, when he felt as if his own legs might give out beneath him?

"I am sure that it will be delightful," she said.

"Are you in possession of a sweet tooth?"

"I am," she admitted.

"Then you are in luck," Gregory told her. "Mr. Gladdish has promised to include some of his wife's gooseberry pie, which is quite famous in this district."

"Pie?" Neville visibly perked up. He turned to Lady Lucinda. "Did he say we were getting pie?"

"I believe he did," she replied.

Neville sighed with pleasure. "Do you like pie, Lady Lucinda?"

The barest hint of exasperation washed over her features as she asked, "What sort of pie, Mr. Berbrooke?"

"Oh, any pie. Sweet, savory, fruit, meat."

"Well . . ." She cleared her throat, glancing about as if the buildings and trees might offer some guidance. "I . . . ah . . . I suppose I like most pies."

And it was in that minute that Gregory was quite certain Neville had fallen in love.

Poor Lady Lucinda.

They walked across the main thoroughfare to a grassy field, and Gregory swept open the sheets, laying them flat upon the ground. Lady Lucinda, clever girl that she was, sat first, then patted a spot for Neville that would guarantee that Gregory and Miss Watson would be forced to share the other patch of cloth.

And then Gregory set about winning her heart.

Four

In which Our Heroine offers advice, Our Hero takes it, and everyone eats too much pie.

He was going about it all wrong.

Lucy glanced over Mr. Berbrooke's shoulder, trying not to frown. Mr. Bridgerton was making a valiant attempt to win Hermione's favor, and Lucy had to admit that under normal circumstances, with a different female, he would have succeeded handily. Lucy thought of the many girls she knew from school—any one of them would be head over heels in love with him by now. *Every* one of them, as a matter of fact.

But not Hermione.

He was trying too hard. Being too attentive, too focused, too . . . too . . . Well, too in love, quite frankly, or at least too infatuated.

Mr. Bridgerton was charming, and he was handsome, and obviously quite intelligent as well, but Hermione had *seen* all this before. Lucy could not even begin to count the number of gentlemen who had pursued her friend in much the same manner. Some were witty, some were earnest. They gave flowers, poetry, candy—one even brought Hermione a puppy (instantly refused by Hermione's mother, who had informed the poor gentleman that the natural habitat of dogs did not include Aubusson carpets, porcelain from the Orient, or herself).

But underneath they were all the same. They hung on her every word, they gazed at her as if she were a Greek goddess come down to earth, and they fell over each other in an attempt to offer the cleverest, most romantic compliments ever to rain down upon her pretty ears. And they never seemed to understand how completely unoriginal they all were.

If Mr. Bridgerton truly wished to pique Hermione's interest, he was going to need to do something different.

"More gooseberry pie, Lady Lucinda?" Mr. Berbrooke asked.

"Yes, please," Lucy murmured, if only to keep him busy with the slicing as she pondered what to do next. She really didn't want Hermione to throw her life away on Mr. Edmonds, and truly, Mr. Bridgerton was perfect. He just needed a little help.

"Oh, look!" Lucy exclaimed. "Hermione doesn't have any pie."

"No pie?" Mr. Berbrooke gasped.

Lucy batted her eyelashes at him, not a mannerism with which she had much practice or skill. "Would you be so kind as to serve her?"

As Mr. Berbrooke nodded, Lucy stood up. "I believe I will stretch my legs," she announced. "There are lovely flowers on the far side of the field. Mr. Bridgerton, do you know anything about the local flora?"

He looked up, surprised by her question. "A bit." But he didn't move.

Hermione was busy assuring Mr. Berbrooke that she adored gooseberry pie, so Lucy took advantage of the moment and jerked her head toward the flowers, giving Mr. Bridgerton the sort of urgent look that generally meant "*Come with me* now."

For a moment he appeared to be puzzled, but he quickly recovered and rose to his feet. "Will you allow me to tell you a bit about the scenery, Lady Lucinda?"

"That would be marvelous," she said, perhaps a touch too enthusiastically. Hermione was staring at her with patent suspicion. But Lucy knew that she would not offer to join them; to do so would encourage Mr. Bridgerton to believe she desired his company.

So Hermione would be left with Mr. Berbrooke and the pie. Lucy shrugged. It was only fair.

"That one, I believe, is a daisy," Mr. Bridgerton said, once they had crossed the field. "And that stalky blue one— Actually, I don't know what it's called."

"Delphinium," Lucy said briskly, "and you must know that I did not summon you to speak of flowers."

"I had an inkling."

She decided to ignore his tone. "I wished to give you some advice."

"Really," he drawled. Except it wasn't a question.

"Really."

"And what might your advice be?"

There was really no way to make it sound any better than it was, so she looked him in the eye and said, "You're going about this all wrong."

"I beg your pardon," he said stiffly.

Lucy stifled a groan. Now she'd pricked his pride, and he would surely be insufferable. "If you want to win Hermione," she said, "you have to do something different."

Mr. Bridgerton stared down at her with an expression that almost bordered on contempt. "I am well able to conduct my own courtships."

"I am sure you are . . . with other ladies. But Hermione is different."

He remained silent, and Lucy knew that she had made her point. He also thought Hermione different, else he wouldn't be making such an effort.

"Everyone does what you do," Lucy said, glancing over at the picnic to make sure that neither Hermione nor Mr. Berbrooke had got up to join them. "Everyone."

"A gentleman does love to be compared to the flock," Mr. Bridgerton murmured.

Lucy had any number of rejoinders for *that,* but she kept her mind on the task at hand and said, "You cannot act like the rest of them. You need to set yourself apart."

"And how do you propose I do that?"

She took a breath. He wasn't going to like her answer. "You must stop being so . . . devoted. Don't treat her like a princess. In fact, you should probably leave her alone for a few days."

His expression turned to distrust. "And allow all the other gentleman to rush in?"

"They will rush in anyway," she said in a matter-of-fact voice. "There is nothing you can do about that."

"Lovely."

Lucy plodded on. "If *you* withdraw, Hermione will be curious as to the reason why."

Mr. Bridgerton looked dubious, so she continued with, "Do not worry, she will know that you're interested. Heavens, after today she'd have to be an idiot not to."

He scowled at that, and Lucy herself couldn't quite believe she was speaking so frankly to a man she barely knew, but desperate times surely called for desperate measures . . . or desperate speech. "She will know, I promise you. Hermione is very intelligent. Not that anyone seems to notice. Most men can't see beyond her face."

"I would like to know her mind," he said softly.

Something in his tone hit Lucy squarely in the chest. She looked up, right into his eyes, and she had the strangest sense that she was somewhere else, and he was somewhere else, and the world was dropping away around them.

He was different from the other gentlemen she'd met. She wasn't sure how, exactly, except that there was something more to him. Something different. Something that made her ache, deep in her chest.

And for a moment she thought she might cry.

But she didn't. Because, really, she couldn't. And she wasn't that sort of female, anyway. She didn't wish to be. And she certainly did not cry when she did not know the reason for it.

"Lady Lucinda?"

She'd stayed silent too long. It was unlike her, and— "She will not wish to allow you to," she blurted out. "Know her mind, I mean. But you can . . ." She cleared her throat, blinked, regained her focus, and then planted her eyes firmly on the small patch of daisies sparkling in the sun. "You can convince her otherwise," she continued. "I am sure that you can. If you are patient. And you are true."

He didn't say anything right away. There was nothing but the faint whistle of the breeze. And then, quietly, he asked, "Why are you helping me?"

Lucy turned back to him and was relieved that this time the earth remained firmly fixed beneath her feet. She was herself again, brisk, no-nonsense, and practical to a fault. And he was just another gentleman vying for Hermione's hand.

All was normal.

"It's you or Mr. Edmonds," she said.

"Is that his name," he murmured.

"He is her father's secretary," she explained. "He is not a bad man, and I don't think he is only after her money, but any fool could see that you are the better match."

Mr. Bridgerton cocked his head to the side. "Why, I wonder, does it sound as if you have just called Miss Watson a fool?"

Lucy turned to him with steel in her eyes. "Do not *ever* question my devotion to Hermione. I could not—" She shot a quick glance at Hermione to make sure she wasn't looking before she lowered her voice and continued. "I could not love her better if she were my blood sister."

To his credit, Mr. Bridgerton gave her a respectful nod and said, "I did you a disservice. My apologies."

Lucy swallowed uncomfortably as she acknowledged his words. He looked as if he meant them, which went a long way toward mollifying her. "Hermione means the world to me," she said. She thought about the school holidays she had spent with the Watson family, and she thought about the lonely visits home. Her returns had never seemed to coincide with those of her brother, and Fennsworth Abbey was a cold and forbidding place with only her uncle for company.

Robert Abernathy had always done his duty by his two charges, but he was rather cold and forbidding as well. Home meant long walks alone, endless reading alone, even meals alone, as Uncle Robert had never shown any interest in dining with her. When he had informed Lucy that she would be attending Miss Moss's, her initial impulse had been to throw her arms around him and gush, "Thank you thank you *thank you*!"

Except that she had never hugged him before, not in the seven years he'd been her guardian. And besides that, he had been seated behind his desk and had already returned his attention to the papers in front of him. Lucy had been dismissed.

When she arrived at school, she had thrown herself into her new life as a student. And she had adored every moment. It was so marvelous just to have people to talk to. Her brother Richard had left for Eton at the age of ten, even before their father had died, and she'd been wandering the halls of the Abbey for nearly a decade with no one but her officious governess for company.

At school people liked her. That had been the best part of all. At home she was nothing more than an afterthought, but at Miss Moss's School for Exceptional Young Ladies the other students sought her company. They asked her questions and actually waited to hear her answer. Lucy might not have been the queen bee of the school, but she had felt that she belonged, and that she had mattered.

She and Hermione had been assigned to share a room that first year at Miss Moss's, and their friendship had been almost instant. By nightfall of that first day, the two were laughing and chattering as if they had known each other all of their lives.

Hermione made her feel . . . better somehow. Not just their friendship, but the knowledge of their friendship. Lucy *liked* being someone's best friend. She liked having one, too, of course, but she really liked knowing that in all the world, there was someone who liked her best. It made her feel confident.

Comfortable.

It was rather like Mr. Bridgerton and what he'd said about his family, actually.

She knew she could count on Hermione. And Hermione knew the same was true of her. And Lucy wasn't sure that there was anyone else in the world she could say that of. Her brother, she supposed. Richard would always come to her aid if she needed him, but they saw each other so rarely these days. It was a pity, really. They had been quite close when they were small. Shut away at Fennsworth Abbey, there was rarely anyone else with whom to play, and so they'd had no choice but to turn to each other. Luckily, they'd got along, more often than not.

She forced her mind back to the present and turned to Mr. Bridgerton. He was standing quite still, regarding her with an expression of polite curiosity, and Lucy had the strangest sense that if she told him everything—about Hermione and Richard and Fennsworth Abbey and how lovely it had been to leave for school . . .

He would have understood. It seemed impossible that he could, coming from such a large and famously close family. He couldn't possibly know what it was to be lonely, to have something to say but no one to say it to. But somehow—it was his eyes, really, suddenly greener than she'd realized, and so focused on her face—

She swallowed. Good heavens, what was happening to her that she could not even finish her own thoughts?

"I only wish for Hermione's happiness," she managed to get out. "I hope you realize that."

He nodded, then flicked his eyes toward the picnic. "Shall we rejoin the others?" he asked. He smiled ruefully. "I do believe Mr. Berbrooke has fed Miss Watson three pieces of pie."

Lucy felt a laugh bubbling within her. "Oh dear."

His tone was charmingly bland as he said, "For the sake of her health, if nothing else, we ought to return."

"Will you think about what I said?" Lucy asked, allowing him to place her hand on his arm.

He nodded. "I will."

She felt herself grip him a little more tightly. "I am right about this. I promise you that I am. No one knows Hermione better than I. And no one else has watched all those gentlemen try—and fail—to win her favor."

He turned, and his eyes caught hers. For a moment they stood perfectly still, and Lucy realized that he was assessing her, taking her measure in a manner that should have been uncomfortable.

But it wasn't. And that was the oddest thing. He was staring at her as if he could see down to her very soul, and it didn't feel the least bit awkward. In fact, it felt oddly . . . nice.

"I would be honored to accept your advice regarding Miss Watson," he said, turning so that they might return to the picnic spot. "And I thank you for offering to help me win her."

"Th-thank you," Lucy stammered, because really, hadn't that been her intention?

But then she realized that she no longer felt quite so nice.

Gregory followed Lady Lucinda's directives to the letter. That evening, he did not approach Miss Watson in the drawing room, where the guests had assembled before supper. When they removed themselves to the dining room, he made no attempt to interfere with the social order and have his seat switched so that he might sit next to her. And once the gentlemen had returned from their port and joined the ladies in the conservatory for a piano recital, he took a seat at the rear, even though she and Lady Lucinda were standing quite alone, and it would have been easy—expected, even—for him to pause and murmur his greetings as he passed by.

But no, he had committed to this possibly ill-advised scheme, and so the back of the room it was. He watched as Miss Watson found a seat three rows ahead, and then settled into his chair, finally allowing himself the indulgence of gazing upon the back of her neck.

Which would have been a perfectly fulfilling pastime were he not *completely* unable to think of anything other than her absolute lack of interest. In him.

Truly, he could have grown two heads and a tail and he would have received nothing more than the polite half-smile she seemed to give everyone. If that.

It was not the sort of reaction Gregory was used to receiving from women. He did not expect universal adulation, but really, when he did make an effort, he usually saw better results than this.

It was damned irritating, actually.

And so he watched the two women, willing them to turn, to squirm, to do something to indicate that they were cognizant of his presence. Finally, after three concertos and a fugue, Lady Lucinda slowly twisted in her seat.

He could easily imagine her thoughts.

Slowly, slowly, act as if you're glancing at the door to see if someone came in. Flick your eyes ever so slightly at Mr. Bridgerton—

He lifted his glass in salute.

She gasped, or at least he hoped she did, and turned quickly around.

He smiled. He probably shouldn't take such joy in her distress, but truly, it was the only bright spot in the evening thus far.

As for Miss Watson—if she could feel the heat of his stare, she gave no indication. Gregory would have liked to have thought that she was studiously ignoring him—that at least might have indicated some sort of awareness. But as he watched her glance idly around the room, dipping her head every so often to whisper something in Lady Lucinda's ear, it became painfully clear that she wasn't ignoring him at all. That would imply that she noticed him.

Which she quite obviously did not.

Gregory felt his jaw clench. While he did not doubt the good intentions behind Lady Lucinda's advice, the advice itself had been quite patently dreadful. And with only five days remaining to the house party, he had wasted valuable time.

"You look bored."

He turned. His sister-in-law had slipped into the seat next to him and was speaking in a low undertone so as not to interfere with the performance.

"Quite a blow to my reputation as a hostess," she added dryly.

"Not at all," he murmured. "You are splendid as always."

Kate turned forward and was silent for a few moments before saying, "She's quite pretty."

Gregory did not bother to pretend that he didn't know what she was talking about. Kate was far too clever for that. But that didn't mean he had to encourage the conversation. "She is," he said simply, keeping his eyes facing front.

"My suspicion," said Kate, "is that her heart is otherwise engaged. She has not encouraged any of the gentlemen's attentions, and they have certainly all tried."

Gregory felt his jaw tense.

"I have heard," Kate continued, surely aware that she was being a bother, not that that would stop her, "that the same has been true all of this spring. The girl gives no indication that she wishes to make a match."

"She fancies her father's secretary," Gregory said. Because, really, what was the point of keeping it a secret? Kate had a way of finding everything out. And perhaps she could be of help.

"Really?" Her voice came out a bit too loud, and she was forced to murmur apologies to her guests. "Really?" she said again, more quietly. "How do you know?"

Gregory opened his mouth to reply, but Kate answered her own question. "Oh, of course," she said, "the Lady Lucinda. She would know everything."

"Everything," Gregory confirmed dryly.

Kate pondered this for a few moments, then stated the obvious. "Her parents cannot be pleased."

"I don't know that they are aware."

"Oh my." Kate sounded sufficiently impressed by this gossipy tidbit that Gregory turned to look at her. Sure enough, her eyes were wide and sparkling.

"Do try to contain yourself," he said.

"But it's the most excitement I've had all spring."

He looked her squarely in the face. "You need to find a hobby."

"Oh, Gregory," she said, giving him a little nudge with her elbow. "Don't allow love to turn you into such a stuff. You're far too much fun for that. Her parents will never allow her to marry the secretary, and she's not one to elope. You need only to wait her out."

He let out an irritated exhale.

Kate patted him comfortingly. "I know, I know, you wish to have things done. Your sort is never one for patience."

"My sort?"

She flicked her hand, which she clearly considered enough of an answer. "Truly, Gregory," she said, "this is for the best."

"That she is in love with someone else?"

"Stop being so dramatic. I meant that it will give you time to be certain of your feelings for her."

Gregory thought of the gut-punched feeling he got every time he looked at her. Good God, especially the back of her neck, strange as that seemed. He couldn't imagine he needed time. This was everything he'd ever imagined love to be. Huge, sudden, and utterly exhilarating.

And somehow crushing at the same time.

"I was surprised you didn't ask to be seated with her at supper," Kate murmured.

Gregory glared at the back of Lady Lucinda's head.

"I can arrange it for tomorrow, if you wish," Kate offered.

"Do."

Kate nodded. "Yes, I— Oh, here we are. The music is ending. Pay attention now and look like we're polite."

He stood to applaud, as did she. "Have you ever *not* chattered all the way through a music recital?" he asked, keeping his eyes front.

"I have a curious aversion to them," she said. But then her lips curved into a wicked little smile. "And a nostalgic sort of a fondness, as well."

"Really?" *Now* he was interested.

"I don't tell tales, of course," she murmured, quite purposefully not looking at him, "but really, have you ever seen me attend the opera?"

Gregory felt his brows lift. Clearly there was an opera singer somewhere in his brother's past. Where *was* his brother, anyway? Anthony seemed to have developed a remarkable talent for avoiding most of the social functions of the house party. Gregory had seen him only twice aside from their interview the night he arrived.

"Where *is* the scintillating Lord Bridgerton?" he asked.

"Oh, somewhere. I don't know. We'll find each other at the end of the day, that is all that matters." Kate turned to him with a remarkably serene smile. Annoyingly serene. "I must mingle," she said, smiling at him as if she hadn't a care in the world. "Do enjoy yourself." And she was off.

Gregory hung back, making polite conversation with a few of the other guests as he surreptitiously watched Miss Watson. She was chatting with two young gentlemen—annoying sops, the both of them—while Lady Lucinda stood politely to the side. And while Miss Watson did not appear to be flirting with either, she certainly was paying them more attention than *he'd* received that evening.

And there was Lady Lucinda, smiling prettily, taking it all in.

Gregory's eyes narrowed. Had she double-crossed him? She didn't seem the sort. But then again, their acquaintance was barely twenty-four hours old. How well did he know her, really? She *could* have an ulterior motive. And she *might* be a very fine actress, with dark, mysterious secrets lying below the surface of her—

Oh, blast it all. He was going mad. He would bet his last penny that Lady Lucinda could not lie to save her life. She was sunny and open and most definitely *not* mysterious. She had meant well, of that much he was certain.

But her advice had been excremental.

He caught her eye. A faint expression of apology seemed to flit across her face, and he thought she might have shrugged.

Shrugged? What the hell did *that* mean?

He took a step forward.

Then he stopped.

Then he thought about taking another step.

No.

Yes.

No.

Maybe?

Damn it. He didn't know what to do. It was a singularly unpleasant sensation.

He looked back at Lady Lucinda, quite certain that his expression was not one of sweetness and light. Really, this was all her fault.

But of course now she wasn't looking at him.

He did not shift his gaze.

She turned back. Her eyes widened, hopefully with alarm.

Good. Now they were getting somewhere. If he couldn't feel the bliss of Miss Watson's regard, then at least he could make Lady Lucinda feel the misery of his.

Truly, there were times that just didn't call for maturity and tact.

He remained at the edge of the room, finally beginning to enjoy himself. There was something perversely entertaining about imagining Lady Lucinda as a small defenseless hare, not quite sure if or when she might meet her untimely end.

Not, of course, that Gregory could ever assign himself the role of hunter. His piss-poor marksmanship guaranteed that he couldn't hit anything that moved, and it was a damned good thing he wasn't responsible for acquiring his own food.

But he *could* imagine himself the fox.

He smiled, his first real one of the evening.

And then he knew that the fates were on his side, because he saw Lady Lucinda make her excuses and slip out the conservatory door, presumably to attend to her needs. As Gregory was standing on his own in the back corner, no one noticed when he exited the room through a different door.

And when Lady Lucinda passed by the doorway to the library, he was able to yank her in without making a sound.

Five

In which Our Hero and Heroine have a most intriguing conversation.

One moment Lucy was walking down the corridor, her nose scrunched in thought as she tried to recall the location of the nearest washroom, and the next she was hurtling through air, or at the very least tripping over her feet, only to find herself bumping up against a decidedly large, decidedly warm, and decidedly human form.

"Don't scream," came a voice. One she knew.

"Mr. Bridgerton?" Good heavens, this seemed out of character. Lucy wasn't quite certain if she ought to be scared.

"We need to talk," he said, letting go of her arm. But he locked the door and pocketed the key.

"Now?" Lucy asked. Her eyes adjusted to the dim light and she realized they were in the library. "Here?" And then a more pertinent question sprang to mind. "Alone?"

He scowled. "I'm not going to ravish you, if that's what worries you."

She felt her jaw clench. She hadn't thought he *would,* but he didn't need to make his honorable behavior sound so much like an insult.

"Well, then, what is this about?" she demanded. "If I am caught here in your company, there will be the devil to pay. I'm practically engaged, you know."

"I know," he said. In *that* sort of tone. As if she'd informed him of it ad nauseam, when she knew for a fact she had not mentioned it more than once. Or possibly twice.

"Well, I am," she grumbled, just knowing that she would think of the perfect retort two hours later.

"What," he demanded, "is going on?"

"What do you mean?" she asked, even though she knew quite well what he was talking about.

"Miss Watson," he ground out.

"Hermione?" As if there was another Miss Watson. But it did buy her a bit of time.

"Your advice," he said, his gaze boring into hers, "was abysmal."

He was correct, of course, but she'd been hoping he might not have noticed.

"Right," she said, eyeing him warily as he crossed his arms. It wasn't the most welcoming of gestures, but she had to admit that he carried it off well. She'd heard that his reputation was one of joviality and fun, neither of which was presently in evidence, but, well, hell hath no fury and all that. She supposed one didn't need to be a woman to feel a tad bit underwhelmed at the prospect of unrequited love.

And as she glanced hesitantly at his handsome face, it occurred to her that he probably didn't have much experience with unrequited love. Really, who *would* say no to this gentleman?

Besides Hermione. But she said no to everyone. He shouldn't take it personally.

"Lady Lucinda?" he drawled, waiting for a response.

"Of course," she stalled, wishing he didn't seem so very *large* in the closed room. "Right. Right."

He lifted a brow. "Right."

She swallowed. His tone was one of vaguely paternal indulgence, as if she were mildly amusing but not quite worthy of notice. She knew that tone well. It was a favorite of older brothers, for use with younger sisters. And any friends they might bring home for school holidays.

She hated that tone.

But she plowed on nonetheless and said, "I agree that my plan did not turn out to be the best course of action, but truthfully, I am not certain that anything else would have been an improvement."

This did not appear to be what he wished to hear. She cleared her throat. Twice. And then again. "I'm terribly sorry," she added, because she did feel badly, and it was her experience that apologies always worked when one wasn't quite certain what to say. "But I really did think—"

"You told me," he interrupted, "that if I ignored Miss Watson—"

"I didn't tell you to *ignore* her!"

"You most certainly did."

"No. No, I did not. I told you to back away a bit. To try to be not quite so obvious in your besottedment."

It wasn't a word, but really, Lucy couldn't be bothered.

"Very well," he replied, and his tone shifted from slightly-superior-older-brother to outright condescension. "If I wasn't meant to ignore her, just what precisely do you think I should have done?"

"Well . . ." She scratched the back of her neck, which suddenly felt as if it were sprouting the most horrid of hives. Or maybe it was just nerves. She'd almost rather the hives. She didn't much like this queasy feeling growing in her stomach as she tried to think of something reasonable to say.

"Other than what I did, that is," he added.

"I'm not sure," she ground out. "I haven't *oceans* of experience with this sort of thing."

"Oh, *now* you tell me."

"Well, it was worth a try," she shot back. "Heaven knows, you certainly weren't succeeding on your own."

His mouth clamped into a line, and she allowed herself a small, satisfied smile for hitting a nerve. She wasn't *normally* a mean-spirited person, but the occasion did seem to call for just a little bit of self-congratulation.

"Very well," he said tightly, and while she would have preferred that he apologized and then said—explicitly—that she was right and he was wrong, she supposed that in *some* circles, "Very well" *might* pass for an acknowledgment of error.

And judging by his face, it was the most she was likely to receive.

She nodded regally. It seemed the best course of action. Act like a queen and maybe she would be treated like one.

"Have you any other brilliant ideas?"

Or not.

"Well," she said, pretending that he'd actually sounded as if he cared about the answer, "I don't think it's so much a question of what to do as why what you did didn't work."

He blinked.

"No one has ever given up on Hermione," Lucy said with a touch of impatience. She hated when people did not understand her meaning immediately. "Her disinterest only makes them redouble their efforts. It's embarrassing, really."

He looked vaguely affronted. "I beg your pardon."

"Not *you,*" Lucy said quickly.

"My relief is palpable."

Lucy should have taken offense at his sarcasm, but his sense of humor was so like her own she couldn't help but enjoy it. "As I was saying," she continued, because she always did like to remain on the topic at hand, "no one ever seems to admit defeat and move on to a more attainable lady. Once everyone realizes that everyone *else* wants her, they seem to go mad. It's as if she's nothing but a prize to be won."

"Not to me," he said quietly.

Her eyes snapped to his face, and she realized instantly that he meant that Hermione was *more* than a prize. He cared for her. He truly cared for her. Lucy wasn't sure why, or even how, as he had barely made her friend's acquaintance. And Hermione hadn't been terribly forthcoming in her conversations, not that she ever was with the gentlemen who pursued her. But Mr. Bridgerton cared for the woman inside, not just the perfect face. Or at least he thought he did.

She nodded slowly, letting all this sink in. "I thought that perhaps if someone actually *stopped* dancing attendance on her, she might find it intriguing. Not," she hastened to assure him, "that Hermione sees all of this gentlemanly attention as her due. Quite to the contrary. To be honest, for the most part it's a nuisance."

"Your flattery knows no bounds." But he was smiling—just a little bit—as he said it.

"I've never been very skilled at flattery," she admitted.

"Apparently not."

She smiled wryly. He hadn't meant his words as an insult, and she wasn't going to take them as such. "She will come around."

"Do you think so?"

"I do. She will have to. Hermione is a romantic, but she understands how the world works. Deep down she knows she cannot marry Mr. Edmonds. It simply cannot be done. Her parents will disown her, or at the very least they will threaten to, and she is not the sort to risk that."

"If she really loved someone," he said softly, "she would risk anything."

Lucy froze. There was something in his voice. Something rough, something powerful. It shivered across her skin, raising goosebumps, leaving her strangely unable to move.

And she had to ask. She had to. She had to *know*. "Would you?" she whispered. "Would you risk anything?"

He didn't move, but his eyes burned. And he didn't hesitate. "Anything."

Her lips parted. With surprise? Awe? Something else?

"Would *you*?" he countered.

"I . . . I'm not sure." She shook her head, and she had the queerest feeling that she didn't quite know herself any longer. Because it ought to have been an easy question. It would have been, just a few days ago. She would have said of course not, and she would have said she was far too practical for that sort of nonsense.

And most of all, she would have said that that sort of love did not exist, anyway.

But something had changed, and she didn't know what. Something had shifted within her, leaving her off-balance.

Unsure.

"I don't know," she said again. "I suppose it would depend."

"On what?" And his voice grew even softer. Impossibly soft, and yet she could make out every word.

"On . . ." She didn't know. How could she not know what it would depend upon? She felt lost, and rootless, and . . . and . . . and then the words just came. Slipped softly from her lips. "On love, I suppose."

"On love."

"Yes." Good heavens, had she ever had such a conversation? Did people actually talk about such things? And were there even any answers?

Or was she the only person in the world who didn't understand?

Something caught in her throat, and Lucy suddenly felt far too alone in her ignorance. He knew, and Hermione knew, and the poets claimed they did as well. It seemed *she* was the only lost soul, the only person who didn't understand what love was, who wasn't even sure it existed, or if it did, whether it existed for her.

"On how it felt," she finally said, because she didn't know what else to say. "On how love felt. How it feels."

His eyes met hers. "Do you think there is a variation?"

She hadn't expected another question. She was still reeling from the last one.

"How love feels," he clarified. "Do you think it could possibly be different for different people? If you loved someone, truly and deeply, wouldn't it feel like . . . like *everything*?"

She didn't know what to say.

He turned and took a few steps toward the window. "It would consume you," he said. "How could it not?"

Lucy just stared at his back, mesmerized by the way his finely cut coat stretched across his shoulders. It was the strangest thing, but she couldn't seem to pull her gaze from the little spot where his hair touched his collar.

She almost jumped when he turned around. "There would be no doubting it," he said, his voice low with the intensity of a true believer. "You would simply know. It would feel like everything you'd ever dreamed, and then it would feel like more."

He stepped toward her. Once. Then again. And then he said, "That, I think, is how love must feel."

And in that moment Lucy knew that she was not destined to feel that way. If it existed—if love existed the way Gregory Bridgerton imagined it—it did not wait for her. She couldn't imagine such a maelstrom of emotion. And she would not enjoy it. That much she knew. She didn't want to feel lost to the whirlwind, at the mercy of something beyond her control.

She didn't want misery. She didn't want despair. And if that meant she also had to forsake bliss and rapture, so be it.

She lifted her eyes to his, made breathless by the gravity of her own revelations. "It's too much," she heard herself say. "It would be too much. I wouldn't . . . I wouldn't . . ."

Slowly, he shook his head. "You would have no choice. It would be beyond your control. It just . . . happens."

Her mouth parted with surprise. "That's what she said."

"Who?"

And when she answered, her voice was strangely detached, as if the words were being drawn straight from her memory. "Hermione," she said. "That's what Hermione said about Mr. Edmonds."

Gregory's lips tightened at the corners. "Did she?"

Lucy slowly nodded. "Almost precisely. She said it just happens. In an instant."

"She said that?" The words sounded like an echo, and indeed, that was all he could do—whisper inane questions, looking for verification, hoping that maybe he had misheard, and she would reply with something entirely different.

But of course she did not. In fact, it was worse than he'd feared. She said, "She was in the garden, that's what she said, just looking at the roses, and then she saw him. And she knew."

Gregory just stared at her. His chest felt hollow, his throat tight.

This wasn't what he wanted to hear. *Damn* it, this was the one thing he didn't want to hear.

She looked up at him then, and her eyes, gray in the dim light of the night, found his in an oddly intimate manner. It was as if he knew her, knew what she would say, and how her face would look when she said it. It was strange, and terrifying, and most of all, discomforting, because this wasn't the Honorable Miss Hermione Watson.

This was Lady Lucinda Abernathy, and she was not the woman with whom he intended to spend the rest of his life.

She was perfectly nice, perfectly intelligent, and certainly more than attractive. But Lucy Abernathy was not for him. And he almost laughed, because it all would have been so much easier if his heart had flipped the first time he saw *her.* She might be practically engaged, but she wasn't in love. Of that he was certain.

But Hermione Watson . . .

"What did she say?" he whispered, dreading the answer.

Lady Lucinda tilted her head to the side, and she looked nothing so much as puzzled. "She said that she didn't even see his face. Just the back of his head—"

Just the back of her neck.

"—and then he turned, and she thought she heard music, and all she could think was—"

I am wrecked.

"—'I am ruined.' That is what she said to me." She looked up at him, her head still tilting curiously to the side. "Can you imagine? Ruined? Of all things. I couldn't quite grasp it."

But *he* could. He could.

Exactly.

He looked at Lady Lucinda, and he saw that she was watching his face. She looked puzzled still. And concerned. And just a little bit bewildered when she asked, "Don't you find it odd?"

"Yes." Just one word, but with his entire heart wrapped around it. Because it *was* strange. It cut like a knife. She wasn't supposed to feel that way about someone else.

This wasn't the way it was supposed to happen.

And then, as if a spell had been broken, Lady Lucinda turned and took a few steps to the right. She peered at the bookshelves—not that she could possibly make out any of the titles in this light—then ran her fingers along the spines.

Gregory watched her hand; he didn't know why. He just watched it as it moved. She was quite elegant, he realized. It wasn't noticeable at first, because her looks were so wholesome and traditional. One expected elegance to shimmer like silk, to glow, to transfix. Elegance was an orchid, not a simple daisy.

But when Lady Lucinda moved, she looked different. She seemed to . . . flow.

She would be a good dancer. He was sure of it.

Although he wasn't quite sure why that mattered.

"I'm sorry," she said, turning quite suddenly around.

"About Miss Watson?"

"Yes. I did not mean to hurt your feelings."

"You didn't," he said, perhaps a little too sharply.

"Oh." She blinked, perhaps with surprise. "I'm glad for that. I didn't mean to."

She wouldn't mean to, he realized. She wasn't the sort.

Her lips parted, but she didn't speak right away. Her eyes seemed to focus beyond his shoulder, as if she were searching behind him for the correct words. "It was just that . . . Well, when you said what you said about love," she began, "it just sounded so familiar. I couldn't quite fathom it."

"Nor could I," he said softly.

She held silent, not quite looking at him. Her lips were pursed—just a touch—and every now and then she would blink. Not a fluttery sort of movement but rather something quite deliberate.

She was thinking, he realized. She was the sort who *thought* about things, probably to the neverending frustration of anyone charged with the task of guiding her through life.

"What will you do now?" she asked.

"About Miss Watson?"

She nodded.

"What do you suggest I do?"

"I'm not sure," she said. "I can speak to her on your behalf, if you would like."

"No." Something about that seemed far too juvenile. And Gregory was only just now beginning to feel that he was truly a man, well and grown, ready to make his mark.

"You can wait, then," she said with a tiny shrug. "Or you can proceed and try again to woo her. She won't have the opportunity to see Mr. Edmonds for at least a month, and I would think . . . eventually . . . she would come to see . . ."

But she didn't finish. And he wanted to know. "Come to see what?" he pressed.

She looked up, as if pulled from a dream. "Why, that you . . . that you . . . just that you are so much *better* than the rest. I don't know why she cannot see it. It's quite obvious to me."

From anyone else it would have been a strange statement. Overly forward, perhaps. Maybe even a coy hint of availability.

But not from her. She was without artifice, the sort of girl a man could trust. Rather like his sisters, he supposed, with a keen wit and a sharp sense of humor. Lucy Abernathy would never inspire poetry, but she would make a very fine friend.

"It will happen," she said, her voice soft but certain. "She will realize. You . . . and Hermione . . . You will be together. I am sure of it."

He watched her lips as she spoke. He didn't know why, but the shape of them was suddenly intriguing . . . the way they moved, formed their consonants and vowels. They were ordinary lips. Nothing about them had attracted his attention before. But now, in the darkened library, with nothing in the air but the soft whisper of their voices . . .

He wondered what it would mean to kiss her.

He stepped back, feeling suddenly and overwhelmingly *wrong.*

"We should return," he said abruptly.

A flicker of hurt passed over her eyes. Damn. He hadn't meant to sound like he was so eager to be rid of her. None of this was her fault. He was just tired. And frustrated. And she was there. And the night was dark. And they were alone.

And it hadn't been desire. It couldn't be desire. He'd been waiting his entire life to react to a woman the way he had to Hermione Watson. He couldn't possibly feel desire for another woman after that. Not Lady Lucinda, not anyone.

It was nothing. *She* was nothing.

No, that was not fair. She was something. Quite a bit, actually. But not for him.

Six

In which Our Hero makes progress.

Dear God, *what* had she said?

That single thought pounded through Lucy's mind as she lay in bed that night, too horrified even to toss and turn. She lay on her back, staring at the ceiling, utterly still, utterly mortified.

And the next morning, as she peered in the mirror, sighing at the weary lavender color beneath her eyes, there it was again—

Oh, Mr. Bridgerton, you are so much better than the rest.

And every time she relived it, the voice in her memory grew higher, more simpering, until she turned into one of those awful creatures—the girls who fluttered and swooned every time someone's older brother came to visit at school.

"Lucy Abernathy," she muttered under her breath, "you silly cow."

"Did you say something?" Hermione looked up at her from her position near the bed. Lucy already had her hand on the doorknob, ready to leave for breakfast.

"Just doing sums in my head," Lucy lied.

Hermione went back to putting on her shoes. "For heaven's sake, *why*?" she said, mostly to herself.

Lucy shrugged, even though Hermione was not looking at her. She always said that she was doing sums in her head when Hermione caught her talking to herself. She had no idea why Hermione believed her; Lucy detested sums, almost as much as she hated fractions and tables. But it seemed like the sort of thing she might do, practical as she was, and Her-mione had never questioned it.

Every now and then Lucy mumbled a number, just to make it more authentic.

"Are you ready to go down?" Lucy asked, twisting the knob. Not that *she* was. The last thing she wished was to see, well, anyone. Mr. Bridgerton in particular, of course, but the thought of facing the world at large was just ghastly.

But she was hungry, and she was going to have to show herself eventually, and she didn't see why her misery ought to wallow on an empty stomach.

As they walked to breakfast, Hermione peered at her curiously. "Are you well, Lucy?" she asked. "You look a little strange."

Lucy fought the urge to laugh. She *was* strange. She was an idiot, and probably shouldn't be let loose in public.

Good God, had she actually told Gregory Bridgerton that he was better than the rest?

She wanted to die. Or at the very least hide under a bed.

But no, she couldn't even manage to feign illness and have a good lying-in. It hadn't even occurred to her to try. She was so ridiculously normal and routineish that she was up and ready to depart for breakfast before she'd even managed a single coherent thought.

Aside from the pondering of her apparent madness, of course. *That* she had no trouble focusing upon.

"Well, you look very fine, anyway," Hermione said as they reached the top of the staircase. "I do like your choice of the green ribbon with the blue dress. I wouldn't have thought of it, but it's very smart. And so lovely with your eyes."

Lucy looked down at her clothing. She had no recollection of dressing herself. It was a miracle she did not look as if she had escaped from a Gypsy circus.

Although . . .

She let out a little sigh. Running off with the Gypsies sounded rather appealing just then, practical even, since she was quite certain she ought never to show her face in polite society again. Clearly she was missing an extremely important connecting vessel between her brain and her mouth, and heaven only knew what might emerge from her lips next.

Good gracious, she might as well have told Gregory Bridgerton that she thought him a god.

Which she did not. Not at all. She merely thought him a rather fine catch for Hermione. And she'd told him so. Hadn't she?

What *had* she said? Precisely, what had she said?

"Lucy?"

What she said was . . . What she said *was*—

She stopped cold.

Dear *God.* He was going to think *she* wanted him.

Hermione walked another few paces before she realized Lucy was no longer in step beside her. "Lucy?"

"Do you know," Lucy said, her voice coming out just a little bit squeaky, "I don't believe I'm hungry after all."

Hermione looked incredulous. "For breakfast?"

It *was* a bit farfetched. Lucy always ate like a sailor at breakfast.

"I . . . ah . . . I think something did not quite agree with me last night. Perhaps the salmon." She put her hand on her belly for added effect. "I think I should lie down."

And never get up.

"You do look a bit green," Hermione said.

Lucy smiled wanly, making a conscious decision to be thankful for small favors.

"Would you like me to bring you something?" Hermione asked.

"Yes," Lucy said fervently, hoping Hermione hadn't heard the rumble of her stomach.

"Oh, but I shouldn't," Hermione said, placing one thoughtful finger to her lips. "You probably shouldn't eat if you are feeling queasy. The last thing you want is to bring it all up again."

"It's not queasiness, exactly," Lucy improvised.

"It's not?"

"It's . . . ah . . . rather difficult to explain, actually. I . . ." Lucy sagged against the wall. Who knew she had it in her to be such a fine actress?

Hermione rushed to her side, concern knitting her brow. "Oh dear," she said, supporting Lucy with an arm around her back. "You look ghastly."

Lucy blinked. Maybe she *was* taking ill. Even better. That would keep her sequestered for days.

"I am returning you to bed," Hermione said, her tone brooking no argument. "And then I will summon Mother. She will know what to do."

Lucy nodded with relief. Lady Watson's remedy for any sort of ailment was chocolate and biscuits. Unorthodox, to be sure, but as it was what Hermione's mother chose whenever she claimed to be ill, she couldn't very well deny it to anyone else.

Hermione guided her back to their bedchamber, even going so far as to remove Lucy's slippers for her before she lay atop the bed. "If I didn't know you so well," Hermione said, tossing the slippers carelessly into the armoire, "I would think you were faking."

"I would never."

"Oh, you would," Hermione said. "You absolutely would. But you could never carry it off. You're far too traditional."

Traditional? What had *that* to do with anything?

Hermione let out a little huff of air. "I'm probably going to have to sit with that wearisome Mr. Bridgerton at breakfast now."

"He's not so dreadful," Lucy said, with perhaps a bit more verve than one might expect from someone with a belly full of bad salmon.

"I suppose not," Hermione acceded. "He's better than most, I daresay."

Lucy winced at the echo of her own words. *So much better than the rest. So much better than the rest.*

It was quite possibly the most appalling thing ever to cross her lips.

"But he is not for me," Hermione continued, oblivious to Lucy's distress. "He will realize it soon enough. And then he will move on to someone else."

Lucy doubted that, but she didn't say anything. What a coil. Hermione was in love with Mr. Edmonds, Mr. Bridgerton was in love with Hermione, and Lucy was *not* in love with Mr. Bridgerton.

But he thought she was.

Which was nonsense, of course. She would never allow that to happen, practically engaged as she was to Lord Haselby.

Haselby. She nearly groaned. This would all be so much easier if she could remember his face.

"Perhaps I'll ring for breakfast," Hermione said, her face lighting up as if she had just discovered a new continent. "Do you think they will send up a tray?"

Oh, blast. There went all her plans. Now Hermione had an excuse to remain in their chamber all day. And the next, too, if Lucy continued to feign illness.

"I don't know why I didn't think of it sooner," Hermione said, heading to the bellpull. "I would much rather remain here with you."

"Don't," Lucy called out, her brain spinning madly.

"Why not?"

Indeed. Lucy thought quickly. "If you have them bring a tray, you might not get what you want."

"But I know what I want. Coddled eggs and toast. Surely they can manage that."

"But *I* don't want coddled eggs and toast." Lucy tried to keep her expression as pitiful and pathetic as she could manage. "You know my taste so well. If you go to the breakfast room, I'm sure you would find something exactly right."

"But I thought you weren't going to eat."

Lucy put her hand back on her belly. "Well, I might want to eat a little."

"Oh, very well," Hermione said, by now sounding more impatient than anything else. "What do you want?"

"Er, perhaps some bacon?"

"With a fishy stomach?"

"I'm not sure it was the fish."

For the longest moment, Hermione just stood there and stared at her. "Just bacon, then?" she finally asked.

"Ehm, and anything else you think I might enjoy," Lucy said, since it would have been easy enough to ring for bacon.

Hermione let out a pent-up breath. "I shall return soon." She regarded Lucy with a slightly suspicious expression. "Don't overexert yourself."

"I won't," Lucy promised. She smiled at the door as it closed behind Hermione. She counted to ten, then hopped out of bed and ran to the wardrobe to straighten her slippers. Once that was done to her satisfaction, she snatched up a book and crawled back in to settle down and read.

All in all, it was turning out to be a lovely morning.

By the time Gregory entered the breakfast room, he was feeling much better. What had happened the night before—it was nothing. Practically forgotten.

It wasn't as if he'd *wanted* to kiss Lady Lucinda. He'd merely wondered about it, which was worlds apart.

He was just a man, after all. He'd wondered about hundreds of women, most of the time without *any* intention of even speaking to them. Everybody wondered. It was whether one acted upon it that made the difference.

What was that his brothers—his happily married brothers, he might add—had once said? Marriage didn't render them *blind.* They might not be looking for other women, but that didn't mean they didn't notice what was standing right in front of them. Whether it was a barmaid with extremely large bosoms or a proper young lady with a—well, with a pair of lips—one couldn't very well not *see* the body part in question.

And if one saw, then of course one would wonder, and—

And nothing. It all added up to nothing.

Which meant Gregory could eat his breakfast with a clear head.

Eggs were good for the soul, he decided. Bacon, too.

The only other occupant of the breakfast room was the fiftyish and perpetually starchy Mr. Snowe, who was thankfully more interested in his newspaper than in conversation. After the obligatory grunts of greeting, Gregory sat down at the opposite end of the table and began to eat.

Excellent sausage this morning. And the toast was exceptional as well. Just the right amount of butter. A bit of salt needed for the eggs, but other than that they were rather tasty.

He tried the salted cod. Not bad. Not bad at all.

He took another bite. Chewed. Enjoyed himself. Thought very deep thoughts about politics and agriculture.

Moved on determinedly to Newtonian physics. He really should have paid more attention at Eton, because he couldn't quite recall the difference between force and work.

Let's see, work was that bit with the foot-pounds, and force was . . .

It wasn't even really *wondering*. Honestly, it could all be blamed on a trick of the light. And his mood. He'd been feeling a bit off. He'd been looking at her mouth because she'd been talking, for heaven's sake. Where else was he meant to look?

He picked up his fork with renewed vigor. Back to the cod. And his tea. Nothing washed everything away like tea.

He took a long sip, peering over the edge of his cup as he heard someone coming down the hall.

And then *she* filled the doorway.

He blinked with surprise, then glanced over her shoulder. She'd come without her extra appendage.

Now that he thought about it, he didn't think he'd ever seen Miss Watson without Lady Lucinda.

"Good morning," he called out, in precisely the right tone. Friendly enough so as not to sound bored, but not *too* friendly. A man never wanted to sound desperate.

Miss Watson looked over at him as he stood, and her face registered absolutely no emotion whatsoever. Not happiness, not ire, nothing but the barest flicker of acknowledgment. It was quite remarkable, really.

"Good morning," she murmured.

Then, hell, why not. "Will you join me?" he asked.

Her lips parted and she paused, as if not quite sure what she wished to do. And then, as if to offer perverse proof that they did in fact share some sort of higher connection, he read her mind.

Truly. He knew exactly what she was thinking.

Oh, very well, I suppose I have to eat breakfast, anyway.

It positively warmed the soul.

"I cannot stay very long," Miss Watson said. "Lucy is unwell, and I promised to bring her a tray."

It was difficult to imagine the indomitable Lady Lucinda taking ill, although Gregory didn't know why. It wasn't as if he *knew* her. Really, it had been nothing but a few conversations. If that. "I trust it is nothing serious," he murmured.

"I don't think so," she replied, taking a plate. She looked up at him, blinking those astounding green eyes. "Did you eat the fish?"

He looked down at his cod. "Now?"

"No, last night."

"I imagine so. I usually eat everything."

Her lips pursed for a moment, then she murmured, "I ate it as well."

Gregory waited for further explanation, but she didn't seem inclined to offer any. So instead he remained on his feet as she placed delicate portions of eggs and ham on her plate. Then, after a moment's deliberation—

Am I really hungry? Because the more food I put on my plate, the longer it will take to consume it. Here. In the breakfast room. With him.

—she took a piece of toast.

Hmmm. Yes, I'm hungry.

Gregory waited until she took a seat across from him, and he sat down. Miss Watson offered him a small smile—the sort that was really nothing more than a shrug of the lips—and proceeded to eat her eggs.

"Did you sleep well?" Gregory asked.

She dabbed at her mouth with her serviette. "Very well, thank you."

"I did not," he announced. Hell, if polite conversation failed to draw her out, perhaps he ought to opt for surprise.

She looked up. "I'm so sorry." And then she looked back down. And ate.

"Terrible dream," he said. "Nightmare, really. Ghastly."

She picked up her knife and cut her bacon. "I'm so sorry," she said, seemingly unaware that she'd uttered those very same words mere moments earlier.

"I can't quite recall what it was," Gregory mused. He was making it all up, of course. He hadn't slept well, but not because of a nightmare. But he was going to get her to talk to him or die trying. "Do you remember your dreams?" he asked.

Her fork stopped midway to her mouth—and there was that delightful connection of the minds again.

In God's name, why is he asking me this?

Well, maybe not in God's name. That would require a bit more emotion than she seemed to possess. At least with him.

"Er, no," she said. "Not usually."

"Really? How intriguing. I recall mine about half of the time, I would estimate."

She nodded.

If I nod, I won't have to come up with something to say.

He plowed on. "My dream from last night was quite vivid. There was a rainstorm. Thunder and lightning. Very dramatic."

She turned her neck, ever so slowly, and looked over her shoulder.

"Miss Watson?"

She turned back. "I thought I heard someone."

I hoped I heard someone.

Really, this mind-reading talent was beginning to grow tedious.

"Right," he said. Well, where was I?"

Miss Watson began to eat very quickly.

Gregory leaned forward. She wasn't going to escape so easily. "Oh, yes, the rain," he said. "It was pouring. Absolute deluge. And the ground began to melt beneath my feet. Dragged me down."

He paused, purposefully, and then kept his eyes on her face until she was forced to say something.

After a few moments of exceedingly awkward silence, she finally moved her gaze from her food to his face. A small piece of egg trembled on the edge of her fork.

"The ground was melting," he said. And almost laughed.

"How . . . unpleasant."

"It *was,*" he said, with great animation. "I thought it would swallow me whole. Have you ever felt like that, Miss Watson?"

Silence. And then— "No. No, I can't say that I have."

He idly fingered his earlobe, and then said, quite offhandedly, "I didn't much like it."

He thought she might spit her tea.

"Well, really," he continued. "Who would?"

And for the first time since he'd met her, he thought he saw the disinterested mask slip from her eyes as she said, with quite a bit of feeling, "I have no idea."

She even shook her head. Three things at once! A complete sentence, a spot of emotion, *and* a shake of the head. By George, he might be getting through to her.

"What happened next, Mr. Bridgerton?"

Good *God,* she had asked him a question. He might tumble from his chair. "Actually," he said, "I woke up."

"That's fortunate."

"I thought so as well. They say if you die in your dreams, you die in your sleep."

Her eyes widened. "They do?"

"*They* being my brothers," he admitted. "You may feel free to assess the information based upon its source."

"I have a brother," she said. "He delights in tormenting me."

Gregory offered her a grave nod. "That is what brothers are meant to do."

"Do you torment your sisters?"

"Mostly just the younger one."

"Because she's smaller."

"No, because she deserves it."

She laughed. "Mr. Bridgerton, you are terrible."

He smiled slowly. "You haven't met Hyacinth."

"If she bothers you enough to make you wish to torment her, I am sure I would adore her."

He sat back, enjoying this feeling of ease. It was nice not to have to work so hard. "Your brother is your elder, then?"

She nodded. "He *does* torment me because I'm smaller."

"You mean you don't deserve it?"

"Of course not."

He couldn't quite tell if she was being facetious. "Where is your brother now?"

"Trinity Hall." She took the last bite of her eggs. "Cambridge. Lucy's brother was there as well. He has been graduated for a year."

Gregory wasn't quite certain why she was telling him this. He wasn't interested in Lucinda Abernathy's brother.

Miss Watson cut another small piece of bacon and lifted her fork to her mouth. Gregory ate as well, stealing glances at her as he chewed. Lord, but she was lovely. He didn't think he'd ever seen another woman with her coloring. It was the skin, really. He imagined that most men thought her beauty came from her hair and eyes, and it was true that those were the features that initially stopped a man cold. But her skin was like alabaster laid over a rose petal.

He paused mid-chew. He had no idea he could be so poetic.

Miss Watson set down her fork. "Well," she said, with the tiniest of sighs, "I suppose I should prepare that plate for Lucy."

He stood immediately to assist her. Good heavens, but she actually sounded as if she didn't wish to leave. Gregory congratulated himself on an extremely productive breakfast.

"I shall find someone to carry it back for you," he said, signaling to a footman.

"Oh, that would be lovely." She smiled gratefully at him, and his heart quite literally skipped a beat. He'd thought it merely a figure of speech, but now he knew it was true. Love really could affect one's internal organs.

"Please do offer Lady Lucinda my well wishes," he said, watching curiously as Miss Watson heaped five slices of meat on the plate.

"Lucy likes bacon," she said.

"I see that."

And then she proceeded to spoon eggs, cod, potatoes, tomatoes, and then on a separate plate muffins and toast.

"Breakfast has always been her favorite meal," Miss Watson said.

"Mine as well."

"I shall tell her that."

"I can't imagine that she will be interested."

A maid had entered the room with a tray, and Miss Watson placed the heaping plates upon it. "Oh, she will," she said breezily. "Lucy is interested in everything. She does sums in her head, even. For entertainment."

"You're joking." Gregory couldn't imagine a less pleasant way to keep oneself occupied.

She placed her hand on her heart. "I swear it to you. I think she must be trying to improve her mind, because she was never very good at maths." She walked to the door, then turned to face him. "Breakfast was lovely, Mr. Bridgerton. Thank you for the company and the conversation."

He inclined his head. "The pleasure was all mine."

Except that it wasn't. She had enjoyed their time together, too. He could see it in her smile. And her eyes.

And he felt like a king.

"Did you know that if you die in your dreams, you die in your sleep?"

Lucy didn't even pause in her cutting of her bacon. "Nonsense," she said. "Who told you that?"

Hermione perched on the edge of the bed. "Mr. Bridgerton."

Now *that* rated above bacon. Lucy looked up immediately. "Then you saw him at breakfast?"

Hermione nodded. "We sat across from each other. He helped me arrange for the tray."

Lucy regarded her massive breakfast with dismay. Usually she managed to hide her ferocious appetite by dallying at the breakfast table, then getting another serving once the first wave of guests had departed.

Oh well, nothing to do about it. Gregory Bridgerton already thought her a widgeon—he might as well think her a widgeon who would weigh twelve stone by the year's end.

"He's rather amusing, actually," Hermione said, absently twirling her hair.

"I've heard he's quite charming."

"Mmmm."

Lucy watched her friend closely. Hermione was gazing out the window, and if she didn't quite have that ridiculous memorizing-a-love-sonnet look to her, she had at least worked her way up to a couplet or two.

"He is extremely handsome," Lucy said. There seemed no harm in confessing it. It wasn't as if she was planning to set her cap for him, and his looks were fine enough that it could be interpreted as a statement of fact rather than opinion.

"Do you think so?" Hermione asked. She turned back to Lucy, her head tilting thoughtfully to the side.

"Oh yes," Lucy replied. "His eyes, particularly. I'm quite partial to hazel eyes. I always have been."

Actually, she'd never considered it one way or the other, but now that she thought about it, hazel eyes *were* rather fine. Bit of brown, bit of green. Best of both worlds.

Hermione looked at her curiously. "I didn't know that."

Lucy shrugged. "I don't tell you everything."

Another lie. Hermione was privy to every boring detail of Lucy's life and had been for three years. Except, of course, for her plans to match Hermione with Mr. Bridgerton.

Mr. Bridgerton. Right. Must return the conversation to the subject of *him*.

"But you must agree," Lucy said in her most pondering of voices, "he's not *too* handsome. It's a good thing, really."

"Mr. Bridgerton?"

"Yes. His nose has a great deal of character, wouldn't you say? And his eyebrows aren't quite even." Lucy frowned. She hadn't realized she was quite so familiar with Gregory Bridgerton's face.

Hermione did nothing but nod, so Lucy continued with "I don't think I should want to be married to someone who was *too* handsome. It must be terribly intimidating. I would feel like a duck every time I opened my mouth."

Hermione giggled at that. "A duck?"

Lucy nodded and decided not to quack. She wondered if the men who courted Hermione worried about the same thing.

"He's quite dark," Hermione said.

"Not so dark." Lucy thought his hair a medium-brown.

"Yes, but Mr. Edmonds is so fair."

Mr. Edmonds did have lovely blond hair, so Lucy decided not to comment. And she knew she had to be very careful at this point. If she pushed Hermione too hard in Mr. Bridgerton's direction, Hermione would surely balk and go right back to being in love with Mr. Edmonds, which, of course, was utter disaster.

No, Lucy was going to need to be subtle. If Hermione was going to switch her devotion to Mr. Bridgerton, she was going to have to figure it out for herself. Or think she did.

"And his family is very smart," Hermione murmured.

"Mr. Edmonds's?" Lucy asked, deliberately misinterpreting.

"No, Mr. Bridgerton's, of course. I have heard such interesting things about them."

"Oh, yes," Lucy said. "I have as well. I rather admire Lady Bridgerton. She's been a marvelous hostess."

Hermione nodded her agreement. "I think she prefers you to me."

"Don't be silly."

"I don't mind," Hermione said with a shrug. "It's not as if she *doesn't* like me. She just likes you better. Women always like you better."

Lucy opened her mouth to contradict but then stopped, realizing that it was true. How odd that she had never noticed it. "Well, it's not as if you'd be marrying *her,*" she said.

Hermione looked at her sharply. "I didn't say I wished to marry Mr. Bridgerton."

"No, of course not," Lucy said, mentally kicking herself. She'd known the words were a mistake the minute they'd escaped her mouth.

"But . . ." Hermione sighed and proceeded to stare off into space.

Lucy leaned forward. So this was what it meant to hang on a word.

And she hung, and she hung . . . until she could bear it no longer. "Hermione?" she finally queried.

Hermione flopped back onto the bed. "Oh, Lucy," she moaned, in tones worthy of Covent Garden, "I'm so confused."

"Confused?" Lucy smiled. This had to be a good thing.

"Yes," Hermione replied, from her decidedly inelegant position atop the bed. "When I was sitting at the table with Mr. Bridgerton—well, actually at first I thought him quite mad—but then I realized I was enjoying myself. He was funny, actually, and made me laugh."

Lucy did not speak, waiting for Hermione to gather the rest of her thoughts.

Hermione made a little noise, half-sigh, half-moan. Wholly distressed. "And then once I realized that, I looked up at him, and I—" She rolled onto her side, leaning on her elbow and propping her head up with one hand. "I *fluttered.*"

Lucy was still trying to digest the *mad* comment. "Fluttered?" she echoed. "What is *fluttered*?"

"My stomach. My heart. My—my something. I don't know what."

"Similar to when you saw Mr. Edmonds for the first time?"

"No. *No.* No." Each no was said with a different emphasis, and Lucy had the distinct sense that Hermione was trying to convince herself of it.

"It wasn't the same at all," Hermione said. "But it was . . . a little bit the same. On a much smaller scale."

"I see," Lucy said, with an admirable amount of gravity, considering that she didn't understand at all. But then again, she never understood this sort of thing. And after her strange conversation with Mr.

Bridgerton the night before, she was quite convinced she never would.

"But wouldn't you think—if I am so desperately in love with Mr. Edmonds—wouldn't you think I would never flutter with anyone else?"

Lucy thought about that. And then she said, "I don't see why love has to be desperate."

Hermione pushed herself up on her elbows and looked at her curiously. "That wasn't my question."

It wasn't? Oughtn't it have been?

"Well," Lucy said, choosing her words carefully, "perhaps it means—"

"I know what you are going to say," Hermione cut in. "You're going to say that it probably means I am not as in love with Mr. Edmonds as I thought. And then you will say that I need to give Mr. Bridgerton a chance. And then you will tell me that I ought to give all of the other gentlemen a chance."

"Well, not *all* of them," Lucy said. But the rest of it was rather close.

"Don't you think this has all occurred to me? Don't you realize how terribly distressing all of this is? To doubt myself so? And good heavens, Lucy, what if this is not the end of it? What if this happens again? With someone else?"

Lucy rather suspected she was not meant to answer, but still she spoke. "There is nothing wrong with doubting yourself, Hermione. Marriage is an enormous undertaking. The biggest choice you will ever make in your life. Once it's done, you can't change your mind."

Lucy took a bite of her bacon, reminding herself how grateful she was that Lord Haselby was so suitable. Her situation could have been ever so much worse. She chewed, swallowed, and said, "You need only to give yourself a bit of time, Hermione. And you should. There is never any good reason to rush into marriage."

There was a long paused before Hermione answered. "I reckon you're right."

"If you are truly meant to be with Mr. Edmonds, he will wait for you." Oh, heavens. Lucy couldn't *believe* she'd just said that.

Hermione jumped from the bed, just so that she could rush to Lucy's side and envelop her in a hug. "Oh, Lucy, that was the sweetest thing you have ever said to me. I know you don't approve of him."

"Well . . ." Lucy cleared her throat, trying to think of an acceptable reply. Something that would make her feel not *quite* so guilty for not having meant it. "It's not that—"

A knock sounded at the door.

Oh, thank goodness.

"Enter," the two girls called out in unison.

A maid came in and bobbed a quick curtsy. "M'lady," she said, looking at Lucy, "Lord Fennsworth has arrived to see you."

Lucy gaped at her. "My *brother*?"

"He is waiting in the rose salon, m'lady. Shall I tell him you will be right down?"

"Yes. Yes, of course."

"Will there be anything else?"

Lucy slowly shook her head. "No, thank you. That will be all."

The maid departed, leaving Lucy and Hermione staring at each other in shock.

"Why do you think Richard is here?" Hermione asked, her eyes wide with interest. She had met Lucy's brother on a number of occasions, and they had always got on well.

"I don't know." Lucy quickly climbed out of bed, all thoughts of feigning an upset stomach forgotten. "I hope nothing is amiss."

Hermione nodded and followed her to the wardrobe. "Has your uncle been unwell?"

"Not that I have been made aware." Lucy fished out her slippers and sat on the edge of the bed to put them back on her feet. "I had best get down to see him. If he is here, it is something important."

Hermione regarded her for a moment, then asked, "Would you like for me to accompany you? I shan't intrude upon your conversation, of course. But I will walk down with you, if you like."

Lucy nodded, and together they departed for the rose salon.

Seven

In which Our Unexpected Guest delivers distressing news.

Gregory had been chatting with his sister-in-law in the breakfast room when the butler informed her of their unexpected guest, and so naturally he decided to accompany her to the rose salon to greet Lord Fennsworth, elder brother to Lady Lucinda. He had nothing better to do, and it somehow seemed he ought to go meet the young earl, given that Miss Watson had been chattering on about him a quarter of an hour earlier. Gregory knew him only by reputation; the four years' difference in their ages had ensured that they had not crossed paths at university, and Fennsworth had not yet chosen to take his place in London society.

Gregory had been expecting a studious, bookish sort; he'd heard that Fennsworth had elected to remain at Cambridge even when school was not in session. Indeed, the gentleman waiting by the window in the rose salon did possess a certain gravitas that made him seem slightly older than his years. But Lord Fennsworth was also tall, fit, and although perhaps a touch shy, he carried himself with an air of self-possession that came from something more primal than a title of nobility.

Lady Lucinda's brother knew who he was, not just what he was born to be called. Gregory liked him immediately.

Until it became obvious that he, like the rest of male humanity, was in love with Hermione Watson.

The only mystery, really, was why Gregory was surprised.

Gregory had to commend him—Fennsworth managed a full minute of inquiries about his sister's welfare before he added, "And Miss Watson? Will she be joining us as well?"

It wasn't so much the words as the tone, and even that not so much as the flicker in his eyes—that spark of eagerness, anticipation.

Oh, call a spade a spade. It was desperate longing, pure and simple. Gregory ought to know—he was quite certain it had flashed through his own eyes more than once in the past few days.

Good God.

Gregory supposed he still found Fennsworth a good enough fellow, even with his annoying infatuation, but really, the entire situation was beginning to grow tiresome.

"We are so pleased to welcome you to Aubrey Hall, Lord Fennsworth," Kate said, once she had informed him that she did not know if Miss Watson would be accompanying his sister down to the rose salon. "I do hope that your presence does not indicate an emergency at home."

"Not at all," Fennsworth replied. "But my uncle has requested that I fetch Lucy and bring her home. He wishes to speak with her on a matter of some importance."

Gregory felt one corner of his lips quirk in an upward direction. "You must be quite devoted to your sister," he said, "to come all this way yourself. Surely you could have simply sent a carriage."

To his credit, Lucy's brother did not appear flustered by the question, but at the same time, he did not have an immediate answer. "Oh no," he said, the words coming out rather quickly after the long pause. "I was more than happy to make the trip. Lucy is good company, and we have not visited for quite some time."

"Must you leave right away?" Kate asked. "I have been so enjoying your sister's company. And we would be honored to count you among our guests as well."

Gregory wondered just what she was about. Kate was going to have to locate another female to even up the numbers if Lord Fennsworth was to join the party. Although he supposed that if Lady Lucinda left, she would have to do the exact same thing.

The young earl hesitated, and Kate took advantage of the moment with a beautifully executed "Oh, do say that you will remain. Even if it cannot be for the duration of the party."

"Well," Fennsworth said, blinking as he considered the invitation. It was clear that he wanted to stay (and Gregory was quite certain he knew the reason why). But title or no, he was still young, and Gregory imagined that he answered to his uncle on all matters pertaining to the family.

And said uncle clearly desired Lady Lucinda's swift return.

"I suppose there would be no harm in taking an extra day," Fennsworth said.

Oh, dandy. He was willing to defy his uncle to gain extra time with Miss Watson. And as Lady Lucinda's brother, he was the one man who Hermione would never brush away with her usual polite boredom. Gregory readied himself for another day of tedious competition.

"Please say you will stay until Friday," Kate said. "We are planning a masked ball for Thursday evening, and I would hate for you to miss it."

Gregory made a mental note to give Kate an extremely ordinary gift for her next birthday. Rocks, maybe.

"It's only one more day," Kate said with a winning smile.

It was at that moment that Lady Lucinda and Miss Watson entered the room, the former in a morning dress of lightish blue and the latter in the same green frock she'd worn to breakfast. Lord Fennsworth took one look at the duo (more at one than the other, and suffice it to say that blood was not thicker than unrequited love), and he murmured, "Friday it is."

"Delightful," Kate said, clasping her hands together. "I shall have a room readied for you straightaway."

"Richard?" Lady Lucinda queried. "Why are you here?" She paused in the doorway and looked from person to person, apparently confused by Kate's and Gregory's presence.

"Lucy," her brother said. "It has been an age."

"Four months," she said, almost unthinkingly, as if some little part of her brain required absolute accuracy, even when it hardly mattered.

"Heavens, that is a long time," Kate said. "We will leave you now, Lord Fennsworth. I am sure you and your sister wish to have a few moments of privacy."

"There is no rush," Fennsworth said, his eyes flicking briefly to Miss Watson. "I would not wish to be rude, and I haven't yet had the opportunity to thank you for your hospitality."

"It wouldn't be rude at all," Gregory put in, anticipating a swift departure from the salon with Miss Watson on his arm.

Lord Fennsworth turned and blinked, as if he'd forgotten Gregory's presence. Not terribly surprising, as Gregory had remained uncharacteristically silent through the exchange.

"Pray do not trouble yourself," the earl said. "Lucy and I will have our conversation later."

"Richard," Lucy said, looking somewhat concerned, "are you certain? I was not expecting you, and if there is anything amiss . . ."

But her brother shook his head. "Nothing that cannot wait. Uncle Robert wishes to speak with you. He asked me to bring you home."

"Now?"

"He did not specify," Fennsworth replied, "but Lady Bridgerton has very graciously asked us to remain until Friday, and I agreed. That is"—he cleared his throat—"assuming you wish to remain."

"Of course," Lucy replied, looking confused and adrift. "But I—well . . . Uncle Robert . . ."

"We should leave," Miss Watson said firmly. "Lucy, you should have a moment with your brother."

Lucy looked at her brother, but he had taken advantage of Miss Watson's entry into the conversation by looking at *her,* and he said, "And how are you, Hermione? It has been far too long."

"Four months," Lucy said.

Miss Watson laughed and smiled warmly at the earl. "I am well, thank you. And Lucy is correct, as always. We last spoke in January, when you visited us at school."

Fennsworth dipped his chin in acknowledgment. "How could I have forgotten? It was such a pleasant few days."

Gregory would have bet his right arm that Fennsworth had known down to the minute how long it had been since he had last laid eyes on Miss Watson. But the lady in question was clearly oblivious to the infatuation, because she just smiled and said, "It was, wasn't it? It was so sweet of you to take us ice skating. You are always such good company."

Good God, how could she be so oblivious? There was no way she would have been so encouraging had she realized the nature of the earl's feelings for her. Gregory was certain of it.

But while it was obvious that Miss Watson was extremely fond of Lord Fennsworth, there was no indication that she held him in any sort of romantic esteem. Gregory consoled himself with the knowledge that the two had certainly known each other for years, and naturally she would be friendly with Fennsworth, given how close she was to Lady Lucinda.

Practically brother and sister, really.

And speaking of Lady Lucinda—Gregory turned in her direction and was not surprised to find that she was frowning. Her brother, who had traveled at least a day to reach her side, now seemed in no hurry whatsoever to speak with her.

And indeed, everyone else had fallen silent, as well. Gregory watched the awkward tableau with interest. Everyone seemed to be glancing about, waiting to see who might speak next. Even Lady Lucinda, whom no one would call shy, seemed not to know what to say.

"Lord Fennsworth," Kate said, thankfully breaking the silence, "you must be famished. Will you have some breakfast?"

"I would appreciate that greatly, Lady Bridgerton."

Kate turned to Lady Lucinda. "I did not see you at breakfast, either. Will you have something now?"

Gregory thought of the massive tray Miss Watson had had brought up for her and wondered how much of it she'd managed to wolf down before having to come meet her brother.

"Of course," Lady Lucinda murmured. "I should like to keep Richard company, in any case."

"Miss Watson," Gregory cut in smoothly, "would you care to take a turn about the gardens? I believe the peonies are in bloom. And those stalky blue things—I always forget what they are called."

"Delphinium." It was Lady Lucinda, of course. He'd known she would not be able to resist. Then she turned and looked at him, her eyes narrowing ever so slightly. "I told you that the other day."

"So you did," he murmured. "I've never had much of a head for details."

"Oh, Lucy remembers everything," Miss Watson said breezily. "And I would be delighted to view the gardens with you. That is, if Lucy and Richard do not mind."

Both assured her that they did not, although Gregory was quite certain he saw a flash of disappointment and—dare he say it—irritation in Lord Fennsworth's eyes.

Gregory smiled.

"I shall find you back in our room?" Miss Watson said to Lucy.

The other girl nodded, and with a feeling of triumph—there was nothing quite like besting one's competition—Gregory placed Miss Watson's hand in the crook of his elbow and led her out of the room.

It was going to be an excellent morning, after all.

Lucy followed her brother and Lady Bridgerton to the breakfast room, which she did not mind one bit, as she had not had a chance to eat very much of what Hermione had brought her earlier. But it did mean that she had to endure a full thirty minutes of meaningless conversation while her brain raced about, imagining all sorts of disasters that could be responsible for her unexpected summons home.

Richard couldn't very well speak to her about anything important with Lady Bridgerton and half of the house party blithering on about coddled eggs and the recent rainfall, so Lucy waited uncomplainingly while he finished (he'd always been an annoyingly slow eater), and then she tried her best not to lose her patience as they strolled out to the side lawn, Richard first asking her about school, then Hermione, and then Hermione's mother, and then her upcoming debut, and then Hermione again, with a side tangent to Hermione's brother, whom he'd apparently run across in Cambridge, and then it was back to the debut, and to what extent she was to share it with Hermione . . .

Until finally Lucy halted in her tracks, planted her hands on her hips, and demanded that he tell her why he was there.

"I told you," he said, not quite meeting her eyes. "Uncle Robert wishes to speak with you."

"But *why*?" It was not a question with an obvious answer. Uncle Robert hadn't cared to speak with her more than a handful of times in the past ten years. If he was planning to start now, there was a reason for it.

Richard cleared his throat a number of times before finally saying, "Well, Luce, I think he plans to marry you off."

"Straightaway?" Lucy whispered, and she didn't know why she was so surprised. She'd known this was coming; she'd been practically engaged for years. And she had told Hermione, on more than one occasion, that a season for her was really quite foolish—why bother with the expense when she was just going to marry Haselby in the end?

But now . . . suddenly . . . she didn't want to do it. At least not so soon. She didn't want to go from schoolgirl to wife, with nothing in between. She wasn't asking for adventure—she didn't even *want* adventure—truly, she wasn't the sort.

She wasn't asking for very much—just a few months of freedom, of laughter.

Of dancing breathlessly, spinning so fast that the candle flames streaked into long snakes of light.

Maybe she was practical. Maybe she was "that old Lucy," as so many had called her at Miss Moss's. But she liked to dance. And she wanted to do it. Now. Before she was old. Before she became Haselby's wife.

"I don't know when," Richard said, looking down at her with . . . was it regret?

Why would it be regret?

"Soon, I think," he said. "Uncle Robert seems somewhat eager to have it done."

Lucy just stared at him, wondering why she couldn't stop thinking about dancing, couldn't stop picturing herself, in a gown of silvery blue, magical and radiant, in the arms of—

"Oh!" She clapped a hand to her mouth, as if that could somehow silence her thoughts.

"What is it?"

"Nothing," she said, shaking her head. Her daydreams did not have a face. They could not. And so she said it again, more firmly, "It was nothing. Nothing at all."

Her brother stooped to examine a wildflower that had somehow missed the discerning eyes of Aubrey Hall's gardeners. It was small, blue, and just beginning to open.

"It's lovely, isn't it?" Richard murmured.

Lucy nodded. Richard had always loved flowers. Wildflowers in particular. They were different that way, she realized. She had always preferred the order of a neatly arranged bed, each bloom in its place, each pattern carefully and lovingly maintained.

But now . . .

She looked down at that little flower, small and delicate, defiantly sprouting where it didn't belong.

And she decided that she liked the wild ones, too.

"I know you were meant to have a season," Richard said apologetically. "But truly, is it so very dreadful? You never really wanted one, did you?"

Lucy swallowed. "No," she said, because she knew it was what he wanted to hear, and she didn't want him to feel any worse than he already did. And she hadn't really cared one way or the other about a season in London. At least not until recently.

Richard pulled the little blue wildflower out by the roots, looked at it quizzically, and stood. "Cheer up, Luce," he said, chucking her lightly on the chin. "Haselby's not a bad sort. You won't mind being married to him."

"I know," she said softly.

"He won't hurt you," he added, and he smiled, that slightly false sort of smile. The kind that was meant to be reassuring and somehow never was.

"I didn't think he would," Lucy said, an edge of . . . of *something* creeping into her voice. "Why would you bring such a thing up?"

"No reason at all," Richard said quickly. "But I know that it is a concern for many women. Not all men give their wives the respect with which Haselby will treat you."

Lucy nodded. Of course. It was true. She'd heard stories. They'd all heard stories.

"It won't be so bad," Richard said. "You'll probably even like him. He's quite agreeable."

Agreeable. It was a good thing. Better than disagreeable.

"He will be the Earl of Davenport someday," Richard added, even though of course she already knew that. "You will be a countess. Quite a prominent one."

There was that. Her schoolfriends had always said she was so lucky to have her prospects already settled, and with such a lofty result. She was the daughter of an earl and the sister of an earl. And she was destined to be the wife of one as well. She had nothing to complain about. Nothing.

But she felt so empty.

It wasn't a bad feeling precisely. But it was disconcerting. And unfamiliar. She felt rootless. She felt adrift.

She felt not like herself. And that was the worst of it.

"You're not surprised, are you, Luce?" Richard asked. "You knew this was coming. We all did."

She nodded. "It is nothing," she said, trying to sound her usual matter-of-fact self. "It is only that it never felt quite so immediate."

"Of course," Richard said. "It is a surprise, that is all. Once you grow used to the idea, it will all seem so much better. Normal, even. After all, you have always known you were to be Haselby's wife. And think of how much you will enjoy planning the wedding. Uncle Robert says it is to be a grand affair. In London, I believe. Davenport insists upon it."

Lucy felt herself nod. She did rather like to plan things. There was such a pleasant feeling of being in charge that came along with it.

"Hermione can be your attendant, as well," Richard added.

"Of course," Lucy murmured. Because, really, who else would she choose?

"Is there a color that doesn't favor her?" Richard asked with a frown. "Because you will be the bride. You don't want to be overshadowed."

Lucy rolled her eyes. That was a brother for you.

He seemed not to realize that he had insulted her, though, and Lucy supposed she shouldn't have been surprised. Hermione's beauty was so legendary that no one took insult with an unfavorable comparison. One would have to be delusional to think otherwise.

"I can't very well put her in black," Lucy said. It was the only hue she could think of that turned Hermione a bit sallow.

"No, no you couldn't, could you?" Richard paused, clearly pondering this, and Lucy stared at him in disbelief. Her brother, who had to be regularly informed of what was fashionable and what was not, was actually *interested* in the shade of Hermione's attendant dress.

"Hermione can wear whatever color she desires," Lucy decided. And why not? Of all the people who would be in attendance, there was no one who meant more to her than her closest friend.

"That's very kind of you," Richard said. He looked at her thoughtfully. "You're a good friend, Lucy."

Lucy knew she should have felt complimented, but instead she just wondered why it had taken him so long to realize it.

Richard gave her a smile, then looked down at the flower, still in his hands. He held it up, twirled it a few times, the stem rolling back and forth between his thumb and index finger. He blinked, his brow furrowing a touch, then he placed the flower in front of her dress. They were the same blue—slightly purple, maybe just a little bit gray.

"You should wear this color," he said. "You look quite lovely just now."

He sounded a little surprised, so Lucy knew that he was not just saying it. "Thank you," she said. She'd always thought the hue made her eyes a bit brighter. Richard was the first person besides Hermione ever to comment on it. "Perhaps I will."

"Shall we walk back to the house?" he asked. "I am sure you will wish to tell Hermione everything."

She paused, then shook her head. "No, thank you. I think I shall remain outside for a short while." She motioned to a spot near the path that led down to the lake. "There is a bench not too far away. And the sun feels rather pleasant on my face."

"Are you certain?" Richard squinted up at the sky. "You're always saying you don't want to get freckles."

"I already have freckles, Richard. And I won't be very long." She hadn't planned to come outside when she'd gone to greet him, so she had not brought her bonnet. But it was early yet in the day. A few minutes of sunshine would not destroy her complexion.

And besides that, she wanted to. Wouldn't it be nice to do something just because she wanted to, and not because it was expected?

Richard nodded. "I will see you at dinner?"

"I believe it is laid at half one."

He grinned. "You would know."

"There is nothing like a brother," she grumbled.

"And there is nothing like a sister." He leaned over and kissed her brow, catching her completely off-guard.

"Oh, Richard," she muttered, aghast at her soppy reaction. She never cried. In fact, she was known for her complete lack of flowerpot tendencies.

"Go on," he said, with enough affection to send one tear rolling down her cheek. Lucy brushed it away, embarrassed that he'd seen it, embarrassed that she'd done it.

Richard squeezed her hand and motioned with his head toward the south lawn. "Go stare at the trees and do whatever you need to do. You'll feel better after you have a few moments to yourself."

"I don't feel poorly," Lucy said quickly. "There is no need for me to feel *better.*"

"Of course not. You are merely surprised."

"Exactly."

Exactly. Exactly. Really, she was delighted, really. She'd been waiting for this moment for years. Wouldn't it be nice to have everything settled? She liked order. She liked being settled.

It was just the surprise. That was all. Rather like when one saw a friend in an unexpected location and almost didn't recognize her. She hadn't expected the announcement now. Here, at the Bridgerton house party. And that was the only reason she felt so odd.

Really.

Eight

In which Our Heroine learns a truth about her brother (but does not believe it), Our Hero learns a secret about Miss Watson (but is not concerned by it), and both learn a truth about themselves (but are not aware of it).

An hour later, Gregory was still congratulating himself on the masterful combination of strategy and timing that had led to his outing with Miss Watson. They had had a perfectly lovely time, and Lord Fennsworth had—well, Fennsworth may have also had a perfectly lovely time, but if so, it had been in the company of his sister and not the lovely Hermione Watson.

Victory was indeed sweet.

As promised, Gregory had taken her on a stroll through the Aubrey Hall gardens, impressing them both with his stupendous recall of six different horticultural names. Delphinium, even, though in truth that was all Lady Lucinda's doing.

The others were, just to give credit where it was due: rose, daisy, peony, hyacinth, and grass. All in all, he thought he'd acquitted himself well. Dctails never had been his forte. And truly, it was all just a game by that point.

Miss Watson appeared to be warming to his company, as well. She might not have been sighing and fluttering her lashes, but the veil of polite disinterest was gone, and twice he had even made her laugh.

She hadn't made *him* laugh, but he wasn't so certain she'd been trying to, and besides, he had certainly smiled. On more than one occasion.

Which was a good thing. Really. It was rather pleasant to once again have his wits about him. He was no longer struck by that punched-in-the-chest feeling, which one would think had to be good for his respiratory health. He was discovering he rather enjoyed breathing, an undertaking he seemed to find difficult while gazing upon the back of Miss Watson's neck.

Gregory frowned, pausing in his solitary jaunt down to the lake. It *was* a rather odd reaction. And surely he'd seen the back of her neck that morning. Hadn't she run ahead to smell one of the flowers?

Hmmm. Perhaps not. He couldn't quite recall.

"Good day, Mr. Bridgerton."

He turned, surprised to see Lady Lucinda sitting by herself on a nearby stone bench. It was an odd location for a bench, he'd always thought, facing nothing but a bunch of trees. But maybe that was the point. Turning one's back on the house—and its many inhabitants. His sister Francesca had often said that after a day or two with the entire Bridgerton family, trees could be quite good company.

Lady Lucinda smiled faintly in greeting, and it struck him that she didn't look quite herself. Her eyes seemed tired, and her posture was not quite straight.

She looks vulnerable, he thought, rather unexpectedly. Her brother must have brought unhappy tidings.

"You're wearing a somber expression," he said, walking politely to her side. "May I join you?"

She nodded, offering him a bit of a smile. But it wasn't a smile. Not quite.

He took a seat beside her. "Did you have an opportunity to visit with your brother?"

She nodded. "He passed along some family news. It was . . . not important."

Gregory tilted his head as he regarded her. She was lying, clearly. But he did not press further. If she'd wanted to share, she would have done. And besides, it wasn't his business in any case.

He was curious, though.

She stared off in the distance, presumably at some tree. "It's quite pleasant here."

It was an oddly bland statement, coming from her.

"Yes," he said. "The lake is just a short walk beyond these trees. I often come in this direction when I wish to think."

She turned suddenly. "You do?"

"Why are you so surprised?"

"I—I don't know." She shrugged. "I suppose you don't seem the sort."

"To think?" Well, really.

"Of course not," she said, giving him a peevish look. "I meant the sort who needed to get away to do so."

"Pardon my presumptuousness, but you don't seem the sort, either."

She thought about that for a moment. "I'm not."

He chuckled at that. "You must have had quite a conversation with your brother."

She blinked in surprise. But she didn't elaborate. Which again didn't seem like her. "What are you here to think about?" she asked.

He opened his mouth to reply, but before he could utter a word, she said, "Hermione, I suppose."

There seemed little point in denying it. "Your brother is in love with her."

That seemed to snap her out of her fog. "*Richard?* Don't be daft."

Gregory looked at her in disbelief. "I can't believe you haven't seen it."

"I can't believe you *have.* For heaven's sake, she thinks of him as a brother."

"That may well be true, but he does not return the sentiment."

"Mr. Br—"

But he halted her with a lifted hand. "Now, now, Lady Lucinda, I daresay I have been witness to more fools in love than you have—"

The laughter quite literally exploded from her mouth. "Mr. Bridgerton," she said, once she was able, "I have been constant companion these last three years to Hermione Watson. *Hermione Watson,*" she added, just in case he hadn't understood her meaning. "Trust me when I tell you there is no one who has been witness to more lovesick fools than I."

For a moment Gregory did not know how to respond. She did have a point.

"Richard is not in love with Hermione," she said with a dismissive shake of her head. And a snort. A ladylike one, but still. She *snorted* at him.

"I beg to differ," he said, because he had seven siblings, and he certainly did not know how to gracefully bow out of an argument.

"He can't be in love with her," she said, sounding quite certain of her statement. "There is someone else."

"Oh, really?" Gregory didn't even bother to get his hopes up.

"Really. He's always nattering on about a girl he met through one of his friends," she said. "I think it was someone's sister. I can't recall her name. Mary, perhaps."

Mary. Hmmph. He *knew* that Fennsworth had no imagination.

"Ergo," Lady Lucinda continued, "he is not in love with Hermione."

At least she seemed rather more like herself. The world seemed a bit steadier with Lucy Abernathy yipping along like a terrier. He'd felt almost off-balance when she'd been staring morosely at the trees.

"Believe what you will," Gregory said with a lofty sigh. "But know this: your brother will be nursing a broken heart ere long."

"Oh, really?" she scoffed. "Because you are so convinced of your own success?"

"Because I'm convinced of his lack of it."

"You don't even know him."

"And now you are defending him? Just moments ago you said he wasn't interested."

"He's not." She bit her lip. "But he is my brother. And if he *were* interested, I would have to support him, wouldn't you think?"

Gregory lifted a brow. "My, how quickly your loyalties shift."

She looked almost apologetic. "He *is* an earl. And you . . . are not."

"You shall make a fine society mama."

Her back stiffened. "I beg your pardon."

"Auctioning your friend off to the highest bidder. You'll be well-practiced by the time you have a daughter."

She jumped to her feet, her eyes flashing with anger and indignation. "That is a terrible thing to say. My most important consideration has always been Hermione's happiness. And if she can be made happy by an earl . . . who happens to be my *brother* . . ."

Oh, brilliant. Now she was going to *try* to match Hermione with Fennsworth. Well done, Gregory. Well done, indeed.

"She can be made happy by me," he said, rising to his feet. And it was true. He'd made her laugh twice this morning, even if she had not done the same for him.

"Of course she can," Lady Lucinda said. "And heavens, she probably will if you don't muck it up. Richard is too young to marry, anyway. He's only two-and-twenty."

Gregory eyed her curiously. Now she sounded as if she were back to him as the best candidate. What was she about, anyway?

"And," she added, impatiently tucking a lock of her dark blond hair behind her ear when the wind whipped it into her face, "he is *not* in love with her. I'm quite certain of it."

Neither one of them seemed to have anything to add to *that,* so, since they were both already on their feet, Gregory motioned toward the house. "Shall we return?"

She nodded, and they departed at a leisurely pace.

"This still does not solve the problem of Mr. Edmonds," Gregory remarked.

She gave him a funny look.

"What was that for?" he demanded.

And she actually giggled. Well, perhaps not a giggle, but she did do that breathy thing with her nose people did when they were rather amused. "It was nothing," she said, still smiling. "I'm rather impressed, actually, that you didn't pretend to not remember his name."

"What, should I have called him Mr. Edwards, and then Mr. Ellington, and then Mr. Edifice, and—"

Lucy gave him an arch look. "You would have lost all of my respect, I assure you."

"The horror. Oh, the horror," he said, laying one hand over his heart.

She glanced at him over her shoulder with a mischievous smile. "It was a near miss."

He looked unconcerned. "I'm a terrible shot, but I do know how to dodge a bullet."

Now *that* made her curious. "I've never known a man who would admit to being a bad shot."

He shrugged. "There are some things one simply can't avoid. I shall always be the Bridgerton who can be bested at close range by his sister."

"The one you told me about?"

"All of them," he admitted.

"Oh." She frowned. There ought to be some sort of prescribed statement for such a situation. What *did* one say when a gentleman confessed to a shortcoming? She couldn't recall ever hearing one do so before, but surely, sometime in the course of history, some gentleman had. And someone would have had to make a reply.

She blinked, waiting for something meaningful to come to mind. Nothing did.

And then—

"Hermione can't dance." It just popped out of her mouth, with no direction whatsoever from her head.

Good gracious, *that* was meant to be meaningful?

He stopped, turning to her with a curious expression. Or maybe it was more that he was startled. Probably both. And he said the only thing she imagined one *could* say under the circumstances:

"I beg your pardon?"

Lucy repeated it, since she couldn't take it back. "She can't dance. That's why she won't dance. Because she can't."

And then she waited for a hole to open up in the ground so that she could jump into it. It didn't help that he was presently staring at her as if she were slightly deranged.

She managed a feeble smile, which was all that filled the impossibly long moment until he finally said, "There must be a reason you are telling this to me."

Lucy let out a nervous exhale. He didn't sound angry—more curious than anything else. And she hadn't *meant* to insult Hermione. But when he said he couldn't shoot, it just seemed to make an odd sort of sense to tell him that Hermione couldn't dance. It fit, really. Men were supposed to shoot, and women were supposed to dance, and trusty best friends were supposed to keep their foolish mouths shut.

Clearly, all three of them needed a bit of instruction.

"I thought to make you feel better," Lucy finally said. "Because you can't shoot."

"Oh, I can *shoot,*" he said. "That's the easy part. I just can't aim."

Lucy grinned. She couldn't help herself. "I could show you."

His head swung around. "Oh, *gad.* Don't tell me *you* know how to shoot."

She perked up. "Quite well, actually."

He shook his head. "The day only needed this."

"It's an admirable skill," she protested.

"I'm sure it is, but I've already four females in my life who can best me. The last thing I need is—oh, gad *again,* please don't say Miss Watson is a crack shot as well."

Lucy blinked. "Do you know, I'm not sure."

"Well, there is still hope there, then."

"Isn't that peculiar?" she murmured.

He gave her a deadpan look. "That I have hope?"

"No, that—" She couldn't say it. Good heavens, it sounded silly even to her.

"Ah, then you must think it peculiar that you don't know whether Miss Watson can shoot."

And there it was. He guessed it, anyway. "Yes," she admitted. "But then again, why would I? Marksmanship wasn't a part of the curriculum at Miss Moss's."

"To the great relief of gentlemen everywhere, I assure you." He gave her a lopsided smile. "Who did teach you?"

"My father," she said, and it was strange, because her lips parted before she answered. For a moment she thought she'd been surprised by the question, but it hadn't been that.

She'd been surprised by her answer.

"Good heavens," he responded, "were you even out of leading strings?"

"Just barely," Lucy said, still puzzling over her odd reaction. It was probably just because she didn't often think of her father. He had been gone so long that there weren't many questions to which the late Earl of Fennsworth constituted the reply.

"He thought it an important skill," she continued. "Even for girls. Our home is near the Dover coast, and there were always smugglers. Most of them were friendly—everyone knew who they were, even the magistrate."

"He must have enjoyed French brandy," Mr. Bridgerton murmured.

Lucy smiled in recollection. "As did my father. But not all of the smugglers were known to us. Some, I'm sure, were quite dangerous. And . . ." She leaned toward him. One really couldn't say something like this without leaning in. Where would the fun be in that?

"And . . . ?" he prompted.

She lowered her voice. "I think there were spies."

"In Dover? Ten years ago? Absolutely there were spies. Although I do wonder at the advisability of arming the infant population."

Lucy laughed. "I was a bit older than *that.* I believe we began when I was seven. Richard continued the lessons once my father had passed on."

"I suppose he's a brilliant marksman as well."

She nodded ruefully. "Sorry."

They resumed their stroll toward the house. "I won't challenge him to a duel, then," he said, somewhat offhandedly.

"I'd rather you didn't."

He turned to her with an expression that could only be called sly. "Why, Lady Lucinda, I do believe you have just declared your affection for me."

Her mouth flapped open like an inarticulate fish. "I have n— what could possibly lead you to that conclusion?" And *why* did her cheeks feel so suddenly hot?

"It could never be a fair match," he said, sounding remarkably at ease with his shortcomings. "Although in all truth, I don't know that there is a man in Britain with whom I could have a fair match."

She still felt somewhat light-headed after her previous surprise, but she managed to say, "I'm sure you overstate."

"No," he said, almost casually. "Your brother would surely leave a bullet in my shoulder." He paused, considering this. "Assuming he wasn't of a mind to put one in my heart."

"Oh, don't be silly."

He shrugged. "Regardless, you must be more concerned for my welfare than you were aware."

"I'm concerned for everybody's welfare," she muttered.

"Yes," he murmured, "you would be."

Lucy drew back. "Why does that sound like an insult?"

"Did it? I can assure you it wasn't meant to."

She stared at him suspiciously for so long that he finally lifted his hands in surrender. "It was a compliment, I swear to you," he said.

"Grudgingly given."

"Not at all!" He glanced over at her, quite obviously unable to suppress a smile.

"You're laughing at me."

"No," he insisted, and then of course he laughed. "Sorry. Now I am."

"You could at least *attempt* to be kind and say that you are laughing *with* me."

"I could." He grinned, and his eyes turned positively devilish. "But it would be a lie."

She almost smacked him on the shoulder. "Oh, you are terrible."

"Bane of my brothers' existence, I assure you."

"Really?" Lucy had never been the bane of anyone's existence, and right then it sounded rather appealing. "How so?"

"Oh, the same as always. I need to settle down, find purpose, apply myself."

"Get married?"

"That, too."

"Is that why you are so enamored of Hermione?"

He paused—just for a moment. But it was there. Lucy felt it.

"No," he said. "It was something else entirely."

"Of course," she said quickly, feeling foolish for having asked. He'd told her all about it the night before—about love just happening, having no choice in the matter. He didn't want Hermione to please his brother; he wanted Hermione because he couldn't *not* want her.

And it made her feel just a little bit more alone.

"We are returned," he said, motioning to the door to the drawing room, which she had not even realized they had reached.

"Yes, of course." She looked at the door, then looked at him, then wondered why it felt so awkward now that they had to say goodbye. "Thank you for the company."

"The pleasure was all mine."

Lucy took a step toward the door, then turned back to face him with a little "Oh!"

His brows rose. "Is something wrong?"

"No. But I must apologize—I turned you quite around. You said you like to go that way—down toward the lake—when you need to think. And you never got to."

He looked at her curiously, his head tilting ever so slightly to the side. And his eyes—oh, she wished she could describe what she saw there. Because she didn't understand it, didn't quite comprehend how it made her tilt her head in concert with his, how it made her feel as if the moment were stretching . . . longer . . . longer . . . until it could last a lifetime.

"Didn't you wish for time for yourself?" she asked, softly . . . so softly it was almost a whisper.

Slowly, he shook his head. "I did," he said, sounding as if the words were coming to him at that very moment, as if the thought itself was new and not quite what he had expected.

"I did," he said again, "but now I don't."

She looked at him, and he looked at her. And the thought quite suddenly popped into her head—

He doesn't know why.

He didn't know why he no longer wanted to be by himself.

And she didn't know why that was meaningful.

Nine

In which Our Story takes a turn.

The following night was the masked ball. It was to be a grand affair, not *too* grand, of course—Gregory's brother Anthony wouldn't stand for that much disruption of his comfortable life in the country. But nevertheless, it was to be the pinnacle of the house party events. All the guests would be there, along with another hundred or so extra attendees—some down from London, others straight from their homes in the country. Every last bedchamber had been aired out and prepared for occupants, and even with that, a good number of partygoers were staying at the homes of neighbors, or, for an unlucky few, at nearby inns.

Kate's original intention had been to throw a fancy dress party—she'd been longing to fashion herself as Medusa (to the surprise of no one)—but she had finally abandoned the idea after Anthony informed her that if she had her way with this, *he* would choose his own costume.

The look he gave her was apparently enough for her to declare an immediate retreat.

She later told Gregory that he had still not forgiven her for costuming him as Cupid at the Billington fancy dress ball the previous year.

"Costume too cherubic?" Gregory murmured.

"But on the bright side," she had replied, "I now know exactly how he must have looked as a baby. Quite darling, actually."

"Until this moment," Gregory said with a wince, "I'm not sure I understood exactly how much my brother loves you."

"Quite a bit." She smiled and nodded. "Quite a bit indeed."

And so a compromise was reached. No costumes, just masks. Anthony didn't mind that one bit, as it would enable him to abandon his duties as host entirely if he so chose (who would notice his absence, after all?), and Kate set to work designing a mask with Medusish snakes jumping out in every direction. (She was unsuccessful.)

At Kate's insistence, Gregory arrived in the ballroom at precisely half eight, the ball's announced start. It meant, of course, that the only guests in attendance were he, his brother, and Kate, but there were enough servants milling about to make it seem not quite so empty, and Anthony declared himself delighted with the gathering.

"It's a much better party without everyone else jostling about," he said happily.

"When did you grow so opposed to social discourse?" Gregory asked, plucking a champagne flute off a proffered tray.

"It's not that at all," Anthony answered with a shrug. "I've simply lost patience for stupidity of any kind."

"He is not aging well," his wife confirmed.

If Anthony took any exception to her comment, he made no show of it. "I simply refuse to deal with idiots," he told Gregory. His face brightened. "It has cut my social obligations in half."

"What's the point of possessing a title if one cannot refuse one's invitations?" Gregory murmured wryly.

"Indeed," was Anthony's reply. "Indeed."

Gregory turned to Kate. "You have no arguments with this?"

"Oh, I have many arguments," she answered, craning her neck as she examined the ballroom for any last-minute disasters. "I always have arguments."

"It's true," Anthony said. "But she knows when she cannot win."

Kate turned to Gregory even though her words were quite clearly directed at her husband. "What I *know* is how to choose my battles."

"Pay her no mind," Anthony said. "That is just her way of admitting defeat."

"And yet he continues," Kate said to no one in particular, "even though he knows that I always win in the end."

Anthony shrugged and gave his brother an uncharacteristically sheepish grin. "She's right, of course." He finished his drink. "But there is no point in surrendering without a fight."

Gregory could only smile. Two bigger fools in love had yet to be born. It was endearing to watch, even if it did leave him with a slight pang of jealousy.

"How fares your courtship?" Kate asked him.

Anthony's ears perked up. "Your courtship?" he echoed, his face assuming its usual *obey-me-I-am-the-viscount* expression. "Who is she?"

Gregory shot Kate an aggravated look. He had not shared his feelings with his brother. He wasn't sure why; surely in part because he hadn't actually *seen* much of Anthony in the past few days. But there was more. It just didn't seem like the sort of thing one wished to share with one's brother. Especially one who was considerably more father than brother.

Not to mention . . . If he didn't succeed . . .

Well, he didn't particularly wish for his family to know.

But he *would* succeed. Why was he doubting himself? Even earlier, when Miss Watson was still treating him like a minor nuisance, he had been sure of the outcome. It made no sense that now—with their friendship growing—he should suddenly doubt himself.

Kate, predictably, ignored Gregory's irritation. "I just adore it when you don't know something," she said to her husband. "Especially when I do."

Anthony turned to Gregory. "You're sure you want to marry one of these?"

"Not that one precisely," Gregory answered. "Something rather like it, though."

Kate's expression turned somewhat pinched at having been called an "it," but she recovered quickly, turning to Anthony and saying, "He has declared his love for—" She let one of her hands flutter in the air as if waving away a foolish idea. "Oh, never mind, I think I won't tell you."

Her phrasing was a bit suspect. She probably had meant to keep it from him all along. Gregory wasn't sure which he found more satisfying—that Kate had honored his secret or that Anthony had been flummoxed.

"See if you can guess," Kate said to Anthony with an arch smile. "That should lend your evening a sense of purpose."

Anthony turned to Gregory with a level stare. "Who is it?"

Gregory shrugged. He always sided with Kate when it came to thwarting his brother. "Far be it from me to deny you a sense of purpose."

Anthony muttered, "Arrogant pup," and Gregory knew that the evening was off to a fine start.

The guests began to trickle in, and within an hour, the ballroom sang with the low buzz of conversation and laughter. Everyone seemed a bit more adventurous with a mask on the face, and soon the banter grew more risqué, the jokes more ribald.

And the laughter . . . It was difficult to put the right word on it, but it was different. There was more than merriment in the air. There was an edge to the excitement, as if the partygoers somehow knew that this was the night to be daring.

To break free.

Because in the morning, no one would know.

All in all, Gregory liked nights like these.

By half nine, however, he was growing frustrated. He could not be positive, but he was almost certain that Miss Watson had not made an appearance. Even with a mask, she would find it nearly impossible to keep her identity a secret. Her hair was too startling, too ethereal in the candlelight for her to pass as anyone else.

But Lady Lucinda, on the other hand . . . She would have no trouble blending in. Her hair was certainly a lovely shade of honeyish blond, but it was nothing unexpected or unique. Half the ladies of the *ton* probably had hair that color.

He glanced around the ballroom. Very well, not half. And maybe not even a quarter. But it wasn't the spun moonlight of her friend's.

He frowned. Miss Watson really ought to have been present by then. As a member of the house party, she need not deal with muddy roads or lame horses or even the long line of carriages waiting out front to deliver the guests. And while he doubted she would have wished to arrive as early as he had done, surely she would not come over an hour late.

If nothing else, Lady Lucinda would not have tolerated it. She was clearly a punctual sort.

In a good way.

As opposed to an insufferable, nagging way.

He smiled to himself. She wasn't like that.

Lady Lucinda was more like Kate, or at least she would be, once she was a bit older. Intelligent, no-nonsense, just a little bit sly.

Rather good fun, actually. She was a good sport, Lady Lucinda was.

But he didn't see her among the guests, either. Or at least he didn't think he did. He couldn't be quite sure. He did see several ladies with hair the approximate shade of hers, but none of them seemed quite right. One of them moved the wrong way—too clunky, maybe even a little bit lumbering. And another was the wrong height. Not very wrong, probably just a few inches. But he could tell.

It wasn't she.

She was probably wherever Miss Watson was. Which he did find somewhat reassuring. Miss Watson could not possibly get into trouble with Lady Lucinda about.

His stomach growled, and he decided to abandon his search for the time being and instead seek sustenance. Kate had, as always, provided a hearty selection of food for her guests to nibble upon during the course of the evening. He went directly to the plate of sandwiches—they looked rather like the ones she'd served the night he'd arrived, and he'd liked those quite well. Ten of them ought to do the trick.

Hmmm. He saw cucumber—a waste of bread if ever he saw one. Cheese—no, not what he was looking for. Perhaps—

"Mr. Bridgerton?"

Lady Lucinda. He'd know that voice anywhere.

He turned. There she was. He congratulated himself. He'd been right about those other masked honey blonds. He definitely hadn't come across her yet this evening.

Her eyes widened, and he realized that her mask, covered with slate blue felt, was the exact color of her eyes. He wondered if Miss Watson had obtained a similar one in green.

"It *is* you, isn't it?"

"How did you know?" he returned.

She blinked. "I don't know. I just did." Then her lips parted—just enough to reveal a tiny little gleam of white teeth, and she said, "It's Lucy. Lady Lucinda."

"I know," he murmured, still looking at her mouth. What was it about masks? It was as if by covering up the top, the bottom was made more intriguing.

Almost mesmerizing.

How was it he hadn't noticed the way her lips tilted ever so slightly up at the corners? Or the freckles on her nose. There were seven of them. Precisely seven, all shaped like ovals, except for that last one, which looked rather like Ireland, actually.

"Were you hungry?" she asked.

He blinked, forced his eyes back to hers.

She motioned to the sandwiches. "The ham is very nice. As is the cucumber. I'm not normally partial to cucumber sandwiches—they never seem to satisfy although I do like the crunch—but these have a bit of soft cheese on them instead of just butter. It was a rather nice surprise."

She paused and looked at him, tilting her head to the side as she awaited his reply.

And he smiled. He couldn't help it. There was something so uncommonly entertaining about her when she was prattling on about food.

He reached out and placed a cucumber sandwich on his plate. "With such a recommendation," he said, "how could I refuse?"

"Well, the ham is nice, too, if you don't like it."

Again, so like her. Wanting everyone to be happy. *Try this. And if you don't like it, try this or this or this or this. And if that doesn't work, have mine.*

She'd never said it, of course, but somehow he knew she would.

She looked down at the serving platter. "I do wish they weren't all mixed up."

He looked at her quizzically. "I beg your pardon?"

"Well," she said—that singular sort of *well* that foretold a long and heartfelt explanation. "Don't you think it would have made far more sense to separate the different types of sandwiches? To put each on its own smaller plate? That way, if you found one you liked, you would know exactly where to go to get another. *Or*"—at this she grew even more animated, as if she were attacking a problem of great societal importance—"*if* there was another. Consider it." She waved at the platter. "There might not be a single ham sandwich left in the stack. And you couldn't very well sift through them all, looking. It would be most impolite."

He regarded her thoughtfully, then said, "You like things to be orderly, don't you?"

"Oh, I do," she said with feeling. "I really do."

Gregory considered his own disorganized ways. He tossed shoes in the wardrobe, left invitations strewn about . . . The year before, he had released his valet-secretary from service for a week to visit his ailing father, and when the poor man had come back, the chaos on Gregory's desk alone had nearly done him in.

Gregory looked at Lady Lucinda's earnest expression and chuckled. He'd probably drive her mad in under a week as well.

"Do you like the sandwich?" she asked, once he'd taken a bite. "The cucumber?"

"Very intriguing," he murmured.

"I wonder, is food meant to be intriguing?"

He finished the sandwich. "I'm not certain."

She nodded absently, then said, "The ham is nice."

They lapsed into a companionable silence as they glanced out across the room. The musicians were playing a lively waltz, and the ladies' skirts were billowing like silken bells as they spun and twirled. It was impossible to watch the scene and not feel as if the night itself were alive . . . restless with energy . . . waiting to make its move.

Something would happen that night. Gregory was sure of it. Someone's life would change.

If he was lucky, it would be his.

His hands began to tingle. His feet, too. It was taking everything he had just to stand still. He wanted to move, he wanted to *do* something. He wanted to set his life in motion, reach out and capture his dreams.

He wanted to move. He couldn't stand still. He—

"Would you like to dance?"

He hadn't meant to ask. But he'd turned, and Lucy was right there beside him, and the words just tumbled out.

Her eyes lit up. Even with the mask, he could see that she was delighted. "Yes," she said, almost sighing as she added, "I love to dance."

He took her hand and led her to the floor. The waltz was in full swing, and they quickly found their place in the music. It seemed to lift them, render them as one. Gregory needed only to press his hand at her waist, and she moved, exactly as he anticipated. They spun, they twirled, the air rushing past their faces so quickly that they had to laugh.

It was perfect. It was breathless. It was as if the music had crept under their skin and was guiding their every movement.

And then it was over.

So quickly. *Too* quickly. The music ended, and for a moment they stood, still in each other's arms, still wrapped in the memory of the music.

"Oh, that was lovely," Lady Lucinda said, and her eyes shone.

Gregory released her and bowed. "You are a superb dancer, Lady Lucinda. I knew you would be."

"Thank you, I—" Her eyes snapped to his. "You did?"

"I—" Why had he said that? He hadn't meant to say that. "You're quite graceful," he finally said, leading her back to the ballroom's perimeter. Far more graceful than Miss Watson, actually, although that did make sense given what Lucy had said about her friend's dancing ability.

"It is in the way you walk," he added, since she seemed to be expecting a more detailed explanation.

And that would have to do, since he wasn't about to examine the notion any further.

"Oh." And her lips moved. Just a little. But it was enough. And it struck him—she looked happy. And he realized that most people didn't. They looked amused, or entertained, or satisfied.

Lady Lucinda looked happy.

He rather liked that.

"I wonder where Hermione is," she said, looking this way and that.

"She didn't arrive with you?" Gregory asked, surprised.

"She did. But then we saw Richard. And he asked her to dance. *Not*," she added with great emphasis, "because he is in love with her. He was merely being polite. That is what one does for one's sister's friends."

"I have four sisters," he reminded her. "I know." But then he remembered. "I thought Miss Watson does not dance."

"She doesn't. But Richard does not know that. No one does. Except me. And you." She looked at him with some urgency. "Please do *not* tell anyone. I beg of you. Hermione would be mortified."

"My lips are sealed," he promised.

"I imagine they went off to find something to drink," Lucy said, leaning slightly to one side as she tried to catch a glimpse of the lemonade table. "Hermione made a comment about being overheated. It is her favorite excuse. It almost always works when someone asks her to dance."

"I don't see them," Gregory said, following her gaze.

"No, you wouldn't." She turned back to face him, giving her head a little shake. "I don't know why I was looking. It was some time ago."

"Longer than one can sip at a drink?"

She chuckled. "No, Hermione can make a glass of lemonade last an entire evening when she needs to. But I think Richard would have lost patience."

It was Gregory's opinion that her brother would gladly cut off his right arm just for the chance to gaze upon Miss Watson while she pretended to drink lemonade, but there was little point in trying to convince Lucy of that.

"I imagine they decided to take a stroll," Lucy said, quite obviously unconcerned.

But Gregory immediately felt an unease. "Outside?"

She shrugged. "I suppose. They are certainly not here in the ballroom. Hermione cannot hide in a crowd. Her hair, you know."

"But do you think it is wise for them to be off alone?" Gregory pressed.

Lady Lucinda looked at him as if she couldn't quite understand the urgency in his voice. "They're hardly off alone," she said. "There are at least two dozen people outside. I looked out through the French doors."

Gregory forced himself to stand perfectly still while he considered what to do. Clearly he needed to find Miss Watson, and quickly, before she was subjected to anything that might be considered irrevocable.

Irrevocable.

Jesus.

Lives could turn on a single moment. If Miss Watson really was off with Lucy's brother . . . If someone caught them . . .

A strange heat began to rise within him, something angry and jealous and entirely unpleasant. Miss Watson might be in danger . . . or she might not. Maybe she welcomed Fennsworth's advances . . .

No. No, she did not. He practically forced the thought down his throat. Miss Watson thought she was in love with that ridiculous Mr. Edmonds, whoever he was. She wouldn't welcome advances from Gregory *or* Lord Fennsworth.

But had Lucy's brother seized an opportunity that *he* had missed? It rankled, lodged itself in his chest like a hot cannonball—this *feeling,* this emotion, this bloody . . . awful . . . pissish . . .

"Mr. Bridgerton?"

Foul. Definitely foul.

"Mr. Bridgerton, is something wrong?"

He moved his head the inch required to face Lady Lucinda, but even so, it took several seconds for him to focus on her features. Her eyes were concerned, her mouth pressed into a worried line.

"You don't look well," she said.

"I'm fine," he ground out.

"But—"

"Fine," he positively snapped.

She drew back. "Of course you are."

How had Fennsworth done it? How had he got Miss Watson off

alone? He was still wet behind the ears, for God's sake, barely out of university and never come down to London. And Gregory was . . . Well, more experienced than that.

He should have been paying more attention.

He should never have allowed this.

"Perhaps I'll look for Hermione," Lucy said, inching away. "I can see that you would prefer to be alone."

"No," he blurted out, with a bit more force than was strictly polite. "I will join you. We shall search together."

"Do you think that's wise?"

"Why wouldn't it be wise?"

"I . . . don't know." She stopped, stared at him with wide, unblinking eyes, finally saying, "I just don't think it is. You yourself just questioned the wisdom of Richard and Hermione going off together."

"You certainly cannot search the house by yourself."

"Of course not," she said, as if he were foolish for even having suggested it. "I was going to find Lady Bridgerton."

Kate? Good God. "Don't do *that,*" he said quickly. And perhaps a bit disdainfully as well, although that hadn't been his intention.

But she clearly took umbrage because her voice was clipped as she asked, "And why not?"

He leaned in, his tone low and urgent. "If Kate finds them, and they are not as they should be, they will be married in less than a fort night. Mark my words."

"Don't be absurd. Of course they will be as they should," she hissed, and it took him aback, actually, because it never occurred to him that she might stand up for herself with quite so much vigor.

"Hermione would never behave in an untoward manner," she continued furiously, "and neither would Richard, for that matter. He is my brother. My *brother.*"

"He loves her," Gregory said simply.

"No. He. *Doesn't.*" Good God, she looked ready to explode. "And even if he did," she railed on, "which he does not, he would *never* dishonor her. Never. He wouldn't. He wouldn't—"

"He wouldn't what?"

She swallowed. "He wouldn't do that to *me.*"

Gregory could not believe her naiveté. "He's not thinking of *you,* Lady Lucinda. In fact, I believe it would be safe to say that you have not crossed his mind even once."

"That is a terrible thing to say."

Gregory shrugged. "He's a man in love. Hence, he is a man insensible."

"Oh, is *that* how it works?" she retorted. "Does that render *you* insensible as well?"

"No," he said tersely, and he realized it was actually true. He had already grown accustomed to this strange fervor. He'd regained his equilibrium. And as a gentleman of considerably more experience, he was, even when Miss Watson was not an issue, more easily in possession of his wits than Fennsworth.

Lady Lucinda gave him a look of disdainful impatience. "Richard is not in love with her. I don't know how many ways I can explain that to you."

"You're wrong," he said flatly. He'd been watching Fennsworth for two days. He'd been watching him watching Miss Watson. Laughing at her jokes. Fetching her a cool drink.

Picking a wildflower, tucking it behind her ear.

If that wasn't love, then Richard Abernathy was the most attentive, caring, and unselfish older brother in the history of man.

And as an older brother himself—one who had frequently been pressed into service dancing attendance upon his sisters' friends—Gregory could categorically say that there did not exist an older brother with such levels of thoughtfulness and devotion.

One loved one's sister, of course, but one did not sacrifice one's every waking minute for the sake of her best friend without some sort of compensation.

Unless a pathetic and unrequited love factored into the equation.

"I am not wrong," Lady Lucinda said, looking very much as if she would like to cross her arms. "And I'm getting Lady Bridgerton."

Gregory closed his hand around her wrist. "That would be a mistake of magnificent proportions."

She yanked, but he did not let go. "Don't patronize me," she hissed.

"I'm not. I'm instructing you."

Her mouth fell open. Really, truly, flappingly open.

Gregory would have enjoyed the sight, were he not so furious with everything else in the world just then.

"You are insufferable," she said, once she'd recovered.

He shrugged. "Occasionally."

"*And* delusional."

"Well done, Lady Lucinda." As one of eight, Gregory could not help but admire any well-placed quip or retort. "But I would be far more likely to admire your verbal skills if I were not trying to stop you from doing something monumentally stupid."

She looked at him through narrowed eyes, and then she said, "I don't care to speak to you any longer."

"Ever?"

"I'm getting Lady Bridgerton," she announced.

"You're getting me? What is the occasion?"

It was the last voice Gregory wanted to hear.

He turned. Kate was standing in front of them both, regarding the tableau with a single lifted brow.

No one spoke.

Kate glanced pointedly at Gregory's hand, still on Lady Lucinda's wrist. He dropped it, quickly stepping back.

"Is there something I should know about?" Kate asked, and her voice was that perfectly awful mix of cultured inquiry and moral authority. Gregory was reminded that his sister-in-law could be a formidable presence when she so chose.

Lady Lucinda—*of course*—spoke immediately. "Mr. Bridgerton seems to feel that Hermione might be in danger."

Kate's demeanor changed instantly. "Danger? Here?"

"No," Gregory ground out, although what he really meant was—*I am going to* kill *you*. Lady Lucinda, to be precise.

"I haven't seen her for some time," the annoying twit continued. "We arrived together, but that was nearly an hour ago."

Kate glanced about, her gaze finally settling on the doors leading outside. "Couldn't she be in the garden? Much of the party has moved abroad."

Lady Lucinda shook her head. "I didn't see her. I looked."

Gregory said nothing. It was as if he were watching the world destructing before his very eyes. And really, what could he possibly say to stop it?

"Not outside?" Kate said.

"I didn't think anything was amiss," Lady Lucinda said, rather officiously. "But Mr. Bridgerton was instantly concerned."

"He was?" Kate's head snapped to face him. "You were? Why?"

"May we speak of this at another time?" Gregory ground out.

Kate immediately dismissed him and looked squarely at Lucy. "Why was he concerned?"

Lucy swallowed. And then she whispered, "I think she might be with my brother."

Kate blanched. "That is not good."

"Richard would never do anything improper," Lucy insisted. "I promise you."

"He is in love with her," Kate said.

Gregory said nothing. Vindication had never felt less sweet.

Lucy looked from Kate to Gregory, her expression almost bordering on panic. "No," she whispered. "No, you're wrong."

"I'm not wrong," Kate said in a serious voice. "And we need to find them. Quickly."

She turned and immediately strode toward the door. Gregory followed, his long legs keeping pace with ease. Lady Lucinda seemed momentarily frozen, and then, jumping into action, she scurried after them both. "He would never do anything against Hermione's will," she said urgently. "I promise you."

Kate stopped. Turned around. Looked at Lucy, her expression frank and perhaps a little sad as well, as if she recognized that the younger woman was, in that moment, losing a bit of her innocence and that she, Kate, regretted having to be the one to deliver the blow.

"He might not have to," Kate said quietly.

Force her. Kate didn't say it, but the words hung in the air all the same.

"He might not have— What do you—"

Gregory saw the moment she realized it. Her eyes, always so changeable, had never looked more gray.

Stricken.

"We have to find them," Lucy whispered.

Kate nodded, and the three of them silently left the room.

Ten

***In which love is triumphant—
but not for Our Hero and Heroine.***

Lucy followed Lady Bridgerton and Gregory into the hallway, trying to stem the anxiety she felt building within her. Her belly felt queer, her breath not quite right.

And her mind wouldn't quite clear. She needed to focus on the matter at hand. She knew she needed to give her full attention to the search, but it felt as if a portion of her mind kept pulling away—dizzy, panicked, and unable to escape a horrible sense of foreboding.

Which she did not understand. Didn't she *want* Hermione to marry her brother? Hadn't she just told Mr. Bridgerton that the match, while improbable, would be superb? Hermione would be her sister in name, not just in feeling, and Lucy could not imagine anything more fitting. But still, she felt . . .

Uneasy.

And a little bit angry as well.

And guilty. Of course. Because what right did she have to feel angry?

"We should search separately," Mr. Bridgerton directed, once they had turned several corners, and the sounds of the masked ball had receded into the distance. He yanked off his mask, and the two ladies followed suit, leaving all three on a small lamp table that was tucked into a recessed nook in the hallway.

Lady Bridgerton shook her head. "We can't. *You* certainly can't find them by yourself," she said to him. "I don't wish to even ponder the consequences of Miss Watson being alone with two unmarried gentlemen."

Not to mention his reaction, Lucy thought. Mr. Bridgerton struck her as an even-tempered man; she wasn't sure that he could come across the pair alone without thinking he had to spout off about honor and the defense of virtue, which always led to disaster. Always. Although given the depth of his feelings for Hermione, his reaction might be a little less honor and virtue and a little more jealous rage.

Even worse, while Mr. Bridgerton might lack the ability to shoot a straight bullet, Lucy had no doubt that he could blacken an eye with lethal speed.

"And *she* can't be alone," Lady Bridgerton continued, motioning in Lucy's direction. "It's dark. And empty. The gentlemen are wearing masks, for heaven's sake. It does loosen the conscience."

"I wouldn't know where to look, either," Lucy added. It was a large house. She'd been there nearly a week, but she doubted she'd seen even half of it.

"We shall remain together," Lady Bridgerton said firmly.

Mr. Bridgerton looked as if he wanted to argue, but he held his temper in check and instead bit off, "Fine. Let's not waste time, then." He strode off, his long legs establishing a pace that neither of the two women was going to find easy to keep up with.

He wrenched open doors and then left them hanging ajar, too driven to reach the next room to leave things as he'd found them. Lucy scrambled behind him, trying rooms on the other side of the hall. Lady Bridgerton was just up ahead, doing the same.

"Oh!" Lucy jumped back, slamming a door shut.

"Did you find them?" Mr. Bridgerton demanded. Both he and Lady Bridgerton immediately moved to her side.

"No," Lucy said, blushing madly. She swallowed. "Someone else."

Lady Bridgerton groaned. "Good God. Please say it wasn't an unmarried lady."

Lucy opened her mouth, but several seconds passed before she said, "I don't know. The masks, you realize."

"They were wearing masks?" Lady Bridgerton asked. "They're married, then. And not to each other."

Lucy desperately wanted to ask how she had reached that conclusion, but she couldn't bring herself to do so, and besides, Mr. Bridgerton quite diverted her thoughts by cutting in front of her and yanking the door open. A feminine shriek split the air, followed by an angry male voice, uttering words Lucy dare not repeat.

"Sorry," Mr. Bridgerton grunted. "Carry on." He shut the door. "Morley," he announced, "and Winstead's wife."

"Oh," Lady Bridgerton said, her lips parting with surprise. "I had no idea."

"Should we do something?" Lucy asked. Good heavens, there were people committing *adultery* not ten feet away from her.

"It's Winstead's problem," Mr. Bridgerton said grimly. "We have our own matters to attend to."

Lucy's feet remained rooted to the spot as he took off again, striding down the hallway. Lady Bridgerton glanced at the door, looking very much as if she wanted to open it and peek inside, but in the end she sighed and followed her brother-in-law.

Lucy just stared at the door, trying to figure out just what it was that was niggling at her mind. The couple on the table —on the *table,* for God's sake—had been a shock, but something else was bothering her. Something about the scene wasn't quite right. Out of place. Out of context.

Or maybe something was sparking a memory.

What *was* it?

"Are you coming?" Lady Bridgerton called.

"Yes," Lucy replied. And then she took advantage of her innocence and youth, and added, "The shock, you know. I just need a moment."

Lady Bridgerton gave her a sympathetic look and nodded, but she carried on her work, inspecting the rooms on the left side of the hall.

What had she seen? There was the man and the woman, of course, and the aforementioned table. Two chairs, pink. One sofa, striped. And one end table, with a vase of cut flowers . . .

Flowers.

That was it.

She knew where they were.

If she was wrong and everybody else was right, and her brother really was in love with Hermione, there was only one place he would have taken her to try to convince her to return the emotion.

The orangery. It was on the other side of the house, far from the ballroom. And it was filled, not just with orange trees, but with flowers. Gorgeous tropical plants that must have cost Lord Bridgerton a fortune to import. Elegant orchids. Rare roses. Even humble wildflowers, brought in and replanted with care and devotion.

There was no place more romantic in the moonlight, and no place her brother would feel more at ease. He loved flowers. He always had, and he possessed an astounding memory for their names, scientific and common. He was always picking something up, rattling off some sort of informational tidbit—this one only opened in the moonlight, that one was related to some such plant brought in from Asia. Lucy had always found it somewhat tedious, but she could see how it might seem romantic, if it weren't one's brother doing the talking.

She looked up the hall. The Bridgertons had stopped to speak to each other, and Lucy could see by their postures that the conversation was intensely felt.

Wouldn't it be best if she were the one to find them? Without *any* of the Bridgertons?

If Lucy found them, she could warn them and avert disaster. If Hermione wanted to marry her brother . . . well, it could be her choice, not something she had to do because she'd been caught unawares.

Lucy knew how to get to the orangery. She could be there in minutes.

She took a cautious step back toward the ballroom. Neither Gregory nor Lady Bridgerton seemed to notice her.

She made her decision.

Six quiet steps, backing up carefully to the corner. And then—one last quick glance thrown down the hall—she stepped out of sight.

And ran.

She picked up her skirts and ran like the wind, or at the very least, as fast as she possibly could in her heavy velvet ball gown. She had no idea how long she would have before the Bridgertons noticed her absence, and while they would not know her destination, she had no doubt that they would find her. All Lucy had to do was find Hermione and Richard first. If she could get to them, warn them, she could push Hermione out the door and claim she'd come across Richard alone.

She would not have much time, but she could do it. She knew she could.

Lucy made it to the main hall, slowing her pace as much as she dared as she passed through. There were servants about, and probably a few late-arriving guests as well, and she couldn't afford to arouse suspicion by running.

She slipped out and into the west hallway, skidding around a corner as she took off again at a run. Her lungs began to burn, and her skin grew damp with perspiration beneath her gown. But she did not slow down. It wasn't far now. She could do it.

She knew she could.

She had to.

And then, amazingly, she was there, at the heavy double doors that led out to the orangery. Her hand landed heavily on one of the doorknobs, and she meant to turn it, but instead she found herself bent over, struggling to catch her breath.

Her eyes stung, and she tried to stand, but when she did she was hit with what felt like a wall of panic. It was physical, palpable, and it rushed at her so quickly that she had to grab on to the wall for support.

Dear God, she didn't want to open that door. She didn't want to see them. She didn't want to know what they had been doing, didn't want to know how or why. She didn't want this, any of this. She wanted it all back as it was, just three days earlier.

Couldn't she have that back? It was just *three days.* Three days, and Hermione would still be in love with Mr. Edmonds, which really wasn't such a problem since nothing would come of it, and Lucy would still be—

She would still be herself, happy and confident, and only practically engaged.

Why did everything have to *change*? Lucy's life had been perfectly acceptable the way it was. Everyone had his place, and all was in perfect order, and she hadn't had to *think* so hard about everything. She hadn't cared about what love meant or how it felt, and her brother wasn't secretly pining for her best friend, and her wedding was a hazy plan for the future, and she had been happy. She had been happy.

And she wanted it all back.

She grasped the knob more tightly, tried to turn it, but her hand wouldn't move. The panic was still there, freezing her muscles, pressing at her chest. She couldn't focus. She couldn't think.

And her legs began to tremble.

Oh, dear God, she was going to fall. Right there in the hallway, inches from her goal, she was going to crumple to the floor. And then—

"Lucy!"

It was Mr. Bridgerton, and he was running to her, and it occurred to her that she'd failed.

She'd failed.

She'd made it to the orangery. She'd made it in time, but then she'd just stood at the door. Like an idiot, she'd stood there, with her fingers on the bloody knob and—

"My God, Lucy, what were you thinking?"

He grabbed her by the shoulders, and Lucy leaned into his strength. She wanted to fall into him and forget. "I'm sorry," she whispered. "I'm sorry."

She did not know what she was sorry for, but she said it all the same.

"This is no place for a woman alone," he said, and his voice sounded different. Hoarse. "Men have been drinking. They use the masks as a license to—"

He fell silent. And then— "People are not themselves."

She nodded, and she finally looked up, pulling her eyes from the floor to his face. And then she saw him. Just saw him. His face, which had become so familiar to her. She seemed to know every feature, from the slight curl of his hair to the tiny scar near his left ear.

She swallowed. Breathed. Not quite the way she was meant to, but she breathed. More slowly, closer to normal.

"I'm sorry," she said again, because she didn't know what else to say.

"My God," he swore, searching her face with urgent eyes, "what happened to you? Are you all right? Did someone—"

His grip loosened slightly as he looked frantically around. "Who did this?" he demanded. "Who made you—"

"No," Lucy said, shaking her head. "It was no one. It was just me. I—I wanted to find them. I thought if I— Well, I didn't want you to— And then I— And then I got here, and I—"

Gregory's eyes moved quickly to the doors to the orangery. "Are they in there?"

"I don't know," Lucy admitted. "I think so. I couldn't—" The panic was finally receding, almost gone, really, and it all seemed so silly now. She felt so stupid. She'd stood there at the door, and she'd done nothing. Nothing.

"I couldn't open the door," she finally whispered. Because she had to tell him. She couldn't explain it—she didn't even understand it—but she had to tell him what had happened.

Because he'd found her.

And that had made the difference.

"Gregory!" Lady Bridgerton burst on the scene, practically hurtling against them, quite clearly out of breath from having tried to keep up. "Lady Lucinda! Why did you— Are you all right?"

She sounded so concerned that Lucy wondered what she looked like. She felt pale. She felt small, actually, but what could possibly be in her face that would cause Lady Bridgerton to look upon her with such obvious worry.

"I'm fine," Lucy said, relieved that she had not seen her as Mr. Bridgerton had. "Just a bit overset. I think I ran too quickly. It was foolish of me. I'm sorry."

"When we turned around and you were gone—" Lady Bridgerton looked as if she were trying to be stern, but worry was creasing her brow, and her eyes were so very kind.

Lucy wanted to cry. No one had ever looked at her like that. Hermione loved her, and Lucy took great comfort in that, but this was different. Lady Bridgerton couldn't have been that much older than she was—ten years, maybe fifteen—but the way she was looking at her . . .

It was almost as if she had a mother.

It was just for a moment. Just a few seconds, really, but she could pretend. And maybe wish, just a little.

Lady Bridgerton hurried closer and put an arm around Lucy's shoulders, drawing her away from Gregory, who allowed his arms to return to his sides. "Are you certain you are all right?" she asked.

Lucy nodded. "I am. Now."

Lady Bridgerton looked over to Gregory. He nodded. Once.

Lucy didn't know what that meant.

"I think they might be in the orangery," she said, and she wasn't quite certain what had caught at her voice—resignation or regret.

"Very well," Lady Bridgerton said, her shoulders pushing back as she went to the door. "There's nothing for it, is there?"

Lucy shook her head. Gregory did nothing.

Lady Bridgerton took a deep breath and pulled open the door. Lucy and Gregory immediately moved forward to peer inside, but the orangery was dark, the only light the moon, shining through the expansive windows.

"Damn."

Lucy's chin drew back in surprise. She'd never heard a woman curse before.

For a moment the trio stood still, and then Lady Bridgerton stepped forward and called out, "Lord Fennsworth! Lord Fennsworth, please reply. Are you here?"

Lucy started to call out for Hermione, but Gregory clamped a hand over her mouth.

"Don't," he whispered in her ear. "If someone else is here, we don't want them to realize we're looking for them both."

Lucy nodded, feeling painfully green. She'd thought she'd known something of the world, but as each day passed, it seemed she understood less and less. Mr. Bridgerton stepped away, moving farther into the room. He stood with his hands on his hips, his stance wide as he scanned the orangery for occupants.

"Lord Fennsworth!" Lady Bridgerton called out again.

This time they heard a rustling. But soft. And slow. As if someone were trying to conceal his presence.

Lucy turned toward the sound, but no one came forward. She bit her lip. Maybe it was just an animal. There were several cats at Aubrey Hall. They slept in a little hutch near the door to the kitchen, but maybe one of them had lost its way and got locked in the orangery.

It had to be a cat. If it were Richard, he'd have come forward when he heard his name.

She looked at Lady Bridgerton, waiting to see what she would do next. The viscountess was looking intently at her brother-in-law, mouthing something and motioning with her hands and pointing in the direction of the noise.

Gregory gave her a nod, then moved forward on silent feet, his long legs crossing the room with impressive speed, until—

Lucy gasped. Before she had time to blink, Gregory had charged forward, a strange, primal sound ripping from his throat. Then he positively leaped through the air, coming down with a thud and a grunt of "I have you!"

"Oh no." Lucy's hand rose to cover her mouth. Mr. Bridgerton had someone pinned to the floor, and his hands looked to be very close to his captive's throat.

Lady Bridgerton rushed toward them, and Lucy, seeing her, finally remembered her own feet and ran to the scene. If it was Richard—*oh, please don't let it be Richard*—she needed to reach him before Mr. Bridgerton killed him.

"Let . . . me . . . *go*!"

"Richard!" Lucy called out shrilly. It was his voice. There could be no mistaking it.

The figure on the floor of the orangery twisted, and then she could see his face.

"Lucy?" He looked stunned.

"Oh, Richard." There was a world of disappointment in those two words.

"Where is she?" Gregory demanded.

"Where is who?"

Lucy felt sick. Richard was feigning ignorance. She knew him too well. He was lying.

"Miss Watson," Gregory ground out.

"I don't know what y—"

A horrible gurgling noise came from Richard's throat.

"Gregory!" Lady Bridgerton grabbed his arm. "Stop!"

He loosened his hold. Barely.

"Maybe she's not here," Lucy said. She knew it wasn't true, but somehow it seemed the best way to salvage the situation. "Richard loves flowers. He always has. And he doesn't like parties."

"It's true," Richard gasped.

"Gregory," Lady Bridgerton said, "you must let him up."

Lucy turned to face her as she spoke, and that was when she saw it. Behind Lady Bridgerton.

Pink. Just a flash. More of a strip, actually, just barely visible through the plants.

Hermione was wearing pink. That very shade.

Lucy's eyes widened. Maybe it was just a flower. There were heaps of pink flowers. She turned back to Richard. Quickly.

Too quickly. Mr. Bridgerton saw her head snapping around.

"What did you see?" he demanded.

"Nothing."

But he didn't believe her. He let go of Richard and began to move in the direction Lucy was looking, but Richard rolled to the side and grabbed one of his ankles. Gregory went down with a yell, and he quickly retaliated, catching hold of Richard's shirt and yanking with enough force to scrape his head along the floor.

"Don't!" Lucy cried, rushing forward. Good God, they were going to kill each other. First Mr. Bridgerton was on top, then Richard, then Mr. Bridgerton, then she couldn't tell *who* was winning, and the whole time they were just *pummeling* each other.

Lucy wanted desperately to separate them, but she didn't see how without risking injury to herself. The two of them were beyond noticing anything so mundane as a human being.

Maybe Lady Bridgerton could stop them. It was her home, and the guests her responsibility. She could attack the situation with more authority than Lucy could hope to muster.

Lucy turned. "Lady Br—"

The words evaporated in her throat. Lady Bridgerton was not where she had been just moments earlier.

Oh *no*.

Lucy twisted frantically about. "Lady Bridgerton? Lady Bridgerton?"

And then there she was, moving back toward Lucy, making her way through the plants, her hand wrapped tightly around Hermione's wrist. Hermione's hair was mussed, and her dress was wrinkled and dirty, and—dear God above—she looked as if she might cry.

"Hermione?" Lucy whispered. What had happened? What had Richard done?

For a moment Hermione did nothing. She just stood there like a guilty puppy, her arm stretched limply in front of her, almost as if she'd forgotten that Lady Bridgerton still had her by the wrist.

"Hermione, what happened?"

Lady Bridgerton let go, and it was almost as if Hermione were water, let loose from a dam. "Oh, Lucy," she cried, her voice catching as she rushed forward. "I'm so sorry."

Lucy stood in shock, embracing her . . . but not quite. Hermione was clutching her like a child, but Lucy didn't quite know what to do with herself. Her arms felt foreign, not quite attached. She looked past Hermione's shoulder, down to the floor. The men had finally stopped thrashing about, but she wasn't sure she cared any longer.

"Hermione?" Lucy stepped back, far enough so that she could see her face. "What happened?"

"Oh, Lucy," Hermione said. *"I fluttered."*

An hour later, Hermione and Richard were engaged to be married. Lady Lucinda had been returned to the party, not that she would be able to concentrate on anything anyone was saying, but Kate had insisted.

Gregory was drunk. Or at the very least, doing his best to get there.

He supposed the night had brought a few small favors. He hadn't actually come across Lord Fennsworth and Miss Watson in flagrante delicto. Whatever they'd been doing—and Gregory was expending a great deal of energy to *not* imagine it—they had stopped when Kate had bellowed Fennsworth's name.

Even now, it all felt like a farce. Hermione had apologized, then

Lucy had apologized, then *Kate* had apologized, which had seemed remarkably out of character until she finished her sentence with, "but you are, as of this moment, engaged to be married."

Fennsworth had looked delighted, the annoying little sod, and then he'd had the gall to give Gregory a triumphant little smirk.

Gregory had kneed him in the balls.

Not *too* hard.

It could have been an accident. Really. They were still on the floor, locked into a stalemate position. It was entirely plausible that his knee could have slipped.

Up.

Whatever the case, Fennsworth had grunted and collapsed. Gregory rolled to the side the second the earl's grip loosened, and he moved fluidly to his feet.

"So sorry," he'd said to the ladies. "I'm not certain what's come over him."

And that, apparently, was that. Miss Watson had apologized to him—after apologizing to first Lucy, then Kate, then Fennsworth, although heaven knew why, as he'd clearly won the evening.

"No apology is needed," Gregory had said tightly.

"No, but I—" She looked distressed, but Gregory didn't much care just then.

"I did have a lovely time at breakfast," she said to him. "I just wanted you to know that."

Why? Why would she *say* that? Did she think it would make him feel better?

Gregory hadn't said a word. He gave her a single nod, and then walked away. The rest of them could sort the details out themselves. He had no ties to the newly affianced couple, no responsibilities to them or to propriety. He didn't care when or how the families were informed.

It was not his concern. None of it was.

So he left. He had a bottle of brandy to locate.

And now here he was. In his brother's office, drinking his brother's liquor, wondering what the hell this all meant. Miss Watson was lost to him now, that much was clear. Unless of course he wanted to kidnap the girl.

Which he did not. Most assuredly. She'd probably squeal like an idiot the whole way. Not to mention the little matter of her possibly having given herself to Fennsworth. Oh, and Gregory destroying his good reputation. There was that. One did not kidnap a gently bred female—especially one affianced to an earl—and expect to emerge with one's good name intact.

He wondered what Fennsworth had said to get her off alone.

He wondered what Hermione had meant when she'd said she fluttered.

He wondered if they would invite him to the wedding.

Hmmm. Probably. Lucy would insist upon it, wouldn't she? Stickler for propriety, that one. Good manners all around.

So what now? After so many years of feeling slightly aimless, of waiting waiting waiting for the pieces of his life to fall into place, he'd thought he finally had it all figured out. He'd found Miss Watson and he was ready to move forward and conquer.

The world had been bright and good and shining with promise.

Oh, very well, the world had been perfectly bright and good and shining with promise before. He hadn't been unhappy in the least. In fact, he hadn't really minded the waiting. He wasn't even sure he'd wanted to find his bride so soon. Just because he knew his true love existed didn't mean he wanted her right away.

He'd had a very pleasant existence before. Hell, most men would give their eyeteeth to trade places.

Not Fennsworth, of course.

Bloody little bugger was probably plotting every last detail of his wedding night that very minute.

Sodding little b—

He tossed back his drink and poured another.

So what did it mean? What did it mean when you met the woman who made you forget how to breathe and she up and married someone else? What was he supposed to do now? Sit and wait until the back of someone else's neck sent him into raptures?

He took another sip. He'd had it with necks. They were highly overrated.

He sat back, plunking his feet on his brother's desk. Anthony would hate it, of course, but was he in the room? No. Had he just discovered the woman he'd hoped to marry in the arms of another man? No. More to the immediate point, had his face recently served as a punching bag for a surprisingly fit young earl?

Definitely not.

Gregory gingerly touched his left cheekbone. And his right eye.

He was not going to look attractive tomorrow, that was for sure.

But neither would Fennsworth, he thought happily.

Happily? He was happy? Who'd have thought?

He let out a long sigh, attempting to assess his sobriety. It had to be the brandy. Happiness was not on the agenda for the evening.

Although . . .

Gregory stood. Just as a test. Bit of scientific inquiry. Could he stand?

He could.

Could he walk?

Yes!

Ah, but could he walk straight?

Almost.

Hmmm. He wasn't nearly as foxed as he'd thought.

He might as well go out. No sense in wasting an unexpectedly fine mood.

He made his way to the door and put his hand on the knob. He stopped, cocking his head in thought.

It had to be the brandy. Really, there was no other explanation for it.

Eleven

In which Our Hero does the one thing he would never have anticipated.

The irony of the evening was not lost on Lucy as she made her way back to her room.

Alone.

After Mr. Bridgerton's panic over Hermione's disappearance . . . after Lucy had been thoroughly scolded for running off by herself in the middle of what was turning out to be a somewhat raucous evening . . . after one couple had been forced to become engaged, for heaven's sake—no one had noticed when Lucy left the masked ball by herself.

She still couldn't believe that Lady Bridgerton had insisted upon returning her to the party. She had practically led Lucy back by the collar, depositing her in the care of someone or other's maiden aunt before retrieving Hermione's mother, who, it must be presumed, had no idea of the excitement that lay in wait for her.

And so Lucy had stood at the edge of the ballroom like a fool, staring at the rest of the guests, wondering how they could possibly not be aware of the events of the evening. It seemed inconceivable that three lives could be upended so completely, and the rest of the world was carrying on as usual.

No, she thought, rather sadly, actually—it was four; there was Mr. Bridgerton to be considered. His plans for the future had been decidedly different at the outset of the evening.

But no, everyone else appeared perfectly normal. They danced, they laughed, they ate sandwiches that were still distressingly mixed up on a single serving platter.

It was the strangest sight. Shouldn't something seem different? Shouldn't someone come up to Lucy and say, eyes quizzical—*You look somewhat altered. Ah, I know. Your brother must have seduced your closest friend.*

No one did, of course, and when Lucy caught sight of herself in a mirror, she was startled to see that she appeared entirely unchanged. A little tired, perhaps, maybe a little pale, but other than that, the same old Lucy.

Blond hair, not *too* blond. Blue eyes—again, not too blue. Awkwardly shaped mouth that never quite held still the way she wanted it to, and the same nondescript nose with the same seven freckles, including the one close to her eye that no one ever noticed but her.

It looked like Ireland. She didn't know why that interested her, but it always had.

She sighed. She'd never been to Ireland, and she probably never would. It seemed silly that this would suddenly bother her, as she didn't even want to go to Ireland.

But if she did wish to, she'd have to ask Lord Haselby, wouldn't she? It wasn't much different from having to ask Uncle Robert for permission to do, well, anything, but somehow . . .

She shook her head. Enough. It had been a strange night, and now she was in a strange mood, stuck in all her strangeness in the middle of a masked ball.

Clearly what she needed to do was go to bed.

And so, after thirty minutes of trying to look as if she were enjoying herself, it finally became apparent that the maiden aunt entrusted with her care did not quite understand the scope of the assignment. It wasn't difficult to deduce; when Lucy had attempted to speak to her, she had squinted through her mask and screeched, "Lift your chin, gel! Do I know you?"

Lucy decided that this was not an opportunity to be wasted, and so she had replied, "I'm sorry. I thought you were someone else," and walked right out of the ballroom.

Alone.

Really, it was almost funny.

Almost.

She wasn't foolish, however, and she'd traversed enough of the house that evening to know that while the guests had spilled to the west and south of the ballroom, they had not ventured to the north wing, where the family kept their private rooms. Strictly speaking, Lucy ought not to go that way, either, but after what she'd been through in the past few hours, she rather thought she deserved a bit of latitude.

But when she reached the long hall that led to the north, she saw a closed door. Lucy blinked with surprise; she'd never noticed a door there before. She supposed the Bridgertons normally left it open. Then her heart sank. Surely it would be locked—what was the purpose of a closed door if not to keep people out?

But the doorknob turned with ease. Lucy carefully shut the door behind her, practically melting with relief. She couldn't face going back to the party. She just wanted to crawl into bed, curl up under the covers, close her eyes, and sleep sleep sleep.

It sounded like heaven. And with any luck, Hermione would not yet have returned. Or better yet, her mother would insist upon her remaining overnight in her room.

Yes, privacy sounded extremely appealing just then.

It was dark as she walked, and quiet, too. After a minute or so, Lucy's eyes adjusted to the dim light. There were no lanterns or candles to illuminate the way, but a few doors had been left open, allowing pale shafts of moonlight to make parallelograms on the carpet. She walked slowly, and with an odd sort of deliberation, each step carefully measured and aimed, as if she were balancing on a thin line, stretching right down the center of the hall.

One, two . . .

Nothing out of the ordinary. She frequently counted her steps. And *always* on the stairs. She'd been surprised when she got to school and realized that other people did not.

. . . three, four . . .

The runner carpet looked monochromatic in the moonlight, but Lucy knew that the big diamonds were red, and the smaller ones were gold. She wondered if it were possible to step only on gold.

. . . five, six . . .

Or maybe red. Red would be easier. This wasn't a night to challenge herself.

. . . seven, eight, n—

"Oomph!"

She crashed into something. Or dear heaven, some*one.* She'd been looking down, following the red diamonds, and she hadn't seen . . . but shouldn't the other person have seen *her*?

Strong hands caught her by the arms and steadied her. And then—

"Lady Lucinda?"

She froze. "Mr. Bridgerton?"

His voice was low and smooth in the darkness. "Now *this* is a coincidence."

She carefully disentangled herself—he had grabbed her by the arms to keep her from falling—and stepped back. He seemed very large in the close confines of the hall. "What are you doing here?" she asked.

He offered her a suspiciously easy grin. "What're *you* doing here?"

"Going to bed. This hallway seemed the best route," she explained, then added with a wry expression, "given my state of unaccompaniment."

He cocked his head. Scrunched his brow. Blinked. And finally: "Is that a word?"

For some reason that made her smile. Not her lips, exactly, but on the inside, where it counted. "I don't think so," she replied, "but really, I can't be bothered."

He smiled faintly, then motioned with his head to the room he must have just exited. "I was in my brother's office. Pondering."

"Pondering?"

"Quite a bit to ponder this evening, wouldn't you say?"

"Yes." She looked around the hall. Just in case there was someone else about, even though she was quite certain there was not. "I really shouldn't be here alone with you."

He nodded gravely. "I wouldn't want to disrupt your practical engagement."

Lucy hadn't even been thinking of *that.* "I meant after what happened with Hermione and—" And then it seemed somehow insensitive to spell it out. "Well, I'm sure you're aware."

"Indeed."

She swallowed, then tried to make it appear as if she weren't looking at his face to see if he was upset.

He just blinked, then he shrugged, and his expression was . . .

Nonchalant?

She chewed on her lip. No, that couldn't be. She must have misread him. He had been a man in love. He had told her so.

But this was none of her business. This required a certain measure of self-remindering (to add another word to her rapidly growing collection), but there it was. It was none of her business. Not one bit.

Well, except for the part about her brother and her best friend. No one could say that *that* didn't concern her. If it had just been Hermione, or just been Richard, there *might* have been an argument that she should keep her nose out of it, but with the both of them—well, clearly she was involved.

As regarded Mr. Bridgerton, however . . . *none* of her business.

She looked at him. His shirt collar was loosened, and she could see a tiny scrap of skin where she knew she ought not look.

None. None! Business. Of hers. None of it.

"Right," she said, ruining her determined tone with a decidedly involuntary cough. Spasm. Coughing spasm. Vaguely punctuated by: "Should be going."

But it came out more like . . . Well, it came out like something that she was quite certain could not be spelled with the twenty-six letters of the English language. Cyrillic might do it. Or possibly Hebrew.

"Are you all right?" he queried.

"Perfectly well," she gasped, then realized she was back to looking at that spot that wasn't even his neck. It was more his chest, which meant that it was more someplace decidedly unsuitable.

She yanked her eyes away, then coughed again, this time on purpose. Because she had to do *some*thing. Otherwise her eyes would be right back where they ought not be.

He watched her, almost a bit owlish in his regard, as she recovered. "Better?"

She nodded.

"I'm glad."

Glad? *Glad?* What did *that* mean?

He shrugged. "I hate it when that happens."

Just that he is a human being, Lucy you dolt. One who knows what a scratchy throat feels like.

She was going mad. She was quite certain of it.

"I should go," she blurted out.

"You should."

"I really should."

But she just stood there.

He was looking at her the *strangest* way. His eyes were narrowed—not in that angry way people usually associated with squinty eyes, but rather as if he were thinking exceptionally hard about something.

Pondering. That was it. He was pondering, just as he'd said.

Except that he was pondering *her.*

"Mr. Bridgerton?" she asked hesitantly. Not that she knew what she might inquire of him when he acknowledged her.

"Do you drink, Lady Lucinda?"

Drink? "I beg your pardon?"

He gave her a sheepish half-smile. "Brandy. I know where my brother keeps the good stuff."

"Oh." *Goodness.* "No, of course not."

"Pity," he murmured.

"I really couldn't," she added, because, well, she felt as if she had to explain.

Even though *of course* she did not drink spirits.

And *of course* he would know that.

He shrugged. "Don't know why I asked."

"I should go," she said.

But he didn't move.

And neither did she.

She wondered what brandy tasted like.

And she wondered if she would ever know.

"How did you enjoy the party?" he asked.

"The party?"

"Weren't you forced to go back?"

She nodded, rolling her eyes. "It was strongly suggested."

"Ah, so then she dragged you."

To Lucy's great surprise, she chuckled. "Rather close to it. And I didn't have my mask, which made me stick out a bit."

"Like a mushroom?"

"Like a—?"

He looked at her dress and nodded at the color. "A blue mushroom."

She glanced at herself and then at him. "Mr. Bridgerton, are you intoxicated?"

He leaned forward with a sly and slightly silly smile. He held up his hand, his thumb and index finger measuring an inch between them. "Just a little bit."

She eyed him dubiously. "Really?"

He looked down at his fingers with a furrowed brow, then added another inch or so to the space between them. "Well, perhaps this much."

Lucy didn't know much about men or much about spirits, but she knew enough about the two of them together to ask, "Isn't that always the case?"

"No." He lifted his brows and stared down his nose at her. "I usually know exactly how drunk I am."

Lucy had no idea what to say to that.

"But do you know, tonight I'm not sure." And he sounded surprised at that.

"Oh." Because she was at her articulate best this evening.

He smiled.

Her stomach felt strange.

She tried to smile back. She really should be going.

So naturally, she did not move.

His head tilted to the side and he let out a thoughtful exhale, and it occurred to her that he was doing exactly what he'd said he'd been doing—pondering. "I was thinking," he said slowly, "that given the events of the evening . . ."

She leaned forward expectantly. Why did people always let their voices trail off just when they were about to say something meaningful? "Mr. Bridgerton?" she nudged, because now he was just staring at some painting on the wall.

His lips twisted thoughtfully. "Wouldn't you think I ought to be a bit more upset?"

Her lips parted with surprise. "You're not upset?" How was that possible?

He shrugged. "Not as much as I should be, given that my heart practically stopped beating the first time I saw Miss Watson."

Lucy smiled tightly.

His head went back to vertical, and he looked at her and blinked—perfectly clear-eyed, as if he had just reached an obvious conclusion. "Which is why I suspect the brandy."

"I see." She didn't, of course, but what else could she say? "You . . . ah . . . you certainly seemed upset."

"I was cross," he explained.

"You're not any longer?"

He thought about that. "Oh, I'm still cross."

And Lucy felt the need to apologize. Which she *knew* was ridiculous, because none of this was her fault. But it was so ingrained in her, this need to apologize for everything. She couldn't help it. She wanted everyone to be happy. She always had. It was neater that way. More orderly.

"I'm sorry I didn't believe you about my brother," she said. "I didn't know. Truly, I didn't know."

He looked down at her, and his eyes were kind. She wasn't sure when it had happened, because a moment ago, he'd been flip and nonchalant. But now . . . he was different.

"I know you didn't," he said. "And there is no need to apologize."

"I was just as startled when we found them as you were."

"I wasn't very startled," he said. Gently, as if he were trying to spare her feelings. Make her feel not such a dunce for not seeing the obvious.

She nodded. "No, I suppose you wouldn't have been. You realized what was happening, and I did not." And truly, she did feel like a half-wit. How could she have been so completely unaware? It was Hermione and her brother, for heaven's sake. If anyone were to detect a budding romance, it ought to have been she.

There was a pause—an awkward one—and then he said, "I will be well."

"Oh, of course you will," Lucy said reassuringly. And then *she* felt reassured, because it felt so lovely and *normal* to be the one trying to make everything right. That's what she did. She scurried about. She made sure everyone was happy and comfortable.

That was who she was.

But then he asked —oh *why* did he ask—"Will you?"

She said nothing.

"Be well," he clarified. "Will you be well"—he paused, then shrugged— "as well?"

"Of course," she said, a little too quickly.

She thought that was the end of it, but then he said, "Are you certain? Because you seemed a little . . ."

She swallowed, waiting uncomfortably for his assessment.

". . . overset," he finished.

"Well, I was surprised," she said, glad to have an answer. "And so naturally I was somewhat disconcerted." But she heard a slight stammer in her voice, and she was wondering which one of them she was trying convince.

He didn't say anything.

She swallowed. It was uncomfortable. *She* was uncomfortable, and yet she kept talking, kept explaining it all. And she said, "I'm not entirely certain what happened."

Still, he did not speak.

"I felt a little . . . Right here . . ." Her hand went to her chest, to the spot where she had felt so paralyzed. She looked up at him, practically begging him with her eyes to say something, to change the subject and end the conversation.

But he didn't. And the silence made her explain.

If he'd asked a question, said even one comforting word, she wouldn't have told him. But the silence was too much. It had to be filled.

"I couldn't move," she said, testing out the words as they left her lips. It was as if by speaking, she was finally confirming what had happened. "I reached the door, and I couldn't open it."

She looked up at him, searching for answers. But of course he did not have any.

"I—I don't know why I was so overcome." Her voice sounded breathy, nervous even. "I mean—it was Hermione. And my brother. I—I'm sorry for your pain, but this is all rather tidy, really. It's nice. Or at least it should be. Hermione will be my sister. I have always wanted a sister."

"They are occasionally entertaining." He said it with a half-smile, and it did make Lucy feel better. It was remarkable how much it did. And it was just enough to cause her words to spill out, this time without hesitation, without even a stammer.

"I could not believe they had gone off together. They should have said something. They should have told me that they cared for one another. I shouldn't have had to discover it that way. It's not right." She grabbed his arm and looked up at him, her eyes earnest and urgent. "It's not right, Mr. Bridgerton. It's not right."

He shook his head, but only slightly. His chin barely moved, and neither did his lips as he said, "No."

"Everything is changing," she whispered, and she wasn't talking about Hermione any longer. But it didn't matter, except that she didn't want to think anymore. Not about that. Not about the future. "It's all changing," she whispered, "and I can't stop it."

Somehow his face was closer as he said, again, "No."

"It's too much." She couldn't stop looking at him, couldn't move her eyes from his, and she was still whispering it—"It's all too much"—when there was no more distance between them.

And his lips . . . they touched hers.

It was a kiss.

She had been kissed.

Her. Lucy. For once it was about her. She was at the center of her world. It was life. And it was happening to *her.*

It was remarkable, because it all felt so *big,* so transforming. And yet it was just a little kiss—soft, just a brush, so light it almost tickled. She felt a rush, a shiver, a tingly lightness in her chest. Her body seemed to come alive, and at the same time freeze into place, as if afraid that the wrong movement might make it all go away.

But she didn't want it to go away. God help her, she wanted this. She wanted this moment, and she wanted this memory, and she wanted . . .

She just *wanted.*

Everything. Anything she could get.

Anything she could feel.

His arms came around her, and she leaned in, sighing against his mouth as her body came into contact with his. This was it, she thought dimly. This was the music. This was a symphony.

This was a flutter. More than a flutter.

His mouth grew more urgent, and she opened to him, reveling in the warmth of his kiss. It spoke to her, called to her soul. His hands were holding her tighter, tighter, and her own snaked around him, finally resting where his hair met his collar.

She hadn't meant to touch him, hadn't even thought about it. Her hands seemed to know where to go, how to find him, bring him closer. Her back arched, and the heat between them grew.

And the kiss went on . . . and on.

She felt it in her belly, she felt it in her toes. This kiss seemed to be everywhere, all across her skin, straight down to her soul.

"Lucy," he whispered, his lips finally leaving hers to blaze a hot trail along her jaw to her ear. "My God, Lucy."

She didn't want to speak, didn't want to do anything to break the moment. She didn't know what to call him, couldn't quite say *Gregory,* but *Mr. Bridgerton* was no longer right.

He was more than that now. More to her.

She'd been right earlier. Everything *was* changing. She didn't feel the same. She felt . . .

Awakened.

Her neck arched as he nipped at her earlobe, and she moaned—soft, incoherent sounds that slid from her lips like a song. She wanted to sink into him. She wanted to slide to the carpet and take him with her. She wanted the weight of him, the heat of him, and she wanted to *touch* him—she wanted to *do* something. She wanted to act. She wanted to be daring.

She moved her hands to his hair, sinking her fingers into the silky strands. He let out a little groan, and just the sound of his voice was enough to make her heart beat faster. He was doing remarkable things to her neck—his lips, his tongue, his teeth—she didn't know which, but one of them was setting her on fire.

His lips moved down the column of her throat, raining fire along her skin. And his hands—they had moved. They were cupping her, pressing her against him, and everything felt so *urgent.*

This was no longer about what she wanted. It was about what she needed.

Was this what had happened to Hermione? Had she innocently gone for a stroll with Richard and then . . . *this*?

Lucy understood it now. She understood what it meant to want something you knew was wrong, to allow it to happen even though it could lead to scandal and—

And then she said it. She tried it. "Gregory," she whispered, testing the name on her lips. It felt like an endearment, an intimacy, almost as if she could change the world and everything around her with one single word.

If she said his name, then he could be hers, and she could forget everything else, she could forget—

Haselby.

Dear God, she was engaged. It was not just an understanding any longer. The papers had been signed. And she was—

"No," she said, pressing her hands on his chest. "No, I can't."

He allowed her to push him away. She turned her head, afraid to look at him. She knew . . . if she saw his face . . .

She was weak. She wouldn't be able to resist.

"Lucy," he said, and she realized that the sound of him was just as hard to bear as his face would have been.

"I can't do this." She shook her head, still not looking at him. "It's wrong."

"Lucy." And this time she felt his fingers on her chin, gently urging her to face him.

"Please allow me to escort you upstairs," he said.

"No!" It came out too loud, and she stopped, swallowing uncomfortably. "I can't risk it," she said, finally allowing her eyes to meet his.

It was a mistake. The way he was looking at her— His eyes were stern, but there was more. A hint of softness, a touch of warmth. And curiosity. As if . . . As if he wasn't quite sure what he was seeing. As if he were looking at her for the very first time.

Dear heaven, that was the part she couldn't bear. She wasn't even sure why. Maybe it was because he was looking at *her.* Maybe it was because the expression was so . . . *him.* Maybe it was both.

Maybe it didn't matter.

But it terrified her all the same.

"I will not be deterred," he said. "Your safety is my responsibility."

Lucy wondered what had happened to the slightly intoxicated, rather jolly man with whom she'd been conversing just moments earlier. In his place was someone else entirely. Someone quite in charge.

"Lucy," he said, and it wasn't exactly a question, more of a reminder. He would have his way in this, and she would have to acknowledge it.

"My room isn't far," she said, trying one last time, anyway. "Truly, I don't need your assistance. It's just up those stairs."

And down the hall and around a corner, but he didn't need to know that.

"I will walk you to the stairs, then."

Lucy knew better than to argue. He would not relent. His voice was quiet, but it had an edge she wasn't quite certain she'd heard there before.

"And I will remain there until you reach your room."

"That's not necessary."

He ignored her. "Knock three times when you do so."

"I'm not going to—"

"If I don't hear your knock, I will come upstairs and personally assure myself of your welfare."

He crossed his arms, and as she looked at him she wondered if he'd have been the same man had he been the firstborn son. There was an unexpected imperiousness to him. He would have made a fine viscount, she decided, although she wasn't certain she would have liked him so well. Lord Bridgerton quite frankly terrified her, although he must have had a softer side, adoring his wife and children as he so obviously did.

Still . . .

"Lucy."

She swallowed and grit her teeth, hating to have to admit that she'd lied. "Very well," she said grudgingly. "If you wish to hear my knock, you had better come to the top of the stairs."

He nodded and followed her, all the way to the top of the seventeen steps.

"I will see you tomorrow," he said.

Lucy said nothing. She had a feeling that would be unwise.

"I will see you tomorrow," he repeated.

She nodded, since it seemed to be required, and she didn't see how she was meant to avoid him, anyway.

And she wanted to see him. She shouldn't want to, and she *knew* she shouldn't do it, but she couldn't help herself.

"I suspect we will be leaving," she said. "I'm meant to return to my uncle, and Richard . . . Well, he will have matters to attend to."

But her explanations did not change his expression. His face was still resolute, his eyes so firmly fixed on hers that she shivered.

"I will see you in the morning," was all he said.

She nodded again, and then left, as quickly as she could without breaking into a run. She rounded the corner and finally saw her room, just three doors down.

But she stopped. Right there at the corner, just out of his sight.

And she knocked three times.

Just because she could.

Twelve

In which nothing is resolved.

When Gregory sat down to breakfast the next day, Kate was already there, grim-faced and weary.

"I'm so sorry," was the first thing she said when she took the seat next to him.

What *was* it with apologies? he wondered. They were positively rampant these past few days.

"I know you had hoped—"

"It is nothing," he interrupted, flicking a glance at the plate of food she'd left on the other side of the table. Two seats down.

"But—"

"Kate," he said, and even he didn't quite recognize his own voice. He sounded older, if that was possible. Harder.

She fell silent, her lips still parted, as if her words had been frozen on her tongue.

"It's nothing," he said again, and turned back to his eggs. He didn't want to talk about it, he didn't want listen to explanations. What was done was done, and there was nothing he could do about it.

Gregory was not certain what Kate was doing while he concentrated on his food—presumably looking around the room, gauging whether any of the guests could hear their conversation. Every now and then he heard her shifting in her seat, unconsciously changing her position in anticipation of saying something.

He moved on to his bacon.

And then—he knew she would not be able to keep her mouth shut for long—"But are you—"

He turned. Looked at her hard. And said one word.

"Don't."

For a moment her expression remained blank. Then her eyes widened, and one corner of her mouth tilted up. Just a little. "How old were you when we met?" she asked.

What the devil was she about? "I don't know," he said impatiently, trying to recall her wedding to his brother. There had been a bloody lot of flowers. He'd been sneezing for weeks, it seemed. "Thirteen, perhaps. Twelve?"

She regarded him curiously. "It must be difficult, I think, to be so very much younger than your brothers."

He set his fork down.

"Anthony and Benedict and Colin—they are all right in a row. Like ducks, I've always thought, although I'm not so foolish to say so. And then—hmmm. How many years between you and Colin?"

"Ten."

"Is that all?" Kate looked surprised, which he wasn't sure he found particularly complimentary.

"It's a full six years from Colin to Anthony," she continued, pressing one finger against her chin as if that were to indicate deep thought. "A bit more than that, actually. But I suppose they are more commonly lumped together, what with Benedict in the middle."

He waited.

"Well, no matter," she said briskly. "Everyone finds his place in life, after all. Now then—"

He stared at her in amazement. How could she change the subject like that? Before he had any idea what she was talking about.

"—I suppose I should inform you of the remainder of the events of last night. After you left." Kate sighed—groaned really—shaking her head. "Lady Watson was a bit put out that her daughter had not been closely supervised, although really, whose fault is that? And *then* she was put out that Miss Watson's London season was over before she had a chance to spend money on a new wardrobe. Because, after all, it is not as if she will make a debut now."

Kate paused, waiting for Gregory to say something. He lifted his brows in the tiniest of shrugs, just enough to say that he had nothing to add to the conversation.

Kate gave him one more second, then continued with: "Lady Watson did come about rather quickly when it was pointed out that Fennsworth is an earl, however young."

She paused, twisting her lips. "He *is* rather young, isn't he?"

"Not so much younger than I am," Gregory said, even though he'd thought Fennsworth the veriest infant the night before.

Kate appeared to give that some thought. "No," she said slowly, "there's a difference. He's not . . . Well, I don't know. Anyway—"

Why did she keep changing the subject just when she started to say something he actually wanted to hear?

"—the betrothal is done," she continued, picking up speed with that, "and I believe that all parties involved are content."

Gregory supposed he did not count as an involved party. But then again, he felt more irritation than anything else. He did not like being beaten. At anything.

Well, except for shooting. He'd long since given up on that.

How was it that it never occurred to him, not even once, that he might not win Miss Watson in the end? He had accepted that it would not be easy, but to him, it was a fait accompli. Predestined.

He'd actually been making progress with her. She had laughed with him, by gad. Laughed. Surely that had to have meant something.

"They are leaving today," Kate said. "All of them. Separately, of course. Lady and Miss Watson are off to prepare for the wedding, and Lord Fennsworth is taking his sister home. It's why he came, after all."

Lucy. He had to see Lucy.

He'd been trying not to think about her.

With mixed results.

But she was there, all the time, hovering at the back of his mind, even while he was stewing over the loss of Miss Watson.

Lucy. It was impossible now to think of her as Lady Lucinda. Even if he hadn't kissed her, she would be Lucy. It was who she was. It fit her perfectly.

But he *had* kissed her. And it had been magnificent.

But most of all, unexpected.

Everything about it had surprised him, even the very fact that he'd done it. It was Lucy. He wasn't supposed to kiss *Lucy.*

But she'd been holding his arm. And her eyes—what was it about her eyes? She'd been looking up at him, searching for something.

Searching *him* for something.

He hadn't meant to do it. It just happened. He'd felt pulled, inexorably tugged toward her, and the space between them had grown smaller and smaller . . .

And then there she was. In his arms.

He'd wanted to melt to the floor, lose himself in her and never let go.

He'd wanted to kiss her until they both fell apart from the passion of it.

He'd wanted to—

Well. He'd wanted to do quite a bit, to tell the truth. But he'd also been a little bit drunk.

Not very. But enough to doubt the veracity of his response.

And he'd been angry. And off-balance.

Not with Lucy, of course, but he was quite certain it had impaired his judgment.

Still, he should see her. She was a gently bred young lady. One didn't kiss one of *those* without making explanations. And he ought to apologize as well, although that didn't really feel like what he wanted to do.

But it was what he *should* do.

He looked up at Kate. "When are they leaving?"

"Lady and Miss Watson? This afternoon, I believe."

No, he almost blurted out, *I meant Lady Lucinda.* But he caught himself and kept his voice unconcerned as he said instead, "And Fennsworth?"

"Soon, I think. Lady Lucinda has already been down for breakfast." Kate thought for a moment. "I believe Fennsworth said he wished to be home by supper. But they can make the journey in one day. They don't live too very far away."

"Near Dover," Gregory murmured absently.

Kate's brow furrowed. "I think you're right."

Gregory frowned at his food. He'd thought to wait here for Lucy; she would not be able to miss breakfast. But if she'd already eaten, then the time of her departure would be growing near.

And he needed to find her.

He stood. A bit abruptly—he knocked his thigh against the edge of the table, causing Kate to look up at him with a startled expression.

"You're not going to finish your breakfast?" she asked.

He shook his head. "I'm not hungry."

She looked at him with patent disbelief. She'd been a member of the family for over ten years, after all. "How is that possible?"

He ignored the question. "I bid you a lovely morning."

"Gregory?"

He turned. He didn't want to, but there was a slight edge to her voice, just enough for him to know he needed to pay attention.

Kate's eyes filled with compassion—and apprehension. "You're not going to seek out Miss Watson, are you?"

"No," he said, and it was almost funny, because that was the last thing on his mind.

Lucy stared at her packed trunks, feeling tired. And sad. And confused.

And heaven knew what else.

Wrung out. That was how she felt. She'd watched the maids with the bath towels, how they twisted and twisted to wring out every last drop of water.

So it had come to this.

She was a bath towel.

"Lucy?"

It was Hermione, quietly entering their room. Lucy had already been asleep when Hermione had returned the night before, and Hermione had been asleep when Lucy had left for breakfast.

When Lucy had returned, Hermione had been gone. In many ways, Lucy had been grateful for that.

"I was with my mother," Hermione explained. "We depart this afternoon."

Lucy nodded. Lady Bridgerton had found her at breakfast and informed her of everyone's plans. By the time she had returned to her bedchamber, her belongings were all packed and ready to be loaded onto a carriage.

That was it, then.

"I wanted to talk with you," Hermione said, perching on the edge of the bed but keeping a respectful distance from Lucy. "I wanted to explain."

Lucy's gaze remained fixed on her trunks. "There is nothing to explain. I'm very happy that you will be marrying Richard." She managed a weary smile. "You shall be my sister now."

"You don't sound happy."

"I'm tired."

Hermione was quiet for a moment, and then, when it was apparent that Lucy was done speaking, she said, "I wanted to make sure that you knew that I was not keeping secrets from you. I would never do that. I hope you know I would never do that."

Lucy nodded, because she did know, even if she had felt abandoned, and perhaps even a little betrayed the night before.

Hermione swallowed, and then her jaw tightened, and then she took a breath. And Lucy knew in that moment that she had been rehearsing her words for hours, tossing them back and forth in her mind, looking for the exact right combination to say what she felt.

It was exactly what Lucy would have done, and yet somehow it made her want to cry.

But for all Hermione's practice, when she spoke she was still changing her mind, choosing new words and phrases. "I really did love— No. No," she said, talking more to herself than to Lucy. "What I mean is, I really did *think* I loved Mr. Edmonds. But I reckon I didn't. Because first there was Mr. Bridgerton, and then . . . Richard."

Lucy looked sharply up. "What do you mean, first there was Mr. Bridgerton?"

"I . . . I'm not sure, actually," Hermione answered, flustered by the question. "When I shared breakfast with him it was as if I was awakened from a long, strange dream. Do you remember, I spoke to you about it? Oh, I didn't hear music or any some such, and I did not even feel . . . Well, I don't know how to explain it, but even though I was not in any way *overcome*—as I was with Mr. Edmonds—I . . . I wondered. About him. And whether maybe I *could* feel something. If I tried. And I did not see how I could possibly be in love with Mr. Edmonds if Mr. Bridgerton made me wonder."

Lucy nodded. Gregory Bridgerton made her wonder, too. But not about whether she could. That she knew. She just wanted to know how to make herself *not.*

But Hermione did not see her distress. Or perhaps Lucy hid it well. Either way, Hermione just continued with her explanation. "And then . . ." she said, "with Richard . . . I'm not certain how it happened, but we were walking, and we were talking, and it all felt so pleasant. But more than pleasant," she hastily added. "Pleasant sounds dull, and it wasn't that. I felt . . . right. Like I'd come home."

Hermione smiled, almost helplessly, as if she couldn't quite believe her good fortune. And Lucy was glad for her. She really was. But she wondered how it was possible to feel so happy and so sad at the same time. Because she was never going to feel that way. And even if she hadn't believed in it before, she did now. And that made it so much worse.

"I am sorry if I did not appear happy for you last night," Lucy said softly. "I am. Very much so. It was the shock, that is all. So many changes all at one time."

"But *good* changes, Lucy," Hermione said, her eyes shining. "Good changes."

Lucy wished she could share her confidence. She wanted to embrace Hermione's optimism, but instead she felt overwhelmed. But she could not say that to her friend. Not now, when she was glowing with happiness.

So Lucy smiled and said, "You will have a good life with Richard." And she meant it, too.

Hermione grasped her hand with both of her own, squeezing tightly with all the friendship and excitement inside of her. "Oh, Lucy, I know it. I have known him for so long, and he's *your* brother, so he has always made me feel safe. Comfortable, really. I don't have to worry about what he thinks of me. You've surely already told him everything, good and bad, and he still believes I'm rather fine."

"He doesn't know you can't dance," Lucy admitted.

"He doesn't?" Hermione shrugged. "I will tell him, then. Perhaps he can teach me. Does he have any talent for it?"

Lucy shook her head.

"Do you see?" Hermione said, her smile wistful and hopeful and joyful all at once. "We are perfectly matched. It has all become so clear. It is so easy to talk with him, and last night . . . I was laughing, and he was laughing, and it just felt so . . . *lovely.* I can't really explain."

But she didn't have to explain. Lucy was terrified that she knew exactly what Hermione meant.

"And then we were in the orangery, and it was so beautiful with the moonlight shining through the glass. It was all dappled and blurry and . . . and then I looked at him." Hermione's eyes grew misty and unfocused, and Lucy knew that she was lost in the memory.

Lost and happy.

"I looked at him," Hermione said again, "and he was looking down at me. I could not look away. I simply could not. And then we kissed. It was . . . I didn't even think about it. It just happened. It was just the most natural, wonderful thing in the world."

Lucy nodded sadly.

"I realized that I didn't understand before. With Mr. Edmonds—

oh, I thought myself so violently in love with him, but I did not know what love was. He was so handsome, and he made me feel shy and excited, but I never longed to kiss him. I never looked at him and leaned in, not because I wanted to, but just because . . . because . . ."

Because what? Lucy wanted to scream. But even if she'd had the inclination, she lacked the energy.

"Because it was where I belonged," Hermione finished softly, and she looked amazed, as if she hadn't herself realized it until that very moment.

Lucy suddenly began to feel very queer. Her muscles felt twitchy, and she had the most insane desire to wrap her hands into fists. What did she *mean*? Why was she saying this? Everyone had spent so much time telling her that love was a thing of magic, something wild and uncontrollable that came like a thunderstorm.

And now it was something else? It was just *comfort*? Something peaceful? Something that actually sounded *nice*? "What happened to hearing music?" she heard herself demand. "To seeing the back of his head and *knowing*?"

Hermione gave her a helpless shrug. "I don't know. But I shouldn't trust it, if I were you."

Lucy closed her eyes in agony. She didn't need Hermione's warning. She would never have trusted that sort of feeling. She wasn't the sort who memorized love sonnets, and she never would be. But the other kind—the one with the laughing, the comfort, the feeling *nice*—that she would trust in a heartbeat.

And dear God, that was what she'd felt with Mr. Bridgerton.

All that and music, too.

Lucy felt the blood drain from her face. She'd heard *music* when she kissed him. It had been a veritable symphony, with soaring crescendos and pounding percussion and even that pulsing little underbeat one never noticed until it crept up and took over the rhythm of one's heart.

Lucy had floated. She'd tingled. She'd felt all those things Hermione had said she'd felt with Mr. Edmonds—and everything she'd said she felt with Richard, as well.

All with one person.

She was in love with him. She was in love with Gregory Bridgerton. The realization couldn't have been more clear . . . or more cruel.

"Lucy?" Hermione asked hesitantly. And then again—"Luce?"

"When is the wedding?" Lucy asked abruptly. Because changing the subject was the only thing she could do. She turned, looked directly at Hermione and held her gaze for the first time in the conversation. "Have you begun making plans? Will it be in Fenchley?"

Details. Details were her salvation. They always had been.

Hermione's expression grew confused, then concerned, and then she said, "I . . . no, I believe it is to be at the Abbey. It's a bit more grand. And . . . are you certain you're all right?"

"Quite well," Lucy said briskly, and she *sounded* like herself, so maybe that would mean she would begin to feel that way, too. "But you did not mention when."

"Oh. Soon. I'm told there were people near the orangery last night. I am not certain what was heard—or repeated—but the whispering has begun, so we will need to have it all settled posthaste." Hermione gave her a sweet smile. "I don't mind. And I don't think Richard does, either."

Lucy wondered which of them would reach the altar first. She hoped it was Hermione.

A knock sounded on the door. It was a maid, followed by two footmen, there to remove Lucy's trunks.

"Richard desires an early start," Lucy explained, even though she had not seen her brother since the events of the previous night. Hermione probably knew more about their plans than she did.

"Think of it, Lucy," Hermione said, walking her to the door. "We shall both be countesses. I of Fennsworth, and you of Davenport. We shall cut quite a dash, we two."

Lucy knew that she was trying to cheer her up, so she used every ounce of her energy to force her smile to reach her eyes as she said, "It will be great fun, won't it?"

Hermione took her hand and squeezed it. "Oh, it will, Lucy. You shall see. We are at the dawn of a new day, and it will be bright, indeed."

Lucy gave her friend a hug. It was the only way she could think to hide her face from view.

Because there was no way she could feign a smile this time.

Gregory found her just in time. She was in the front drive, surprisingly alone, save for the handful of servants scurrying about. He could see her profile, chin tipped slightly up as she watched her trunks being loaded onto the carriage. She looked . . . composed. Carefully held.

"Lady Lucinda," he called out.

She went quite still before she turned. And when she did, her eyes looked pained.

"I am glad I caught you," he said, although he was no longer sure that he was. She was not happy to see him. He had not been expecting that.

"Mr. Bridgerton," she said. Her lips were pinched at the corners, as if she thought she was smiling.

There were a hundred different things he could have said, so of course he chose the least meaningful and most obvious. "You're leaving."

"Yes," she said, after the barest of pauses. "Richard desires an early start."

Gregory looked around. "Is he here?"

"Not yet. I imagine he is saying goodbye to Hermione."

"Ah. Yes." He cleared his throat. "Of course."

He looked at her, and she looked at him, and they were quiet.

Awkward.

"I wanted to say that I am sorry," he said.

She . . . she didn't smile. He wasn't sure what her expression was, but it wasn't a smile. "Of course," she said.

Of course? *Of course?*

"I accept." She looked slightly over his shoulder. "Please, do not think of it again."

It was what she had to say, to be sure, but it still niggled at Gregory. He had kissed her, and it had been stupendous, and if he wished to remember it, he damned well would.

"Will I see you in London?" he asked.

She looked up at him then, her eyes finally meeting his. She was searching for something. She was searching for something in him, and he did not think she found it.

She looked too somber, too tired.

Too not like *her.*

"I expect you shall," she replied. "But it won't be the same. I am engaged, you see."

"*Practically* engaged," he reminded her, smiling.

"No." She shook her head, slow and resigned. "I truly am now. That is why Richard came to fetch me home. My uncle has finalized the agreements. I believe the banns will be read soon. It is done."

His lips parted with surprise. "I see," he said, and his mind raced. And raced and raced, and got absolutely nowhere. "I wish you the best," he said, because what else could he say?

She nodded, then tilted her head toward the wide green lawn in front of the house. "I believe I shall take a turn around the garden. I have a long ride ahead of me."

"Of course," he said, giving her a polite bow. She did not wish for his company. She could not have made herself more clear if she had spoken the words.

"It has been lovely knowing you," she said. Her eyes caught his, and for the first time in the conversation, he *saw* her, saw right down to everything inside of her, weary and bruised.

And he saw that she was saying goodbye.

"I am sorry . . ." She stopped, looked to the side. At a stone wall. "I am sorry that everything did not work out as you had hoped."

I'm not, he thought, and he realized that it was true. He had a sudden flash of his life married to Hermione Watson, and he was . . .

Bored.

Good God, how was it he was only just now realizing it? He and Miss Watson were not suited at all, and in truth, he had made a narrow escape.

He wasn't likely to trust his judgment next time when it came to matters of the heart, but that seemed far more preferable to a dull marriage. He supposed he had Lady Lucinda to thank for that, although he wasn't sure why. She had not prevented his marriage to Miss Watson; in fact, she had encouraged it at every turn.

But somehow she was responsible for his coming to his senses. If there was any one true thing to be known that morning, that was it.

Lucy motioned to the lawn again. "I shall take that stroll," she said.

He nodded his greeting and watched her as she walked off. Her hair was smoothed neatly into a bun, the blond strands catching the sunlight like honey and butter.

He waited for quite some time, not because he expected her to turn around, or even because he hoped she would.

It was just in case.

Because she might. She might turn around, and she might have something to say to him, and then he might reply, and she might—

But she didn't. She kept on walking. She did not turn, did not look back, and so he spent his final minutes watching the back of her neck. And all he could think was—

Something is not right.

But for the life of him, he did not know what.

Thirteen

In which Our Heroine sees a glimpse of her future.

One month later

The food was exquisite, the table settings magnificent, the surroundings beyond opulent.

Lucy, however, was miserable.

Lord Haselby and his father, the Earl of Davenport, had come to Fennsworth House in London for supper. It had been Lucy's idea, a fact which she now found painfully ironic. Her wedding was a mere week away, and yet until this night she hadn't even seen her future husband. Not since the wedding had shifted from probable to imminent, anyway.

She and her uncle had arrived in London a fortnight earlier, and after eleven days had passed without a glimpse of her intended, she had approached her uncle and asked if they might arrange some sort of gathering. He had looked rather irritated, although not, Lucy was fairly certain, because he thought the request foolish. No, her mere presence was all it required to bring on such an expression. She was standing in front of him, and he had been forced to look up.

Uncle Robert did not like to be interrupted.

But he apparently saw the wisdom in allowing an affianced couple to share a word or two before they met at a church, so he had curtly told her that he would make the arrangements.

Buoyed by her small victory, Lucy had also asked if she might attend one of the many social events that were taking place practically right outside her door. The London social season had begun, and each night Lucy stood at her window, watching the elegant carriages roll by. Once there had been a party directly across St. James's Square from Fennsworth House. The line of carriages had snaked around the square, and Lucy had snuffed the candles in her room so that she would not be silhouetted in the window as she watched the proceedings. A number of partygoers had grown impatient with the wait, and since the weather was so fine, they had disembarked on her side of the square and walked the rest of the way.

Lucy had told herself that she just wanted to see the gowns, but in her heart she knew the truth.

She was looking for Mr. Bridgerton.

She didn't know what she would do if she actually *saw* him. Duck out of sight, she supposed. He had to know that this was her home, and surely he would be curious enough to glance at the façade, even if her presence in London was not a widely known fact.

But he didn't attend that party, or if he did, his carriage had deposited him right at the front doorstep.

Or maybe he wasn't in London at all. Lucy had no way of knowing. She was trapped in the house with her uncle and her aging, slightly deaf aunt Harriet, who had been brought in for the sake of propriety. Lucy left the house for trips to the dressmaker and walks in the park, but other than that, she was completely on her own, with an uncle who did not speak, and an aunt who could not hear.

So she was not generally privy to gossip. About Gregory Bridgerton or anyone, for that matter.

And even on the odd occasion when she did see someone she knew, she couldn't very well *ask* after him. People would think she was interested, which of course she was, but no one, absolutely no one, could ever know of it.

She was marrying someone else. In a week. And even if she weren't, Gregory Bridgerton had shown no sign that he might be interested in taking Haselby's place.

He had kissed her, that was true, and he had seemed concerned for her welfare, but if he was of the belief that a kiss demanded a proposal of marriage, he had made no indication. He had not known that her engagement to Haselby had been finalized—not when he'd kissed her, and not the following morning when they had stood awkwardly in the drive. He could only have believed that he was kissing a girl who was entirely unattached. One simply did not *do* such a thing unless one was ready and willing to step up to the altar.

But not Gregory. When she *had* finally told him, he hadn't looked stricken. He hadn't even looked mildly upset. There had been no pleas to reconsider, or to try to find a way out of it. All she'd seen in his face—and she had *looked,* oh, how she'd looked—was . . . nothing.

His face, his eyes—they had been almost blank. Maybe a touch of surprise, but no sorrow or relief. Nothing to indicate that her engagement meant anything to him, one way or another.

Oh, she did not think him a cad, and she was quite sure he would have married her, had it been necessary. But no one had seen them, and thus, as far as the rest of the world was concerned, it had never happened.

There were no consequences. For either of them.

But wouldn't it have been nice if he'd seemed just a little bit upset? He'd kissed her, and the earth had *shook*—surely he'd felt it. Shouldn't he have wanted more? Shouldn't he have wanted, if not to marry her, then at least the possibility of doing so?

Instead he'd said, "I wish you the best," and it had sounded so final. As she'd stood there, watching her trunks being loaded into the carriage, she had *felt* her heart breaking. Felt it, right there in her chest. It had *hurt.* And as she walked away, it had just got worse, pressing and squeezing until she thought it would steal her very breath. She'd begun to move faster—as fast as she could while maintaining a normal gait, and then finally she rounded a corner and collapsed onto a bench, letting her face fall helplessly into her hands.

And prayed that no one saw her.

She'd wanted to look back. She'd wanted to steal one last glance at him and memorize his stance—that singular way he held himself when he stood, hands behind his back, legs slightly apart. Lucy knew that hundreds of men stood the same way, but on him it was different. He could be facing the other direction, yards and yards away, and she would know it was he.

He walked differently, too, a little bit loose and easygoing, as if a small part of his heart was still seven years old. It was in the shoulders, the hips maybe—the sort of thing almost no one would notice, but Lucy had always paid attention to details.

But she hadn't looked back. It would have only made it worse. He probably wasn't watching her, but if he were . . . and he saw her turn around . . .

It would have been devastating. She wasn't sure why, but it would. She didn't want him to see her face. She had managed to remain composed through their conversation, but once she turned away, she had felt herself change. Her lips had parted, and she'd sucked in a huge breath, and it was as if she had hollowed herself out.

It was awful. And she didn't want him to see it.

Besides, he wasn't interested. He had all but fallen over himself to apologize for the kiss. She knew it was what he had to do; society dictated it (or if not that, then a quick trip to the altar). But it hurt all the same. She'd wanted to think he'd felt at least a tiny fraction of what she had. Not that anything could come of it, but it would have made her feel better.

Or maybe worse.

And in the end, it didn't matter. It didn't matter what her heart did or didn't know, because she couldn't do anything with it. What was the point of feelings if one couldn't use them toward a tangible end? She had to be practical. It was what she was. It was her only constant in a world that was spinning far too quickly for her comfort.

But still—here in London—she wanted to see him. It was silly and it was foolish and it was most certainly unadvisable, but she wanted it all the same. She didn't even have to speak with him. In fact she probably *shouldn't* speak with him. But a glimpse . . .

A glimpse wouldn't hurt anyone.

But when she had asked Uncle Robert if she might attend a party, he had refused, stating that there was little point in wasting time or money on the season when she was already in possession of the desired outcome—a proposal of marriage.

Furthermore, he informed her, Lord Davenport wished for Lucy to be introduced to society as Lady Haselby, not as Lady Lucinda Abernathy. Lucy wasn't sure why this was important, especially as quite a few members of society already knew her as Lady Lucinda Abernathy, both from school and the "polishing" she and Hermione had undergone that spring. But Uncle Robert had indicated (in his inimitable manner, that is to say, without a word) that the interview was over, and he had already returned his attention to the papers on his desk.

For a brief moment, Lucy had remained in place. If she said his name, he might look up. Or he might not. But if he did, his patience would be thin, and she would feel like an annoyance, and she wouldn't receive any answers to her questions, anyway.

So she just nodded and left the room. Although heaven only knew why she had bothered to nod. Uncle Robert never looked back up once he dismissed her.

And now here she was, at the supper she herself had requested, and she was wishing—fervently—that she had never opened her mouth. Haselby was fine, perfectly pleasant even. But his father . . .

Lucy prayed that she would not be living at the Davenport residence. Please *please* let Haselby have his own home.

In Wales. Or maybe France.

Lord Davenport had, after complaining about the weather, the House of Commons, and the opera (which he found, respectively, rainy, full of ill-bred idiots, and *by God not even in English!*) then turned his critical eye on her.

It had taken all of Lucy's fortitude not to back up as he descended upon her. He looked rather like an overweight fish, with bulbous eyes and thick, fleshy lips. Truly, Lucy would not have been surprised if he had torn off his shirt to reveal gills and scales.

And then . . . *eeeeuhh* . . . she shuddered just to remember it. He stepped close, so close that his hot, stale breath puffed around her face.

She stood rigidly, with the perfect posture that had been drilled into her since birth.

He told her to show her teeth.

It had been humiliating.

Lord Davenport had inspected her like a broodmare, even going so far as to place his hands on her hips to measure them for potential childbirth! Lucy had gasped and glanced frantically at her uncle for help, but he was stone-faced and staring resolutely at a spot that was not her face.

And now that they had sat to eat . . . good heavens! Lord Davenport was *interrogating* her. He had asked every conceivable question about her health, covering areas she was quite certain were not suitable for mixed company, and then, just when she thought the worst of it was over—

"Can you do your tables?"

Lucy blinked. "I beg your pardon?"

"Your tables," he said impatiently. "Sixes, sevens."

For a moment Lucy could not speak. He wanted her to do *maths*?

"Well?" he demanded.

"Of course," she stammered. She looked again to her uncle, but he was maintaining his expression of determined disinterest.

"Show me." Davenport's mouth settled into a firm line in his jowly cheeks. "Sevens will do."

"I . . . ah . . ." Utterly desperate, she even tried to catch Aunt Harriet's eye, but she was completely oblivious to the proceedings and in fact had not uttered a word since the evening had begun.

"Father," Haselby interrupted, "surely you—"

"It's all about breeding," Lord Davenport said curtly. "The future of the family lies in her womb. We have a right to know what we're getting."

Lucy's lips parted in shock. Then she realized she'd moved a hand to her abdomen. Hastily she allowed it to drop. Her eyes shot back and forth between father and son, not sure whether she was supposed to speak.

"The last thing you want is a woman who thinks too much," Lord Davenport was saying, "but she ought to be able to do something as basic as multiplication. Good God, son, think of the ramifications."

Lucy looked to Haselby. He looked back. Apologetically.

She swallowed and shut her eyes for a fortifying moment. When she opened them, Lord Davenport was staring straight at her, and his lips were parting, and she realized he was going to speak again, which she positively could not bear, and—

"Seven, fourteen, twenty-one," she blurted out, cutting him off as best she could. "Twenty-eight, thirty-five, forty-two . . ."

She wondered what he would do if she botched it. Would he call off the marriage?

". . . forty-nine, fifty-six . . ."

It was tempting. So tempting.

". . . sixty-three, seventy, seventy-seven . . ."

She looked at her uncle. He was eating. He wasn't even looking at her.

". . . eighty-two, eighty-nine . . ."

"Eh, that's enough," Lord Davenport announced, coming in right atop the *eighty-two.*

The giddy feeling in her chest quickly drained away. She'd rebelled—possibly for the first time in her entire life—and no one had noticed. She'd waited too long.

She wondered what else she should have done already.

"Well done," Haselby said, with an encouraging smile.

Lucy managed a little smile in return. He really wasn't bad. In fact, if not for Gregory, she would have thought him a rather fine choice. Haselby's hair was perhaps a little thin, and actually *he* was a little thin as well, but that wasn't really anything to complain about. Especially as his personality—surely the most important aspect of any man—was perfectly agreeable. They had managed a short conversation before supper while his father and her uncle were discussing politics, and he had been quite charming. He'd even made a dry, sideways sort of joke about his father, accompanied by a roll of the eyes that had made Lucy chuckle.

Truly, she shouldn't complain.

And she didn't. She wouldn't. She just wished for something else.

"I trust you acquitted yourself acceptably at Miss Moss's?" Lord Davenport asked, his eyes narrowed just enough to make his query not precisely friendly.

"Yes, of course," Lucy replied, blinking with surprise. She'd thought the conversation had veered away from her.

"Excellent institution," Davenport said, chewing on a piece of roasted lamb. "They know what a girl should and should not know. Winslow's daughter went there. Fordham's, too."

"Yes," Lucy murmured, since a reply seemed to be expected. "They are both very sweet girls," she lied. Sybilla Winslow was a nasty little tyrant who thought it good fun to pinch the upper arms of the younger students.

But for the first time that evening, Lord Davenport appeared to be pleased with her. "You know them well, then?" he asked.

"Er, somewhat," Lucy hedged. "Lady Joanna was a bit older, but it's not a large school. One can't really *not* know the other students."

"Good." Lord Davenport nodded approvingly, his jowls quivering with the movement.

Lucy tried not to look.

"These are the people you will need to know," he went on. "Connections that you must cultivate."

Lucy nodded dutifully, all the while making a mental list of all the places she would rather be. Paris, Venice, Greece, although weren't they at war? No matter. She would still rather be in Greece.

". . . responsibility to the name . . . certain standards of behavior . . ."

Was it very hot in the Orient? She'd always admired Chinese vases.

". . . will not tolerate any deviation from . . ."

What was the name of that dreadful section of town? St. Giles? Yes, she'd rather be there as well.

". . . obligations. Obligations!"

This last was accompanied by a fist on the table, causing the silver to rattle and Lucy to jerk in her seat. Even Aunt Harriet looked up from her food.

Lucy snapped to attention, and because all eyes were on her, she said, "Yes?"

Lord Davenport leaned in, almost menacingly. "Someday you will be Lady Davenport. You will have obligations. Many obligations."

Lucy managed to stretch her lips just enough to count as a response. Dear God, when would this evening end?

Lord Davenport leaned in, and even though the table was wide and laden with food, Lucy instinctively backed away. "You cannot take lightly your responsibilities," he continued, his voice rising scarily in volume. "Do you understand me, gel?"

Lucy wondered what would happen if she clasped her hands to her head and shouted it out.

God in heaven, put an end to this torture!!!

Yes, she thought, almost analytically, that might very well put him off. Maybe he would judge her unsound of mind and—

"Of course, Lord Davenport," she heard herself say.

She was a coward. A miserable coward.

And then, as if he were some sort of wind-up toy that someone had twisted off, Lord Davenport sat back in his seat, perfectly composed. "I am glad to hear of it," he said dabbing at the corner of his mouth with his serviette. "I am reassured to see that they still teach deference and respect at Miss Moss's. I do not regret my choice in having sent you there."

Lucy's fork halted halfway to her mouth. "I did not realize you had made the arrangements."

"I had to do something," he grunted, looking at her as if she were of feeble mind. "You haven't a mother to make sure you are properly schooled for your role in life. There are things you will need to know to be a countess. Skills you must possess."

"Of course," she said deferentially, having decided that a show of absolute meekness and obedience would be the quickest way to put an end to the torture. "Er, and thank you."

"For what?" Haselby asked.

Lucy turned to her fiancé. He appeared to be genuinely curious.

"Why, for having me sent to Miss Moss's," she explained, carefully directing her answer at Haselby. Maybe if she didn't *look* at Lord Davenport, he would forget she was there.

"Did you enjoy it, then?" Haselby asked.

"Yes, very much," she replied, somewhat surprised at how very *nice* it felt to be asked a polite question. "It was lovely. I was extremely happy there."

Haselby opened his mouth to reply, but to Lucy's horror, the voice that emerged was that of his father.

"It's not about what makes one happy!" came Lord Davenport's blustery roar.

Lucy could not take her eyes off the sight of Haselby's still-open mouth. *Really,* she thought, in a strange moment of absolute calm, *that had been almost frightening.*

Haselby shut his mouth and turned to his father with a tight smile. "What is about, then?" he inquired, and Lucy could not help but be impressed at the absolute lack of displeasure in his voice.

"It is about what one learns," his father answered, letting one of his fists bang down on the table in a most unseemly manner. "And who one befriends."

"Well, I did master the multiplication tables," Lucy put in mildly, not that anyone was listening to her.

"She will be a countess," Davenport boomed. "A countess!"

Haselby regarded his father equably. "She will only be a countess when you die," he murmured.

Lucy's mouth fell open.

"So really," Haselby continued, casually popping a minuscule bite of fish into his mouth, "it won't matter much to you, will it?"

Lucy turned to Lord Davenport, her eyes very very wide.

The earl's skin flushed. It was a horrible color—angry, dusky, and deep, made worse by the vein that was positively jumping in his left temple. He was staring at Haselby, his eyes narrowed with rage. There was no malice there, no wish to do ill or harm, but although it made absolutely no sense, Lucy would have sworn in that moment that Davenport hated his son.

And Haselby just said, "Fine weather we're having." And he smiled.

Smiled!

Lucy gaped at him. It was pouring and had been for days. But more to the point, didn't he realize that his father was one cheeky comment away from an apoplectic fit? Lord Davenport looked ready to spit, and Lucy was quite certain she could hear his teeth grinding from across the table.

And then, as the room practically pulsed with fury, Uncle Robert stepped into the breach. "I am pleased we have decided to hold the wedding here in London," he said, his voice even and smooth and tinged with finality, as if to say—*We are done with that, then.* "As you know," he continued, while everyone else regained his composure, "Fennsworth was married at the Abbey just two weeks ago, and while it does put one in the mind of ancestral history—I believe the last seven earls held their weddings in residence—really, hardly anyone was able to attend."

Lucy suspected that had as much to do with the hurried nature of the event as with its location, but this didn't seem the time to weigh in on the topic. And she had loved the wedding for its smallness. Richard and Hermione had been so very happy, and everyone in attendance had come out of love and friendship. It had truly been a joyous occasion.

Until they had left the next day for their honeymoon trip to Brighton. Lucy had never felt so miserable and alone as when she'd stood in the drive and waved them away.

They would be back soon, she reminded herself. Before her own wedding. Hermione would be her only attendant, and Richard was to give her away.

And in the meantime she had Aunt Harriet to keep her company. And Lord Davenport. And Haselby, who was either utterly brilliant or completely insane.

A bubble of laughter—ironic, absurd, and highly inappropriate—pressed in her throat, escaping through her nose with an inelegant snort.

"Enh?" Lord Davenport grunted.

"It is nothing," she hastily said, coughing as best she could. "A bit of food. Fishbone, probably."

It was almost funny. It would have been funny, even, if she'd been reading it in a book. It would have had to have been a satire, she decided, because it certainly wasn't a romance.

And she couldn't bear to think it might turn out a tragedy.

She looked around the table at the three men who presently made up her life. She was going to have to make the best of it. There was nothing else to do. There was no sense in remaining miserable, no matter how difficult it was to look on the bright side. And truly, it could have been worse.

So she did what she did best and tried to look at it all from a practical standpoint, mentally cataloguing all the ways it could have been worse.

But instead, Gregory Bridgerton's face kept coming to mind—and all the ways it could have been better.

Fourteen

In which Our Hero and Heroine are reunited, and the birds of London are ecstatic.

When Gregory saw her, right there in Hyde Park his first day back in London, his first thought was—

Well, of course.

It seemed only natural that he would come across Lucy Abernathy in what was literally his first hour out and about in London. He didn't know *why*; there was no logical reason for them to cross paths. But she had been much in his thoughts since they had parted ways in Kent. And even though he'd thought her still off at Fennsworth, he was strangely unsurprised that hers would be the first familiar face he'd see upon his return after a month in the country.

He'd arrived in town the night before, uncommonly weary after a long trip on flooded roads, and he'd gone straight to bed. When he woke—rather earlier than usual, actually—the world was still wet from the rains, but the sun had popped out and was shining brightly.

Gregory had immediately dressed to go out. He loved the way the air smelled clean after a good, stormy rain—even in London. No, *especially* in London. It was the only time the city smelled like that—thick and fresh, almost like leaves.

Gregory kept a small suite of rooms in a tidy little building in Marylebone, and though his furnishings were spare and simple, he rather liked the place. It felt like home.

His brother and his mother had, on multiple occasions, invited him to live with them. His friends thought him mad to refuse; both residences were considerably more opulent and more to the point, better staffed than his humble abode. But he preferred his independence. It wasn't that he minded them telling him what to do—they knew he wasn't going to listen, and he knew he wasn't going to listen, but for the most part, everyone remained rather good-natured about it.

It was the scrutiny he couldn't quite tolerate. Even if his mother was pretending not to interfere in his life, he knew that she was always watching him, taking notc of his social schedule.

And *commenting* on it. Violet Bridgerton could, when the inclination struck, converse on the topic of young ladies, dance cards, and the intersection thereof (as pertained to her unmarried son) with a speed and facility that could make a grown man's head spin.

And frequently did.

There was this young lady and that young lady and would he please be sure to dance with both of them—twice—at the next soiree, and above all, he must never, ever forget the *other* young lady. The one off by the wall, didn't he see her, standing by herself. Her aunt, he must recall, was a close personal friend.

Gregory's mother had a lot of close personal friends.

Violet Bridgerton had successfully ushered seven of her eight children into happy marriages, and now Gregory was bearing the sole brunt of her matchmaking fervor. He adored her, of course, and he adored that she cared so much for his well-being and happiness, but at times she made him want to pull his hair out.

And Anthony was worse. He didn't even have to *say* anything. His mere presence was usually enough to make Gregory feel that he was somehow not living up to the family name. It was difficult to make one's way in the world with the mighty Lord Bridgerton constantly looking over one's shoulder. As far as Gregory could determine, his eldest brother had never made a mistake in his life.

Which made his own all the more egregious.

But, as luck would have it, this was a problem more easily solved than not. Gregory had simply moved out. It required a fair portion of his allowance to maintain his own residence, small though it was, but it was worth it, every last penny.

Even something as simple as this—just leaving the house without anyone wondering why or where (or in his mother's case, to *whom*)—it was lovely. Fortifying. It was strange how a mere stroll could make one feel like one's own man, but it did.

And then there she was. Lucy Abernathy. In Hyde Park when by all rights she ought to still be in Kent.

She was sitting on a bench, tossing bits of bread at a scruffy lot of birds, and Gregory was reminded of that day he'd stumbled upon her at the back of Aubrey Hall. She had been sitting on a bench then as well, and she had seemed so subdued. In retrospect, Gregory realized that her brother had probably just told her that her engagement had been finalized.

He wondered why she hadn't said anything to him.

He wished she'd said something to him.

If he had known that she was spoken for, he would never have kissed her. It went against every code of conduct to which he held himself. A gentleman did not poach upon another man's bride. It was simply not done. If he had known the truth, he would have stepped away from her that night, and he would have—

He froze. He didn't know what he would have done. How was it that he had rewritten the scene in his mind countless times, and he only now realized that he had never quite got to the point where he pushed her away?

If he had known, would he have set her on her way right at that first moment? He'd had to take hold of her arms to steady her, but he could have shifted her toward her destination when he let go. It would not have been difficult—just a little shuffle of the feet. He could have ended it then, before anything had had a chance to begin.

But instead, he had smiled, and he had asked her what she was doing there, and then—good *God,* what had he been thinking—he'd asked her if she drank brandy.

After that—well, he wasn't sure how it had happened, but he remembered it all. Every last detail. The way she was looking at him, her hand on his arm. She'd been clutching him, and for a moment it had almost felt like she needed him. He could be her rock, her center.

He had never been anyone's center.

But it wasn't that. He hadn't kissed her for that. He'd kissed her because . . .

Because . . .

Hell, he didn't know *why* he'd kissed her. There had just been that moment—that strange, inscrutable moment—and it had all been so quiet—a fabulous, magical, mesmerizing silence that seemed to seep into him and steal his breath.

The house had been full, teeming with guests, even, but the hallway had been theirs alone. Lucy had been gazing up at him, her eyes searching, and then . . . somehow . . . she was closer. He didn't recall moving, or lowering his head, but her face was just a few inches away. And the next he knew . . .

He was kissing her.

From that moment on, he had been quite simply gone. It was as if he'd lost all knowledge of words, of rationality and thought. His mind had become a strange, preverbal thing. The world was color and sound, heat and sensation. It was as if his mind had been subsumed by his body.

And now he wondered—when he let himself wonder—if he could have stopped it. If she hadn't said no, if she hadn't pressed her hands to his chest and told him to stop—

Would he have done so on his own?

Could he have done so?

He straightened his shoulders. Squared his jaw. Of course he could have. She was Lucy, for heaven's sake. She was quite wonderful, in quite a number of ways, but she wasn't the sort men lost their heads over. It had been a temporary aberration. Momentary insanity brought on by a strange and unsettling evening.

Even now, sitting on a bench in Hyde Park with a small fleet of pigeons at her feet, she was clearly the same old Lucy. She hadn't seen him yet, and it felt almost luxurious just to observe. She was on her own, save for her maid, who was twiddling her thumbs two benches over.

And her mouth was moving.

Gregory smiled. Lucy was talking to the birds. Telling them something. Most likely she was giving them directions, perhaps setting a date for future bread-tossing engagements.

Or telling them to chew with their beaks closed.

He chuckled. He couldn't help himself.

She turned. She turned, and she saw him. Her eyes widened, and her lips parted, and it hit him squarely in the chest—

It was *good* to see her.

Which struck him as a rather odd sort of reaction, given how they'd parted.

"Lady Lucinda," he said, walking forward. "This is a surprise. I had not thought you were in London."

For a moment it seemed she could not decide how to act, and then she smiled—perhaps a bit more hesitantly than he was accustomed to—and held forward a slice of bread.

"For the pigeons?" he murmured. "Or me?"

Her smile changed, grew more familiar. "Whichever you prefer. Although I should warn you—it's a bit stale."

His lips twitched. "You've tried it, then?"

And then it was as if none of it had happened. The kiss, the awkward conversation the morning after . . . it was gone. They were back to their odd little friendship, and all was right with the world.

Her mouth was pursed, as if she thought she ought to be scolding him, and he was chuckling, because it was such good fun to bait her.

"It's my second breakfast," she said, utterly deadpan.

He sat on the opposite end of the bench and began to tear his bread into bits. When he had a good-sized handful, he tossed them all at once, then sat back to watch the ensuing frenzy of beaks and feathers.

Lucy, he noticed, was tossing her crumbs methodically, one after another, precisely three seconds apart.

He counted. How could he not?

"The flock has abandoned me," she said with a frown.

Gregory grinned as the last pigeon hopped to the feast of Bridgerton. He threw down another handful. "I always host the best parties."

She turned, her chin dipping as she gave him a dry glance over her shoulder. "You are insufferable."

He gave her a wicked look. "It is one of my finest qualities."

"According to whom?"

"Well, my mother seems to like me quite well," he said modestly.

She sputtered with laughter.

It felt like a victory.

"My sister . . . not as much."

One of her brows lifted. "The one you are fond of torturing?"

"I don't torture her because I *like* to," he said, in a rather instructing sort of tone. "I do it because it is *necessary*."

"To whom?"

"To all Britain," he said. "Trust me."

She looked at him dubiously. "She can't be that bad."

"I suppose not," he said. "My mother seems to like her quite well, much as that baffles me."

She laughed again, and the sound was . . . *good*. A nondescript word, to be sure, but somehow it got right to the heart of it. Her laughter came from within—warm, rich, and true.

Then she turned, and her eyes grew quite serious. "You like to tease, but I would bet all that I have that you would lay down your life for her."

He pretended to consider this. "How much do you have?"

"For shame, Mr. Bridgerton. You're avoiding the question."

"Of course I would," he said quietly. "She's my little sister. Mine to torture and mine to protect."

"Isn't she married now?"

He shrugged, gazing out across the park. "Yes, I suppose St. Clair can take care of her now, God help him." He turned, flashing her a lopsided smile. "Sorry."

But she wasn't so high in the instep to take offense. And in fact, she surprised him utterly by saying—with considerable feeling, "There is no need to apologize. There are times when only the Lord's name will properly convey one's desperation."

"Why do I feel you are speaking from recent experience?"

"Last night," she confirmed.

"Really?" He leaned in, terribly interested. "What happened?"

But she just shook her head. "It was nothing."

"Not if *you* were blaspheming."

She sighed. "I did tell you you were insufferable, didn't I?"

"Once today, and almost certainly several times before."

She gave him a dry look, the blue of her eyes sharpening as they fixed upon him. "You've been counting?"

He paused. It was an odd question, not because she'd asked it—for heaven's sake, he would have asked the very thing, had he been given the same bait. Rather, it was odd because he had the eerie feeling that if he thought about it long enough, he might actually know the answer.

He liked talking with Lucy Abernathy. And when she said something to him . . .

He remembered it.

Peculiar, that.

"I wonder," he said, since it seemed a good time to change the topic. "Is *sufferable* a word?"

She considered that. "I think it must be, don't you?"

"No one has ever uttered it in my presence."

"This surprises you?"

He smiled slowly. With appreciation. "You, Lady Lucinda, have a smart mouth."

Her brows arched, and in that moment she was positively devilish. "It is one of my best-kept secrets."

He started to laugh.

"I'm more than just a busybody, you know."

The laughter grew. Deep in his belly it rumbled, until he was shaking with it.

She was watching him with an indulgent smile, and for some reason he found that calming. She looked warm . . . peaceful, even.

And he was happy to be with her. Here on this bench. It was rather pleasant simply to be in her company. So he turned. Smiled. "Do you have another piece of bread?"

She handed him three. "I brought the entire loaf."

He started tearing them up. "Are you trying to fatten the flock?"

"I have a taste for pigeon pie," she returned, resuming her slow, miserly feeding schedule.

Gregory was quite sure it was his imagination, but he would have sworn the birds were looking longingly in his direction. "Do you come here often?" he asked.

She didn't answer right away, and her head tilted, almost as if she had to think about her answer.

Which was odd, as it was a rather simple question.

"I like to feed the birds," she said. "It's relaxing."

He hurled another handful of bread chunks and quirked a smile. "Do you think so?"

Her eyes narrowed and she tossed her next piece with a precise, almost military little flick of her wrist. The following piece went out the same way. And the one after that, as well. She turned to him with pursed lips. "It is if you're not trying to incite a riot."

"Me?" he returned, all innocence. "You are the one forcing them to battle to the death, all for one pathetic crumb of stale bread."

"It's a very fine loaf of bread, well-baked and extremely tasty, I'll have you know."

"On matters of nourishment," he said with overdone graciousness, "I shall always defer to you."

Lucy regarded him dryly. "Most women would not find that complimentary."

"Ah, but you are not most women. And," he added, "I have seen you eat breakfast."

Her lips parted, but before she could gasp her indignation, he cut in with: "That was a compliment, by the way."

Lucy shook her head. He really was insufferable. And she was *so* thankful for that. When she'd first seen him, just standing there watching her as she fed the birds, her stomach had dropped, and she'd felt queasy, and she didn't know what to say or how to act, or really, anything.

But then he'd ambled forward, and he'd been so . . . *himself.* He'd put her immediately at ease, which, under the circumstances, was really quite astonishing.

She was, after all, in love with him.

But then he'd smiled, that lazy, familiar smile of his, and he'd made some sort of joke about the pigeons, and before she knew it, she was smiling in return. And she felt like herself, which was so reassuring.

She hadn't felt like herself for weeks.

And so, in the spirit of making the best of things, she had decided not to dwell upon her inappropriate affection for him and instead be thankful that she could be in his presence without turning into an awkward, stammering fool.

There *were* small favors left in the world, apparently.

"Have you been in London all this time?" she asked him, quite determined to maintain a pleasant and perfectly normal conversation.

He drew back in surprise. Clearly, he had not expected that question. "No. I only just returned last night."

"I see." Lucy paused to digest that. It was strange, but she hadn't even considered that he might not be in town. But it would explain—Well, she wasn't sure what it would explain. That she hadn't caught a glimpse of him? It wasn't as if she'd been anywhere besides her home, the park, and the dressmaker. "Were you at Aubrey Hall, then?"

"No, I left shortly after you departed and went to visit my brother. He lives with his wife and children off in Wiltshire, quite blissfully away from all that is civilized."

"Wiltshire isn't so very far away."

He shrugged. "Half the time they don't even receive the *Times.* They claim they are not interested."

"How odd." Lucy didn't know anyone who did not receive the newspaper, even in the most remote of counties.

He nodded. "I found it rather refreshing this time, however. I have no idea what anyone is doing, and I don't mind it a bit."

"Are you normally such a gossip?"

He gave her a sideways look. "Men don't gossip. We talk."

"I see," she said. "That explains so much."

He chuckled. "Have *you* been in town long? I had assumed you were also rusticating."

"Two weeks," she replied. "We arrived just after the wedding."

"We? Are your brother and Miss Watson here, then?"

She hated that she was listening for eagerness in his voice, but she supposed it couldn't be helped. "She is Lady Fennsworth now, and no, they are on their honeymoon trip. I am here with my uncle."

"For the season?"

"For my wedding."

That stopped the easy flow of conversation.

She reached into her bag and pulled out another slice of bread. "It is to take place in a week."

He stared at her in shock. "That soon?"

"Uncle Robert says there is no point in dragging it out."

"I see."

And maybe he did. Maybe there was some sort of etiquette to all this that she, sheltered girl from the country that she was, had not been taught. Maybe there *was* no point in postponing the inevitable. Maybe it was all a part of that making the best of things philosophy she was working so diligently to espouse.

"Well," he said. He blinked a few times, and she realized that he did not know what to say. It was a most uncharacteristic response and one she found gratifying. It was a bit like Hermione not knowing how to dance. If Gregory Bridgerton could be at a loss for words, then there was hope for the rest of humanity.

Finally he settled upon: "My felicitations."

"Thank you." She wondered if he had received an invitation. Uncle Robert and Lord Davenport were determined to hold the ceremony in front of absolutely everyone. It was, they said, to be her grand debut, and they wanted all the world to know that she was Haselby's wife.

"It is to be at St. George's," she said, for no reason whatsoever.

"Here in London?" He sounded surprised. "I would have thought you would marry from Fennsworth Abbey."

It was most peculiar, Lucy thought, how *not* painful this was—discussing her upcoming wedding with him. She felt more numb, actually. "It was what my uncle wanted," she explained, reaching into her basket for another slice of bread.

"Your uncle remains the head of the household?" Gregory asked, regarding her with mild curiosity. "Your brother is the earl. Hasn't he reached his majority?"

Lucy tossed the entire slice to the ground, then watched with morbid interest as the pigeons went a bit mad. "He has," she replied. "Last year. But he was content to allow my uncle to handle the family's affairs while he was conducting his postgraduate studies at

Cambridge. I expect that he will assume his place soon now that he is"—she offered him an apologetic smile—"married."

"Do not worry over my sensibilities," he assured her. "I am quite recovered."

"Truly?"

He gave her a small, one-shouldered shrug. "Truth be told, I count myself lucky."

She pulled out another slice of bread, but her fingers froze before pinching off a piece. "You do?" she asked, turning to him with interest. "How is that possible?"

He blinked with surprise. "You *are* direct, aren't you?"

And she blushed. She felt it, pink and warm and just *horrible* on her cheeks. "I'm sorry," she said. "That was terribly rude of me. It is only that you were so very much—"

"Say no more," he cut her off, and then she felt even worse, because she had been about to describe—probably in meticulous detail—how lovesick he'd been over Hermione. Which, had she been in his position, she'd not wish recounted.

"I'm sorry," she said.

He turned. Regarded her with a contemplative sort of curiosity. "You say that quite frequently."

"I'm sorry?"

"Yes."

"I . . . I don't know." Her teeth ground together, and she felt quite tense. Uncomfortable. Why would he point out such a thing? "It's what I do," she said, and she said it firmly, because . . . Well, because. That ought to be enough of a reason.

He nodded. And that made her feel even worse. "It's who I am," she added defensively, even though he'd been agreeing with her, for heaven's sake. "I smooth things over and I make things right."

And at that, she hurled the last piece of bread to the ground.

His brows rose, and they both turned in unison to watch the ensuing chaos. "Well done," he murmured.

"I make the best of things," she said. "Always."

"It's a commendable trait," he said softly.

And at that, somehow, she was angry. Really, truly, beastly angry. She didn't want to be commended for knowing how to settle for second-best. That was like winning a prize for the prettiest shoes in a footrace. Irrelevant and *not* the point.

"And what of you?" she asked, her voice growing strident. "Do you make the best of things? Is that why you claim yourself recovered? Weren't you the one who waxed rhapsodic over the mere thought of love? You said it was *everything,* that it gave you no choice. You said—"

She cut herself off, horrified by her tone. He was staring at her as if she'd gone mad, and maybe she had.

"You said many things," she mumbled, hoping that might end the conversation.

She ought to go. She had been sitting on the bench for at least fifteen minutes before he'd arrived, and it was damp and breezy, and her maid wasn't dressed warmly enough, and if she thought long and hard enough about it, she probably had a hundred things she needed to do at home.

Or at least a book she could read.

"I am sorry if I upset you," Gregory said quietly.

She couldn't quite bring herself to look at him.

"But I did not lie to you," he said. "Truthfully, I no longer think of Miss—excuse me, Lady Fennsworth—with any great frequency, except, perhaps, to realize that we should not have been well-suited after all."

She turned to him, and she realized she wanted to believe him. She really did.

Because if he could forget Hermione, maybe she could forget him.

"I don't know how to explain it," he said, and he shook his head, as if he were every bit as perplexed as she. "But if ever you fall madly and inexplicably in love . . ."

Lucy froze. *He wasn't going to say it. Surely, he couldn't say it.*

He shrugged. "Well, I shouldn't trust it."

Dear God. Hermione's words. Exactly.

She tried to remember how she had replied to Hermione. Because she had to say something. Otherwise, he would notice the silence, and then he'd turn, and he'd see her looking so unnerved. And then he would ask questions, and she wouldn't know the answers, and—

"It's not likely to happen to me," she said, the words practically pouring from her mouth.

He turned, but she kept her face scrupulously forward. And she wished desperately that she had not tossed out all the bread. It would be far easier to avoid looking at him if she could pretend to be involved with something else.

"You don't believe that you will fall in love?" he asked.

"Well, perhaps," she said, trying to sound blithe and sophisticated. "But not *that.*"

"That?"

She took a breath, hating that he was forcing her to explain. "That desperate sort of thing you and Hermione now disavow," she said. "I'm not the sort, don't you think?"

She bit her lip, then finally allowed herself to turn in his direction. Because what if he could tell that she was lying? What if he sensed that she was already in love—with him? She would be embarrassed beyond comprehension, but wouldn't it be better to *know* that he knew? At least then, she wouldn't have to wonder.

Ignorance wasn't bliss. Not for someone like her.

"It is all beside the point, anyway," she continued, because she couldn't bear the silence. "I am marrying Lord Haselby in one week, and I would *never* stray from my vows. I—"

"Haselby?" Gregory's entire body twisted as he swung around to face her. "You're marrying *Haselby*?"

"Yes," she said, blinking furiously. What sort of reaction was *that*? "I thought you knew."

"No, I didn't—" He looked shocked. Stupefied.

Good heavens.

He shook his head. "I can't imagine why I didn't know."

"It wasn't a secret."

"No," he said, a bit forcefully. "I mean, no. No, of course not. I did not mean to imply."

"Do you hold Lord Haselby in low esteem?" she asked, choosing her words with extreme care.

"No," Gregory replied, shaking his head—but just a little, as if he were not quite aware that he was doing it. "No. I've known him for a number of years. We were at college together. And university."

"Are you of an age, then?" Lucy asked, and it occurred to her that something was a bit wrong if she did not know the age of her fiancé. But then again, she wasn't certain of Gregory's age, either.

He nodded. "He's quite . . . affable. He will treat you well." He cleared his throat. "Gently."

"Gently?" she echoed. It seemed an odd choice of words.

His eyes met hers, and it was only then that she realized he had not precisely looked at her since she'd told him the name of her fiancé. But he didn't speak. Instead he just stared at her, his eyes so intense that they seemed to change color. They were brown with green, then green with brown, and then it all seemed almost to blur.

"What is it?" she whispered.

"It is of no account," he said, but he did not sound like himself. "I . . ." And then he turned away, broke the spell. "My sister," he said, clearing his throat. "She is hosting a soiree tomorrow evening. Would you like to attend?"

"Oh yes, that would be lovely," Lucy said, even though she knew she should not. But it had been so long since she'd had any sort of social interaction, and she wasn't going to be able to spend time in his company once she was married. She ought not torture herself now, longing for something she could not have, but she couldn't help it.

Gather ye rosebuds.

Now. Because really, when else—

"Oh, but I *can't,*" she said, disappointment turning her voice to nearly a whine.

"Why not?"

"It is my uncle," she replied, sighing. "And Lord Davenport—Haselby's father."

"I know who he is."

"Of course. I'm sor—" She cut herself off. She wasn't going to say it. "They don't wish for me to make my bow yet."

"I beg your pardon. Why?"

Lucy shrugged. "There is no point in my being introduced to society as Lady Lucinda Abernathy when I'm to be Lady Haselby in a week."

"That's ridiculous."

"It is what they say." She frowned. "And I don't think they wish to suffer the expense, either."

"You will attend tomorrow evening," Gregory said firmly. "I shall see to it."

"You?" Lucy asked dubiously.

"Not *me,*" he answered, as if she'd gone mad. "My mother. Trust me, when it comes to matters of social discourse and niceties, she can accomplish anything. Have you a chaperone?"

Lucy nodded. "My aunt Harriet. She is a bit frail, but I am certain she could attend a party if my uncle allowed it."

"He will allow it," Gregory said confidently. "The sister in question is my eldest. Daphne." He then clarified: "Her grace the Duchess of Hastings. Your uncle would not say no to a duchess, would he?"

"I don't think so," she said slowly. Lucy could not think of anyone who would say no to a duchess.

"It's settled, then," Gregory said. "You shall be hearing from Daphne by afternoon." He stood, offering his hand to help her up.

She swallowed. It would be bittersweet to touch him, but she placed her hand in his. It felt warm, and comfortable. And safe.

"Thank you," she murmured, taking her hand back so that she might wrap both around the handle of her basket. She nodded at her maid, who immediately began walking to her side.

"Until tomorrow," he said, bowing almost formally as he bade her farewell.

"Until tomorrow," Lucy echoed, wondering if it were true. She had never known her uncle to change his mind before. But maybe . . .

Possibly.

Hopefully.

Fifteen

In which Our Hero learns that he is not, and probably never will be, as wise as his mother.

One hour later, Gregory was waiting in the drawing room at Number Five, Bruton Street, his mother's London home since she had insisted upon vacating Bridgerton House upon Anthony's marriage. It had been his home, too, until he had found his own lodgings several years earlier. His mother lived there alone now, ever since his younger sister had married. Gregory made a point of calling upon her at least twice a week when he was in London, but it never ceased to surprise him how quiet the house seemed now.

"Darling!" his mother exclaimed, sailing into the room with a wide smile. "I had not thought to see you until this evening. How was your journey? And tell me everything about Benedict and Sophie and the children. It is a crime how infrequently I see my grandchildren."

Gregory smiled indulgently. His mother had visited Wiltshire just one month earlier, and did so several times per year. He dutifully passed along news of Benedict's four children, with added emphasis on little Violet, her namesake. Then, once she had exhausted her supply of questions, he said, "Actually, Mother, I have a favor to ask of you."

Violet's posture was always superb, but still, she seemed to straighten a bit. "You do? What is it you need?"

He told her about Lucy, keeping the tale as brief as possible, lest she reach any inappropriate conclusions about his interest in her.

His mother tended to view any unmarried female as a potential bride. Even those with a wedding scheduled for the week's end.

"Of course I will assist you," she said. "This will be easy."

"Her uncle is determined to keep her sequestered," Gregory reminded her.

She waved away his warning. "Child's play, my dear son. Leave this to me. I shall make short work of it."

Gregory decided not to pursue the subject further. If his mother said she knew how to ensure someone's attendance at a ball, then he believed her. Continued questioning would only lead her to believe he had an ulterior motive.

Which he did not.

He simply liked Lucy. Considered her a friend. And he wished for her to have a bit of fun.

It was admirable, really.

"I shall have your sister send an invitation with a personal note," Violet mused. "And perhaps I shall call upon her uncle directly. I shall lie and tell him I met her in the park."

"Lie?" Gregory's lips twitched. "You?"

His mother's smile was positively diabolical. "It won't matter if he does not believe me. It is one of the advantages of advanced years. No one dares to countermand an old dragon like me."

Gregory lifted his brows, refusing to fall for her bait. Violet Bridgerton might have been the mother of eight adult children, but with her milky, unlined complexion and wide smile, she did not look like anyone who could be termed old. In fact, Gregory had often wondered why she did not remarry. There was no shortage of dashing widowers clamoring to take her in to supper or stand up for a dance. Gregory suspected any one of them would have leaped at the chance to marry his mother, if only she would indicate interest.

But she did not, and Gregory had to admit that he was rather selfishly glad of it. Despite her meddling, there was something quite comforting in her single-minded devotion to her children and grandchildren.

His father had been dead for over two dozen years. Gregory hadn't even the slightest memory of the man. But his mother had spoken of him often, and whenever she did, her voice changed. Her eyes softened, and the corners of her lips moved—just a little, just enough for Gregory to see the memories on her face.

It was in those moments that he understood why she was so adamant that her children choose their spouses for love.

He'd always planned to comply. It was ironic, really, given the farce with Miss Watson.

Just then a maid arrived with a tea tray, which she set on the low table between them.

"Cook made your favorite biscuits," his mother said, handing him a cup prepared exactly as he liked it—no sugar, one tiny splash of milk.

"You anticipated my visit?" he asked.

"Not this afternoon, no," Violet said, taking a sip of her own tea. "But I knew you could not stay away for long. Eventually you would need sustenance."

Gregory offered her a lopsided smile. It was true. Like many men of his age and status, he did not have room in his apartments for a proper kitchen. He ate at parties, and at his club, and, of course, at the homes of his mother and siblings.

"Thank you," he murmured, accepting the plate onto which she'd piled six biscuits.

Violet regarded the tea tray for a moment, her head cocked slightly to the side, then placed two on her own plate. "I am quite touched," she said, looking up at him, "that you seek my assistance with Lady Lucinda."

"Are you?" he asked curiously. "Who else would I turn to with such a matter?"

She took a delicate bite of her biscuit. "No, I am the obvious choice, of course, but you must realize that you rarely turn to your family when you need something."

Gregory went still, then turned slowly in her direction. His mother's eyes—so blue and so unsettlingly perceptive—were fixed on his face. What could she possibly have meant by that? No one could love his family better than he did.

"That cannot be true," he finally said.

But his mother just smiled. "Do you think not?"

His jaw clenched. "I *do* think not."

"Oh, do not take offense," she said, reaching across the table to pat him on the arm. "I do not mean to say that you do not love us. But you do prefer to do things for yourself."

"Such as?"

"Oh, finding yourself a wife—"

He cut her off right then and there. "Are you trying to tell me that Anthony, Benedict, and Colin welcomed your interference when they were looking for wives?"

"No, of course not. No man does. But—" She flitted one of her hands through the air, as if she could erase the sentence. "Forgive me. It was a poor example."

She let out a small sigh as she gazed out the window, and Gregory realized that she was prepared to let the subject drop. To his surprise, however, he was not.

"What is wrong with preferring to do things for oneself?" he asked.

She turned to him, looking for all the world as if she had not just introduced a potentially discomforting topic. "Why, nothing. I am quite proud that I raised such self-sufficient sons. After all, three of you must make your own way in the world." She paused, considering this, then added, "With some help from Anthony, of course. I should be quite disappointed if he did not watch out for the rest of you."

"Anthony is exceedingly generous," Gregory said quietly.

"Yes, he is, isn't he?" Violet said, smiling. "With his money *and* his time. He is quite like your father in this way." She looked at him with wistful eyes. "I am so sorry you never knew him."

"Anthony was a good father to me." Gregory said it because he knew it would bring her joy, but he also said it because it was true.

His mother's lips pursed and tightened, and for a moment Gregory thought she might cry. He immediately retrieved his handkerchief and held it out to her.

"No, no, that's not necessary," she said, even as she took it and dabbed her eyes. "I am quite all right. Merely a little—" She swallowed, then smiled. But her eyes still glistened. "Someday you will understand—when you have children of your own—how lovely it was to hear that."

She set the handkerchief down and picked up her tea. Sipping it thoughtfully, she let out a little sigh of contentment.

Gregory smiled to himself. His mother adored tea. It went quite beyond the usual British devotion. She claimed it helped her to think, which he would normally have lauded as a good thing, except that all too often *he* was the subject of her thoughts, and after her third cup she had usually devised a frighteningly thorough plan to marry him off to the daughter of whichever friend she had most recently paid a morning call to.

But this time, apparently, her mind was not on marriage. She set her cup down, and, just when he thought she was ready to change the subject, she said, "But he is not your father."

He paused, his own teacup halfway to his mouth. "I beg your pardon."

"Anthony. He is not your father."

"Yes?" he said slowly, because really, what could possibly be her point?

"He is your brother," she continued. "As are Benedict and Colin, and when you were small—oh, how you wished to be a part of their affairs."

Gregory held himself very still.

"But of course they were not interested in bringing you along, and really, who can blame them?"

"Who indeed?" he murmured tightly.

"Oh, do not take offense, Gregory," his mother said, turning to him with an expression that was a little bit contrite and little bit impatient. "They were wonderful brothers, and truly, very patient most of the time."

"Most of the time?"

"Some of the time," she amended. "But you were so much smaller than they were. There simply wasn't much in common for you to do. And then when you grew older, well . . ."

Her words trailed off, and she sighed. Gregory leaned forward. "Well?" he prompted.

"Oh, it's nothing."

"Mother."

"Very well," she said, and he knew right then and there that she knew *exactly* what she was saying, and that any sighs and lingering words were entirely for effect.

"I think that you think you must prove yourself to them," Violet said.

He regarded her with surprise. "Don't I?"

His mother's lips parted, but she made no sound for several seconds. "No," she finally said. "Why would you think you would?"

What a silly question. It was because— It was because—

"It's not the sort of thing one can easily put into words," he muttered.

"Really?" She sipped at her tea. "I must say, that was not the sort of reaction I had anticipated."

Gregory felt his jaw clench. "What, precisely, did you anticipate?"

"Precisely?" She looked up at him with just enough humor in her eyes to completely irritate him. "I'm not certain that I can be precise, but I suppose I had expected you to deny it."

"Just because I do not wish it to be the case does not render it untrue," he said with a deliberately casual shrug.

"Your brothers respect you," Violet said.

"I did not say they do not."

"They recognize that you are your own man."

That, Gregory thought, was not precisely true.

"It is not a sign of weakness to ask for help," Violet continued.

"I have never believed that it was," he replied. "Didn't I just seek your assistance?"

"With a matter that could only be handled by a female," she said, somewhat dismissively. "You had no choice but to call on me."

It was true, so Gregory made no comment.

"You are used to having things done for you," she said.

"Mother."

"Hyacinth is the same way," she said quickly. "I think it must be a symptom of being the youngest. And truly, I did not mean to imply that either of you is lazy or spoiled or mean-spirited in any way."

"What did you mean, then?" he asked.

She looked up with a slightly mischievous smile. "Precisely?"

He felt a bit of his tension slipping away. "Precisely," he said, with a nod to acknowledge her wordplay.

"I merely meant that you have never had to work particularly hard for anything. You're quite lucky that way. Good things seem to happen to you."

"And as my mother, you are bothered by this . . . how?"

"Oh, Gregory," she said with a sigh. "I am not bothered at all. I wish you nothing but good things. You know that."

He wasn't quite sure what the proper response might be to this, so he held silent, merely lifting his brows in question.

"I've made a muddle of this, haven't I?" Violet said with a frown. "All I am trying to say is that you have never had to expend much of an effort to achieve your goals. Whether that is a result of your abilities or your goals, I am not certain."

He did not speak. His eyes found a particularly intricate spot in the patterned fabric covering the walls, and he was riveted, unable to focus on anything else as his mind churned.

And yearned.

And then, before he even realized what he was thinking, he asked, "What has this to do with my brothers?"

She blinked uncomprehendingly, and then finally murmured, "Oh, you mean about your feeling the need to prove yourself?"

He nodded.

She pursed her lips. Thought. And then said, "I'm not sure."

He opened his mouth. That was not the answer he had been expecting.

"I don't know everything," she said, and he suspected it was the first time that particular collection of words had ever crossed her lips.

"I suppose," she said, slowly and thoughtfully, "that you . . . Well, it's an odd combination, I should think. Or perhaps not so odd, when one has so many older brothers and sisters."

Gregory waited as she collected her thoughts. The room was quiet, the air utterly still, and yet it felt as if something were bearing down on him, pressing at him from all sides.

He did not know what she was going to say, but somehow . . .

He knew . . .

It mattered.

Maybe more than anything else he'd ever heard.

"You don't wish to ask for help," his mother said, "because it is so important to you that your brothers see you as a man grown. And yet at the same time . . . Well, life has come easily to you, and so I think sometimes you don't try."

His lips parted.

"It is not that you refuse to try," she hastened to add. "Just that most of the time you don't have to. And when something is going to require too much effort . . . If it is something you cannot manage yourself, you decide that it is not worth the bother."

Gregory found his eyes pulling back toward that spot on the wall, the one where the vine twisted so curiously. "I know what it means to work for something," he said in a quiet voice. He turned to her then, looking her full in the face. "To want it desperately and to know that it might not be yours."

"Do you? I'm glad." She reached for her tea, then apparently changed her mind and looked up. "Did you get it?"

"No."

Her eyes turned a little bit sad. "I'm sorry."

"I'm not," he said stiffly. "Not any longer."

"Oh. Well." She shifted in her seat. "Then I am not sorry. I imagine you are a better man for it now."

Gregory's initial impulse leaned toward offense, but to his great surprise, he found himself saying, "I believe you are correct."

To his even greater surprise, he meant it.

His mother smiled wisely. "I am so glad you are able to see it in that light. Most men cannot." She glanced up at the clock and let out a chirp of surprise. "Oh dear, the time. I promised Portia Featherington that I would call upon her this afternoon."

Gregory stood as his mother rose to her feet.

"Do not worry about Lady Lucinda," she said, hurrying to the door. "I shall take care of everything. And please, finish your tea. I do worry about you, living all by yourself with no woman to care for you. Another year of this, and you will waste away to skin and bones."

He walked her to the door. "As nudges toward matrimony go, that was particularly unsubtle."

"Was it?" She gave him an arch look. "How nice for me that I no longer even try for subtlety. I have found that most men do not notice anything that is not clearly spelled out, anyway."

"Even your sons."

"*Especially* my sons."

He smiled wryly. "I asked for that, didn't I?"

"You practically wrote me an invitation."

He tried to accompany her to the main hall, but she shooed him away. "No, no, that's not necessary. Go and finish your tea. I asked the kitchen to bring up sandwiches when you were announced. They should arrive at any moment and will surely go to waste if you don't eat them."

Gregory's stomach grumbled at that exact moment, so he bowed and said, "You are a superb mother, did you know that?"

"Because I feed you?"

"Well, yes, but perhaps for a few other things as well."

She stood on her toes and kissed him on the cheek. "You are no longer my darling boy, are you?"

Gregory smiled. It had been her endearment for him for as long as he remembered. "I am for as long as you wish it, Mother. As long as you wish it."

Sixteen

In which Our Hero falls in love. Again.

When it came to social machinations, Violet Bridgerton was every bit as accomplished as she claimed, and indeed, when Gregory arrived at Hastings House the following evening, his sister Daphne, the current Duchess of Hastings, informed him that Lady Lucinda Abernathy would indeed be attending the ball.

He found himself rather unaccountably pleased at the outcome. Lucy had looked so disappointed when she'd told him that she would not be able to go, and really, shouldn't the girl enjoy one last night of revelry before she married Haselby?

Haselby.

Gregory still couldn't quite believe it. How could he have not known that she was marrying Haselby? There was nothing he could do to stop it, and really, it wasn't his place, but dear God, it was *Haselby.*

Shouldn't Lucy be told?

Haselby was a perfectly amiable fellow, and, Gregory had to allow, in possession of a more than acceptable wit. He wouldn't beat her, and he wouldn't be unkind, but he didn't . . . he couldn't . . .

He would not be a husband to her.

Just the thought of it left him grim. Lucy wasn't going to have a regular marriage, because Haselby didn't *like* women. Not the way a man was meant to.

Haselby would be kind to her, and he'd probably provide her with an exceedingly generous allowance, which was more than many women had in their marriages, regardless of their husbands' proclivities.

But it did not seem fair that, of all people, Lucy was destined for such a life. She deserved so much more. A house full of children. And dogs. Perhaps a cat or two. She seemed the sort who'd want a menagerie.

And flowers. In Lucy's home there would be flowers everywhere, he was certain of it. Pink peonies, yellow roses, and that stalky blue thing she liked so well.

Delphinium. That was it.

He paused. Remembered. Delphinium.

Lucy might claim that her brother was the horticulturalist of the family, but Gregory could not imagine her living in a home without color.

There would be laughter and noise and splendid disarray—despite her attempts to keep every corner of her life neat and tidy. He could see her easily in his mind's eye, fussing and organizing, trying to keep everyone on a proper schedule.

It almost made him laugh aloud, just to think of it. It wouldn't matter if there was a fleet of servants dusting and straightening and shining and sweeping. With children nothing was ever quite where one put it.

Lucy was a manager. It was what made her happy, and she ought to have a household to manage.

Children. Lots of them.

Maybe eight.

He glanced around the ballroom, which was slowly beginning to fill. He didn't see Lucy, and it wasn't so crowded yet that he might miss her. He did, however, see his mother.

She was heading his way.

"Gregory," she said, reaching out to him with both hands when she reached him, "you look especially handsome this evening."

He took her hands and raised them to his lips. "Said with all the honesty and impartiality of a mother," he murmured.

"Nonsense," she said with a smile. "It is a fact that all of my children are exceedingly intelligent and good-looking. If it were merely my opinion, don't you think someone would have corrected me by now?"

"As if any would dare."

"Well, yes, I suppose," she replied, maintaining an impressively impassive face. "But I shall be stubborn and insist that the point is moot."

"As you wish, Mother," he said with perfect solemnity. "As you wish."

"Has Lady Lucinda arrived?"

Gregory shook his head. "Not yet."

"Isn't it odd that I haven't met her," she mused. "One would think, if she has been in town a fortnight already . . . Ah well, it matters not. I am certain I will find her delightful if you made such an effort to secure her attendance this evening."

Gregory gave her a look. He knew this tone. It was a perfect blend of nonchalance and utter precision, usually utilized whilst digging for information. His mother was a master at it.

And sure enough, she was discreetly patting her hair and not quite looking at him as she said, "You said you were introduced while you were visiting Anthony, did you not?"

He saw no reason to pretend he did not know what she was about.

"She is engaged to be married, Mother," he said with great emphasis. And then for good measure he added, "In one week."

"Yes, yes, I know. To Lord Davenport's son. It is a long-standing match, I understand."

Gregory nodded. He couldn't imagine that his mother knew the truth about Haselby. It was not a well-known fact. There were whispers, of course. There were always whispers. But none would dare repeat them in the presence of ladies.

"I received an invitation to the wedding," Violet said.

"Did you?"

"It's to be a very large affair, I understand."

Gregory clenched his teeth a bit. "She is to be a countess."

"Yes, I suppose. It's not the sort of thing one can do up small."

"No."

Violet sighed. "I adore weddings."

"Do you?"

"Yes." She sighed again, with even more drama, not that Gregory would have imagined it possible. "It is all so romantic," she added. "The bride, the groom . . ."

"Both are considered standard in the ceremony, I understand."

His mother shot him a peevish look. "How could I have raised a son who is so unromantic?"

Gregory decided there could not possibly be an answer to that.

"Fie on you, then," Violet said, "I plan to attend. I almost never refuse an invitation to a wedding."

And then came *the voice*. "Who is getting married?"

Gregory turned. It was his younger sister, Hyacinth. Dressed in blue and poking her nose into everyone else's business as usual.

"Lord Haselby and Lady Lucinda Abernathy," Violet answered.

"Oh yes." Hyacinth frowned. "I received an invitation. At St. George's, is it not?"

Violet nodded. "Followed by a reception at Fennsworth House."

Hyacinth glanced around the room. She did that quite frequently, even when she was not searching for anyone in particular. "Isn't it odd that I haven't met her? She is sister to the Earl of Fennsworth, is she not?" She shrugged. "Odd that I have not met him, either."

"I don't believe Lady Lucinda is 'out,' " Gregory said. "Not formally, at least."

"Then tonight will be her debut," his mother said. "How exciting for us all."

Hyacinth turned to her brother with razor-sharp eyes. "And how is it that you are acquainted with Lady Lucinda, Gregory?"

He opened his mouth, but she was already saying, "And do not say that you are not, because Daphne has already told me everything."

"Then why are you asking?"

Hyacinth scowled. "She did not tell me how you *met*."

"You might wish to revisit your understanding of the word *everything*." Gregory turned to his mother. "Vocabulary and comprehension were never her strong suits."

Violet rolled her eyes. "Every day I marvel that the two of you managed to reach adulthood."

"Afraid we'd kill each other?" Gregory quipped.

"No, that I'd do the job myself."

"Well," Hyacinth stated, as if the previous minute of conversation had never taken place, "Daphne said that you were most anxious that Lady Lucinda receive an invitation, and Mother, I understand, even penned a note saying how much she enjoys her company, which as we all know is a baldfaced lie, as none of us has ever met the—"

"Do you ever cease talking?" Gregory interrupted.

"Not for you," Hyacinth replied. "How *do* you know her? And more to the point, how well? *And* why are you so eager to extend an invitation to a woman who will be married in a week?"

And then, amazingly, Hyacinth *did* stop talking.

"I was wondering that myself," Violet murmured.

Gregory looked from his sister to his mother and decided he hadn't meant any of that rot he'd said to Lucy about large families being a comfort. They were a nuisance and an intrusion and a whole host of other things, the words for which he could not quite retrieve at that moment.

Which may have been for the best, as none of them were likely to have been polite.

Nonetheless, he turned to the two women with extreme patience and said, "I was introduced to Lady Lucinda in Kent. At Kate and Anthony's house party last month. And I asked Daphne to invite her this evening because she is an amiable young lady, and I happened upon her yesterday in the park. Her uncle has denied her a season, and I thought it would be a kind deed to provide her with an opportunity to escape for one evening."

He lifted his brows, silently daring them to respond.

They did, of course. Not with words—words would never have been as effective as the dubious stares they were hurling in his direction.

"Oh, for heaven's sake," he nearly burst out. "She is *engaged.* To be married."

This had little visible effect.

Gregory scowled. "Do I appear to be attempting to put a halt to the nuptials?"

Hyacinth blinked. Several times, the way she always did when she was thinking far too hard about something not her affair. But to his great surprise, she let out a little *hmm* of acquiescence and said, "I suppose not." She glanced about the room. "I should like to meet her, though."

"I'm sure you will," Gregory replied, and he congratulated himself, as he did at least once a month, on not strangling his sister.

"Kate wrote that she is lovely," Violet said.

Gregory turned to her with a sinking feeling. "*Kate* wrote to you?" Good God, what had she revealed? It was bad enough that Anthony knew about the fiasco with Miss Watson—he had figured it out, of course—but if his mother found out, his life would be utter hell.

She would kill him with kindness. He was sure of it.

"Kate writes twice a month," Violet replied with a delicate, one-shouldered shrug. "She tells me everything."

"Is Anthony aware?" Gregory muttered.

"I have no idea," Violet said, giving him a superior look. "It's really none of his business."

Good God.

Gregory just managed to not say it aloud.

"I gather," his mother continued, "that her brother was caught in a compromising position with Lord Watson's daughter."

"Really?" Hyacinth had been perusing the crowd, but she swung back for that.

Violet nodded thoughtfully. "I had wondered why that wedding was so rushed."

"Well, that's why," Gregory said, a little bit like a grunt.

"Hmmmm." This, from Hyacinth.

It was the sort of sound one never wished to hear from Hyacinth.

Violet turned to her daughter and said, "It was quite the to-do."

"Actually," Gregory said, growing more irritated by the second, "it was all handled discreetly."

"There are always whispers," Hyacinth said.

"Don't you add to them," Violet warned her.

"I won't say a word," Hyacinth promised, waving her hand as if she had never spoken out of turn in her life.

Gregory let out a snort. "Oh, *please*."

"I won't," she protested. "I am superb with a secret as long as I *know* it is a secret."

"Ah, so what you mean, then, is that you possess no sense of discretion?"

Hyacinth narrowed her eyes.

Gregory lifted his brows.

"How *old* are you?" Violet interjected. "Goodness, the two of you haven't changed a bit since you were in leading strings. I half expect you to start pulling each other's hair right on the spot."

Gregory clamped his jaw into a line and stared resolutely ahead. There was nothing quite like a rebuke from one's mother to make one feel three feet tall.

"Oh, don't be a stuff, Mother," Hyacinth said, taking the scolding with a smile. "He knows I only tease him so because I love him best." She smiled up at him, sunny and warm.

Gregory sighed, because it was true, and because he felt the same way, and because it was, nonetheless, exhausting to be her brother. But the two of them were quite a bit younger than the rest of their siblings, and as a result, had always been a bit of a pair.

"He returns the sentiment, by the way," Hyacinth said to Violet, "but as a man, he would never say as much."

Violet nodded. "It's true."

Hyacinth turned to Gregory. "And just to be perfectly clear, I never pulled your hair."

Surely his signal to leave. Or lose his sanity. Really, it was up to him.

"Hyacinth," Gregory said, "I adore you. You know it. Mother, I adore you as well. And now I am leaving."

"Wait!" Violet called out.

He turned around. He should have known it wouldn't be that easy.

"Would you be my escort?"

"To what?"

"Why, to the wedding, of course."

Gad, *what* was that awful taste in his mouth? "Whose wedding? Lady Lucinda's?"

His mother gazed at him with the most innocent blue eyes. "I shouldn't like to go alone."

He jerked his head in his sister's direction. "Take Hyacinth."

"She'll wish to go with Gareth," Violet replied.

Gareth St. Clair was Hyacinth's husband of nearly four years. Gregory liked him immensely, and the two had developed a rather fine friendship, which was how he knew that Gareth would rather peel his eyelids back (and leave them that way for an indefinite amount of time) than sit through a long, drawn-out, all-day society affair.

Whereas Hyacinth was, as she did not mind putting it, *always* interested in gossip, which meant that she surely would not wish to miss such an important wedding. Someone would drink too much, and someone else would dance too close, and Hyacinth would *hate* to be the last to hear of it.

"Gregory?" his mother prompted.

"I'm not going."

"But—"

"I wasn't invited."

"Surely an oversight. One that will be corrected, I am certain, after your efforts this evening."

"Mother, as much as I would like to wish Lady Lucinda well, I have no desire to attend her or anyone's wedding. They are such sentimental affairs."

Silence.

Never a good sign.

He looked at Hyacinth. She was regarding him with large owlish eyes. "You like weddings," she said.

He grunted. It seemed the best response.

"You do," she said. "At my wedding, you—"

"Hyacinth, you are my sister. It is different."

"Yes, but you also attended Felicity Albansdale's wedding, and I distinctly recall—"

Gregory turned his back on her before she could recount his merriness. "Mother," he said, "thank you for the invitation, but I do not wish to attend Lady Lucinda's wedding."

Violet opened her mouth as if to ask a question, but then she closed it. "Very well," she said.

Gregory was instantly suspicious. It was not like his mother to capitulate so quickly. Further prying into her motives, however, would eliminate any chance of a quick escape.

It was an easy decision.

"I bid you both *adieu*," he said.

"Where you going?" Hyacinth demanded. "And why are you speaking French?"

He turned to his mother. "She is all yours."

"Yes," Violet sighed. "I know."

Hyacinth immediately turned on her. "What does *that* mean?"

"Oh, for heaven's sake, Hyacinth, you—"

Gregory took advantage of the moment and slipped away while their attention was fixed on each other.

The party was growing more crowded, and it occurred to him that Lucy might very well have arrived while he was speaking with his mother and sister. If so, she wouldn't have made it very far into the ballroom, however, and so he began to make his way toward the receiving line. It was a slow process; he had been out of town for over a month, and everyone seemed to have something to say to him, none of it remotely of interest.

"Best of luck with it," he murmured to Lord Trevelstam, who was trying to interest him in a horse he could not afford. "I am sure you will have no difficulty—"

His voice left him.

He could not speak.

He could not *think*.

Good God, not again.

"Bridgerton?"

Across the room, just by the door. Three gentlemen, an elderly lady, two matrons, and—

Her.

It was her. And he was being pulled, as sure as if there were a rope between them. He needed to reach her side.

"Bridgerton, is something—"

"I beg your pardon," Gregory managed to say, brushing past Trevelstam.

It was her. Except . . .

It was a different her. It wasn't Hermione Watson. It was— He wasn't sure who she was; he could see her only from the back. But there it was—that same splendid and terrible feeling. It made him dizzy. It made him ecstatic. His lungs were hollow. *He* was hollow.

And he wanted her.

It was just as he'd always imagined it—that magical, almost incandescent sense of knowing that his life was complete, that *she* was the one.

Except that he'd done this before. And Hermione Watson *hadn't* been the one.

Dear God, could a man fall insanely, stupidly in love twice?

Hadn't he just told Lucy to be wary and scared, that if she was ever overcome with such a feeling, she should not trust it?

And yet . . .

And yet there she was.

And there *he* was.

And it was happening all over again.

It was just as it had been with Hermione. No, it was worse. His body tingled; he couldn't keep his toes still in his boots. He wanted to jump out of his skin, rush across the room and . . . just . . . just . . .

Just *see* her.

He wanted her to turn. He wanted to see her face. He wanted to know who she was.

He wanted to know *her.*

No.

No, he told himself, trying to force his feet in the other direction. This was madness. He should leave. He should leave right now.

But he couldn't. Even with every rational corner of his soul screaming at him to turn around and walk away, he was rooted to the spot, waiting for her to turn.

Praying for her to turn.

And then she did.

And she was—

Lucy.

He stumbled as if struck.

Lucy?

No. It couldn't be possible. He knew Lucy.

She did not do this to him.

He had seen her dozens of times, kissed her even, and never once felt like this, as if the world might swallow him whole if he did not reach her side and take her hand in his.

There had to be an explanation. He had felt this way before. With Hermione.

But this time—it wasn't quite the same. With Hermione it had been dizzying, new. There had been the thrill of discovery, of conquest. But this was Lucy.

It was Lucy, and—

It all came flooding back. The tilt of her head as she explained why sandwiches ought to be properly sorted. The delightfully peeved look on her face when she had tried to explain to him why he was doing everything wrong in his courtship of Miss Watson.

The way it had felt so right simply to sit on a bench with her in Hyde Park and throw bread at the pigeons.

And the kiss. Dear God, *the kiss.*

He still dreamed about that kiss.

And he wanted her to dream about it, too.

He took a step. Just one—slightly forward and to the side so that he could better see her profile. It was all so familiar now—the tilt of her head, the way her lips moved when she spoke. How could he not have recognized her instantly, even from the back? The memories had been there, tucked away in the recesses of his mind, but he hadn't wanted—no he hadn't allowed himself—to acknowledge his presence.

And then she saw him. Lucy saw him. He saw it first in her eyes, which widened and sparkled, and then in the curve of her lips.

She smiled. For him.

It filled him. To near bursting, it filled him. It was just one smile, but it was all he needed.

He began to walk. He could barely feel his feet, had almost no conscious control over his body. He simply moved, knowing from deep within that he had to reach her.

"Lucy," he said, once he was next to her, forgetting that they were surrounded by strangers, and worse, friends, and he should not presume to use her given name.

But nothing else felt right on his lips.

"Mr. Bridgerton," she said, but her eyes said, *Gregory.*

And he knew.

He loved her.

It was the strangest, most wonderful sensation. It was exhilarating. It was as if the world had suddenly become open to him. Clear. He understood. He understood everything he needed to know, and it was all right there in her eyes.

"Lady Lucinda," he said, bowing deeply over her hand. "May I have this dance?"

Seventeen

In which Our Hero's sister moves things along.

It was heaven.

Forget angels, forget St. Peter and glittering harpsichords. Heaven was a dance in the arms of one's true love. And when the one in question had a mere week before marrying someone else entirely, aforementioned one had to grab heaven tightly, with both hands.

Metaphorically speaking.

Lucy grinned as she bobbed and twirled. Now there was an image. What would people say if she charged forward and grabbed him with both hands?

And never let go.

Most would say she was mad. A few that she was in love. The shrewd would say both.

"What are you thinking about?" Gregory asked. He was looking at her . . . differently.

She turned away, turned back. She felt daring, almost magical. "Wouldn't you care to know?"

He stepped around the lady to his left and returned to his place. "I would," he answered, smiling wolfishly at her.

But she just smiled and shook her head. Right now she wanted to pretend she was someone else. Someone a little less conventional. Someone a great deal more impulsive.

She did not want to be the same old Lucy. Not tonight. She was sick of planning, sick of placating, sick of never doing anything without first thinking through every possibility and consequence.

If I do this, then that will happen, but if I do that, then this, this, and the other thing will happen, which will yield an entirely different result, which could mean that—

It was enough to make a girl dizzy. It was enough to make her feel paralyzed, unable to take the reins of her own life.

But not tonight. Tonight, somehow, through some amazing miracle named the Duchess of Hastings—or perhaps the dowager Lady Bridgerton, Lucy was not quite certain—she was wearing a gown of the most exquisite green silk, attending the most glittering ball she could ever have imagined.

And she was dancing with the man she was quite certain she would love until the end of time.

"You look different," he said.

"I feel different." She touched his hand as they stepped past each other. His fingers gripped hers when they should have just brushed by. She looked up and saw that he was gazing at her. His eyes were warm and intense and he was watching her the same way—

Dear God, he was watching her the way he'd watched Hermione.

Her body began to tingle. She felt it in the tips of her toes, in places she did not dare to contemplate.

They stepped past each other again, but this time he leaned in, perhaps a bit more than he ought, and said, "I feel different as well."

Her head snapped around, but he had already turned so that his back was to her. How was he different? Why? What did he *mean*?

She circled around the gentleman to her left, then moved past Gregory.

"Are you glad you attended this evening?" he murmured.

She nodded, since she had moved too far away to answer without speaking too loudly.

But then they were together again, and he whispered, "So am I."

They moved back to their original places and held still as a different couple began to process. Lucy looked up. At him. At his eyes.

They never moved from her face.

And even in the flickering light of the night—the hundreds of candles and torches that lit the glittering ballroom—she could see the gleam there. The way he was looking at her—it was hot and possessive and proud.

It made her shiver.

It made her doubt her ability to stand.

And then the music was done, and Lucy realized that some things must truly be ingrained because she was curtsying and smiling and nodding at the woman next to her as if her entire life had not been altered in the course of the previous dance.

Gregory took her hand and led her to the side of the ballroom, back to where the chaperones milled about, watching their charges over the rims of their glasses of lemonade. But before they reached their destination, he leaned down and whispered in her ear.

"I need to speak with you."

Her eyes flew to his.

"Privately," he added.

She felt him slow their pace, presumably to allow them more time to speak before she was returned to Aunt Harriet. "What is it?" she asked. "Is something amiss?"

He shook his head. "Not any longer."

And she let herself hope. Just a little, because she could not bear to ponder the heartbreak if she was wrong, but maybe . . . Maybe he loved her. Maybe he wished to marry her. Her wedding was less than a week away, but she had not said her vows.

Maybe there was a chance. Maybe there was a way.

She searched Gregory's face for clues, for answers. But when she pressed him for more information, he just shook his head and whispered, "The library. It is two doors down from the ladies' retiring room. Meet me there in thirty minutes."

"Are you mad?"

He smiled. "Just a little."

"Gregory, I—"

He gazed into her eyes, and it silenced her. The way he was looking at her—

It took her breath away.

"I cannot," she whispered, because no matter what they might feel for each other, she was still engaged to another man. And even if she were not, such behavior could only lead to scandal. "I can't be alone with you. You know that."

"You must."

She tried to shake her head, but she could not make herself move.

"Lucy," he said, "you must."

She nodded. It was probably the biggest mistake she would ever make, but she could not say no.

"Mrs. Abernathy," Gregory said, his voice sounding overly loud as he greeted her aunt Harriet. "I return Lady Lucinda to your care."

Aunt Harriet nodded, even though Lucy suspected she had no idea what Gregory had said to her, and then she turned to Lucy and yelled, "I'm sitting down!"

Gregory chuckled, then said, "I must dance with others."

"Of course," Lucy replied, even though she rather suspected she was not wholly cognizant of the various intricacies involved in scheduling an illicit meeting. "I see someone I know," she lied, and then, to her great relief, she actually did see someone she knew—an acquaintance from school. Not a good friend, but still, a familiar enough face to offer greetings.

But before Lucy could even flex her foot, she heard a female voice call out Gregory's name.

Lucy could not see who it was, but she could see Gregory. He had shut his eyes and looked quite pained.

"Gregory!"

The voice had drawn close, and so Lucy turned to her left to see a young woman who could only be one of Gregory's sisters. The younger one, most probably, else she was remarkably well-preserved.

"This must be Lady Lucinda," the woman said. Her hair, Lucy noted, was the precise shade of Gregory's—a rich, warm chestnut. But her eyes were blue, sharp and acute.

"Lady Lucinda," Gregory said, sounding a bit like a man with a chore, "may I present my sister, Lady St. Clair."

"Hyacinth," she said firmly. "We must dispense with the formalities. I am certain we shall be great friends. Now then, you must tell me all about yourself. And then I wish to hear about Anthony and Kate's party last month. I had wished to go, but we had a previous engagement. I heard it was vastly entertaining."

Startled by the human whirlwind in front of her, Lucy looked to Gregory for advice, but he just shrugged and said, "This would be the one I am fond of torturing."

Hyacinth turned to him. "I beg your pardon."

Gregory bowed. "I must go."

And then Hyacinth Bridgerton St. Clair did the oddest thing. Her eyes narrowed, and she looked from her brother to Lucy and back again. And then again. And then one more time. And then she said, "You'll need my help."

"Hy—" Gregory began.

"You will," she cut in. "You have plans. Do not try to deny it."

Lucy could not believe that Hyacinth had deduced all that from one bow and an *I must go.* She opened her mouth to ask a question, but all she got out was, "How—" before Gregory cut her off with a warning look.

"I know that you have something up your sleeve," Hyacinth said to Gregory. "Else you would not have gone to such lengths to secure her attendance this evening."

"He was just being kind," Lucy tried to say.

"Don't be silly," Hyacinth said, giving her a reassuring pat on the arm. "He would never do that."

"That's not true," Lucy protested. Gregory might be a bit of a devil, but his heart was good and true, and she would not countenance anyone—even his sister—saying otherwise.

Hyacinth regarded her with a delighted smile. "I like you," she said slowly, as if she were deciding upon it right then and there. "You are wrong, of course, but I like you, anyway." She turned to her brother. "I like her."

"Yes, you've said as much."

"And you need my help."

Lucy watched as brother and sister exchanged a glance that she couldn't begin to understand.

"You will need my help," Hyacinth said softly. "Tonight, and l ater, too."

Gregory stared at his sister intently, and then he said, in a voice so quiet that Lucy had to lean forward to hear it, "I need to speak with Lady Lucinda. Alone."

Hyacinth smiled. Just a touch. "I can arrange that."

Lucy had a feeling she could do anything.

"When?" Hyacinth asked.

"Whenever is easiest," Gregory replied.

Hyacinth glanced around the room, although for the life of her, Lucy could not imagine what sort of information she was gleaning that could possibly be pertinent to the decision at hand.

"One hour," she announced, with all the precision of a military general. "Gregory, you go off and do whatever it is you do at these affairs. Dance. Fetch lemonade. Be seen with that Whitford girl whose parents have been dangling after you for months.

"You," Hyacinth continued, turning to Lucy with an authoritarian gleam in her eye, "shall remain with me. I shall introduce you to everyone you need to know."

"Who do I need to know?" Lucy asked.

"I'm not sure yet. It really doesn't matter."

Lucy could only stare at her in awe.

"In precisely fifty-five minutes," Hyacinth said, "Lady Lucinda will tear her dress."

"I will?"

"*I* will," Hyacinth replied. "I'm good at that sort of thing."

"You're going to tear her dress?" Gregory asked doubtfully. "Right here in the ballroom?"

"Don't worry over the details," Hyacinth said, waving him off dismissively. "Just go and do your part, and meet her in Daphne's dressing room in one hour."

"In the duchess's bedchamber?" Lucy croaked. She couldn't possibly.

"She's Daphne to us," Hyacinth said. "Now then, everyone, off with you."

Lucy just stared at her and blinked. Wasn't she meant to stay at Hyacinth's side?

"That means him," Hyacinth said.

And then Gregory did the most startling thing. He took Lucy's hand. Right there, in the middle of the ballroom where anyone might see, he took her hand and kissed it. "I leave you in good hands," he told her, stepping back with a polite nod. He gave his sister a look of warning before adding, "As difficult as that might be to believe."

Then he went off, presumably to dote on some poor unsuspecting female who had no idea she was nothing but an innocent pawn in his sister's master plan.

Lucy looked back at Hyacinth, somewhat exhausted by the entire encounter. Hyacinth was beaming at her.

"Well done," she said, although to Lucy it sounded more like she was congratulating herself. "Now then," she continued, "why does my brother need to speak with you? And don't say that you have no idea, because I will not believe you."

Lucy pondered the wisdom of various replies and finally decided upon "I have no idea." It wasn't precisely the truth, but she wasn't about to divulge her most secret hopes and dreams to a woman she'd met only minutes earlier, no matter whose sister she might be.

And it made her feel as if she might have won the point.

"Really?" Hyacinth looked suspicious.

"Really."

Hyacinth was clearly unconvinced. "Well, you're clever, at least. I shall grant you that."

Lucy decided she would not be cowed. "Do you know," she said,

"I thought I was the most organized and managing person I knew, but I think you're worse."

Hyacinth laughed. "Oh, I am not at all organized. But I *am* managing. And we shall get on famously." She looped her arm through Lucy's. "Like sisters."

One hour later, Lucy had realized three things about Hyacinth, Lady St. Clair.

First, she knew everyone. And everything about everyone.

Second, she was a wealth of information about her brother. Lucy had not needed to ask a single question, but by the time they left the ballroom, she knew Gregory's favorite color (blue) and food (cheese, any sort), and that as a child he had spoken with a lisp.

Lucy had also learned that one should never make the mistake of underestimating Gregory's younger sister. Not only had Hyacinth torn Lucy's dress, she had carried it out with enough flair and cunning so that four people were aware of the mishap (and the need for repair). And she had done all her damage to the hem, so as to conveniently preserve Lucy's modesty.

It was really quite impressive.

"I've done this before," Hyacinth confided as she guided her out of the ballroom.

Lucy was unsurprised.

"It's a useful talent," Hyacinth added, sounding utterly serious. "Here, this way."

Lucy followed her up a back staircase.

"There are very few excuses available to women who wish to leave a social function," Hyacinth continued, displaying a remarkable talent for sticking to her chosen topic like glue. "It behooves us to master every weapon in our arsenal."

Lucy was beginning to believe that she'd led a very sheltered life.

"Ah, here we are." Hyacinth pushed open a door. She peered in. "He's not here yet. Good. That gives me time."

"For what?"

"To mend your dress. I confess I forgot that detail when I formulated my plan. But I know where Daphne keeps needles."

Lucy watched as Hyacinth strode to a dressing table and opened a drawer.

"Right where I thought they were," Hyacinth said with a triumphant smile. "I do love it when I am right. It makes life so much more convenient, wouldn't you agree?"

Lucy nodded, but her mind was on her own question. And then she asked it—"Why are you helping me?"

Hyacinth looked at her as if she were daft. "You can't go back in with a torn dress. Not after we told everyone we'd gone off to mend it."

"No, not that."

"Oh." Hyacinth held up a needle and regarded it thoughtfully. "This will do. What color thread, do you think?"

"White, and you did not answer my question."

Hyacinth ripped a piece of thread off a spool and slid it through the eye of the needle. "I like you," she said. "And I love my brother."

"You know that I am engaged to be married," Lucy said quietly.

"I know." Hyacinth knelt at Lucy's feet, and with quick, sloppy stitches began to sew.

"In a *week.* Less than a week."

"I know. I was invited."

"Oh." Lucy supposed she ought to have known that. "Erm, do you plan to attend?"

Hyacinth looked up. "Do you?"

Lucy's lips parted. Until that moment, the idea of not marrying Haselby was a wispy, far-fetched thing, more of a *oh-how-I-wish-I-did-not-have-to-marry-him* sort of feeling. But now, with Hyacinth watching her so carefully, it began to feel a bit more firm. Still impossible, of course, or at least . . .

Well, maybe . . .

Maybe not quite impossible. Maybe only mostly impossible.

"The papers are signed," Lucy said.

Hyacinth turned back to her sewing. "Are they?"

"My uncle *chose* him," Lucy said, wondering just who she was trying to convince. "It has been arranged for ages."

"Mmmm."

Mmmm? What the devil did *that* mean?

"And he hasn't . . . Your brother hasn't . . ." Lucy fought for words, mortified that she was unburdening herself to a near stranger, to Gregory's own sister, for heaven's sake. But Hyacinth wasn't *saying* anything; she was just sitting there with her eyes focused on the needle looping in and out of Lucy's hem. And if Hyacinth didn't say anything, then Lucy had to. Because— Because—

Well, because she did.

"He has made me no promises," Lucy said, her voice nearly shaking with it. "He stated no intentions."

At that, Hyacinth did look up. She glanced around the room, as if to say, *Look at us, mending your gown in the bedchamber of the Duchess of Hastings.* And she murmured, "Hasn't he?"

Lucy closed her eyes in agony. She was not like Hyacinth St. Clair. One needed only a quarter of an hour in her company to know that she would dare anything, take any chance to secure her own happiness. She would defy convention, stand up to the harshest of critics, and emerge entirely intact, in body and spirit.

Lucy was not so hardy. She wasn't ruled by passions. Her muse had always been good sense. Pragmatism.

Hadn't she been the one to tell Hermione that she needed to marry a man of whom her parents would approve?

Hadn't she told Gregory that she didn't want a violent, overwhelming love? That she just wasn't the sort?

She wasn't that kind of person. She wasn't. When her governess had made line drawings for her to fill, she had always colored between the lines.

"I don't think I can do it," Lucy whispered.

Hyacinth held her gaze for an agonizingly long moment before turning back to her sewing. "I misjudged you," she said softly.

It hit Lucy like a slap in the face.

"Wh . . . wh . . ."

What did you say?

But Lucy's lips would not form the words. She did not wish to hear the answer. And Hyacinth was back to her brisk self, looking up with an irritated expression as she said, "Don't fidget so much."

"Sorry," Lucy mumbled. And she thought—*I've said it again. I am so predictable, so utterly conventional and unimaginative.*

"You're still moving."

"Oh." Good God, could she do nothing right this evening? "Sorry."

Hyacinth jabbed her with the needle. "You're *still* moving."

"I am not!" Lucy almost yelled.

Hyacinth smiled to herself. "That's better."

Lucy looked down and scowled. "Am I bleeding?"

"If you are," Hyacinth said, rising to her feet, "it's nobody's fault but your own."

"I beg your pardon."

But Hyacinth was already standing, a satisfied smile on her face. "There," she announced, motioning to her handiwork. "Certainly not as good as new, but it will pass any inspection this evening."

Lucy knelt to inspect her hem. Hyacinth had been generous in her self-praise. The stitching was a mess.

"I've never been gifted with a needle," Hyacinth said with an unconcerned shrug.

Lucy stood, fighting the impulse to rip the stitches out and fix them herself. "You might have told me," she muttered.

Hyacinth's lips curved into a slow, sly smile. "My, my," she said, "you've turned prickly all of a sudden."

And then Lucy shocked herself by saying, "*You've* been hurtful."

"Possibly," Hyacinth replied, sounding as if she didn't much care one way or the other. She glanced toward the door with a quizzical expression. "He ought to have been here by now."

Lucy's heart thumped strangely in her chest. "You still plan to help me?" she whispered.

Hyacinth turned back. "I am hoping," she replied, her eyes meeting Lucy's with cool assessment, "that you have misjudged yourself."

Gregory was ten minutes late to the assignation. It couldn't be helped; once he had danced with one young lady, it had become apparent that he was required to repeat the favor for a half-dozen others. And although it was difficult to keep his attention on the conversations he was meant to be conducting, he did not mind the delay. It meant that Lucy and Hyacinth were well gone before he slipped out the door. He intended to find some way to make Lucy his wife, but there was no need to go looking for scandal.

He made his way to his sister's bedchamber; he had spent countless hours at Hastings House and knew his way around. When he reached his destination, he entered without knocking, the well-oiled hinges of the door giving way without a sound.

"Gregory."

Hyacinth's voice came first. She was standing next to Lucy, who looked . . .

Stricken.

What had Hyacinth done to her?

"Lucy?" he asked, rushing forward. "Is something wrong?"

Lucy shook her head. "It is of no account."

He turned to his sister with accusing eyes.

Hyacinth shrugged. "I will be in the next room."

"Listening at the door?"

"I shall wait at Daphne's escritoire," she said. "It is halfway across the room, and before you make an objection, I cannot go farther.

If someone comes you will need me to rush in to make everything respectable."

Her point was a valid one, loath as Gregory was to admit it, so he gave her a curt nod and watched her leave the room, waiting for the click of the door latch before speaking.

"Did she say something unkind?" he asked Lucy. "She can be disgracefully tactless, but her heart is usually in the right place."

Lucy shook her head. "No," she said softly. "I think she might have said exactly the right thing."

"Lucy?" He stared at her in question.

Her eyes, which had seemed so cloudy, appeared to focus. "What was it you needed to tell me?" she asked.

"Lucy," he said, wondering how best to approach this. He'd been rehearsing speeches in his mind the entire time he'd been dancing downstairs, but now that he was here, he didn't know what to say.

Or rather, he did. But he didn't know the order, and he didn't know the tone. Did he tell her he loved her? Bare his heart to a woman who intended to marry another? Or did he opt for the safer route and explain why she could not marry Haselby?

A month ago, the choice would have been obvious. He was a romantic, fond of grand gestures. He would have declared his love, certain of a happy reception. He would have taken her hand. Dropped to his knees.

He would have kissed her.

But now . . .

He was no longer quite so certain. He trusted Lucy, but he did not trust fate.

"You can't marry Haselby," he said.

Her eyes widened. "What do you mean?"

"You can't marry him," he replied, avoiding the question. "It will be a disaster. It will . . . You must trust me. You must not marry him."

She shook her head. "Why are you telling me this?"

Because I want you for myself.

"Because . . . because . . ." He fought for words. "Because you have become my friend. And I wish for your happiness. He will not be a good husband to you, Lucy."

"Why not?" Her voice was low, hollow, and heartbreakingly unlike her.

"He . . ." Dear God, how did he say it? Would she even understand what he meant?

"He doesn't . . ." He swallowed. There had to be a gentle way to say it. "He doesn't . . . Some people . . ."

He looked at her. Her lower lip was quivering.

"He prefers men," he said, getting the words out as quickly as he was able. "To women. Some men are like that."

And then he waited. For the longest moment she made no reaction, just stood there like a tragic statue. Every now and then she would blink, but beyond that, nothing. And then finally—

"Why?"

Why? He didn't understand. "Why is he—"

"No," she said forcefully. "Why did you tell me? Why would you say it?"

"I told you—"

"No, you didn't do it to be kind. Why did you tell me? Was it just to be cruel? To make me feel the way you feel, because Hermione married my brother and not you?"

"No!" The word burst out of him, and he was holding her, his hands wrapped around her upper arms. "No, Lucy," he said again. "I would never. I want you to be happy. I want . . ."

Her. He wanted her, and he didn't know how to say it. Not then, not when she was looking at him as if he'd broken her heart.

"I could have been happy with him," she whispered.

"No. No, you couldn't. You don't understand, he—"

"Yes, I could," she cried out. "Maybe I wouldn't have loved him, but I could have been happy. It was what I expected. Do you understand, it was what I was prepared for. And you . . . you . . ." She wrenched herself away, turning until he could no longer see her face. "You ruined it."

"How?"

She raised her eyes to his, and the look in them was so stark, so deep, he could not breathe. And she said, "Because you made me want you instead."

His heart slammed in his chest. "Lucy," he said, because he could not say anything else. "Lucy."

"I don't know what to do," she confessed.

"Kiss me." He took her face in his hands. "Just kiss me."

This time, when he kissed her, it was different. She was the same woman in his arms, but *he* was not the same man. His need for her was deeper, more elemental.

He loved her.

He kissed her with everything he had, every breath, every last beat of his heart. His lips found her cheek, her brow, her ears, and all the while, he whispered her name like a prayer—

Lucy Lucy Lucy.

He wanted her. He needed her.

She was like air.

Food.

Water.

His mouth moved to her neck, then down to the lacy edge of her bodice. Her skin burned hot beneath him, and as his fingers slid the gown from one of her shoulders, she gasped—

But she did not stop him.

"Gregory," she whispered, her fingers digging into his hair as his lips moved along her collarbone. "Gregory, oh my G— Gregory."

His hand moved reverently over the curve of her shoulder. Her skin glowed pale and milky smooth in the candlelight, and he was struck by an intense sense of possession. Of pride.

No other man had seen her thus, and he prayed that no other man ever would.

"You can't marry him, Lucy," he whispered urgently, his words hot against her skin.

"Gregory, don't," she moaned.

"You can't." And then, because he knew he could not allow this to go any further, he straightened, pressing one last kiss against her lips before setting her back, forcing her to look him in the eye.

"You cannot marry him," he said again.

"Gregory, what can I—"

He gripped her arms. Hard. And he said it.

"I love you."

Her lips parted. She could not speak.

"I love you," he said again.

Lucy had suspected—she'd hoped—but she hadn't really allowed herself to believe. And so, when she finally found words of her own, they were: "You do?"

He smiled, and then he laughed, and then he rested his forehead on hers. "With all of my heart," he vowed. "I only just realized it. I'm a fool. A blind man. A—"

"No," she cut in, shaking her head. "Do not berate yourself. No one ever notices me straightaway when Hermione is about."

His fingers gripped her all the tighter. "She does not hold a candle to you."

A warm feeling began to spread through her bones. Not desire, not passion, just pure, unadulterated happiness. "You really mean it," she whispered.

"Enough to move heaven and earth to make sure you do not go through with your wedding to Haselby."

She blanched.

"Lucy?"

No. She could do it. She would do it. It was almost funny, really. She had spent three years telling Hermione that she had to be practical, follow the rules. She'd scoffed when Hermione had gone on about love and passion and hearing music. And now . . .

She took a deep, fortifying breath. And now she was going to break her engagement.

That had been arranged for years.

To the son of an earl.

Five days before the wedding.

Dear God, the scandal.

She stepped back, lifting her chin so that she could see Gregory's face. His eyes were watching her with all the love she herself felt.

"I love you," she whispered, because she had not yet said it. "I love you, too."

For once she was going to stop thinking about everyone else. She wasn't going to take what she was given and make the best of it. She was going to reach for her own happiness, make her own destiny.

She was not going to do what was expected.

She was going to do what *she* wanted.

It was time.

She squeezed Gregory's hands. And she smiled. It was no tentative thing, but wide and confident, full of her hopes, full of her dreams—and the knowledge that she would achieve them all.

It would be difficult. It would be frightening.

But it would be worth it.

"I will speak with my uncle," she said, the words firm and sure. "Tomorrow."

Gregory pulled her against him for one last kiss, quick and passionate with promise. "Shall I accompany you?" he asked. "Call upon him so that I might reassure him of my intentions?"

The new Lucy, the daring and bold Lucy, asked, "And what *are* your intentions?"

Gregory's eyes widened with surprise, then approval, and then his hands took hers.

She felt what he was doing before she realized it by sight. His hands seemed to slide along hers as he descended . . .

Until he was on one knee, looking up at her as if there could be no more beautiful woman in all creation.

Her hand flew to her mouth, and she realized she was shaking.

"Lady Lucinda Abernathy," he said, his voice fervent and sure, "will you do me the very great honor of becoming my wife?"

She tried to speak. She tried to nod.

"Marry me, Lucy," he said. "Marry me."

And this time she did. "Yes." And then, "Yes! Oh, yes!"

"I will make you happy," he said, standing to embrace her. "I promise you."

"There is no need to promise." She shook her head, blinking back the tears. "There is no way you could not."

He opened his mouth, presumably to say more, but he was cut off by a knock at the door, soft but quick.

Hyacinth.

"Go," Gregory said. "Let Hyacinth take you back to the ballroom. I will follow later."

Lucy nodded, tugging at her gown until everything was back in its proper place. "My hair," she whispered, her eyes flying to his.

"It's lovely," he assured her. "You look perfect."

She hurried to the door. "Are you certain?"

I love you, he mouthed. And his eyes said the same.

Lucy pulled open the door, and Hyacinth rushed in. "Good heavens, the two of you are slow," she said. "We need to be getting back. Now."

She strode to the door to the corridor, then stopped, looking first at Lucy, then at her brother. Her gaze settled on Lucy, and she lifted one brow in question.

Lucy held herself tall. "You did not misjudge me," she said quietly.

Hyacinth's eyes widened, and then her lips curved. "Good."

And it was, Lucy realized. It was very good, indeed.

Eighteen

In which Our Heroine makes a terrible discovery.

She could do this.

She could.

She needed only to knock.

And yet there she stood, outside her uncle's study door, her fingers curled into a fist, as if *ready* to knock on the door.

But not quite.

How long had she stood like this? Five minutes? Ten? Either way, it was enough to brand her a ridiculous ninny. A coward.

How did this happen? *Why* did it happen? At school she had been known as capable and pragmatic. She was the girl who knew how to get things done. She was not shy. She was not fearful.

But when it came to Uncle Robert . . .

She sighed. She had always been like this with her uncle. He was so stern, so taciturn.

So unlike her own laughing father had been.

She'd felt like a butterfly when she left for school, but whenever she returned, it was as if she had been stuffed right back in her tight little cocoon. She became drab, quiet.

Lonely.

But not this time. She took a breath, squared her shoulders. This time she would say what she needed to say. She would make herself heard.

She lifted her hand. She knocked.

She waited.

"Enter."

"Uncle Robert," she said, letting herself into his study. It felt dark, even with the late afternoon sunlight slanting in through the window.

"Lucinda," he said, glancing briefly up before returning to his papers. "What is it?"

"I need to speak with you."

He made a notation, scowled at his handiwork, then blotted his ink. "Speak."

Lucy cleared her throat. This would be a great deal easier if he would just *look up* at her. She hated speaking to the top of his head, hated it.

"Uncle Robert," she said again.

He grunted a response but kept on writing.

"Uncle Robert."

She saw his movements slow, and then, finally, he looked up. "What is it, Lucinda?" he asked, clearly annoyed.

"We need to have a conversation about Lord Haselby." There. She had said it.

"Is there a problem?" he asked slowly.

"No," she heard herself say, even though that wasn't at all the truth. But it was what she always said if someone asked if there was a problem. It was one of those things that just came out, like *Excuse me,* or *I beg your pardon.*

It was what she'd been trained to say.

Is there a problem?

No, of course not. No, don't mind my wishes. No, please don't worry yourself on my account.

"Lucinda?" Her uncle's voice was sharp, almost jarring.

"No," she said again, louder this time, as if the volume would give her courage. "I mean yes, there is a problem. And I need to speak with you about it."

Her uncle gave her a bored look.

"Uncle Robert," she began, feeling as if she were tiptoeing through a field of hedgehogs, "did you know . . ." She bit her lip, glancing everywhere but at his face. "That is to say, were you aware . . ."

"Out with it," he snapped.

"Lord Haselby," Lucy said quickly, desperate just to get it over with. "He doesn't like women."

For a moment Uncle Robert did nothing but stare. And then he . . .

Laughed.

He *laughed.*

"Uncle Robert?" Lucy's heart began to beat far too quickly. "Did you know this?"

"Of course I knew it," he snapped. "Why do you think his father is so eager to have you? He knows you won't talk."

Why wouldn't she talk?

"You should be thanking me," Uncle Robert said harshly, cutting into her thoughts. "Half the men of the *ton* are brutes. I'm giving you to the only one who won't bother you."

"But—"

"Do you have any idea how many women would love to take your place?"

"That is not the point, Uncle Robert."

His eyes turned to ice. "I beg your pardon."

Lucy stood perfectly still, suddenly realizing that this was it. This was her moment. She had never countermanded him before, and she probably never would again.

She swallowed. And then she said it. "I do not wish to marry Lord Haselby."

Silence. But his eyes . . .

His eyes were thunderous.

Lucy met his stare with cool detachment. She could feel a strange new strength growing inside of her. She would not back down. Not now, not when the rest of her life was at stake.

Her uncle's lips pursed and twisted, even as the rest of his face seemed to be made of stone. Finally, just when Lucy was certain that the silence would break her, he asked, his voice clipped, "May I ask why?"

"I—I want children," Lucy said, latching on to the first excuse she could think of.

"Oh, you'll have them," he said.

He smiled then, and her blood turned to ice.

"Uncle Robert?" she whispered.

"He may not like women, but he will be able to do the job often enough to sire a brat off you. And if he can't . . ." He shrugged.

"What?" Lucy felt panic rising in her chest. "What do you mean?"

"Davenport will take care of it."

"His father?" Lucy gasped.

"Either way, it is a direct male heir, and that is all that is important."

Lucy's hand flew to her mouth. "Oh, I can't. I can't." She thought of Lord Davenport, with his horrible breath and jiggly jowls. And his cruel, cruel eyes. He would not be kind. She didn't know how she knew, but he wouldn't be kind.

Her uncle leaned forward in his seat, his eyes narrowing menacingly. "We all have our positions in life, Lucinda, and yours is to be a nobleman's wife. Your duty is to provide an heir. And you will do it, in whatever fashion Davenport deems necessary."

Lucy swallowed. She had always done as she was told. She had always accepted that the world worked in certain ways. Dreams could be adjusted; the social order could not.

Take what you are given, and make the best of things.

It was what she had always said. It was what she had always done.

But not this time.

She looked up, directly into her uncle's eyes. "I won't do it," she said, and her voice did not waver. "I won't marry him."

"What . . . did . . . you . . . say?" Each word came out like its own little sentence, pointy and cold.

Lucy swallowed. "I said—"

"I know what you said!" he roared, slamming his hands on his desk as he rose to his feet. "How dare you question me? I have raised you, fed you, given you every bloody thing you need. I have looked after and protected this family for ten years, when none of it—*none of it*—will come to me."

"Uncle Robert," she tried to say. But she could barely hear her own voice. Every word he had said was true. He did not own this house. He did not own the Abbey or any of the other Fennsworth holdings. He had nothing other than what Richard might choose to give him once he fully assumed his position as earl.

"I am your guardian," her uncle said, his voice so low it shook. "Do you understand? You will marry Haselby, and we will never speak of this again."

Lucy stared at her uncle in horror. He had been her guardian for ten years, and in all that time, she had never seen him lose his temper. His displeasure was always served cold.

"It's that Bridgerton idiot, isn't it?" he bit off, angrily swiping at some books on his desk. They tumbled to the floor with a loud thud.

Lucy jumped back.

"Tell me!"

She said nothing, watching her uncle warily as he advanced upon her.

"Tell me!" he roared.

"Yes," she said quickly, taking another step back. "How did you— How did you know?"

"Do you think I'm an idiot? His mother and his sister *both* beg the favor of your company on the same day?" He swore under his breath. "They were obviously plotting to steal you away."

"But you let me go to the ball."

"Because his sister is a duchess, you little fool! Even Davenport agreed that you had to attend."

"But—"

"Christ above," Uncle Robert swore, shocking Lucy into silence. "I cannot believe your stupidity. Has he even promised marriage? Are you really prepared to toss over the heir to an earldom for the *possibility* of a viscount's fourth son?"

"Yes," Lucy whispered.

Her uncle must have seen the determination on her face, because he paled. "What have you done?" he demanded. "Have you let him touch you?"

Lucy thought of their kiss, and she blushed.

"You stupid cow," he hissed. "Well, lucky for you Haselby won't know how to tell a virgin from a whore."

"Uncle Robert!" Lucy shook with horror. She had not grown so bold that she could brazenly allow him to think her impure. "I would never— I didn't— How could you think it of me?"

"Because you are acting like a bloody idiot," he snapped. "As of this minute, you will not leave this house until you leave for your wedding. If I have to post guards at your bedchamber door, I will."

"No!" Lucy cried out. "How could you do this to me? What does it matter? We don't need their money. We don't need their connections. Why can't I marry for love?"

At first her uncle did not react. He stood as if frozen, the only movement a vein pounding in his temple. And then, just when Lucy thought she might begin to breathe again, he cursed violently and lunged toward her, pinning her against the wall.

"Uncle Robert!" she gasped. His hand was on her chin, forcing her head into an unnatural position. She tried to swallow, but it was almost impossible with her neck arched so tightly. "Don't," she managed to get out, but it was barely a whimper. "Please . . . Stop."

But his grip only tightened, and his forearm pressed against her collarbone, the bones of his wrist digging painfully into her skin.

"You will marry Lord Haselby," he hissed. "You'll marry him, and I will tell you why."

Lucy said nothing, just stared at him with frantic eyes.

"You, my dear Lucinda, are the final payment of a long-standing debt to Lord Davenport."

"What do you mean?" she whispered.

"Blackmail," Uncle Robert said in a grim voice. "We have been paying Davenport for years."

"But why?" Lucy asked. What could they have possibly done to warrant blackmail?

Her uncle's lip curled mockingly. "Your father, the beloved eighth Earl of Fennsworth, was a traitor."

Lucy gasped, and it felt as if her throat were tightening, tying itself into a knot. It couldn't be true. She'd thought perhaps an extramarital affair. Maybe an earl who wasn't really an Abernathy. But treason? Dear God . . . *no.*

"Uncle Robert," she said, trying to reason with him. "There must be a mistake. A misunderstanding. My father . . . He was not a traitor."

"Oh, I assure you he was, and Davenport knows it."

Lucy thought of her father. She could still see him in her mind—tall, handsome, with laughing blue eyes. He had spent money far too freely; even as a small child she had known that. But he was not a traitor. He could not have been. He had a gentleman's honor. She remembered that. It was in the way he'd stood, the things he'd taught her.

"You are lying," she said, the words burning in her throat. "Or misinformed."

"There is proof," her uncle said, abruptly releasing her and striding across the room to his decanter of brandy. He poured a glass and took a long gulp. "And Davenport has it."

"How?"

"I don't know how," he snapped. "I only know that he does. I have seen it."

Lucy swallowed and hugged her arms to her chest, still trying to absorb what he was telling her. "What sort of proof?"

"Letters," he said grimly. "Written in your father's hand."

"They could be forged."

"They have his seal!" he thundered, slamming his glass down.

Lucy's eyes widened as she watched the brandy slosh over the side of the glass and off the edge of the desk.

"Do you think I would accept something like this without verifying it myself?" her uncle demanded. "There was information—details—things only your father could have known. Do you think I would have paid Davenport's blackmail all these years if there was a chance it was false?"

Lucy shook her head. Her uncle was many things, but he was not a fool.

"He came to me six months after your father died. I have been paying him ever since."

"But why me?" she asked.

Her uncle chuckled bitterly. "Because you will be the perfect upstanding, obedient bride. You will make up for Haselby's deficiencies. Davenport had to get the boy married to someone, and he needed a family that would not talk." He gave her a level stare. "Which we will not. We cannot. And he knows it."

She shook her head in agreement. She would never speak of such things, whether she was Haselby's wife or not. She *liked* Haselby. She did not wish to make life difficult for him. But neither did she wish to be his wife.

"If you do not marry him," her uncle said slowly, "the entire Abernathy family will be ruined. Do you understand?"

Lucy stood frozen.

"We are not speaking of a childhood transgression, a Gypsy in the family tree. Your father committed high treason. He sold state secrets to the French, passed them off to agents posing as smugglers on the coast."

"But why?" Lucy whispered. "We didn't need the money."

"How do you think we *got* the money?" her uncle returned caustically. "And your father—" He swore under his breath. "He always had a taste for danger. He probably did it for the thrill of it. Isn't that a joke upon us all? The very earldom is in danger, and all because your father wanted a spot of adventure."

"Father wasn't like that," Lucy said, but inside she wasn't so sure. She had been just eight when he had been killed by a footpad in London. She had been told that he had come to the defense of a lady, but what if that, too, was a lie? Had he been killed because of his traitorous actions? He was her father, but how much did she truly know of him?

But Uncle Robert didn't appear to have heard her comment. "If you do not marry Haselby," he said, his words low and precise, "Lord

Davenport will reveal the truth about your father, and you will bring shame upon the entire house of Fennsworth."

Lucy shook her head. Surely there was another way. This couldn't rest all upon her shoulders.

"You think not?" Uncle Robert laughed scornfully. "Who do you think will suffer, Lucinda? You? Well, yes, I suppose you will suffer, but we can always pack you off to some school and let you moulder away as an instructor. You'd probably enjoy it."

He took a few steps in her direction, his eyes never leaving her face. "But do think of your brother," he said. "How will he fare as the son of a known traitor? The king will almost certainly strip him of his title. And most of his fortune as well."

"No," Lucy said. *No.* She didn't want to believe it. Richard had done nothing wrong. Surely he couldn't be blamed for his father's sins.

She sank into a chair, desperately trying to sort through her thoughts and emotions.

Treason. How could her father have done such a thing? It went against everything she'd been brought up to believe in. Hadn't her father loved England? Hadn't he told her that the Abernathys had a sacred duty to all Britain?

Or had that been Uncle Robert? Lucy shut her eyes tightly, trying to remember. Someone had said that to her. She was sure of it. She could remember where she'd stood, in front of the portrait of the first earl. She remembered the smell of the air, and the exact words, and—blast it all, she remembered everything save the person who'd spoken them.

She opened her eyes and looked at her uncle. It had probably been he. It sounded like something he would say. He did not choose to speak with her very often, but when he did, duty was always a popular topic.

"Oh, Father," she whispered. How could he have done this? To sell secrets to Napoleon—he'd jeopardized the lives of thousands of British soldiers. Or even—

Her stomach churned. Dear God, he may have been responsible for their deaths. Who knew what he had revealed to the enemy, how many lives had been lost because of his actions?

"It is up to you, Lucinda," her uncle said. "It is the only way to end it."

She shook her head, uncomprehending. "What do you mean?"

"Once you are a Davenport, there can be no more blackmail. Any shame they bring upon us would fall on their shoulders as well." He walked to the window, leaning heavily on the sill as he looked out. "After ten years, I will finally— *We* will finally be free."

Lucy said nothing. There was nothing to say. Uncle Robert peered at her over his shoulder, then turned and walked toward her, watching her closely the entire way. "I see you finally grasp the gravity of the situation," he said.

She looked at him with haunted eyes. There was no compassion in his face, no sympathy or affection. Just a cold mask of duty. He had done what was expected of him, and she would have to do the same.

She thought of Gregory, of his face when he had asked her to marry him. He loved her. She did not know what manner of miracle had brought it about, but he loved her.

And she loved him.

God above, it was almost funny. She, who had always mocked romantic love, had fallen. Completely and hopelessly, she'd fallen in love—enough to throw aside everything she'd thought she believed in. For Gregory she was willing to step into scandal and chaos. For Gregory she would brave the gossip and the whispers and the innuendo.

She, who went mad when her shoes were out of order in her wardrobe, was prepared to jilt the son of an earl four days before the wedding! If that wasn't love, she did not know what was.

Except now it was over. Her hopes, her dreams, the risks she longed to take—they were all over.

She had no choice. If she defied Lord Davenport, her family would be ruined. She thought of Richard and Hermione—so happy, so in love. How could she consign them to a life of shame and poverty?

If she married Haselby her life would not be what she wanted for herself, but she would not suffer. Haselby was reasonable. He was kind. If she appealed to him, surely he would protect her from his father. And her life would be . . .

Comfortable.

Routine.

Far better than Richard and Hermione would fare if her father's shame was made public. Her sacrifice was nothing compared to what her family would be forced to endure if she refused.

Hadn't she once wanted nothing more than comfort and routine? Couldn't she learn to want this again?

"I will marry him," she said, sightlessly gazing at the window. It was raining. When had it begun to rain?

"Good."

Lucy sat in her chair, utterly still. She could feel the energy draining from her body, sliding through her limbs, seeping out her fingers and toes. Lord, she was tired. Weary. And she kept thinking that she wanted to cry.

But she had no tears. Even after she'd risen and walked slowly back to her room—she had no tears.

The next day, when the butler asked her if she was at home for Mr. Bridgerton, and she shook her head—she had no tears.

And the day after that, when she was forced to repeat the same gesture—she had no tears.

But the day after that, after spending twenty-hours holding his calling card, gently sliding her finger over his name, of tracing each letter—THE HON. GREGORY BRIDGERTON—she began to feel them, pricking behind her eyes.

Then she caught sight of him standing on the pavement, looking up at the façade of Fennsworth House.

And he saw her. She knew he did; his eyes widened and his body tensed, and she could feel it, every ounce of his bewilderment and anger.

She let the curtain drop. Quickly. And she stood there, trembling, shaking, and yet still unable to move. Her feet were frozen to the floor, and she began to feel it again—that awful rushing panic in her belly.

It was wrong. It was all so wrong, and yet she knew she was doing what had to be done.

She stood there. At the window, staring at the ripples in the curtain. She stood there as her limbs grew tense and tight, and she stood there as she forced herself to breathe. She stood there as her heart began to squeeze, harder and harder, and she stood there as it all slowly began to subside.

Then, somehow, she made her way to the bed and lay down.

And then, finally, she found her tears.

Nineteen

In which Our Hero takes matters—and Our Heroine—into his own hands.

By Friday Gregory was desperate.

Thrice he'd called upon Lucy at Fennsworth House. Thrice he'd been turned away.

He was running out of time.

They were running out of time.

What the *hell* was going on? Even if Lucy's uncle had denied her request to stop the wedding—and he could not have been pleased; she was, after all, attempting to jilt a future earl—surely Lucy would have attempted to contact him.

She loved him.

He knew it the way he knew his own voice, his own heart. He knew it the way he knew the earth was round and her eyes were blue and that two plus two would always *always* be four.

Lucy loved him. She did not lie. She could not lie.

She *would* not lie. Not about something like this.

Which meant that something was wrong. There could be no other explanation.

He had looked for her in the park, waiting for hours at the bench where she liked to feed pigeons, but she had not appeared. He had watched her door, hoping he might intercept her on her way to carry out errands, but she had not ventured outside.

And then, after the third time he had been refused entry, he saw her. Just a glimpse through the window; she'd let the curtains fall quickly. But it had been enough. He'd not been able to see her face—not well enough to gauge her expression. But there had been something in the way she moved, in the hurried, almost frantic release of the curtains.

Something was wrong.

Was she being held against her will? Had she been drugged? Gregory's mind raced with the possibilities, each more dire than the last.

And now it was Friday night. Her wedding was in less than twelve hours. And there was not a whisper—not a peep—of gossip. If there were even a hint that the Haselby-Abernathy wedding might not take place as planned, Gregory would have heard about it. If nothing else, Hyacinth would have said something. Hyacinth knew everything, usually before the subjects of the rumors themselves.

Gregory stood in the shadows across the street from Fennsworth House and leaned against the trunk of a tree, staring, just staring. Was that her window? The one through which he'd seen her earlier that day? There was no candlelight peeking through, but the draperies were probably heavy and thick. Or perhaps she'd gone to bed. It was late.

And she had a wedding in the morning.

Good God.

He could not let her marry Lord Haselby. He could not. If there was one thing he knew in his heart, it was that he and Lucinda Abernathy were meant to be husband and wife. Hers was the face he was supposed to gaze upon over eggs and bacon and kippers and cod and toast every morning.

A snort of laughter pressed through his nose, but it was that nervous, desperate kind of laughter, the sound one made when the only alternative was to cry. Lucy had to marry him, if only so that they could eat masses and masses of food together every morning.

He looked at her window.

What he *hoped* was her window. With his luck he was mooning over the servants' washroom.

How long he stood there he did not know. For the first time in his memory, he felt powerless, and at least this—watching a bloody window—was something he could control.

He thought about his life. Charmed, for sure. Plenty of money, lovely family, scads of friends. He had his health, he had his sanity, and until the fiasco with Hermione Watson, an unshakable belief in his own sense of judgment. He might not be the most disciplined of men, and perhaps he should have paid more attention to all those things Anthony liked to pester him about, but he knew what was right, and he knew what was wrong, and he'd known—he had absolutely *known*—that his life would play out on a happy and contented canvas.

He was simply that sort of person.

He wasn't melancholy. He wasn't given to fits of temper.

And he'd never had to work very hard.

He looked up at the window, thoughtfully.

He'd grown complacent. So sure of his own happy ending that he hadn't believed—he *still* couldn't quite believe—that he might not get what he wanted.

He had proposed. She had accepted. True, she had been promised to Haselby, and still was, for that matter.

But wasn't true love supposed to triumph? Hadn't it done so for all his brothers and sisters? Why the hell was he so unlucky?

He thought about his mother, remembered the look on her face when she had so skillfully dissected his character. She had got most everything right, he realized.

But only most.

It was true that he had never had to work very hard at anything. But that was only part of the story. He was not indolent. He would work his fingers to the very bone if only . . .

If only he had a reason.

He stared at the window.

He had a reason now.

He'd been waiting, he realized. Waiting for Lucy to convince her uncle to release her from her engagement. Waiting for the puzzle pieces that made up his life to fall into position so that he could fit the last one in its place with a triumphant "Aha!"

Waiting.

Waiting for love. Waiting for a calling.

Waiting for clarity, for that moment when he would know exactly how to proceed.

It was time to stop waiting, time to forget about fate and destiny.

It was time to act. To work.

Hard.

No one was going to hand him that second-to-last piece of the puzzle; he had to find it for himself.

He needed to see Lucy. And it had to be now, since it appeared he was forbidden to call upon her in a more conventional manner.

He crossed the street, then slipped around the corner to the back of the house. The ground floor windows were tightly shut, and all was dark. Higher on the façade, a few curtains fluttered in the breeze, but there was no way Gregory could scale the building without killing himself.

He took stock of his surroundings. To the left, the street. To the right, the alley and mews. And in front of him . . .

The servants' entrance.

He regarded it thoughtfully. Well, why not?

He stepped forward and placed his hand on the knob.

It turned.

Gregory almost laughed with delight. At the very least, he went back to believing—well, perhaps just a little—about fate and destiny and all that rot. Surely this was not a usual occurrence. A servant must have sneaked out, perhaps to make his own assignation. If the door was unlocked, then clearly Gregory was meant to go inside.

Or he was mad in the head.

He decided to believe in fate.

Gregory shut the door quietly behind him, then gave his eyes a minute to become accustomed to the dark. He appeared to be in a large pantry, with the kitchen off to the right. There was a decent chance that some of the lower servants slept nearby, so he removed his boots, carrying them in one hand as he ventured deeper into the house.

His stockinged feet were silent as he crept up the back stairs, making his way to the second floor—the one he thought housed Lucy's bedchamber. He paused on the landing, stopping for a brief moment of sanity before stepping out into the hall.

What was he thinking? He hadn't the slightest clue what might happen if he were caught here. Was he breaking a law? Probably. He couldn't imagine how he might not be. And while his position as brother to a viscount would keep him from the gallows, it would not wipe his slate clean when the home he'd chosen to invade belonged to an earl.

But he had to see Lucy. He was done with waiting.

He took a moment on the landing to orient himself, then walked toward the front of the house. There were two doors at the end. He paused, painting a picture of the house's façade in his mind, then reached for the one on the left. If Lucy had indeed been in her own room when he'd seen her, then this was the correct door. If not . . .

Well, then, he hadn't a clue. Not a clue. And here he was, prowling in the Earl of Fennsworth's house after midnight.

Good God.

He turned the knob slowly, letting out a relieved breath when it made no clicks or squeaks. He opened the door just far enough to fit his body through the opening, then carefully shut it behind him, only then taking the time to examine the room.

It was dark, with scarcely any moonlight filtering in around the window coverings. His eyes had already adjusted to the dimness, however, and he could make out various pieces of furniture—a dressing table, a wardrobe . . .

A bed.

It was a heavy, substantial thing, with a canopy and full drapes that closed around it. If there was indeed someone inside, she slept quietly—no snoring, no rustling, nothing.

That's how Lucy would sleep, he suddenly thought. Like the dead. She was no delicate flower, his Lucy, and she would not tolerate anything less than a perfectly restful night. It seemed odd that he would be so certain of this, but he was.

He *knew* her, he realized. He truly knew her. Not just the usual things. In fact, he *didn't* know the usual things. He did not know her favorite color. Nor could he guess her favorite animal or food.

But somehow it didn't matter if he didn't know if she preferred pink or blue or purple or black. He knew her heart. He *wanted* her heart.

And he could not allow her to marry someone else.

Carefully, he drew back the curtains.

There was no one there.

Gregory swore under his breath, until he realized that the sheets were mussed, the pillow with a fresh indent of someone's head.

He whirled around just in time to see a candlestick swinging wildly through the air at him.

Letting out a surprised grunt, he ducked, but not fast enough to avoid a glancing blow to his temple. He swore again, this time in full voice, and then he heard—

"Gregory?"

He blinked. "Lucy?"

She rushed forward. "What are you doing here?"

He motioned impatiently toward the bed. "Why aren't you asleep?"

"Because I'm getting married tomorrow."

"Well, that's why I'm here."

She stared at him dumbly, as if his presence was so unexpected that she could not muster the correct reaction. "I thought you were an intruder," she finally said, motioning to the candlestick.

He allowed himself the tiniest of smiles. "Not to put too fine a point on it," he murmured, "but I am."

For a moment it looked as if she might return the smile. But instead she hugged her arms to her chest and said, "You must go. Right now."

"Not until you speak with me."

Her eyes slid to a point over his shoulder. "There is nothing to say."

"What about 'I love you'?"

"Don't say that," she whispered.

He stepped forward. "I love you."

"Gregory, please."

Even closer. "I love you."

She took a breath. Squared her shoulders. "I am marrying Lord Haselby tomorrow."

"No," he said, "you're not."

Her lips parted.

He reached out and captured her hand in his. She did not pull away.

"Lucy," he whispered.

She closed her eyes.

"Be with me," he said.

Slowly, she shook her head. "Please don't."

He tugged her closer and pulled the candlestick from her slackening fingers. "Be with me, Lucy Abernathy. Be my love, be my wife."

She opened her eyes, but she held his gaze for only a moment before twisting away. "You're making it so much worse," she whispered.

The pain in her voice was unbearable. "Lucy," he said, touching her cheek, "let me help you."

She shook her head, but she paused as her cheek settled into his palm. Not for long. Barely a second. But he felt it.

"You can't marry him," he said, tilting her face toward his. "You won't be happy."

Her eyes glistened as they met his. In the dim light of the night, they looked a dark, dark gray, and achingly sad. He could imagine the entire world there, in the depths of her gaze. Everything he needed to know, everything he might *ever* need to know—it was there, within her.

"You won't be happy, Lucy," he whispered. "You know that you won't."

Still, she didn't speak. The only sound was her breath, moving quietly across her lips. And then, finally—

"I will be content."

"*Content?*" he echoed. His hand dropped from her face, falling to his side as he stepped back. "You will be content?"

She nodded.

"And that's *enough*?"

She nodded again, but smaller this time.

Anger began to spark within him. She was willing to toss him away for that? Why wasn't she willing to fight?

She loved him, but did she love him enough?

"Is it his position?" he demanded. "Does it mean so much to you to be a countess?"

She waited too long before replying, and he knew she was lying when she said, "Yes."

"I don't believe you," he said, and his voice sounded terrible. Wounded. Angry. He looked at his hand, blinking with surprise as he realized he was still holding the candlestick. He wanted to hurl it at the wall. Instead he set it down. His hands were not quite steady, he saw.

He looked at her. She said nothing.

"Lucy," he begged, "just tell me. Let me help you."

She swallowed, and he realized she was no longer looking at his face.

He took her hands in his. She tensed, but she did not pull away. Their bodies were facing each other, and he could see the ragged rise and fall of her chest.

It matched what he felt in his own.

"I love you," he said. Because if he kept saying it, maybe it would be enough. Maybe the words would fill the room, surround her and sneak beneath her skin. Maybe she would finally realize that there were certain things that could not be denied.

"We belong together," he said. "For eternity."

Her eyes closed. One single, heavy blink. But when she opened them again, she looked shattered.

"Lucy," he said, trying to put his very soul into one single word. "Lucy, tell me—"

"Please don't say that," she said, turning her head so that she was not quite looking at him. Her voice caught and shook. "Say anything else, but not that."

"Why not?"

And then she whispered, "Because it's true."

His breath caught, and in one swift movement he pulled her to him. It was not an embrace; not quite. Their fingers were entwined, their arms bent so that their hands met between their shoulders.

He whispered her name.

Lucy's lips parted.

He whispered it again, so soft that the words were more of a motion than a sound.

Lucy Lucy.

She held still, barely breathing. His body was so close to hers, yet not quite touching. There was heat, though, filling the space between them, swirling through her nightgown, trembling along her skin.

She tingled.

"Let me kiss you," he whispered. "One more time. Let me kiss you one more time, and if you tell me to go, I swear that I will."

Lucy could feel herself slipping, sliding into need, falling into a hazy place of love and desire where right was not quite so identifiable from wrong.

She loved him. She loved him so much, and he could not be hers. Her heart was racing, her breath was shaking, and all she could think was that she would never feel this way again. No one would ever look at her the way Gregory was, right at that very moment. In less than a day she was to marry a man who wouldn't even wish to kiss her.

She would never feel this strange curling in the core of her womanhood, the fluttering in her belly. This was the last time she'd stare at someone's lips and *ache* for them to touch hers.

Dear God, she wanted him. She wanted *this.* Before it was too late.

And he loved her. He loved her. He'd said it, and even though she couldn't quite believe it, she believed *him.*

She licked her lips.

"Lucy," he whispered, her name a question, a statement, and a plea—all in one.

She nodded. And then, because she knew she could not lie to herself or to him, she said the words.

"Kiss me."

There would be no pretending later, no claiming she had been swept away by passion, stripped of her ability to think. The decision was hers. And she'd made it.

For a moment Gregory did not move, but she knew that he heard her. His breath sucked raggedly into him, and his eyes turned positively liquid as he gazed at her. "Lucy," he said, his voice husky and deep and rough and a hundred other things that turned her bones to milk.

His lips found the hollow where her jaw met her neck. "Lucy," he murmured.

She wanted to say something in return, but she could not. It had taken all she had just to ask for his kiss.

"I love you," he whispered, trailing the words along her neck to her collarbone. "I love you. I love you."

They were the most painful, wonderful, horrible, magnificent words he could have said. She wanted to cry—with happiness *and* sorrow.

Pleasure and pain.

And she understood—for the first time in her life—she understood the prickly joy of complete selfishness. She shouldn't be doing this. She knew she shouldn't, and she knew he probably thought that this meant that she would find a way out of her commitment to Haselby.

She was lying to him. As surely as if she'd said the words.

But she could not help herself.

This was her moment. Her one moment to hold bliss in her hands. And it would have to last a lifetime.

Emboldened by the fire within her, she pressed her hands roughly to his cheeks, pulling his mouth against hers for a torrid kiss. She had no idea what she was doing—she was sure there must be rules to all this, but she did not care. She just wanted to kiss him. She couldn't stop herself.

One of his hands moved to her hips, burning through the thin fabric of her nightgown. Then it stole around to her bottom, squeezing and cupping, and there was no more space between them. She felt herself sliding down, and then they were on the bed, and she was on her back, his body pressed against hers, the heat and the weight of it exquisitely male.

She felt like a woman.

She felt like a goddess.

She felt like she could wrap herself around him and never let go.

"Gregory," she whispered, finding her voice as she twined her fingers in his hair.

He stilled, and she knew he was waiting for her to say more.

"I love you," she said, because it was true, and because she needed *some*thing to be true. Tomorrow he would hate her. Tomorrow she would betray him, but in this, at least, she would not lie.

"I want you," she said, when he lifted his head to gaze into her eyes. He stared at her long and hard, and she knew that he was giving her one last chance to back out.

"I want you," she said again, because she wanted him beyond words. She wanted him to kiss her, to take her, and to forget that she was not whispering words of love.

"Lu—"

She placed a finger to his mouth. And she whispered, "I want to be yours." And then she added, "Tonight."

His body shuddered, his breath moving audibly over his lips. He groaned something, maybe her name, and then his mouth met hers in a kiss that gave and took and burned and consumed until Lucy could not help but move underneath him. Her hands slid to his neck, then inside his coat, her fingers desperately seeking heat and skin. With a roughly mumbled curse, he rose up, still straddling her, and yanked off the coat and cravat.

She stared at him with wide eyes. He was removing his shirt, not slowly or with finesse, but with a frantic speed that underscored his desire.

He was not in control. She might not be in control, but neither was he. He was as much a slave to this fire as she was.

He tossed his shirt aside, and she gasped at the sight of him, the light sprinkling of hair across his chest, the muscles that sculpted and stretched under his skin.

He was beautiful. She hadn't realized a man could be beautiful, but it was the only word that could possibly describe him. She lifted one hand and gingerly placed it against his skin. His blood leaped and pulsed beneath, and she nearly pulled away.

"No," he said, covering her hand with his own. He wrapped his fingers around hers and then took her to his heart.

He looked into her eyes.

She could not look away.

And then he was back, his body hard and hot against hers, his hands everywhere and his lips everywhere else. And her nightgown— It no longer seemed to be covering quite so much of her. It was up against her thighs, then pooled around her waist. He was touching her—not *there,* but close. Skimming along her belly, scorching her skin.

"Gregory," she gasped, because somehow his fingers had found her breast.

"Oh, Lucy," he groaned, cupping her, squeezing, tickling the tip, and—

Oh, dear God. How was it possible that she felt it *there*?

Her hips arched and bucked, and she needed to be closer. She needed something she couldn't quite identify, something that would fill her, complete her.

He was tugging at her nightgown now, and it slipped over her head, leaving her scandalously bare. One of her hands instinctively rose to cover her, but he grabbed her wrist and held it against his own chest. He was straddling her, sitting upright, staring down at her as if . . . as if . . .

As if she were beautiful.

He was looking at her the way men always looked at Hermione, except somehow there was *more*. More passion, more desire.

She felt worshipped.

"Lucy," he murmured, lightly caressing the side of her breast. "I feel . . . I think . . ."

His lips parted, and he shook his head. Slowly, as if he did not quite understand what was happening to him. "I have been waiting for this," he whispered. "For my entire life. I didn't even know. I didn't know."

She took his hand and brought it to her mouth, kissing the palm. She understood.

His breath quickened, and then he slid off of her, his hands moving to the fastenings of his breeches.

Her eyes widened, and she watched.

"I will be gentle," he vowed. "I promise you."

"I'm not worried," she said, managing a wobbly smile.

His lips curved in return. "You look worried."

"I'm not." But still, her eyes wandered.

Gregory chuckled, lying down beside her. "It might hurt. I'm told it does at the beginning."

She shook her head. "I don't care."

He let his hand wander down her arm. "Just remember, if there is pain, it will get better."

She felt it beginning again, that slow burning in her belly. "How much better?" she asked, her voice breathy and unfamiliar.

He smiled as his fingers found her hip. "Quite a bit, I'm told."

"Quite a bit," she asked, now barely able to speak, "or . . . rather a lot?"

He moved over her, his skin finding every inch of hers. It was wicked.

It was bliss.

"Rather a lot," he answered, nipping lightly at her neck. "More than rather a lot, actually."

She felt her legs slide open, and his body nestled in the space between them. She could feel him, hard and hot and pressing against her. She stiffened, and he must have felt it, because his lips crooned a soft, "Shhhh," at her ear.

From there he moved down.

And down.

And down.

His mouth trailed fire along her neck to the hollow of her shoulder, and then—

Oh, dear God.

His hand was cupping her breast, making it round and plump, and his mouth found the tip.

She jerked beneath him.

He chuckled, and his other hand found her shoulder, holding her immobile while he continued his torture, pausing only to move to the other side.

"Gregory," Lucy whimpered, because she did not know what else to say. She was lost to the sensation, completely helpless against his sensual onslaught. She couldn't explain, she couldn't fix or rationalize. She could only feel, and it was the most terrifying, thrilling thing imaginable.

With one last nip, he released her breast and brought his face back up to hers. His breathing was ragged, his muscles tense.

"Touch me," he said hoarsely.

Her lips parted, and her eyes found his.

"Anywhere," he begged.

It was only then that Lucy realized that her hands were at her sides, gripping the sheets as if they could keep her sane. "I'm sorry," she said, and then, amazingly, she began to laugh.

One side of his mouth curved up. "We're going to have to break you of that habit," he murmured.

She brought her hands to his back, lightly exploring his skin. "You don't want me to apologize?" she asked. When he joked, when he teased—it made her comfortable. It made her bold.

"Not for this," he groaned.

She rubbed her feet against his calves. "Ever?"

And then his hands started doing unspeakable things. "Do you want me to apologize?"

"No," she gasped. He was touching her intimately, in ways she didn't know she could be touched. It should have been the most awful thing in the world, but it wasn't. It made her stretch, arch, squirm. She had no idea what it was she was feeling—she couldn't have described it with Shakespeare himself at her disposal.

But she wanted more. It was her only thought, the only thing she knew.

Gregory was leading her somewhere. She felt pulled, taken, transported.

And she wanted it all.

"Please," she begged, the word slipping unbidden from her lips. "Please . . ."

But Gregory, too, was beyond words. He said her name. Over and over he said it, as if his lips had lost the memory of anything else.

"Lucy," he whispered, his mouth moving to the hollow between her breasts.

"Lucy," he moaned, slipping one finger inside of her.

And then he gasped it. *"Lucy!"*

She had touched him. Softly, tentatively.

But it was she. It was her hand, her caress, and it felt as if he'd been set on fire.

"I'm sorry," she said, yanking her hand away.

"*Don't* apologize," he ground out, not because he was angry but because he could barely speak. He found her hand and dragged it back. "This is how much I want you," he said, wrapping her around him. "With everything I have, everything I am."

His nose was barely an inch from hers. Their breath mingled, and their eyes . . .

It was like they were one.

"I love you," he murmured, moving into position. Her hand slid away, then moved to his back.

"I love you, too," she whispered, and then her eyes widened, as if she were stunned that she'd said it.

But he didn't care. It didn't matter if she'd meant to tell him or not. She'd said it, and she could never take it back. She was his.

And he was hers. As he held himself still, pressing ever so softly at her entrance, he realized that he was at the edge of a precipice. His life was now one of two parts: before and after.

He would never love another woman again.

He *could* never love another woman again.

Not after this. Not as long as Lucy walked the same earth. There could be no one else.

It was terrifying, this precipice. Terrifying, and thrilling, and—

He jumped.

She let out a little gasp as he pushed forward, but when he looked down at her, she did not seem to be in pain. Her head was thrown back, and each breath was accompanied by a little moan, as if she could not quite keep her desire inside.

Her legs wrapped around his, feet running down the length of his calves. And her hips were arching, pressing, begging him to continue.

"I don't want to hurt you," he said, every muscle in his body straining to move forward. He had never wanted anything the way he wanted her in that moment. And yet he had never felt less greedy. This had to be for her. He could not hurt her.

"You're not," she groaned, and then he couldn't help himself. He captured her breast in his mouth as he pushed through her final barrier, embedding himself fully within her.

If she'd felt pain, she didn't care. She let out a quiet shriek of pleasure, and her hands grabbed wildly at his head. She writhed beneath him, and when he attempted to move to her other breast, her fingers grew merciless, holding him in place with a ferocious intensity.

And all the while, his body claiming her, moving in a rhythm that was beyond thought or control.

"Lucy Lucy Lucy," he moaned, finally tearing himself away from her breast. It was too hard. It was too much. He needed room to breathe, to gasp, to suck in the air that never quite seemed to make it to his lungs.

"Lucy!"

He should wait. He was trying to wait. But she was grabbing at him, digging her nails into his shoulders, and her body was arching off the bed with enough strength to lift him as well.

And then he felt her. Tensing, squeezing, shuddering around him, and he let go.

He let go, and the world quite simply exploded.

"I love you," he gasped as he collapsed atop her. He'd thought himself beyond words, but there they were.

They were his companion now. Three little words.

I love you.

He would never be without them.

And that was a splendid thing.

Twenty

In which Our Hero has a very bad morning.

Sometime later, after sleep, and then more passion, and then not quite sleep, but a peaceful quiet and stillness, and then more passion—because they just could not help themselves—it was time for Gregory to go.

It was the most difficult thing he had ever done, and yet he was still able to do it with joy in his heart because he knew that this was not the end. It was not even goodbye; it was nothing so permanent as that. But the hour was growing dangerous. Dawn would arrive shortly, and while he had every intention of marrying Lucy as soon as he could manage it, he would not put her through the shame of being caught in bed with him on the morning of her wedding to another man.

There was also Haselby to consider. Gregory did not know him well, but he had always seemed an affable fellow and did not deserve the public humiliation that would follow.

"Lucy," Gregory whispered, nudging her cheek with his nose, "it is near to morning."

She made a sleepy sound, then turned her head. "Yes," she said. Just *Yes,* not *It's all so unfair* or *It shouldn't have to be this way.* But that was Lucy. She was pragmatic and prudent and charmingly reasonable, and he loved her for all that and more. She didn't want to change the world. She just wanted to make it lovely and wonderful for the people she loved.

The fact that she had done this—that she had let him make love to her and was planning to call off her wedding *now,* the very morning of the ceremony—it only showed him how deeply she cared for him. Lucy didn't look for attention and drama. She craved stability and routine, and for her to make the leap she was preparing for—

It humbled him.

"You should come with me," he said. "Now. We should leave together before the household wakes."

Her bottom lip stretched a bit from side to side in an *oh dear*-ish expression that was so fetching he simply had to kiss her. Lightly, since he had no time to get carried away, and just a little peck on the corner of her mouth. Nothing that interfered with her answer, which was a disappointing "I cannot."

He drew back. "You cannot remain."

But she was shaking her head. "I . . . I must do the right thing."

He looked at her quizzically.

"I must behave with honor," she explained. She sat then, her fingers clutching the bedclothes so tightly that her knuckles turned white. She looked nervous, which he supposed made sense. He felt on the edge of a brand-new dawn, whereas she—

She still had a rather large mountain to scale before she reached her happy ending.

He reached out, trying to take one of her hands, but she was not receptive. It wasn't that she was tugging away from him; rather, it almost felt as if she was not even aware of his touch.

"I cannot sneak away and allow Lord Haselby to wait in vain at the church," she said, the words rushing out, tumbling from her lips as her eyes turned to his, wide and imploring.

But just for a moment.

Then she turned away.

She swallowed. He could not see her face, but he could see it in the way she moved.

She said, softly, "Surely you understand that."

And he did. It was one of the things he loved best about her. She had such a strong sense of right and wrong, sometimes to the point of intractability. But she was never moralistic, never condescending.

"I will watch for you," he said.

Her head turned sharply, and her eyes widened in question.

"You may need my assistance," he said softly.

"No, it won't be necessary. I'm sure I can—"

"I insist," he said, with enough force to silence her. "This shall be our signal." He held up his hand, fingers together, palm out. He twisted at the wrist then, once, to bring his palm around to face him, and then again, to return it to its original position. "I shall watch for you. If you need my help, come to the window and make the signal."

She opened her mouth, as if she might protest one more time, but in the end she merely nodded.

He stood then, opening the heavy draperies that ringed her bed as he searched for his clothing. His garments were strewn about—his breeches here, his shirt remarkably over there, but he quickly gathered what he needed and dressed.

Lucy remained in bed, sitting up with the sheets tucked under her arm. He found her modesty charming, and he almost teased her for it. But instead he decided just to offer an amused smile. It had been a momentous night for her; she should not be made to feel embarrassed for her innocence.

He walked to the window to peer out. Dawn had not yet broken, but the sky hung with anticipation, the horizon painted with that faint shimmer of light one saw only before the sunrise. It glowed gently, a serene purplish-blue, and was so beautiful he beckoned to her to join him. He turned his back while she donned her nightgown and then, once she had padded across the room in her bare feet, he pulled her gently against him, her back to his chest. He rested his chin on top of her head.

"Look," he whispered.

The night seemed to dance, sparkling and tingling, as if the air itself understood that nothing would ever be the same. Dawn was waiting on the other side of the horizon, and already the stars were beginning to look less bright in the sky.

If he could have frozen time, he would have done so. Never had he experienced a single moment that was so magical, so . . . full. Everything was there, everything that was good and honest and true. And he finally understood the difference between happiness and contentment, and how lucky and blessed he was to feel both, in such breathtaking quantities.

It was Lucy. She completed him. She made his life everything he had known it could someday be.

This was his dream. It was coming true, all around him, right there in his arms.

And then, right as they were standing at the window, one of the stars shot through the sky. It made a wide, shallow arc, and it almost seemed to Gregory that he heard it as it traveled, sparking and crackling until it disappeared from sight.

It made him kiss her. He supposed a rainbow would do the same, or a four-leafed clover, or even a simple snowflake, landing on his sleeve without melting. It was simply impossible to enjoy one of nature's small miracles and *not* kiss her. He kissed her neck, and then he turned her around in his arms so that he could kiss her mouth, and her brow, and even her nose.

All seven freckles, too. God, he loved her freckles.

"I love you," he whispered.

She laid her cheek against his chest, and her voice was hoarse, almost choked as she said, "I love you, too."

"Are you certain you will not come with me now?" He knew her answer, but he asked, anyway.

As expected, she nodded. "I must do this myself."

"How will your uncle react?"

"I'm . . . not sure."

He stepped back, taking her by the shoulders and even bending at the knees so that his eyes would not lose contact with hers. "Will he hurt you?"

"No," she said, quickly enough so that he believed her. "No. I promise you."

"Will he try to force you to marry Haselby? Lock you in your room? Because I could stay. If you think you will need me, I could remain right here." It would create an even worse scandal than what currently lay ahead for them, but if it was a question of her safety . . .

There was nothing he would not do.

"Gregory—"

He silenced her with a shake of his head. "Do you understand," he began, "how completely and utterly this goes against my every instinct, leaving you here to face this by yourself?"

Her lips parted and her eyes—

They filled with tears.

"I have sworn in my heart to protect you," he said, his voice passionate and fierce and maybe even a little bit revelatory. Because today, he realized, was the day he truly became a man. After twenty-six years of an amiable and, yes, aimless existence, he had finally found his purpose.

He finally knew why he had been born.

"I have sworn it in my heart," he said, "and I will swear it before

God just as soon as we are able. And it is like acid in my chest to leave you alone."

His hand found hers, and their fingers twined.

"It is not right," he said, his words low but fierce.

Slowly, she nodded her agreement. "But it is what must be done."

"If there is a problem," he said, "if you sense danger, you must promise to signal. I will come for you. You can take refuge with my mother. Or any one of my sisters. They won't mind the scandal. They would care only for your happiness."

She swallowed, and then she smiled, and her eyes grew wistful. "Your family must be lovely."

He took her hands and squeezed them. "They are *your* family now." He waited for her to say something, but she did not. He brought her hands to his lips and kissed them each in turn. "Soon," he whispered, "this will all be behind us."

She nodded, then glanced over her shoulder at the door. "The servants will be waking shortly."

And he left. He slipped out the door, boots in hand, and crept out the way he'd come in.

It was still dark when he reached the small park that filled the square across from her home. There were hours yet before the wedding, and surely he had enough time to return home to change his clothing.

But he was not prepared to chance it. He had told her he would protect her, and he would never break that promise.

But then it occurred to him—he did not need to do this alone. In fact, he should not do it alone. If Lucy needed him, she would need him well and full. If Gregory had to resort to force, he could certainly use an extra set of hands.

He had never gone to his brothers for help, never begged them to extricate him from a tight spot. He was a relatively young man. He had drunk spirits, gambled, dallied with women.

But he had never drunk too much, or gambled more than he had, or, until the previous night, dallied with a woman who risked her reputation to be with him.

He had not sought responsibility, but neither had he chased trouble.

His brothers had always seen him as a boy. Even now, in his twenty-sixth year, he suspected they did not view him as quite fully grown. And so he did not ask for help. He did not place himself in any position where he might need it.

Until now.

One of his older brothers lived not very far away. Less than a quarter of a mile, certainly, maybe even closer to an eighth. Gregory could be there and back in twenty minutes, including the time it took to yank Colin from his bed.

Gregory had just rolled his shoulders back and forth, loosening up in preparation for a sprint, when he spied a chimney sweep, walking across the street. He was young—twelve, maybe thirteen—and certainly eager for a guinea.

And the promise of another, should he deliver Gregory's message to his brother.

Gregory watched him tear around the corner, then he crossed back to the public garden. There was no place to sit, no place even to stand where he might not be immediately visible from Fennsworth House.

And so he climbed a tree. He sat on a low, thick branch, leaned against the trunk, and waited.

Someday, he told himself, he would laugh about this. Someday they would tell this tale to their grandchildren, and it would all sound very romantic and exciting.

As for now . . .

Romantic, yes. Exciting, not so much.

He rubbed his hands together.

Most of all, it was cold.

He shrugged, waiting for himself to stop noticing it. He never did, but he didn't care. What were a few blue fingertips against the rest of his life?

He smiled, lifting his gaze to her window. There she was, he thought. Right there, behind that curtain. And he loved her.

He loved her.

He thought of his friends, most of them cynics, always casting a bored eye over the latest selection of debutantes, sighing that marriage was such a chore, that ladies were interchangeable, and that love was best left to the poets.

Fools, the lot of them.

Love existed.

It was right there, in the air, in the wind, in the water. One only had to wait for it.

To watch for it.

And fight for it.

And he would. As God was his witness, he would. Lucy had only to signal, and he would retrieve her.

He was a man in love.

Nothing could stop him.

"This is not, you realize, how I had intended to spend my Saturday morning."

Gregory answered only with a nod. His brother had arrived four hours earlier, greeting him with a characteristically understated "This is interesting."

Gregory had told Colin everything, even down to the events of the night before. He did not like telling tales of Lucy, but one really could not ask one's brother to sit in a tree for hours without explaining why. And Gregory had found a certain comfort in unburdening himself to Colin. He had not lectured. He had not judged.

In fact, he had understood.

When Gregory had finished his tale, tersely explaining why he was waiting outside Fennsworth House, Colin had simply nodded and said, "I don't suppose you have something to eat."

Gregory shook his head and grinned.

It was good to have a brother.

"Rather poor planning on your part," Colin muttered. But he was smiling, too.

They turned back to the house, which had long since begun to show signs of life. Curtains had been pulled back, candles lit and then snuffed as dawn had given way to morning.

"Shouldn't she have come out by now?" Colin asked, squinting at the door.

Gregory frowned. He had been wondering the same thing. He had been telling himself that her absence boded well. If her uncle were going to force her to marry Haselby, wouldn't she have left for the church by now? By his pocket watch, which admittedly wasn't the most accurate of timepieces, the ceremony was due to begin in less than an hour.

But she had not signaled for his help, either.

And that did not sit well with him.

Suddenly Colin perked up.

"What is it?"

Colin motioned to the right with his head. "A carriage," he said, "being brought 'round from the mews."

Gregory's eyes widened with horror as the front door to Fennsworth House opened. Servants spilled out, laughing and cheering as the vehicle came to a stop in front of Fennsworth House.

It was white, open, and festooned with perfectly pink flowers and wide rosy ribbons, trailing behind, fluttering in the light breeze.

It was a wedding carriage.

And no one seemed to find that odd.

Gregory's skin began to tingle. His muscles burned.

"Not yet," Colin said, placing a restraining hand on Gregory's arm.

Gregory shook his head. His peripheral vision was beginning to fade from view, and all he could see was that damned carriage.

"I have to get her," he said. "I have to go."

"Wait," Colin instructed. "Wait to see what happens. She might not come out. She might—"

But she did come out.

Not first. That was her brother, his new wife on his arm.

Then came an older man—her uncle, most probably—and that ancient woman Gregory had met at his sister's ball.

And then . . .

Lucy.

In a wedding dress.

"Dear God," he whispered.

She was walking freely. No one was forcing her.

Hermione said something to her, whispered in her ear.

And Lucy smiled.

She smiled.

Gregory began to gasp.

The pain was palpable. Real. It shot through his gut, squeezed at his organs until he could no longer move.

He could only stare.

And think.

"Did she tell you she wasn't going to go through with it?" Colin whispered.

Gregory tried to say yes, but the word strangled him. He tried to recall their last conversation, every last word of it. She had said she must behave with honor. She had said she must do what was right. She had said that she loved him.

But she had never said that she would not marry Haselby.

"Oh my God," he whispered.

His brother laid his hand over his own. "I'm sorry," he said.

Gregory watched as Lucy stepped up into the open carriage. The servants were still cheering. Hermione was fussing with her hair, adjusting the veil, then laughing when the wind lifted the gauzy fabric in the air.

This could not be happening.

There had to be an explanation.

"No," Gregory said, because it was the only word he could think to say. "No."

Then he remembered. The hand signal. The wave. She would do it. She would signal to him. Whatever had transpired in the house, she had not been able to halt the proceedings. But now, out in the open, where he could see, she would signal.

She had to. She knew he could see her.

She knew he was out there.

Watching her.

He swallowed convulsively, never taking his eyes off her right hand.

"Is everyone here?" he heard Lucy's brother call out.

He did not hear Lucy's voice in the chorus of replies, but no one was questioning her presence.

She was the bride.

And he was a fool, watching her ride away.

"I'm sorry," Colin said quietly, as they watched the carriage disappear around the corner.

"It doesn't make sense," Gregory whispered.

Colin jumped down out of the tree and silently held out his hand to Gregory.

"It doesn't make sense," Gregory said again, too bewildered to do anything but let his brother help him down. "She wouldn't do this. She loves me."

He looked at Colin. His eyes were kind, but pitying.

"No," Gregory said. "No. You don't know her. She would not—No. You don't know her."

And Colin, whose only experience with Lady Lucinda Abernathy was the moment in which she had broken his brother's heart, asked, "Do *you* know her?"

Gregory stepped back as if struck. "Yes," he said. "Yes, I do."

Colin didn't say anything, but his brows rose, as if to ask, *Well, then?*

Gregory turned, his eyes moving to the corner around which Lucy had so recently disappeared. For a moment he stood absolutely still, his only movement a deliberate, thoughtful blink of his eyes.

He turned back around, looked his brother in the face. "I know her," he said. "I do."

Colin's lips drew together, as if trying to form a question, but Gregory had already turned away.

He was looking at that corner again.

And then he began to run.

Twenty-one

In which Our Hero risks everything.

"Are you ready?"

Lucy regarded the splendid interior of St. George's—the bright stained glass, the elegant arches, the piles and piles of flowers brought in to celebrate her marriage.

She thought about Lord Haselby, standing with the priest at the altar.

She thought about the guests, all more-than-three-hundred of them, all waiting for her to enter on her brother's arm.

And she thought about Gregory, who had surely seen her climb up into the bridal carriage, dressed in her wedding finery.

"Lucy," Hermione repeated, "are you ready?"

Lucy wondered what Hermione might do if she said no.

Hermione was a romantic.

Impractical.

She would probably tell Lucy that she did not have to go through with it, that it did not matter that they were standing just outside the doors to the church sanctuary, or that the prime minister himself was seated inside.

Hermione would tell her that it did not matter that papers had been signed and banns had been read, in three different parishes. It did not matter that by fleeing the church Lucy would create the scandal of the decade. She would tell Lucy that she did not have to do it, that she should not settle for a marriage of convenience when she could have one of passion and love. She would say—

"Lucy?"

(Is what she actually said.)

Lucy turned, blinking in confusion, because the Hermione of her imagination had been giving quite an impassioned speech.

Hermione smiled gently. "Are you ready?"

And Lucy, because she was Lucy, because she would always be Lucy, nodded.

She could do nothing else.

Richard joined them. "I cannot believe you are getting married," he said to Lucy, but not before gazing warmly at his wife.

"I am not so very much younger than you are, Richard," Lucy reminded him. She tilted her head toward the new Lady Fennsworth. "And I am two months older than Hermione."

Richard grinned boyishly. "Yes, but she is not my sister."

Lucy smiled at that, and she was grateful for it. She needed smiles. Every last one she could manage.

It was her wedding day. She had been bathed and perfumed and dressed in what had to be the most luxurious gown she had ever laid eyes upon, and she felt . . .

Empty.

She could not imagine what Gregory thought of her. She had deliberately allowed him to think that she planned to call off the wedding. It was terrible of her, cruel and dishonest, but she did not know what else to do. She was a coward, and she could not bear to see his face when she told him she still intended to marry Haselby.

Good God, how could she have explained it? He would have insisted that there was another way, but he was an idealist, and he had never faced true adversity. There *wasn't* another way. Not this time. Not without sacrificing her family.

She let out a long breath. She could do this. Truly. She could. She could.

She closed her eyes, her head bobbing a half inch or so as the words echoed in her mind.

I can do this. I can. I can.

"Lucy?" came Hermione's concerned voice. "Are you unwell?"

Lucy opened her eyes, and said the only thing Hermione would possibly believe. "Just doing sums in my head."

Hermione shook her head. "I hope Lord Haselby likes maths, because I vow, Lucy, you are mad."

"Perhaps."

Hermione looked at her quizzically.

"What is it?" Lucy asked.

Hermione blinked several times before finally replying. "It is nothing, really," she said. "Just that that sounded quite unlike you."

"I don't know what you mean."

"To agree with me when I call you mad? That's not at all what you would say."

"Well, it's obviously what I did say," Lucy grumbled, "so I don't know what—"

"Oh, pish. The Lucy I know would say something like, 'Mathematics is a very extremely important endeavor, and really, Hermione, you ought to consider practicing sums yourself.' "

Lucy winced. "Am I truly so officious?"

"Yes," Hermione replied, as if she were mad even to question it. "But it's what I love best about you."

And Lucy managed another smile.

Maybe everything would be all right. Maybe she would be happy. If she could manage two smiles in one morning, then surely it couldn't be that bad. She needed only to keep moving forward, in her mind and her body. She needed to have this thing done, to make it permanent, so she could place Gregory in her past and at least pretend to embrace her new life as Lord Haselby's wife.

But Hermione was asking Richard if she might have a moment alone with Lucy, and then she was taking her hands, leaning in and whispering, "Lucy, are you certain you wish to do this?"

Lucy looked up at her in surprise. Why was Hermione asking her this? Right at the moment when she most wanted to run.

Hadn't she been smiling? Hadn't Hermione seen her smiling?

Lucy swallowed. She tried to straighten her shoulders. "Yes," she said. "Yes, of course. Why would you ask such a thing?"

Hermione did not answer right away. But her eyes—those huge, green eyes that rendered grown men senseless—they answered for her.

Lucy swallowed and turned away, unable to bear what she saw there.

And Hermione whispered, *"Lucy."*

That was all. Just Lucy.

Lucy turned back. She wanted to ask Hermione what she meant. She wanted to ask why she said her name as if it were a tragedy. But she didn't. She couldn't. And so she hoped Hermione saw her questions in her eyes.

She did. Hermione touched her cheek, smiling sadly. "You look like the saddest bride I've ever seen."

Lucy closed her eyes. "I'm not sad. I just feel . . ."

But she didn't know what she felt. What was she supposed to feel? No one had trained her for this. In all her education, with her nurse, and governess, and three years at Miss Moss's, no one had given her lessons in *this.*

Why hadn't anyone realized that this was far more important than needlework or country dances?

"I feel . . ." And then she understood. "I feel like I'm saying goodbye."

Hermione blinked with surprise. "To whom?"

To myself.

And she was. She was saying goodbye to herself, and everything she might have become.

She felt her brother's hand on her arm. "It's time to begin," he said.

She nodded.

"Where is your bouquet?" Hermione asked, then answered herself with, "Oh. Right there." She retrieved the flowers, along with her own, from a nearby table and handed them to Lucy. "You shall be happy," she whispered, as she kissed Lucy's cheek. "You must. I simply will not tolerate a world in which you are not."

Lucy's lips wobbled.

"Oh dear," Hermione said. "I sound like you now. Do you see what a good influence you are?" And then, with one last blown kiss, she entered the chapel.

"Your turn," Richard said.

"Almost," Lucy answered.

And then it was.

She was in the church, walking down the aisle. She was at the front, nodding at the priest, looking at Haselby and reminding herself that despite . . . well, despite certain habits she did not quite understand, he would make a perfectly acceptable husband.

This was what she had to do.

If she said no . . .

She could not say no.

She could see Hermione out of the corner of her eye, standing beside her with a serene smile. She and Richard had arrived in London two nights earlier, and they had been so *happy.* They laughed and they teased and they spoke of the improvements they planned to make at Fennsworth Abbey. An orangery, they had laughed. They wanted an orangery. And a nursery.

How could Lucy take that from them? How could she cast them into a life of shame and poverty?

She heard Haselby's voice, answering, "I will," and then it was her turn.

Wilt thou have this Man to thy Wedded Husband, to live together after God's ordinance in the holy estate of Matrimony? Wilt thou obey him, and serve him, love, honor, and keep him in sickness and in health; and, forsaking all other, keep thee only unto him, so long as ye both shall live?

She swallowed and tried not to think of Gregory. "I will."

She had given her consent. Was it done, then? She didn't feel different. She was still the same old Lucy, except she was standing in front of more people than she ever cared to stand in front of again, and her brother was giving her away.

The priest placed her right hand in Haselby's, and he pledged his troth, his voice loud, firm, and clear.

They separated, and then Lucy took his hand.

I, Lucinda Margaret Catherine . . .

"I, Lucinda Margaret Catherine . . ."

. . . take thee, Arthur Fitzwilliam George . . .

". . . take thee, Arthur Fitzwilliam George . . ."

She said it. She repeated after the priest, word for word. She said her part, right up until she meant to give Haselby her troth, right up until—

The doors to the chapel slammed open.

She turned around. Everyone turned around.

Gregory.

Dear God.

He looked like a madman, breathing so hard he was barely able to speak.

He staggered forward, clutching the edges of the pew for support, and she heard him say—

"Don't."

Lucy's heart stopped.

"Don't do it."

Her bouquet slipped from her hands. She couldn't move, couldn't speak, couldn't do anything but stand there like a statue as he walked toward her, seemingly oblivious to the hundreds of people staring at him.

"Don't do it," he said again.

And no one was talking. Why was no one talking? Surely someone would rush forward, grab Gregory by the arms, haul him away—

But no one did. It was a spectacle. It was theater, and it seemed no one wanted to miss the ending.

And then—

Right there.

Right there in front of everyone, he stopped.

He stopped. And he said, "I love you."

Beside her Hermione murmured, "Oh my goodness."

Lucy wanted to cry.

"I love you," he said again, and he just kept walking, his eyes never leaving her face.

"Don't do it," he said, finally reaching the front of the church. "Don't marry him."

"Gregory," she whispered, "why are you doing this?"

"I love you," he said, as if there could be no other explanation.

A little moan choked in her throat. Tears burned her eyes, and her entire body felt stiff. Stiff and frozen. One little wind, one little *breath* would knock her over. And she couldn't manage to think anything but *Why*?

And *No.*

And *Please.*

And—oh heavens, *Lord Haselby*!

She looked up at him, at the groom who had found himself demoted to a supporting role. He had been standing silently this entire time, watching the unfolding drama with as much interest as the audience. With her eyes she pleaded with him for guidance, but he just shook his head. It was a tiny movement, far too subtle for anyone else to discern, but she saw it, and she knew what it meant.

It is up to you.

She turned back to Gregory. His eyes burned, and he sank to one knee.

Don't, she tried to say. But she could not move her lips. She could not find her voice.

"Marry me," Gregory said, and she *felt* him in his voice. It wrapped around her body, kissed her, embraced her. "Marry *me.*"

And oh dear Lord, she wanted to. More than anything, she wanted to sink to her knees and take his face in her hands. She wanted to kiss him, she wanted to shout out her love for him—here, in front of everyone she knew, possibly everyone she ever would know.

But she had wanted all of that the day before, and the day before that. Nothing had changed. Her world had become more public, but it had not changed.

Her father was still a traitor.

Her family was still being blackmailed.

The fate of her brother and Hermione was still in her hands.

She looked at Gregory, aching for him, aching for them both.

"Marry me," he whispered.

Her lips parted, and she said—

"No."

Twenty-two

In which all hell breaks loose.

All hell broke loose.

Lord Davenport charged forward, as did Lucy's uncle and Gregory's brother, who had just tripped up the steps to the church after chasing Gregory across Mayfair.

Lucy's brother dashed forward to move both Lucy and Hermione from the melee, but Lord Haselby, who had been watching the events with the air of an intrigued spectator, calmly took the arm of his intended and said, "I will see to her."

As for Lucy, she stumbled backward, her mouth open with shock as Lord Davenport leaped atop Gregory, landing belly down like a—well, like nothing Lucy had ever seen.

"I have him!" Davenport yelled triumphantly, only to be smacked soundly with a reticule belonging to Hyacinth St. Clair.

Lucy closed her eyes.

"Not the wedding of your dreams, I imagine," Haselby murmured in her ear.

Lucy shook her head, too numb to do anything else. She should help Gregory. Really, she should. But she felt positively drained of energy, and besides, she was too cowardly to face him again.

What if he rejected her?

What if she could not resist him?

"I do hope he will be able to get out from under my father," Haselby continued, his tone as mild as if he were watching a not-terribly-exciting horse race. "The man weighs twenty stone, not that he would admit it."

Lucy turned to him, unable to believe how calm he was given the near riot that had broken out in the church. Even the prime minister appeared to be fending off a largish, plumpish lady in an elaborately fruited bonnet who was swatting at anyone who moved.

"I don't think she can see," Haselby said, following Lucy's gaze. "Her grapes are drooping."

Who *was* this man she had—dear heavens, had she married him yet? They had agreed to something, of that she was certain, but no one had declared them man and wife. But either way, Haselby was bizarrely calm, given the events of the morning.

"Why didn't you say anything?" Lucy asked.

He turned, regarding her curiously. "You mean while your Mr. Bridgerton was professing his love?"

No, while the priest was droning on about the sacrament of marriage, she wanted to snap.

Instead, she nodded.

Haselby cocked his head to the side. "I suppose I wanted to see what you'd do."

She stared at him in disbelief. What would he have done if she'd said yes?

"I am honored, by the way," Haselby said. "And I shall be a kind husband to you. You needn't worry on that score."

But Lucy could not speak. Lord Davenport had been removed from Gregory, and even though some other gentleman she did not recognize was pulling him back, he was struggling to reach her.

"Please," she whispered, even though no one could possibly hear her, not even Haselby, who had stepped down to aid the prime minister. "Please don't."

But Gregory was unrelenting, and even with two men pulling at him, one friendly and one not, he managed to reach the bottom of the steps. He lifted his face, and his eyes burned into hers. They were raw, stark with anguish and incomprehension, and Lucy nearly stumbled from the unleashed pain she saw there.

"Why?" he demanded.

Her entire body began to shake. Could she lie to him? Could she do it? Here, in a church, after she had hurt him in the most personal and the most public way imaginable.

"Why?"

"Because I had to," she whispered.

His eyes flared with something—disappointment? No. Hope? No, not that, either. It was something else. Something she could not quite identify.

He opened his mouth to speak, to ask her something, but it was at that moment that the two men holding him were joined by a third, and together they managed to haul him from the church.

Lucy hugged her arms to her body, barely able to stand as she watched him being dragged away.

"How could you?"

She turned. Hyacinth St. Clair had crept up behind her and was glaring at her as if she were the very devil.

"You don't understand," Lucy said.

But Hyacinth's eyes blazed with fury. "You are weak," she hissed. "You do not deserve him."

Lucy shook her head, not quite sure if she was agreeing with her or not.

"I hope you—"

"Hyacinth!"

Lucy's eyes darted to the side. Another woman had approached. It was Gregory's mother. They had been introduced at the ball at Hastings House.

"That will be enough," she said sternly.

Lucy swallowed, blinking back tears.

Lady Bridgerton turned to her. "Forgive us," she said, pulling her daughter away.

Lucy watched them depart, and she had the strangest sense that all this was happening to someone else, that maybe it was just a dream, just a nightmare, or perhaps she was caught up in a scene from a lurid novel. Maybe her entire life was a figment of someone else's imagination. Maybe if she just closed her eyes—

"Shall we get on with it?"

She swallowed. It was Lord Haselby. His father was next to him, uttering the same sentiment, but in far less gracious words.

Lucy nodded.

"Good," Davenport grunted. "Sensible girl."

Lucy wondered what it meant to be complimented by Lord Davenport. Surely nothing good.

But still, she allowed him to lead her back to the altar. And she stood there in front of half of the congregation who had not elected to follow the spectacle outside.

And she married Haselby.

"What were you thinking?"

It took Gregory a moment to realize that his mother was demanding this of Colin, and not of him. They were seated in her carriage, to which he had been dragged once they had left the church. Gregory did not know where they were going. In random circles, most probably. Anywhere that wasn't St. George's.

"I tried to stop him," Colin protested.

Violet Bridgerton looked as angry as any of them had ever seen her. "You obviously did not try hard enough."

"Do you have any idea how fast he can run?"

"Very fast," Hyacinth confirmed without looking at them. She was seated diagonally to Gregory, staring out the window through narrowed eyes.

Gregory said nothing.

"Oh, Gregory," Violet sighed. "Oh, my poor son."

"You shall have to leave town," Hyacinth said.

"She is right," their mother put in. "It can't be helped."

Gregory said nothing. What had Lucy meant—*Because I had to?* What did that *mean*?

"I shall never receive her," Hyacinth growled.

"She will be a countess," Colin reminded her.

"I don't care if she is the bloody queen of—"

"Hyacinth!" This, from their mother.

"Well, I don't," Hyacinth snapped. "No one has the right to treat my brother like that. No one!"

Violet and Colin stared at her. Colin looked amused. Violet, alarmed.

"I shall ruin her," Hyacinth continued.

"No," Gregory said in a low voice, "you won't."

The rest of his family fell silent, and Gregory suspected that they had not, until the moment he'd spoken, realized that he had not been taking part in the conversation.

"You will leave her alone," he said.

Hyacinth ground her teeth together.

He brought his eyes to hers, hard and steely with purpose. "And if your paths should ever cross," he continued, "you shall be all that is amiable and kind. Do you understand me?"

Hyacinth said nothing.

"Do you understand me?" he roared.

His family stared at him in shock. He never lost his temper. Never.

And then Hyacinth, who'd never possessed a highly developed sense of tact, said, "No, as a matter of fact."

"I beg your pardon?" Gregory, said, his voice dripping ice at the very moment Colin turned to her and hissed, "Shut *up*."

"I don't understand you," Hyacinth continued, jamming her elbow into Colin's ribs. "How can you possibly possess sympathy for her? If this had happened to me, wouldn't you—"

"This didn't happen to you," Gregory bit off. "And you do not know her. You do not know the reasons for her actions."

"Do *you*?" Hyacinth demanded.

He didn't. And it was killing him.

"Turn the other cheek, Hyacinth," her mother said softly.

Hyacinth sat back, her bearing tense with anger, but she held her tongue.

"Perhaps you could stay with Benedict and Sophie in Wiltshire," Violet suggested. "I believe Anthony and Kate are expected in town soon, so you cannot go to Aubrey Hall, although I am sure they would not mind if you resided there in their absence."

Gregory just stared out the window. He did not wish to go to the country.

"You could travel," Colin said. "Italy is particularly pleasant this time of year. And you haven't been, have you?"

Gregory shook his head, only half listening. He did not wish to go to Italy.

Because I had to, she'd said.

Not because she wished it. Not because it was sensible.

Because she had to.

What did that mean?

Had she been forced? Was she being blackmailed?

What could she have possibly done to warrant blackmail?

"It would have been very difficult for her not to go through with it," Violet suddenly said, placing a sympathetic hand on his arm. "Lord Davenport is not a man anyone would wish as an enemy. And really, right there in the church, with everyone looking on . . . Well," she said with a resigned sigh, "one would have to be extremely brave. And resilient." She paused, shaking her head. "And prepared."

"Prepared?" Colin queried.

"For what came next," Violet clarified. "It would have been a huge scandal."

"It already is a huge scandal," Gregory muttered.

"Yes, but not as much as if she'd said yes," his mother said. "Not that I am glad for the outcome. You know I wish you nothing but your heart's happiness. But she will be looked upon approvingly for her choice. She will be viewed as a sensible girl."

Gregory felt one corner of his mouth lift into a wry smile. "And I, a lovesick fool."

No one contradicted him.

After a moment his mother said, "You are taking this rather well, I must say."

Indeed.

"I would have thought—" She broke off. "Well, it matters not what I would have thought, merely what actually is."

"No," Gregory said, turning sharply to look at her. "What would you have thought? How should I be acting?"

"It is not a question of *should,*" his mother said, clearly flustered by the sudden questions. "Merely that I would have thought you would seem . . . angrier."

He stared at her for a long moment, then turned back to the window. They were traveling along Piccadilly, heading west toward Hyde Park. Why *wasn't* he angrier? Why wasn't he putting his fist through the wall? He'd had to be dragged from the church and forcibly stuffed into the carriage, but once that had been done, he had been overcome by a bizarre, almost preternatural calm.

And then something his mother had said echoed in his mind.

You know I wish you nothing but your heart's happiness.

His heart's happiness.

Lucy loved him. He was certain of it. He had seen it in her eyes, even in the moment she'd refused him. He knew it because she had told him so, and she did not lie about such things. He had felt it in the way she had kissed him, and in the warmth of her embrace.

She loved him. And whatever had made her go ahead with her marriage to Haselby, it was bigger than she was. Stronger.

She needed his help.

"Gregory?" his mother said softly.

He turned. Blinked.

"You started in your seat," she said.

Had he? He hadn't even noticed. But his senses had sharpened, and when he looked down, he saw that he was flexing his fingers.

"Stop the carriage."

Everyone turned to face him. Even Hyacinth, who had been determinedly glaring out the window.

"Stop the carriage," he said again.

"Why?" his mother asked, clearly suspicious.

"I need air," he replied, and it wasn't even a lie.

Colin knocked on the wall. "I'll walk with you."

"No. I prefer to be alone."

His mother's eyes widened. "Gregory . . . You don't plan to . . ."

"Storm the church?" he finished for her. He leaned back, giving her a casually lopsided smile. "I believe I've embarrassed myself enough for one day, wouldn't you think?"

"They'll have said their vows by now, anyway," Hyacinth put in.

Gregory fought the urge to glare at his sister, who never seemed to miss an opportunity to poke, prod, or twist. "Precisely," he replied.

"I would feel better if you weren't alone," Violet said, her blue eyes still filled with concern.

"Let him go," Colin said softly.

Gregory turned to his older brother in surprise. He had not expected to be championed by him.

"He is a man," Colin added. "He can make his own decisions."

Even Hyacinth did not attempt to contradict.

The carriage had already come to a halt, and the driver was waiting outside the door. At Colin's nod, he opened it.

"I wish you wouldn't go," Violet said.

Gregory kissed her cheek. "I need air," he said. "That is all."

He hopped down, but before he could shut the door, Colin leaned out.

"Don't do anything foolish," Colin said quietly.

"Nothing foolish," Gregory promised him, "only what is necessary."

He took stock of his location, and then, as his mother's carriage had not moved, deliberately set off to the south.

Away from St. George's.

But once he reached the next street he doubled around.

Running.

Twenty-three

In which Our Hero risks everything. Again.

In the ten years since her uncle had become her guardian, Lucy had never known him to host a party. He was not one to smile upon any sort of unnecessary expense—in truth, he was not one to smile at all. So it was with some suspicion that she approached the lavish fête being thrown in her honor at Fennsworth House following the wedding ceremony.

Lord Davenport had surely insisted upon it. Uncle Robert would have been content to serve tea cakes at the church and be done with it.

But no, the wedding must be an event, in the most extravagant sense of the word, and so as soon as the ceremony was over, Lucy was whisked to her soon-to-be-former home and given just enough time in her soon-to-be-former bedchamber to splash some cool water on her face before she was summoned to greet her guests below.

It was remarkable, she thought as she nodded and received the well wishes of the attendees, just how good the *ton* was at pretending nothing had happened.

Oh, they would be speaking of nothing else tomorrow, and she could probably look forward to being the main topic of conversation for the next few months, even. And certainly for the next year no one would say her name without appending, "You know the one. With the *wedding*."

Which would surely be followed by, "Ohhhhhhhh. *She's* the one."

But for now, to her face, there was nothing but "Such a happy occasion," and "You make a beautiful bride." And of course, for the sly and daring—"Lovely ceremony, Lady Haselby."

Lady Haselby.

She tested it out in her mind. She was Lady Haselby now.

She could have been Mrs. Bridgerton.

Lady Lucinda Bridgerton, she supposed, as she was not required to surrender her honorific upon marriage to a commoner. It was a nice name—not as lofty as Lady Haselby, perhaps, and certainly nothing compared to the Countess of Davenport, but—

She swallowed, somehow managing not to dislodge the smile she'd affixed to her face five minutes earlier.

She would have liked to have been Lady Lucinda Bridgerton.

She *liked* Lady Lucinda Bridgerton. She was a happy sort, with a ready smile and a life that was full and complete. She had a dog, maybe two, and several children. Her house was warm and cozy, she drank tea with her friends, and she laughed.

Lady Lucinda Bridgerton laughed.

But she would never be that woman. She had married Lord Haselby, and now she was his wife, and try as she might, she could not picture where her life might lead. She did not know what it meant to be Lady Haselby.

The party hummed along, and Lucy danced her obligatory dance with her new husband, who was, she was relieved to note, quite accomplished. Then she danced with her brother, which nearly made her cry, and then her uncle, because it was expected.

"You did the right thing, Lucy," he said.

She said nothing. She didn't trust herself to do so.

"I am proud of you."

She almost laughed. "You have never been proud of me before."

"I am now."

It did not escape her notice that this was not a contradiction.

Her uncle returned her to the side of the ballroom floor, and then—dear *God*—she had to dance with Lord Davenport.

Which she did, because she knew her duty. On this day, especially, she knew her duty.

At least she did not have to speak. Lord Davenport was at his most effusive, and more than carried the conversation for the both of them. He was delighted with Lucy. She was a magnificent asset to the family.

And so on and so forth until Lucy realized that she had managed to endear herself to him in the most indelible manner possible. She had not simply agreed to marry his dubiously reputationed son; she had affirmed the decision in front of the entire *ton* in a scene worthy of Drury Lane.

Lucy moved her head discreetly to the side. When Lord Davenport was excited, spittle tended to fly from his mouth with alarming speed and accuracy. Truly, she wasn't sure which was worse—Lord Davenport's disdain or his everlasting gratitude.

But Lucy managed to avoid her new father-in-law for most of the festivities, thank heavens. She managed to avoid most everyone, which was surprisingly undifficult, given that she was the bride. She didn't want to see Lord Davenport, because she detested him, and she didn't want to see her uncle, because she rather suspected she detested him, as well. She didn't want to see Lord Haselby, because that would only lead to thoughts of her upcoming wedding night, and she didn't want to see Hermione, because she would ask questions, and then Lucy would cry.

And she didn't want to see her brother, because he was sure to be with Hermione, and besides that, she was feeling rather bitter, alternating with feeling rather guilty for feeling bitter. It wasn't Richard's fault that he was deliriously happy and she was not.

But all the same, she'd rather not have to see him.

Which left the guests, most of whom she did not know. And none of whom she wished to meet.

So she found a spot in the corner, and after a couple of hours, everyone had drunk so much that no one seemed to notice that the bride was sitting by herself.

And certainly no one took note when she escaped to her bedchamber to take a short rest. It was probably very bad manners for a bride to avoid her own party, but at that moment, Lucy simply did not care. People would think she'd gone off to relieve herself, if anyone noticed her absence. And somehow it seemed appropriate for her to be alone on this day.

She slipped up the back stairs, lest she come across any wandering guests, and with a sigh of relief, she stepped into her room and shut the door behind her.

She leaned her back against the door, slowly deflating until it felt like there was nothing left within her.

And she thought—*Now I shall cry.*

She wanted to. Truly, she did. She felt as if she'd been holding it inside for hours, just waiting for a private moment. But the tears would not come. She was too numb, too dazed by the events of the last twenty-four hours. And so she stood there, staring at her bed.

Remembering.

Dear heaven, had it been only twelve hours earlier that she had lain there, wrapped in his arms? It seemed like years. It was as if her life were now neatly divided in two, and she was most firmly in *after.*

She closed her eyes. Maybe if she didn't see it, it would go away.

Maybe if she—

"Lucy."

She froze. Dear God, *no.*

"Lucy."

Slowly, she opened her eyes. And whispered, "Gregory?"

He looked a mess, windblown and dirty as only a mad ride on horseback could do to a man. He must have sneaked in the same way he'd done the night before. He must have been waiting for her.

She opened her mouth, tried to speak.

"Lucy," he said again, and his voice flowed through her, melted around her.

She swallowed. "Why are you here?"

He stepped toward her, and her heart just *ached* from it. His face was so handsome, and so dear, and so perfectly wonderfully familiar. She knew the slope of his cheeks, and the exact shade of his eyes, brownish near the iris, melting into green at the edge.

And his mouth—she knew that mouth, the look of it, the feel of it. She knew his smile, and she knew his frown, and she knew—

She knew far too much.

"You shouldn't be here," she said, the catch in her voice belying the stillness of her posture.

He took another step in her direction. There was no anger in his eyes, which she did not understand. But the way he was looking at her—it was hot, and it was possessive, and it was nothing a married woman should ever allow from a man who was not her husband.

"I had to know why," he said. "I couldn't let you go. Not until I knew why."

"Don't," she whispered. "Please don't do this."

Please don't make me regret. Please don't make me long and wish and wonder.

She hugged her arms to her chest, as if maybe . . . maybe she could squeeze so tight that she could pull herself inside out. And then she wouldn't have to see, she wouldn't have to hear. She could just be alone, and—

"Lucy—"

"Don't," she said again, sharply this time.

Don't.

Don't make me believe in love.

But he moved ever closer. Slowly, but without hesitation. "Lucy," he said, his voice warm and full of purpose. "Just tell me why. That is all I ask. I will walk away and promise never to approach you again, but I must know why."

She shook her head. "I can't tell you."

"You won't tell me," he corrected.

"No," she cried out, choking on the word. "I can't! Please, Gregory. You must go."

For a long moment he said nothing. He just watched her face, and she could practically *see* him thinking.

She shouldn't allow this, she thought, a bubble of panic beginning to rise within her. She should scream. Have him ejected. She should run from the room before he could ruin her careful plans for the future. But instead she just stood there, and he said—

"You're being blackmailed."

It wasn't a question.

She did not answer, but she knew that her face gave her away.

"Lucy," he said, his voice soft and careful, "I can help you. Whatever it is, I can make it right."

"No," she said, "you can't, and you're a fool to—" She cut herself off, too furious to speak. What made him think he could rush in and fix things when he knew nothing of her travails? Did he think she had given in for something small? Something that could be easily overcome?

She was not that weak.

"You don't know," she said. "You have no idea."

"Then tell me."

Her muscles were shaking, and she felt hot . . . cold . . . everything in between.

"Lucy," he said, and his voice was so calm, so even—it was like a fork, poking her right where she could least tolerate it.

"You can't fix this," she ground out.

"That is not true. There is nothing anyone could hold over you that could not be overcome."

"By what?" she demanded. "Rainbows and sprites and the everlasting good wishes of your family? It won't work, Gregory. It won't.

The Bridgertons may be powerful, but you cannot change the past, and you cannot bend the future to suit your whims."

"Lucy," he said, reaching out for her.

"No. No!" She pushed him away, rejected his offer of comfort. "You don't understand. You can't possibly. You are all so happy, so perfect."

"We are not."

"You *are.* You don't even know that you are, and you can't conceive that the rest of us are not, that we might struggle and try and be good and still not receive what we wish for."

Through it all, he watched her. Just watched her and let her stand by herself, hugging her arms to her body, looking small and pale and heartbreakingly alone.

And then he asked it.

"Do you love me?"

She closed her eyes. "Don't ask me that."

"Do you?"

He saw her jaw tighten, saw the way her shoulders tensed and rose, and he knew she was trying to shake her head.

Gregory walked toward her—slowly, respectfully.

She was hurting. She was hurting so much that it spread through the air, wrapped around him, around his heart. He ached for her. It was a physical thing, terrible and sharp, and for the first time he was beginning to doubt his own ability to make it go away.

"Do you love me?" he asked.

"Gregory—"

"Do you love me?"

"I can't—"

He placed his hands on her shoulders. She flinched, but she did not move away.

He touched her chin, nudged her face until he could lose himself in the blue of her eyes. "Do you love me?"

"Yes," she sobbed, collapsing into his arms. "But I can't. Don't you understand? I shouldn't. I have to make it stop."

For a moment Gregory could not move. Her admission should have come as a relief, and in a way it did, but more than that, he felt his blood begin to race.

He believed in love.

Wasn't that the one thing that had been a constant in his life?

He believed in love.

He believed in its power, in its fundamental goodness, its rightness.

He revered it for its strength, respected it for its rarity.

And he knew, right then, right there, as she cried in his arms, that he would dare anything for it.

For love.

"Lucy," he whispered, an idea beginning to form in his mind. It was mad, bad, and thoroughly inadvisable, but he could not escape the one thought that was rushing through his brain.

She had not consummated her marriage.

They still had a chance.

"Lucy."

She pulled away. "I must return. They will be missing me."

But he captured her hand. "Don't go back."

Her eyes grew huge. "What do you mean?"

"Come with me. Come with me now." He felt giddy, dangerous, and just a little bit mad. "You are not his wife yet. You can have it annulled."

"Oh no." She shook her head, tugging her arm away from him. "No, Gregory."

"Yes. Yes." And the more he thought about it, the more it made sense. They hadn't much time; after this evening it would be impossible for her to say that she was untouched. Gregory's own actions had made sure of that. If they had any chance of being together, it had to be now.

He couldn't kidnap her; there was no way he could remove her from the house without raising an alarm. But he could buy them a bit of time. Enough so that he could sort out what to do.

He pulled her closer.

"No," she said, her voice growing louder. She started really yanking on her arm now, and he could see the panic growing in her eyes.

"Lucy, yes," he said.

"I will scream," she said.

"No one will hear you."

She stared at him in shock, and even he could not believe what he was saying.

"Are you threatening me?" she asked.

He shook his head. "No. I'm saving you." And then, before he had the opportunity to reconsider his actions, he grabbed her around her middle, threw her over his shoulder, and ran from the room.

Twenty-four

In which Our Hero leaves Our Heroine in an awkward position.

"You are tying me to a water closet?"

"Sorry," he said, tying two scarves into such expert knots that she almost worried that he had done this before. "I couldn't very well leave you in your room. That's the first place anyone would look." He tightened the knots, then tested them for strength. "It was the first place *I* looked."

"But a water closet!"

"On the third floor," he added helpfully. "It will take hours before anyone finds you here."

Lucy clenched her jaw, desperately trying to contain the fury that was rising within her.

He had lashed her hands together. *Behind her back.*

Good Lord, she had not known it was possible to be so angry with another person.

It wasn't just an emotional reaction—her entire body had erupted with it. She felt hot and prickly, and even though she knew it would do no good, she jerked her arms against the piping of the water closet, grinding her teeth and letting out a frustrated grunt when it did nothing but produce a dull clang.

"Please don't struggle," he said, dropping a kiss on the top of her head. "It is only going to leave you tired and sore." He looked up, examining the structure of the water closet. "Or you'll break the pipe, and surely that cannot be a hygienic prospect."

"Gregory, you have to let me go."

He crouched so that his face was on a level with hers. "I cannot," he said. "Not while there is still a chance for us to be together."

"Please," she pleaded, "this is madness. You must return me. I will be ruined."

"I will marry you," he said.

"I'm already married!"

"Not quite," he said with a wolfish smile.

"I said my vows!"

"But you did not consummate them. You can still get an annulment."

"That is not the point!" she cried out, struggling fruitlessly as he stood and walked to the door. "You don't understand the situation, and you are selfishly putting your own needs and happiness above those of others."

At that, he stopped. His hand was on the doorknob, but he stopped, and when he turned around, the look in his eyes nearly broke her heart.

"You're happy?" he asked. Softly, and with such love that she wanted to cry.

"No," she whispered, "but—"

"I've never seen a bride who looked so sad."

She closed her eyes, deflated. It was an echo of what Hermione had said, and she knew it was true. And even then, as she looked up at him, her shoulders aching, she could not escape the beatings of her own heart.

She loved him.

She would always love him.

And she hated him, too, for making her want what she could not have. She hated him for loving her so much that he would risk everything to be together. And most of all, she hated him for turning her into the instrument that would destroy her family.

Until she'd met Gregory, Hermione and Richard were the only two people in the world for whom she truly cared. And now they would be ruined, brought far lower and into greater unhappiness than Lucy could ever imagine with Haselby.

Gregory thought that it would take hours for someone to find her here, but she knew better. No one would locate her for days. She could not remember the last time anyone had wandered up here. She was in the nanny's washroom—but Fennsworth House had not had a nanny in residence for years.

When her disappearance was noticed, first they would check her room. Then they'd try a few sensible alternatives—the library, the sitting room, a washroom that had not been in disuse for half a decade . . .

And then, when she was not found, it would be assumed that she'd run off. And after what had happened at the church, no one would think she'd left on her own.

She would be ruined. And so would everyone else.

"It is not a question of my own happiness," she finally said, her voice quiet, almost broken. "Gregory, I beg of you, please don't do this. This is not just about me. My family— We will be ruined, all of us."

He walked to her side and sat. And then he said, simply, "Tell me."

She did. He would not give in otherwise, of that she was certain.

She told him everything. About her father, and the written proof of his treason. She told him about the blackmail. She told him how she was the final payment and the only thing that would keep her brother from being stripped of his title.

Lucy stared straight ahead throughout the telling, and for that, Gregory was grateful. Because what she said—it shook him to his very core.

All day Gregory had been trying to imagine what terrible secret could possibly induce her to marry Haselby. He'd run twice through London, first to the church and then here, to Fennsworth House. He had had plenty of time to think, to wonder. But never—not once—had his imagination led him to this.

"So you see," she said, "it is nothing so common as an illegitimate child, nothing so racy as an extramarital affair. My father—an earl of the realm—committed treason. *Treason.*" And then she laughed. *Laughed.*

The way people did when what they really wanted was to cry.

"It's an ugly thing," she finished, her voice low and resigned. "There is no escaping it."

She turned to him for a response, but he had none.

Treason. Good God, he could not think of anything worse. There were many ways—many *many* ways—one could get oneself thrown out of society, but nothing was as unforgivable as treason. There wasn't a man, woman, or child in Britain who had not lost someone to Napoleon. The wounds were still too fresh, and even if they weren't . . .

It was *treason.*

A gentleman did not forsake his country.

It was ingrained in the soul of every man of Britain.

If the truth about Lucy's father were known, the earldom of

Fennsworth would be dissolved. Lucy's brother would be left destitute. He and Hermione would almost certainly have to emigrate.

And Lucy would . . .

Well, Lucy would probably survive the scandal, especially if her surname was changed to Bridgerton, but she would never forgive herself. Of that, Gregory was certain.

And finally, he understood.

He looked at her. She was pale and drawn, and her hands were clenched tightly in her lap. "My family has been good and true," she said, her voice shaking with emotion. "The Abernathys have been loyal to the crown since the first earl was invested in the fifteenth century. And my father has shamed us all. I cannot allow it to be revealed. I cannot." She swallowed awkwardly and then sadly said, "You should see your face. Even you don't want me now."

"No," he said, almost blurting out the word. "No. That is not true. That could never be true." He took her hands, held them in his own, savoring the shape of them, the arch of her fingers and the delicate heat of her skin.

"I am sorry," he said. "It should not have taken me so long to collect myself. I had not imagined treason."

She shook her head. "How could you?"

"But it does not change how I feel." He took her face in his hands, aching to kiss her but knowing he could not.

Not yet.

"What your father did— It is reprehensible. It is—" He swore under his breath. "I will be honest with you. It leaves me sick. But you—*you,* Lucy—you are innocent. You did nothing wrong, and you should not have to pay for his sins."

"Neither should my brother," she said quietly, "but if I do not complete my marriage to Haselby, Richard will—"

"Shhh." Gregory pressed a finger to her lips. "Listen to me. I love you."

Her eyes filled with tears.

"I love you," he said again. "There is nothing in this world or the next that could ever make me stop loving you."

"You felt that way about Hermione," she whispered.

"No," he said, almost smiling at how silly it all seemed now. "I had been waiting so long to fall in love that I wanted the love more than the woman. I never loved Hermione, just the idea of her. But with you . . . It's different, Lucy. It's deeper. It's . . . it's . . ."

He struggled for words, but there were none. Words simply did not exist to explain what he felt for her. "It's *me,*" he finally said, appalled at the inelegance of it. "Without you, I . . . I am . . ."

"Gregory," she whispered, "you don't have to—"

"I am nothing," he cut in, because he wasn't going to allow her to tell him that he didn't have to explain. "Without you, I am nothing."

She smiled. It was a sad smile, but it was true, and it felt as if he'd been waiting years for that smile. "That's not true," she said. "You know that it's not."

He shook his head. "An exaggeration, perhaps, but that is all. You make me better, Lucy. You make me wish, and hope, and aspire. You make me want to *do* things."

Tears began to trickle down her cheeks.

With the pads of his thumbs he brushed them away. "You are the finest person I know," he said, "the most honorable human being I have ever met. You make me laugh. And you make me *think.* And I . . ." He took a deep breath. "I love you."

And again. "I love you."

And again. "I love you." He shook his head helplessly. "I don't know how else to say it."

She turned away then, twisting her head so that his hands slid from her face to her shoulders, and finally, away from her body completely. Gregory could not see her face, but he could hear her—the quiet, broken sound of her breathing, the soft whimper in her voice.

"I love you," she finally answered, still not looking at him. "You know that I do. I will not demean us both by lying about it. And if it were only me, I would do anything—anything for that love. I would risk poverty, ruin. I would move to America, I would move to darkest Africa if that were the only way to be with you."

She let out a long, shaky breath. "I cannot be so selfish as to bring down the two people who have loved me so well and for so long."

"Lucy . . ." He had no idea what he wanted to tell her, just that he didn't want her to finish. He knew he did not want to hear what she had to say.

But she cut him off with—"Don't, Gregory. Please. I'm sorry. I cannot do it, and if you love me as you say you do, you will bring me back now, before Lord Davenport realizes I've gone missing."

Gregory squeezed his fingers into fists, then flexed them wide and straight. He knew what he should do. He should release her, let her run downstairs to the party. He should sneak back out the servants' door and vow never to approach her again.

She had promised to love, honor, and obey another man. She was supposed to forsake all others.

Surely, he fell under that aegis.

And yet he couldn't give up.

Not yet.

"One hour," he said, moving into a crouching position beside her. "Just give me one hour."

She turned, her eyes doubtful and astonished and maybe—*maybe*—just a little bit hopeful as well. "One hour?" she echoed. "What do you think you can—"

"I don't know," he said honestly. "But I will promise you this. If I cannot find a way to free you from this blackmail in one hour, I will return for you. And I will release you."

"To return to Haselby?" she whispered, and she sounded—

Did she sound disappointed? Even a little?

"Yes," he said. Because in truth it was the only thing he could say. Much as he wished to throw caution to the wind, he knew that he could not steal her away. She would be respectable, as he would marry her as soon as Haselby agreed to the annulment, but she would never be happy.

And he knew that he could not live with himself.

"You will not be ruined if you go missing for one hour," he said to her. "You can simply tell people you were overset. You wished to take a nap. I am sure that Hermione will corroborate your story if you ask her to."

Lucy nodded. "Will you release my bindings?"

He gave his head a tiny shake and stood. "I would trust you with my life, Lucy, but not with your own. You're far too honorable for your own good."

"Gregory!"

He shrugged as he walked to the door. "Your conscience will get the better of you. You know that it will."

"What if I promise—"

"Sorry." One corner of his mouth stretched into a not quite apologetic expression. "I won't believe you."

He took one last look at her before he left. And he had to smile, which seemed ludicrous, given that he had one hour to neutralize the blackmail threat against Lucy's family and extract her from her marriage. During her wedding reception.

By comparison, moving heaven and earth seemed a far better prospect.

But when he turned to Lucy, and saw her sitting there, on the floor, she looked . . .

Like herself again.

"Gregory," she said, "you cannot leave me here. What if someone finds you and removes you from the house? Who will know I am here? And what if . . . and what if . . . and then what if . . ."

He smiled, enjoying her officiousness too much to actually listen to her words. She was definitely herself again.

"When this is all over," he said, "I shall bring you a sandwich."

That stopped her short. "A sandwich? A *sandwich*?"

He twisted the doorknob but didn't yet pull. "You want a sandwich, don't you? You always want a sandwich."

"You've gone mad," she said.

He couldn't believe she'd only just come to the conclusion. "Don't yell," he warned.

"You know I can't," she muttered.

It was true. The last thing she wanted was to be found. If Gregory was not successful, she would need to be able to slip back into the party with as little fuss as possible.

"Goodbye, Lucy," he said. "I love you."

She looked up. And she whispered, "One hour. Do you really think you can do it?"

He nodded. It was what she needed to see, and it was what he needed to pretend.

And as he closed the door behind him, he could have sworn he heard her murmur, "Good luck."

He paused for one deep breath before heading for the stairs. He was going to need more than luck; he was going to need a bloody miracle.

The odds were against him. The odds were *extremely* against him. But Gregory had always been one to cheer for the underdog. And if there was any sense of justice in the world, any existential fairness floating through the air . . . If *Do unto others* offered any sort of payback, surely he was due.

Love existed.

He knew that it did. And he would be damned if it did not exist for him.

Gregory's first stop was Lucy's bedchamber, on the second floor. He couldn't very well stroll into the ballroom and request an audience with one of the guests, but he thought there was a chance that someone had noticed Lucy's absence and gone off looking for her. God willing it would be someone sympathetic to their cause, someone who actually cared about Lucy's happiness.

But when Gregory slipped inside the room, all was exactly as he'd left it. "Damn," he muttered, striding back to the door. Now he was going to have to figure out how to speak to her brother—or Haselby, he supposed—without attracting attention.

He placed his hand on the knob and yanked, but the weight of the door was all wrong, and Gregory wasn't certain which happened first—the feminine shriek of surprise or the soft, warm body tumbling into his.

"You!"

"You!" he said in return. "Thank God."

It was Hermione. The one person he *knew* cared for Lucy's happiness above all else.

"What are you doing here?" she hissed. But she closed the door to the corridor, surely a good sign.

"I had to talk to Lucy."

"She married Lord Haselby."

He shook his head. "It has not been consummated."

Her mouth quite literally fell open. "Good God, you don't mean to—"

"I will be honest with you," he cut in. "I don't know what I mean to do, other than find a way to free her."

Hermione stared at him for several seconds. And then, seemingly out of nowhere, she said, "She loves you."

"She told you that?"

She shook her head. "No, but it's obvious. Or at least with hindsight it is." She paced the room, then turned suddenly around. "Then why did she marry Lord Haselby? I know she feels strongly about honoring commitments, but surely she could have ended it before today."

"She is being blackmailed," Gregory said grimly.

Hermione's eyes grew very large. "With what?"

"I can't tell you."

To her credit, she did not waste time protesting. Instead, she looked up at him, her eyes sharp and steady. "What can I do to help?"

Five minutes later, Gregory found himself in the company of both Lord Haselby and Lucy's brother. He would have preferred to have done without the latter, who looked as if he might cheerfully decapitate Gregory were it not for the presence of his wife.

Who had his arm in a viselike grip.

"Where is Lucy?" Richard demanded.

"She is safe," Gregory replied.

"Pardon me if I am not reassured," Richard retorted.

"Richard, stop," Hermione cut in, forcibly pulling him back. "Mr. Bridgerton is not going to hurt her. He has her best interests at heart."

"Oh, really?" Richard drawled.

Hermione glared at him with more animation than Gregory had ever seen on her pretty face. "He loves her," she declared.

"Indeed."

All eyes turned to Lord Haselby, who had been standing by the door, watching the scene with a strange expression of amusement.

No one seemed to know what to say.

"Well, he certainly made it clear this morning," Haselby continued, settling into a chair with remarkably easy grace. "Wouldn't you agree?"

"Er, yes?" Richard answered, and Gregory couldn't really blame him for his uncertain tone. Haselby did seem to be taking this in a most uncommon manner. Calm. So calm that Gregory's pulse seemed to feel the need to race twice as fast, if only to make up for Haselby's shortcomings.

"She loves me," Gregory told him, balling his hand into a fist behind his back—not in preparation for violence, but rather because if he didn't move *some* part of his body, he was liable to jump out of his skin. "I'm sorry to say it, but—"

"No, no, not at all," Haselby said with a wave. "I'm quite aware she doesn't love *me.* Which is really for the best, as I'm sure we can all agree."

Gregory wasn't sure whether he was meant to answer that. Richard was flushing madly, and Hermione looked completely confused.

"Will you release her?" Gregory asked. He did not have time to dance around the subject.

"If I weren't willing to do that, do you really think I'd be standing here speaking with you in the same tones I use to discuss the weather?"

"Er . . . no?"

Haselby smiled. Slightly. "My father will not be pleased. A state of affairs which normally brings me great joy, to be sure, but it does present a host of difficulties. We shall have to proceed with caution."

"Shouldn't Lucy be here?" Hermione asked.

Richard resumed his glaring. "Where *is* my sister?"

"Upstairs," Gregory said curtly. That narrowed it down to only thirty-odd rooms.

"Upstairs *where*?" Richard ground out.

Gregory ignored the question. It really wasn't the best time to reveal that she was presently tied to a water closet.

He turned back to Haselby, who was still seated, one leg crossed casually over the other. He was examining his fingernails.

Gregory felt ready to climb the walls. How could the bloody man sit there so calmly? This was the single most critical conversation either of them would ever have, and all he could do was inspect his *manicure*?

"Will you release her?" Gregory ground out.

Haselby looked up at him and blinked. "I said I would."

"But will you reveal her secrets?"

At that, Haselby's entire demeanor changed. His body seemed to tighten, and his eyes grew deadly sharp. "I have no idea what you're talking about," he said, each word crisp and precise.

"Nor do I," Richard added, stepping close.

Gregory turned briefly in his direction. "She is being blackmailed."

"Not," Haselby said sharply, "by me."

"My apologies," Gregory said quietly. Blackmail was an ugly thing. "I did not mean to imply."

"I always wondered why she agreed to marry me," Haselby said softly.

"It *was* arranged by her uncle," Hermione put in. Then, when everyone turned to her in mild surprise, she added, "Well, you know Lucy. She's not the sort to rebel. She *likes* order."

"All the same," Haselby said, "she did have a rather dramatic opportunity to get out of it." He paused, cocking his head to the side. "It's my father, isn't it?"

Gregory's chin jerked in a single, grim nod.

"That is not surprising. He is rather eager to have me married. Well, then—" Haselby brought his hands together, twining his fingers and squeezing them down. "What shall we do? Call his bluff, I imagine."

Gregory shook his head. "We can't."

"Oh, come now. It can't be that bad. What on earth could Lady Lucinda have done?"

"We really should get her," Hermione said again. And then, when the three men turned to her again, she added, "How would you like your fate to be discussed in your absence?"

Richard stepped in front of Gregory. "Tell me," he said.

Gregory did not pretend to misunderstand. "It is bad."

"Tell me."

"It is your father," Gregory said in a quiet voice. And he proceeded to relate what Lucy had told to him.

"She did it for us," Hermione whispered once Gregory was done. She turned to her husband, clutching his hand. "She did it to save us. Oh, *Lucy*."

But Richard just shook his head. "It's not true," he said.

Gregory tried to keep the pity out of his eyes as he said, "There is proof."

"Oh, really? What sort of proof?"

"Lucy says there is written proof."

"Has she seen it?" Richard demanded. "Would she even know how to tell if something were faked?"

Gregory took a long breath. He could not blame Lucy's brother for his reaction. He supposed he would be the same, were such a thing to come to light about his own father.

"Lucy doesn't know," Richard continued, still shaking his head. "She was too young. Father wouldn't have done such a thing. It is inconceivable."

"You were young as well," Gregory said gently.

"I was old enough to know my own father," Richard snapped, "and he was not a traitor. Someone has deceived Lucy."

Gregory turned to Haselby. "Your father?"

"Is not that clever," Haselby finished. "He would cheerfully commit blackmail, but he would do it with the truth, not a lie. He is intelligent, but he is not creative."

Richard stepped forward. "But my uncle is."

Gregory turned to him with urgency. "Do you think he has lied to Lucy?"

"He certainly said the one thing to her that would guarantee that she would not back out of the marriage," Richard said bitterly.

"But why does *he* need her to marry Lord Haselby?" Hermione asked.

They all looked to the man in question.

"I have no idea," he said.

"He must have secrets of his own," Gregory said.

Richard shook his head. "Not debts."

"He's not getting any money in the settlement," Haselby remarked.

Everyone turned to look at him.

"I may have let my father choose my bride," he said with a shrug, "but I wasn't about to marry without reading the contracts."

"Secrets, then," Gregory said.

"Perhaps in concert with Lord Davenport," Hermione added. She turned to Haselby. "So sorry."

He waved off her apology. "Think nothing of it."

"What should we do now?" Richard asked.

"Get Lucy," Hermione immediately answered.

Gregory nodded briskly. "She is right."

"No," said Haselby, rising to his feet. "We need my father."

"Your father?" Richard bit off. "He's hardly sympathetic to our cause."

"Perhaps, and I'm the first to say he's intolerable for more than three minutes at a time, but he will have answers. And for all of his venom, he is mostly harmless."

"Mostly?" Hermione echoed.

Haselby appeared to consider that. "Mostly."

"We need to act," Gregory said. "Now. Haselby, you and Fennsworth will locate your father and interrogate him. Find out the truth. Lady Fennsworth and I will retrieve Lucy and bring her back here, where Lady Fennsworth will remain with her." He turned to Richard. "I apologize for the arrangements, but I must have your wife with me to safeguard Lucy's reputation should someone discover us. She's been gone nearly an hour now. Someone is bound to notice."

Richard gave him a curt nod, but it was clear he was not happy with the situation. Still, he had no choice. His honor demanded that he be the one to question Lord Davenport.

"Good," Gregory said. "Then we are agreed. I will meet the two of you back in . . ."

He paused. Aside from Lucy's room and the upstairs washroom, he had no knowledge of the layout of the house.

"Meet us in the library," Richard instructed. "It is on the ground floor, facing east." He took a step toward the door, then turned back and said to Gregory, "Wait here. I will return in a moment."

Gregory was eager to be off, but Richard's grave expression had been enough to convince him to remain in place. Sure enough, when Lucy's brother returned, barely a minute later, he carried with him two guns.

He held one out to Gregory.

Good God.

"You may need this," Richard said.

"Heaven help us if I do," Gregory said under his breath.

"Beg pardon?"

Gregory shook his head.

"Godspeed, then." Richard nodded at Haselby, and the two of them departed, moving swiftly down the hall.

Gregory beckoned to Hermione. "Let us go," he said, leading her in the opposite direction. "And do try not to judge me when you see where I am leading you."

He heard her chuckle as they ascended the stairs. "Why," she said, "do I suspect that, if anything, I shall judge you very clever indeed?"

"I did not trust her to remain in place," Gregory confessed, taking the steps two at a time. When they reached the top, he turned to face her. "It was heavy-handed, but there was nothing else I could do. All I needed was a bit of time."

Hermione nodded. "Where are we going?"

"To the nanny's washroom," he confessed. "I tied her to the water closet."

"You tied her to the— Oh my, I cannot wait to see this."

But when they opened the door to the small washroom, Lucy was gone.

And every indication was that she had not left willingly.

Twenty-five

In which we learn what happened, a mere ten minutes earlier.

Had it been an hour? Surely it had been an hour.

Lucy took a deep breath and tried to calm her racing nerves. Why hadn't anyone thought to install a clock in the washroom? Shouldn't someone have realized that *eventually* someone would find herself tied to the water closet and *might* wish to know the hour?

Really, it was just a matter of time.

Lucy drummed the fingers of her right hand against the floor. Quickly, quickly, index to pinky, index to pinky. Her left hand was tied so that the pads of her fingers faced up, so she flexed, then bent, then flexed, then bent, then—

"Eeeeeuuuuuhhh!"

Lucy groaned with frustration.

Groaned? Grunted.

Groanted.

It should have been a word.

Surely it had been an hour. It must have been an hour.

And then . . .

Footsteps.

Lucy jerked to attention, glaring at the door. She was furious. And hopeful. And terrified. And nervous. And—

Good God, she wasn't meant to possess this many simultaneous emotions. One at a time was all she could manage. Maybe two.

The knob turned and the door jerked backward, and—

Jerked? Lucy had about one second to sense the wrongness of this. Gregory wouldn't jerk the door open. He would have—

"Uncle Robert?"

"You," he said, his voice low and furious.

"I—"

"You little whore," he bit off.

Lucy flinched. She knew he held no great affection for her, but still, it hurt.

"You don't understand," she blurted out, because she had no idea what she should say, and she refused—she absolutely *refused* to say, "I'm sorry."

She was done with apologizing. Done.

"Oh, really?" he spat out, crouching down to her level. "Just what don't I understand? The part about your fleeing your wedding?"

"I didn't flee," she shot back. "I was abducted! Or didn't you notice that I am *tied to the water closet*?"

His eyes narrowed menacingly. And Lucy began to feel scared.

She shrank back, her breath growing shallow. She had long feared her uncle—the ice of his temper, the cold, flat stare of his disdain.

But she had never felt frightened.

"Where is he?" her uncle demanded.

Lucy did not pretend to misunderstand. "I don't know."

"Tell me!"

"I don't know!" she protested. "Do you think he would have tied me up if he trusted me?"

Her uncle stood and cursed. "It doesn't make sense."

"What do you mean?" Lucy asked carefully. She wasn't sure what was going on, and she wasn't sure just whose wife she would be, at the end of the proverbial day, but she was fairly certain that she ought to stall for time.

And reveal nothing. Nothing of import.

"This! You!" her uncle spat out. "Why would he abduct you and leave you here, in Fennsworth House?"

"Well," Lucy said slowly. "I don't think he could have got me out without someone seeing."

"He couldn't have got into the party without someone seeing, either."

"I'm not sure what you mean."

"How," her uncle demanded, leaning down and putting his face far too close to hers, "did he grab you without your consent?"

Lucy let out a short puff of a breath. The truth was easy. And innocuous. "I went to my room to lie down," she said. "He was waiting for me there."

"He knew which room was yours?"

She swallowed. "Apparently."

Her uncle stared at her for an uncomfortably long moment. "People have begun to notice your absence," he muttered.

Lucy said nothing.

"It can't be helped, though."

She blinked. What was he talking about?

He shook his head. "It's the only way."

"I—I beg your pardon?" And then she realized—he wasn't talking to her. He was talking to himself.

"Uncle Robert?" she whispered.

But he was already slicing through her bindings.

Slicing? *Slicing?* Why did he have a knife?

"Let's go," he grunted.

"Back to the party?"

He let out a grim chuckle. "You'd like that, wouldn't you?"

Panic began to rise in her chest. "Where are you taking me?"

He yanked her to her feet, one of his arms wrapped viselike around her. "To your husband."

She managed to twist just far enough to look at his face. "My—Lord Haselby?"

"Have you another husband?"

"But isn't he at the party?"

"Stop asking so many questions."

She looked frantically about. "But where are you taking me?"

"You are not going to ruin this for me," he hissed. "Do you understand?"

"No," she pleaded. Because she didn't. She no longer understood anything.

He yanked her hard against him. "I want you to listen to me, because I will say this only once."

She nodded. She wasn't facing him, but she knew he could feel her head move against his chest.

"This marriage will go forward," he said, his voice deadly and low. "And I will personally see to it that it is consummated tonight."

"What?"

"*Don't* argue with me."

"But—" She dug her heels in as he started to drag her to the door.

"For God's sake, don't fight me," he muttered. "It's nothing that you wouldn't have had to do, anyway. The only difference is that you will have an audience."

"An audience?"

"Indelicate, but I will have my proof."

She began to struggle in earnest, managing to free one arm long enough to swing wildly through the air. He quickly restrained her, but his momentary shift in posture allowed her to kick him hard in the shins.

"God *damn* it," he muttered, wrenching her close. "Cease!"

She kicked out again, knocking over an empty chamber pot.

"Stop it!" He jammed something against her ribs. "Now!"

Lucy stilled instantly. "Is that a knife?" she whispered.

"Remember this," he said, his words hot and ugly against her ear. "I cannot kill you, but I can cause you great pain."

She swallowed a sob. "I am your niece."

"I don't care."

She swallowed and asked, her voice quiet, "Did you ever?"

He nudged her toward the door. "Care?"

She nodded.

For a moment there was silence, and Lucy was left with no means to interpret it. She could not see her uncle's face, could sense no change in his stance. She could do nothing but stare at the door, at his hand as he reached for the knob.

And then he said, "No."

She had her answer, then.

"You were a duty," he clarified. "One I fulfilled, and one I am pleased to discharge. Now come with me, and don't say a word."

Lucy nodded. His knife was pressing ever harder against her ribs and already she had heard a soft crunching sound as it poked through the stiff fabric of her bodice.

She let him move her along the corridor and down the stairs. Gregory was here, she kept telling herself. He was here, and he would find her. Fennsworth House was large, but it was not massive. There were only so many places her uncle could stash her.

And there were hundreds of guests on the ground floor.

And Lord Haselby—surely he would not consent to such a scheme.

There were at least a dozen reasons her uncle would not succeed in this.

A dozen. Twelve. Maybe more. And she needed only one—just one to foil his plot.

But this was of little comfort when he stopped and yanked a blindfold over her eyes.

And even less when he threw her into a room and tied her up.

"I will be back," he bit off, leaving her on her bottom in a corner, bound hand and foot.

She heard his footsteps move across the room, and then it burst from her lips—a single word, the only word that mattered—

"Why?"

His footsteps stopped.

"Why, Uncle Robert?"

This couldn't be just about the family honor. Hadn't she already proved herself on that score? Shouldn't he trust her for that?

"Why?" she asked again, praying he had a conscience. Surely he couldn't have looked after her and Richard for so many years without some sense of right and wrong.

"You know why," he finally said, but she knew that he was lying. He had waited far too long before answering.

"Go, then," she said bitterly. There was no point in stalling him. It would be far better if Gregory found her alone.

But he didn't move. And even through her blindfold she could feel his suspicion.

"What are you waiting for?" she cried out.

"I'm not sure," he said slowly. And then she heard him turn.

His footsteps drew closer.

Slowly.

Slowly . . .

And then—

"Where is she?" Hermione gasped.

Gregory strode into the small room, his eyes taking in everything—the cut bindings, the overturned chamber pot. "Someone took her," he said grimly.

"Her uncle?"

"Or Davenport. They are the only two with reason to—" He shook his head. "No, they cannot do her harm. They need the marriage to be legal and binding. And long-standing. Davenport wants an heir off Lucy."

Hermione nodded.

Gregory turned to her. "You know the house. Where could she be?"

Hermione was shaking her head. "I don't know. I don't know. If it's her uncle—"

"Assume it's her uncle," Gregory ordered. He wasn't sure that Davenport was agile enough to abduct Lucy, and besides that, if what Haselby had said about his father was true, then Robert Abernathy was the man with secrets.

He was the man with something to lose.

"His study," Hermione whispered. "He is always in his study."

"Where is it?"

"On the ground floor. It looks out the back."

"He wouldn't risk it," Gregory said. "Too close to the ballroom."

"Then his bedchamber. If he means to avoid the public rooms, then that is where he would take her. That or her own chamber."

Gregory took her arm and preceded her out the door. They made their way down one flight of stairs, pausing before opening the door that led from the servants' stairs to the second floor landing.

"Point out his door to me," he said, "and then go."

"I'm not—"

"Find your husband," he ordered. "Bring him back."

Hermione looked conflicted, but she nodded and did as he asked.

"Go," he said, once he knew where to go. "Quickly."

She ran down the stairs as Gregory crept along the hall. He reached the door Hermione had indicated and carefully pressed his ear to it.

"What are you waiting for?"

It was Lucy. Muffled through the heavy wood door, but it was she.

"I don't know," came a male voice, and Gregory realized that he could not identify it. He'd had few conversations with Lord Davenport and none with her uncle. He had no idea who was holding her hostage.

He held his breath and slowly turned the knob.

With his left hand.

With his right hand he pulled out his gun.

God help them all if he had to use it.

He managed to get the door open a crack—just enough to peer in without being noticed.

His heart stopped.

Lucy was bound and blindfolded, huddled in the far corner of the room. Her uncle was standing in front of her, a gun pointed between her eyes.

"What are you up to?" he asked her, his voice chilling in its softness.

Lucy did not say anything, but her chin shook, as if she was trying too hard to hold her head steady.

"Why do you wish for me to leave?" her uncle demanded.

"I don't know."

"Tell me." He lunged forward, jamming his gun between her ribs. And then, when she did not answer quickly enough, he yanked up her blindfold, leaving them nose to nose. "Tell me!"

"Because I can't bear the waiting," she whispered, her voice quivering. "Because—"

Gregory stepped quietly into the room and pointed his gun at the center of Robert Abernathy's back. *"Release her."*

Lucy's uncle froze.

Gregory's hand tightened around the trigger. "Release Lucy and step slowly away."

"I don't think so," Abernathy said, and he turned just enough so that Gregory could see that his gun was now resting against Lucy's temple.

Somehow, Gregory held steady. He would never know how, but his arm held firm. His hand did not quiver.

"Drop your gun," her uncle ordered.

Gregory did not move. His eyes flicked to Lucy, then back to her uncle. Would he hurt her? Could he? Gregory still wasn't certain just why, precisely, Robert Abernathy needed Lucy to marry Haselby, but it was clear that he did.

Which meant that he could not kill her.

Gregory gritted his teeth and tightened his finger on the trigger. "Release Lucy," he said, his voice low, strong, and steady.

"Drop your gun!" Abernathy roared, and a horrible, choking sound flew from Lucy's mouth as one of his arms jammed up and under her ribs.

Good God, he was mad. His eyes were wild, darting around the room, and his hand—the one with the gun—was shaking.

He would shoot her. Gregory realized that in one sickening flash. Whatever Robert Abernathy had done—he thought he had nothing left to lose. And he would not care whom he brought down with him.

Gregory began to bend at his knees, never taking his eyes off Lucy's uncle.

"Don't do it," Lucy cried out. "He won't hurt me. He can't."

"Oh, I can," her uncle replied, and he smiled.

Gregory's blood ran cold. He would try—dear God, he would try with everything he had to make sure that they both came through this alive and unhurt, but if there was a choice—if only one of them was to walk out the door . . .

It would be Lucy.

This, he realized, was love. It was that sense of rightness, yes. And it was the passion, too, and the lovely knowledge that he could happily wake up next to her for the rest of his life.

But it was more than all that. It was this feeling, this knowledge, this *certainty* that he would give his life for her. There was no question. No hesitation. If he dropped his gun, Robert Abernathy would surely shoot him.

But Lucy would live.

Gregory lowered himself into a crouch. "Don't hurt her," he said softly.

"Don't let go!" Lucy cried out. "He won't—"

"Shut up!" her uncle snapped, and the barrel of his gun pressed even harder against her.

"Not another word, Lucy," Gregory warned. He still wasn't sure how the hell he was going to get out of this, but he knew that the key was to keep Robert Abernathy as calm and as sane as possible.

Lucy's lips parted, but then their eyes met . . .

And she closed them.

She trusted him. Dear God, she trusted him to keep her safe, to keep them both safe, and he felt like a fraud, because all he was doing was stalling for time, keeping all the bullets in all the guns until someone else arrived.

"I won't hurt you, Abernathy," Gregory said.

"Then drop the gun."

He kept his arm outstretched, the gun now positioned sideways so he could lay it down.

But he did not let go.

And he did not take his eyes off Robert Abernathy's face as he asked, "Why do you need her to marry Lord Haselby?"

"She didn't tell you?" he sneered.

"She told me what you told her."

Lucy's uncle began to shake.

"I spoke with Lord Fennsworth," Gregory said quietly. "He was somewhat surprised by your characterization of his father."

Lucy's uncle did not respond, but his throat moved, his Adam's apple shifting up and down in a convulsive swallow.

"In fact," Gregory continued, "he was quite convinced that you must be in error." He kept his voice smooth, even. Unmocking. He spoke as if at a dinner party. He did not wish to provoke; he only wished to converse.

"Richard knows nothing," Lucy's uncle replied.

"I spoke with Lord Haselby as well," Gregory said. "He was also surprised. He did not realize that his father had been blackmailing you."

Lucy's uncle glared at him.

"He is speaking with him now," Gregory said softly.

No one spoke. No one moved. Gregory's muscles were screaming. He had been in his crouch for several minutes, balancing on the balls of his feet. His arm, still outstretched, still holding the gun sideways but steady, felt like it was on fire.

He looked at the gun.

He looked at Lucy.

She was shaking her head. Slowly, and with small motions. Her lips made no sound, but he could easily make out her words.

Go.

And *please.*

Amazingly, Gregory felt himself smile. He shook his head, and he whispered, "Never."

"What did you say?" Abernathy demanded.

Gregory said the only thing that came to mind. "I love your niece."

Abernathy looked at him as if he'd gone mad. "I don't care."

Gregory took a gamble. "I love her enough to keep your secrets."

Robert Abernathy blanched. He went absolutely bloodless, and utterly still.

"It was you," Gregory said softly.

Lucy twisted. "Uncle Robert?"

"Shut up," he snapped.

"Did you lie to me?" she asked, and her voice sounded almost wounded. "Did you?"

"Lucy, *don't,*" Gregory said.

But she was already shaking her head. "It wasn't my father, was it? It was *you.* Lord Davenport was blackmailing you for your *own* misdeeds."

Her uncle said nothing, but they all saw the truth in his eyes.

"Oh, Uncle Robert," she whispered sadly, "how could you?"

"I had nothing," he hissed. "Nothing. Just your father's droppings and leftovers."

Lucy turned ashen. "Did you kill him?"

"No," her uncle replied. Nothing else. Just no.

"Please," she said, her voice small and pained. "Do not lie to me. Not about this."

Her uncle let out an aggravated breath and said, "I know only what the authorities told me. He was found near a gambling hell, shot in the chest and robbed of all of his valuables."

Lucy watched him for a moment, and then, her eyes brimming with tears, gave a little nod.

Gregory rose slowly to his feet. "It is over, Abernathy," he said. "Haselby knows, as does Fennsworth. You cannot force Lucy to do your bidding."

Lucy's uncle gripped her more tightly. "I can use her to get away."

"Indeed you can. By letting her go."

Abernathy laughed at that. It was a bitter, caustic sound.

"We have nothing to gain by exposing you," Gregory said carefully. "Better to allow you to quietly leave the country."

"It will never be quiet," Lucy's uncle mocked. "If she does not marry that freakish fop, Davenport will shout it from here to Scotland. And the family will be ruined."

"No." Gregory shook his head. "They won't. You were never the earl. You were never their father. There will be a scandal; that cannot be avoided. But Lucy's brother will not lose his title, and it will all blow over when people begin to recall that they'd never quite liked you."

In the blink of an eye, Lucy's uncle moved the gun from her belly to her neck. "You watch what you say," he snapped.

Gregory blanched and took a step back.

And then they all heard it.

A thunder of footsteps. Moving quickly down the hall.

"Put the gun down," Gregory said. "You have only a moment before—"

The doorway filled with people. Richard, Haselby, Davenport, Hermione—they all dashed in, unaware of the deadly confrontation taking place.

Lucy's uncle jumped back, wildly pointing his gun at the lot of them. "Stay away," he yelled. "Get out! All of you!" His eyes flashed like those of a cornered animal, and his arm waved back and forth, leaving no one untargeted.

But Richard stepped forward. "You bastard," he hissed. "I will see you in—"

A gun fired.

Gregory watched in horror as Lucy fell to the ground. A guttural cry ripped from his throat; his own gun rose.

He aimed.

He fired.

And for the first time in his life, he hit his mark.

Well, almost.

Lucy's uncle was not a large man, but nonetheless, when he landed on top of her, it hurt. The air was forced completely from her lungs, leaving her gasping and choking, her eyes squeezed shut from the pain.

"Lucy!"

It was Gregory, tearing her uncle from atop her.

"Where are you hurt?" he demanded, and his hands were everywhere, frantic in their motions as he searched for a wound.

"I didn't—" She fought for breath. "He didn't—" She managed to look at her chest. It was covered with blood. "Oh my heavens."

"I can't find it," Gregory said. He took her chin, positioning her face so that she was looking directly into his eyes.

And she almost didn't recognize him.

His eyes . . . his beautiful hazel eyes . . . they looked lost, nearly empty. And it almost seemed to take away whatever it was that made him . . . *him.*

"Lucy," he said, his voice hoarse with emotion, "*please.* Speak to me."

"I'm not hurt," she finally got out.

His hands froze. "The blood."

"It's not mine." She looked up at him and brought her hand to his cheek. He was shaking. Oh dear God, he was shaking. She had never seen him thus, never imagined he could be brought to this point.

The look in his eyes— She realized it now. It had been terror.

"I'm not hurt," she whispered. "Please . . . don't . . . it's all right, darling." She didn't know what she was saying; she only wanted to comfort him.

His breath was ragged, and when he spoke, his words were broken, unfinished. "I thought I'd— I don't know what I thought."

Something wet touched her finger, and she brushed it gently away. "It's over now," she said. "It's over now, and—"

And suddenly she became aware of the rest of the people in the room. "Well, I think it's over," she said hesitantly, pushing herself into a seated position. Was her uncle dead? She knew he'd been shot. By Gregory or Richard, she did not know which. Both had fired their weapons.

But Uncle Robert had not been mortally wounded. He had pulled himself to the side of the room and was propped up against the wall, clutching his shoulder and staring ahead with a defeated expression.

Lucy scowled at him. "You're lucky he's not a better shot."

Gregory made a rather strange, snorting sound.

Over in the corner, Richard and Hermione were clutching each other, but they both appeared unharmed. Lord Davenport was bellowing about something, she wasn't sure what, and Lord Haselby—good God, her *husband*—was leaning idly against the doorjamb, watching the scene.

He caught her eye and smiled. Just a bit. No teeth, of course; he never smiled quite so broadly.

"I'm sorry," she said.

"Don't be."

Gregory rose to his knees beside her, one arm draped protectively over her shoulder. Haselby viewed the tableau with patent amusement, and perhaps just a touch of pleasure as well.

"Do you still desire that annulment?" he asked.

Lucy nodded.

"I'll have the papers drawn up tomorrow."

"Are you certain?" Lucy asked, concerned. He was a lovely man, really. She didn't want his reputation to suffer.

"Lucy!"

She turned quickly to Gregory. "Sorry. I didn't mean— I just—"

Haselby gave her a wave. "Please, don't trouble yourself. It was the best thing that could possibly have happened. Shootings, blackmail, treason . . . No one will ever look to *me* as the cause of the annulment now."

"Oh. Well, that's good," Lucy said brightly. She rose to her feet because, well, it seemed only polite, given how generous he was being. "But do you still wish for a wife? Because I could help you find one, once I'm settled, that is."

Gregory's eyes practically rolled back in his head. "Good *God,* Lucy."

She watched as he stood. "I feel I must make this right. He thought he was getting a wife. In a way, it's not precisely fair."

Gregory closed his eyes for a long moment. "It is a good thing I love you so well," he said wearily, "because otherwise, I should have to fit you with a muzzle."

Lucy's mouth fell open. "Gregory!" And then, "Hermione!"

"Sorry!" Hermione said, one hand still clapped over her mouth to muffle her laughter. "But you *are* well-matched."

Haselby strolled into the room and handed her uncle a handkerchief. "You'll want to staunch that," he murmured. He turned back to Lucy. "I don't really want a wife, as I'm sure you're aware, but I suppose I must find some way to procreate or the title'll go to my odious cousin. Which would be a shame, really. The House of Lords would surely elect to disband if ever he decided to take up his seat."

Lucy just looked at him and blinked.

Haselby smiled. "So, yes, I should be grateful if you found someone suitable."

"Of course," she murmured.

"You'll need my approval, too," Lord Davenport blustered, marching forward.

Gregory turned to him with unveiled disgust. "You," he bit off, "may shut up. Immediately."

Davenport drew back in a huff. "Do you have any idea to whom you are speaking, you little whelp?"

Gregory's eyes narrowed and he rose to his feet. "To a man in a very precarious position."

"I beg your pardon."

"You will cease your blackmail immediately," Gregory said sharply.

Lord Davenport jerked his head toward Lucy's uncle. "He was a traitor!"

"And you chose not to turn him in," Gregory snapped, "which I would imagine the king would find equally reprehensible."

Lord Davenport staggered back as if struck.

Gregory rose to his feet, pulling Lucy up along with him. "You," he said to Lucy's uncle, "will leave the country. Tomorrow. Don't return."

"I shall pay his passage," Richard bit off. "No more."

"You are more generous than I would have been," Gregory muttered.

"I want him gone," Richard said in a tight voice. "If I can hasten his departure, I am happy to bear the expense."

Gregory turned to Lord Davenport. "You will never breathe a word of this. Do you understand?"

"And you," Gregory said, turning to Haselby. "Thank you."

Haselby acknowledged him with a gracious nod. "I can't help it. I'm a romantic." He shrugged. "It does get one in trouble from time to time, but we can't change our nature, can we?"

Gregory let his head shake slowly from side to side as a wide smile began to spread across his face.

"You have no idea," he murmured, taking Lucy's hand. He couldn't quite bear to be separated from her just then, even by a few inches.

Their fingers twined, and he looked down at her. Her eyes were shining with love, and Gregory had the most overwhelming, absurd desire to laugh. Just because he could.

Just because he loved her.

But then he noticed that her lips were tightening, too. Around the corners, stifling her own laughter.

And right there, in front of the oddest assortment of witnesses, he swept her into his arms and kissed her with every last drop of his hopelessly romantic soul.

Eventually—very eventually—Lord Haselby cleared his throat.

Hermione pretended to look away, and Richard said, "About that wedding . . ."

With great reluctance, Gregory pulled away. He looked to the left. He looked to the right. He looked back at Lucy.

And he kissed her again.

Because, really, it had been a long day.

And he deserved a little indulgence.

And God only knew how long it would be before he could actually marry her.

But mostly, he kissed her because . . .

Because . . .

He smiled, taking her head in his hands and letting his nose rest against hers. "I love you, you know."

She smiled back. "I know."

And he finally realized why he was going to kiss her again.

Just because.

Epilogue

In which Our Hero and Heroine exhibit the industriousness of which we knew they were capable.

The first time, Gregory had been a wreck.

The second time was even worse. The memory of the first time had done little to calm his nerves. Just the opposite, in fact. Now that he had a better understanding of what was happening (Lucy had spared him no detail, a pox on her meticulous little soul) every little noise was subject to morbid scrutiny and speculation.

It was a damned good thing men couldn't have children. Gregory took no shame in admitting that the human race would have died out generations earlier.

Or at the very least, *he* would not have contributed to the current batch of mischievous little Bridgertons.

But Lucy seemed not to mind childbirth, as long as she could later describe the experience to him in relentless detail.

Whenever she wished.

And so by the third time, Gregory was a little more himself. He still sat outside the door, and he still held his breath when he heard a particularly unpleasant groan, but all in all, he wasn't wracked with anxiety.

The fourth time he brought a book.

The fifth, just a newspaper. (It did seem to be getting quicker with every child. Convenient, that.)

The sixth child caught him completely unawares. He'd popped out for a quick visit with a friend, and by the time he'd returned, Lucy was sitting up with the babe in her arms, a cheerful and not the least bit tired smile on her face.

Lucy frequently reminded him of his absence, however, so he took great care to be present for the arrival of number seven. Which he was, as long as one did not deduct points for his having abandoned his post outside her door in search of a middle-of-the-night snack.

At seven, Gregory thought they ought to be done. Seven was a perfectly fine number of children, and, as he told Lucy, he could barely recall what she looked like when she wasn't expecting.

"Well enough for you to make sure I'm expecting again," Lucy had replied pertly.

He couldn't very well argue with that, so he'd kissed her on the forehead and gone off to visit Hyacinth, to expound upon the many reasons seven was the ideal number of children. (Hyacinth was not amused.)

But then, sure enough, six months after the seventh, Lucy sheepishly told him that she was expecting another baby.

"No more," Gregory announced. "We can scarcely afford the ones we already possess." (This was not true; Lucy's dowry had been exceedingly generous, and Gregory had discovered that he possessed a shrewd eye for investments.)

But really, eight *had* to be enough.

Not that he was willing to curtail his nocturnal activities with Lucy, but there *were* things a man could do—things he probably already should have done, to tell the truth.

And so, since he was convinced that this would be his final child, he decided he might as well see what this was all about, and despite the horrified reaction of the midwife, he remained at Lucy's side through the birth (at her shoulder, of course.)

"She's an expert at this," the doctor said, lifting the sheet to take a peek. "Truly, I'm superfluous at this point."

Gregory looked at Lucy. She had brought her embroidery.

She shrugged. "It really does get easier every time."

And sure enough, when the time came, Lucy laid down her work, gave a little grunt, and—

Whoosh!

Gregory blinked as he looked at the squalling infant, all wrinkled and red. "Well, that was much less involved than I'd expected," he said.

Lucy gave him a peevish expression. "If you'd been present the first time, you would have—ohhhhhhh!"

Gregory snapped back to face her. "What is it?"

"I don't know," Lucy replied, her eyes filling with panic. "But this is not right."

"Now, now," the midwife said, "you're just—"

"I know what I am supposed to feel," Lucy snapped. "And this is not it."

The doctor handed the new baby—a girl, Gregory was pleased to learn—to the midwife and returned to Lucy's side. He laid his hands upon her belly. "Hmmmm."

"Hmmmm?" Lucy returned. And not with a great deal of patience.

The doctor lifted the sheet and peered below.

"Gah!" Gregory let out, returning to Lucy's shoulder. "Didn't mean to see that."

"What is going on?" Lucy demanded. "What do you—ohhhhhhh!"

Whoosh!

"Good heavens," the midwife exclaimed. "There are two."

No, Gregory thought, feeling decidedly queasy, there were nine.

Nine children.

Nine.

It was only one less than ten.

Which possessed two digits. If he did this again, he would be in the double-digits of fatherhood.

"Oh dear Lord," he whispered.

"Gregory?" Lucy said.

"I need to sit down."

Lucy smiled wanly. "Well, your mother will be pleased, at the very least."

He nodded, barely able to think. Nine children. What did one do with nine children?

Love them, he supposed.

He looked at his wife. Her hair was disheveled, her face was puffy, and the bags under her eyes had bypassed lavender and were well on their way to purplish-gray.

He thought she was beautiful.

Love existed, he thought to himself.

And it was grand.

He smiled.

Nine times grand.

Which was very grand, indeed.